Look what people are saying about D.B. Reynolds's VAMPIRES IN AMERICA

"Did I mention that the sizzling sex factor in this book is reaching the combustible stage? It is a wonder my Kindle didn't burn up."
—La Deetda Reads on DECEPTION

"It's the brilliance of her characters and the staying power of the world she has created that always keeps me coming back for more."
—KT Book Reviews on DECEPTION

"D.B. Reynolds has outdone herself with this exhilarating story; and VINCENT is a worthy addition to Reynolds's always excellent Vampires in America series."
—Fresh Fiction

"Terrific writing, strong characters and world building, excellent storylines all help make Vampires in America a must read. Aden is one of the best so far." A TOP BOOK OF THE YEAR!
—On Top Down Under Book Reviews

"In one of the most compelling vampire books I've read in a while, Reynolds blends an excellent mix of paranormal elements, suspense and combustible attraction."
—RT Book Reviews on LUCAS

"Remarkably fresh and stunningly beautiful! Sophia is as enchanting as she is dangerous!"
—Fresh Fiction

"Move over Raphael, there's a new Lord in town."
—Bitten by Paranormal Romance on JABRIL

Also by D.B. Reynolds from ImaJinn Books

VAMPIRES IN AMERICA

Raphael

Jabril

Rajmund

Sophia

Duncan

Lucas

Aden

Vincent

Vampires in America: THE VAMPIRE WARS

Deception

Christian

The Cyn and Raphael Novellas

Betrayed

Hunted

Unforgiven

Christian

Vampires in America: The Vampire Wars
Book 10

by

D.B. Reynolds

IMAJINN

ImaJinn Books

This is a work of fiction. Names, characters, places and incidents are either the products of the author's imagination or are used fictitiously. Any resemblance to actual persons (living or dead), events or locations is entirely coincidental.

IMAJINN

ImaJinn Books
PO BOX 300921
Memphis, TN 38130
Print ISBN: 978-1-61194-669-7

ImaJinn Books is an Imprint of BelleBooks, Inc.

ImaJinn Books was founded by Linda Kichline.

We at ImaJinn Books enjoy hearing from readers. Visit our websites
ImaJinnBooks.com
BelleBooks.com
BellBridgeBooks.com

10 9 8 7 6 5 4 3 2 1

Cover design: Debra Dixon
Interior design: Hank Smith
Photo/Art credits:
Man © Georgerudy | Dreamstime.com
Texas road © Neutronman | Dreamstime.com
:Lcfx:01:

Dedication

To all of my little people, some of whom aren't so little anymore,
and some who won't be reading this until they're much older!

Andrew, Xander, Jack, Blake, Zara, and Kristopher
Evan, Kate, Ian, and Leah
Love you all.

"We cannot enter into alliance with neighboring princes until we are acquainted with their designs."

—Sun Tzu, *The Art of War*

Prologue

Nice, France . . . six months earlier

"THIS IS YOUR plan, Mathilde?" Christian Duvall didn't look at his Sire when he asked the question. He didn't want her to understand yet just how troubled he was by what she'd revealed to him.

"It is," she answered. There was more than a touch of pride putting a shine on her usual arrogance.

Christian looked up and met her crystal blue eyes. He'd never seen eyes that color before or since meeting Mathilde, and he'd often wondered if she used some of her considerable power to augment their pristine beauty. She was vain enough to do it, but it seemed like a waste of energy, even for someone as self-centered as Mathilde.

"It seems . . . unnecessarily risky," he said finally. "Why not simply grant permission to those of your children who wish to challenge for a territory of their own in North America?"

Mathilde's gaze narrowed. "I'm not doing this for them. I want to see that arrogant bastard brought low. I want to see his face when I claim his territory for myself."

"You mean Raphael."

"Of course I mean Raphael. Haven't you been listening to anything I've said?"

Christian smiled to take the edge off her temper. He was still a favorite of hers, although not perhaps for much longer. Certainly not once he told her what he really thought about this misbegotten scheme of hers.

"I've listened to every word." Christian crossed his arms over his chest, eyeing her thoughtfully. "You seem quite confident you'll succeed."

"Because I am. Not even Raphael can stand against so many of us."

"If you fail, he will kill you."

"I shall be certain not to fail then," she said, laughing as she placed a dainty hand on his forearm. "How could I do otherwise with you by my side?"

Christian stared down at her. "But I will not be by your side, my lady," he said gently.

Mathilde's eyes sparked with power, a blue fire there and gone so quickly, he almost missed it before her gaze shuttered and she smiled. "Of course you will, my Christian. I would not leave you behind on such a momentous undertaking."

He wasn't fooled. He'd known Mathilde too long to miss the calculating cruelty behind that charming smile. He very carefully gathered his power, keeping it buried beneath his shields, but ready on a moment's notice. He didn't want to provoke her, but he'd long ago grown too powerful for her to command him.

"You don't understand," he said patiently. "I will not undertake this fool's errand with you. It is a bad plan, but even more, it goes against everything that it means to be Vampire. We fight for what we want. We do not use untrustworthy magical devices or an army to hold our opponent captive while pretending to issue a challenge. This is trickery, not victory. And it will not work. Do you think Raphael has no allies? No loyal children of his own to fight against you?"

"And do you take me for a fool who has not considered such things?" she snapped, then smoothed the anger from her expression, like shedding a mask. "You will anchor the power circle to hold him prisoner," she ordered calmly. "And when the North American West is mine, you may name your prize."

Christian shook his head. "You're not hearing me, Mathilde. I *will not* join you in this."

Mathilde stared at him, the skin over her fine cheekbones stretching taut as she fought to contain the rage he could feel bubbling beneath her skin. But she wouldn't fight him directly. He was too powerful, and she might lose. It was the same reason she was resorting to such underhanded tactics with Raphael.

"I am your Sire," she ground out. "You are mine to command."

"You are my Sire," Christian agreed quietly. "But I have not been yours to command for a very long time."

Her power brushed over his skin, probing. It was an unpleasant, un-*clean* feeling. But her probing clearly argued against any attempt to force his compliance, because once again, her expression went from furious to charming in the blink of an eye.

"Very well, you may assist in taking North America's Southern Territory instead. Vincent is still consolidating his power in Mexico, and with Raphael neutralized, Anthony will be badly weakened. Hubert intends to challenge for the South. He will help me subdue Raphael initially, before departing for Texas, where I've promised him my help in staking his claim. You bring far more power to his cause than I intended to offer, but this will ensure his cooperation in taking Raphael down, so perhaps it's for the best."

Christian eyed Mathilde, his expression carefully blank. He didn't dispute her orders; he didn't say anything. He had every intention of journeying to Texas. He even intended to challenge Anthony's hold over the South. But not on behalf of fucking Hubert. He was going to claim the South for himself, and he'd kill Hubert or anyone else who tried to stop him.

That was the vampire way.

Chapter One

Malibu, CA . . . present day

THE HEAVY STEEL gate rolled back on nearly silent wheels, and Christian lowered the back window of the Lincoln he'd hired to drive him from the airport. He'd considered renting a car and driving himself. Maybe something sporty, with a convertible top and a responsive engine. He loved fast cars, and he'd never driven up the California coast. It was supposed to be spectacular. Though perhaps not so much at night.

The lack of scenery wasn't what had changed his mind, however. It was the desire to impress, to be taken seriously by the very powerful and very dangerous vampire lord he was about to meet. He'd been a little surprised that Raphael had agreed to meet him so quickly, given Mathilde's underhanded attack. She'd actually succeeded in the kidnapping part of her plan, but unfortunately for her, she hadn't been able to hold him. And Raphael's revenge had been terrible, just as Christian had warned her it would be. It wasn't only Mathilde who'd paid the ultimate price, but every one of the master vampires she'd assembled for her so-called power circle.

Malibu's wet ocean air drifted in through the open window, carrying a fresh, briny scent as Christian studied the expansive estate. The turn off Pacific Coast Highway had taken them through an established grove of trees before they reached the main entrance. As they rolled past the gate, the road curved and dropped several feet to reveal the main residence.

The big house had clean, modern lines, with balconies on every level. A large swimming pool shone a brilliant blue to one side, and a combination of security and landscape lighting illuminated every exterior inch of the building. The town car rolled to a stop by a broad set of stairs with glass inset doors at the top.

Christian climbed out of the car, then waited as a pair of vampires came to escort him. They were dressed in black combat-style clothing, hulking and silent as they scanned his person with two different detection devices. They didn't pat him down as they might have a human, however. One didn't touch a vampire as powerful as Christian without his permission—something he wasn't about to give to two vampires he didn't know or trust.

The two guards finished their scan, but didn't step away immediately. One of them was muttering into a wireless communication device, obviously checking in with his superior. It was plain that Raphael took his security seriously, and Christian had no doubt that Raphael's people were hyper-vigilant about this visit, given his own ties to Mathilde. He hadn't been part of the Hawaii operation, but he *was* Mathilde's child, and he'd originally come to this continent at the invitation of Enrique, the now dead Lord of Mexico who'd conspired with Mathilde against his fellow North American lords.

Christian wouldn't go down without a fight if that was Raphael's intent, but he didn't think the Western Lord had agreed to this visit just so he could kill him.

Christian still didn't know the precise details of what had gone down in Hawaii, although he'd heard wild rumors about the role of Raphael's mate in his ultimate victory. But regardless of the specifics, there was no question of the outcome. Mathilde was dead, and while he'd experienced a momentary pang of loss in the moment she died—a response hardwired into him since she was his Sire—his overwhelming reaction had been one of relief. He'd already been in Texas by then, already making his own plans. Christian was a powerful vampire, and it spoke to Anthony's weakness that he'd been able to cross into the Southern Territory without raising any red flags on the vampire lord's radar. He'd been in the territory for months, had purchased properties within a few miles of Anthony's estate in Houston, and had even visited the estate incognito during a large gathering. In his mind, that meant the Southern lord was unaware of his presence, which made him too weak to rule.

Since then, of course, Anthony had announced his decision to abdicate, which opened the territory to an official challenge. Christian hadn't met with Anthony yet, but he'd been to a couple of social affairs on the estate. Everything he saw told him Anthony's hold on the territory was fragile. If he hadn't abdicated already, Christian would have challenged him outright. But he had, and Christian had felt it wise, given his connection to Mathilde, to initiate contact with Raphael to make nice with his future allies.

The guard completed the check-in with his superior, then stepped back, clearing a path for Christian to proceed up the stairs, albeit with the two guards flanking him.

"Is there somewhere my driver can wait?" Christian asked.

The guard immediately signaled yet another black-clad vampire who ran around the car and exchanged a few words with the driver, who drove smoothly away from the front entrance and parked near a multi-bay garage on the other side of the courtyard.

"This way," the guard told Christian, and all three of them—Christian and his two escorts—proceeded smartly up the stairs and into a mar-ble-floored foyer. A huge crystal chandelier sparkled brightly over a grand staircase directly in front of him. His escorts didn't pause, but steered him straight for the stairs, and up to the second floor. They turned right, then left, down a thickly-carpeted hallway, passing several closed doors.

But Christian didn't so much as glance away from their destination. He knew exactly where they were going. He could feel Raphael's tremendous power simmering up ahead, like a giant beast curled in its lair. He kept his own power carefully tamped down, not permitting even a spark to leak through his shields. He didn't want the smallest hint of a provocation when he stood before Raphael.

His escorts stopped in front of a pair of huge, black walnut doors, big enough to have stood in the grandest cathedral back home in France. The wood was beautifully carved, with elegant bronze inlays depicting a shad-owy garden. It was a fantastic work of art, and Christian wondered if Raphael had found the doors in an ancient building and brought them to Malibu, or if he'd had them created just for this purpose. Did he have such an artist among his vampire children? That would be a treasure indeed.

The doors whispered open as soon as they'd come to a full stop. One of his escorts nodded at the huge vampire standing in the now-open door-way, then, without a word, the two guards started back the way they'd come. Christian barely registered their departure, his attention focused entirely on the sizeable Japanese vampire blocking entrance to the room. The vamp was close to seven feet of muscle and attitude, and every ounce of that attitude was saying he didn't trust Christian at all.

Christian couldn't blame him, but he wasn't going to tremble before him either. "I believe Lord Raphael is expecting me," he said calmly, meeting the big vampire's cold, black eyes.

The gatekeeper's only reaction was to rake those eyes over Christian from head to toe, before meeting his gaze head-on once again with an unfriendly glare. Someone, perhaps Raphael, must have given a telepathic order at that point, because the huge vampire uttered a soft grunt and stood aside in silent invitation to enter.

Christian gave a slight tilt of his head in acknowledgment, then walked past the door guard and into the room where Raphael waited.

It was an office of sorts, though not many could afford the view visible beyond the wall of windows framing the desk. The moon rode low in the sky, sheening the black ocean with a silvery light and creating the perfect celestial backdrop for Raphael. Christian's first thought was just how wealthy the Western Vampire Lord had to be to afford such an estate, but then he remembered that Raphael had claimed this property hundreds of years before it had become the favorite playground of the rich and famous.

And the thought of all those centuries that Raphael had survived was even more daunting than any consideration of his wealth.

As Christian approached the desk, he passed an entire wall of shelves, filled floor to ceiling with books. He itched to get closer, to take a look at the volumes stacked there. Some appeared to be newer titles, but many of them had the look of ancient tomes, and on the very top shelves were what appeared to be actual scrolls.

He sighed inwardly, cautioning himself to pay attention to the 8000-pound gorilla sitting behind his desk, rather than lusting after his books.

This was not to suggest that Raphael resembled a gorilla. Most of the older vampires were good-looking. That seemed to go hand in hand with the vampire symbiote, part of its natural survival strategy. Something to make vampires more attractive to their prey, and thus better predators, which then extended the life of the symbiote. But Christian had met enough vampires over the years to recognize when the symbiote had been given more to work with from the very beginning. Raphael was one of those. He'd probably been beautiful as a human long before he'd become a vampire. Add in the power and charisma fairly radiating from him, and there probably wasn't a human alive who would want to resist his seduction.

On the other hand, given the stunning woman standing next to Raphael, her green eyes glaring hatred at Christian, he doubted the vampire lord went hunting for blood prey at all anymore.

The woman had to be Raphael's mate, Cynthia Leighton. Rumor ran rife all over the South that she'd been the one who took out Lord Jabril not so long ago. By all accounts, Jabril had been a sociopath who murdered and raped at will, and no one still alive seemed to mourn his death. But that only made it even more impressive that Leighton had defeated him. It also explained Raphael's unusual role as the power behind the throne in the South.

Normally, when a vampire lord was assassinated, the vampire who killed him became the next lord. But as a human, Leighton couldn't rule even if she'd wanted to. So when she'd killed Jabril, it had left the territory wide open to a potential bloodbath of challenges as vampires vied to become the next lord. It had also made her a target for those who wanted to make absolutely certain that their path to the throne was clear. Hence Raphael's decision to step in and establish Anthony as Lord of the South, with the full weight of his enormous power behind him.

With Raphael doing everything he could to establish a stable North American alliance, he wouldn't have wanted an unstable South on his border. But more importantly, by quietly and firmly settling the question of succession, it protected Leighton from anyone who thought to take the South by assassinating her.

Seeing Raphael and Leighton together now, noting the body language between them, Christian had a feeling it was Raphael's desire to protect his mate that had dictated his actions.

But what Christian would really like to know was why Anthony was leaving. Why now? And how much did Raphael have to do with it? He doubted he was going to get those answers tonight, however. It was highly unlikely that the Western Lord would volunteer the information himself, and his people were notoriously close-lipped about their lord's business.

He came to a stop in front of the wide desk. "Lord Raphael," he said, tipping just slightly into a bow from the waist in recognition of Raphael's position as Lord of the West . . . and a scary, fucking vampire lord.

"Christian Duvall," Raphael acknowledged, the silver gleam of his eyes hinting at his power. "My mate, Cynthia Leighton," he said, touching the woman's leg briefly.

"My lady," Christian said politely, despite the hostility radiating from her every pore.

No one introduced the two other vampires standing to Raphael's right, but Christian had done his research before coming here, and didn't need an introduction. The black vampire was Jared Lincoln, Raphael's lieutenant. And standing next to him was Juro, who was Raphael's longtime security chief. He was also an identical copy to the huge vampire who'd admitted Christian to the room, and who now stood guarding the door—or blocking it, depending on one's perspective.

"Gentlemen," Christian said, ignoring the fact that they were both eyeing him with only slightly less hostility than Leighton was.

"Are you here about Mathilde, Christian?" Raphael asked, getting right to the point. "She was your Sire, I believe."

"She was, my lord. But as you know, she was not universally beloved among her people."

"Why would I know that?"

Christian regarded him for a moment. "You spent time in her court. It was long before I was turned, but Mathilde spoke of you often."

"In nothing but the most glowing terms, I'm sure," Raphael said dryly.

Christian permitted himself a small smile. "Not exactly, my lord. Your rejection of her advances were, in part, what drove her to undertake such a reckless invasion."

"You were privy to her plans?"

He nodded. "She wanted me to anchor the power circle which was intended to imprison you. I declined."

"Why?" Cynthia Leighton demanded. "Were you afraid she'd lose?"

Christian switched his attention to her. "The probability of Mathilde's victory, or lack of it, had no bearing on my decision. Although I did warn her that her plan was likely to fail."

"But you didn't bother to warn anyone else," she said bitterly.

He regarded her quizzically. "It is not the vampire way, my lady. We live by a single rule . . . you keep what you win. And winning means challenging your opponent and besting him. I did not endorse Mathilde's decision to resort to trickery against Lord Raphael, but she was my Sire. My duty was to maintain her confidence, whether or not I approved of her plans. On the other hand, I owed no allegiance to Lord Raphael. It was his burden to survive Mathilde's plot, no matter how underhanded or ill-conceived."

He nodded in Raphael's direction. "Your mate understands, my lady, even if you do not."

His words didn't have the hoped-for effect on the woman. If anything, she seemed even angrier than before. He saw Raphael's hand stroke the back of her thigh in a move both possessive and soothing. Although the gesture didn't seem to cool her anger any more than Christian's explanation had. She was every bit as fierce as the rumors had painted her.

"So, then, why are you here?" Raphael asked.

"As I said, my lord, I did not agree with Mathilde's strategy. I urged her to reconsider, but she was blinded by her hatred for you."

Raphael gave him a look that said, *Get to the point!*

"As you know, Anthony intends to abdicate in favor of whoever wins a territorial challenge. I wish to compete, and I want your permission to do so."

Raphael tilted his head, staring at him from beneath lowered brows. "You don't need my permission. I don't rule the South."

"Not in name, my lord. And I mean no disrespect to you or to Anthony, but everyone knows it is *your* power that holds the South together."

He braced himself for an angry response, but Raphael seemed mildly amused instead. "Assuming that's true . . . why would I grant this blessing you seek? What do I gain? You are, after all, the child of my enemy. My very *dead* enemy."

"I want only to compete fairly, my lord, as vampires have done for centuries." He deliberately met Raphael's hard, glittering gaze. "As for what you gain . . . when I win, you will gain a powerful ally in the war which we all know is coming. Mathilde is dead. But Hubert is not, nor Berkhard. And there are others."

Raphael's gaze sharpened shrewdly. "And being such a staunch ally, you will, of course, want to share everything you know of their plans."

Christian was silent for a moment. He'd intended to share what he knew, but not until after he was Lord of the South, when they'd become allies in fact. If he told Raphael everything he knew right now, the Western

Lord could simply decide to kill him before he could leave tonight. Telling him would be an act of trust, something not easy to come by in the world of powerful vampires.

"Trust is not a common currency in our world," Christian said.

"And yet, we must start somewhere," Raphael replied.

Oddly, had it been Mathilde on the other side of that desk, he would never have considered turning over what he knew. Not until he'd achieved his own goal of ruling the South, and had the power of a territory behind him. But Raphael had a reputation for integrity among his own people, and he was right . . . if they were to be allies, they had to start somewhere.

"I would be happy to tell you what I know, as a gesture of goodwill between us."

Raphael shared a glance with his two vampire advisors, but it was Leighton who spoke. "What happened to your vaunted duty to your Sire?" she sneered.

"Mathilde is dead, my lady," Christian said gently. "And I owe her allies nothing. My fate is now mine alone." But he returned his attention to Raphael and said, "One more thing, my lord."

Raphael gave him a questioning look.

"I will be bringing my lieutenant into the territory. I am not the only contender for the South, and I want someone loyal at my back."

"Where is he now?" Juro asked, speaking for the first time.

Christian regarded the big vampire. "Mexico," he said, letting his amusement show. "The lately-departed Enrique was very generous in his welcome to Mathilde and her allies. I doubt even Vincent understands yet just how many European vampires are roaming his territory."

Raphael frowned. "Very well. Bring in your lieutenant. I will speak to Anthony, and Vincent, too. I expect Vincent, at least, will eventually want to speak to you directly, but you can begin tonight by briefing my people on everything you know about your colleague's plans for the continent."

Christian smiled slightly to cover the irritation he was feeling. "With respect, my lord, they are not, nor have they ever been, my colleagues."

There was no reason for him to linger after that. And since no one had offered him a seat, he was still standing, which made his departure easier. His gaze skimmed the vampire lord's still-glaring mate, and rested on Raphael.

"My lord," he said.

Raphael gave him an almost imperceptible nod, but Christian figured that was all he was going to get. So he did the same, then turned and walked out of the room, keenly aware of Juro looming up behind him.

"We'll use the conference room," Juro said, drawing his attention to a pair of open double doors on his left. Christian veered into the designated room, just as Jared exited Raphael's office and headed his way. So far, the visit had gone as well as Christian could have hoped, but it still pissed him off. He was not their enemy, though he easily could have been. If he'd been anchoring that damned power circle, as Mathilde had wanted, it wouldn't have collapsed quite so easily, and maybe not at all. He frowned at the thought, and made a note to somehow find out what had gone wrong in Hawaii. He didn't mourn its failure, but it would be . . . educational to know the details. One never knew when obscure bits of information might come in handy. He was a vampire lord, after all. Or he soon would be. He didn't even entertain the possibility that he would fail in the South. It wasn't going to happen.

He strolled over to the conference room's far window. It had the same spectacular view as the one from Raphael's office, although it was displayed less dramatically—no floor-to-ceiling windows here. Putting the windows at his back, he watched silently as Jared and Juro moved around the room. They were both powerful vampires, and seemed eminently confident that they were in control.

But then, Christian was still hiding his true strength. He was over 230 years old, and more powerful than either of these two. And he was tired of being treated like a second-class citizen.

He didn't move from where he stood, didn't make any grand gestures or call attention to what he was doing. He simply smiled between the two of them, and then slowly released a taste of his true power. Not all at once—doing so might have alarmed Raphael—and not the full measure of his power, either. The only time a smart vampire showed his full strength was in battle. It was always better to keep one's enemies guessing.

But he revealed enough to let Juro and Jared know exactly whom they were dealing with. He studied their faces as they took in the truth. They were good at concealing their reactions, but Christian caught the slight widening of Jared's eyes, the subtle shifting of Juro's stance, as if readying himself for an attack.

"Relax, gentlemen," he said. "We're allies now, right?"

Juro's gaze narrowed slightly. "For better or worse," he growled.

Christian let that hang in the air a few moments, then said, "The night will not last forever, and I want to be safely out of Raphael's territory before the dawn, even if that means sleeping on an airplane between here and Houston. But since we're all such great friends, perhaps I can simply summarize the information, then e-mail you the details."

Juro snorted his opinion of their friendliness, but Christian only smiled.

"The most important thing you need to know about Hubert," he told them, "is the army of vampires he's been building in Mexico."

That got their attention.

Chapter Two

IT WAS LATER than Christian would have liked before he was finally able to bid good-bye to Malibu. The one advantage of the late hour was that traffic back to the airport was virtually nonexistent. He called the pilot of the private jet he'd chartered to let him know he was on his way, then he called his lieutenant, Marc Forest. Christian had turned Marc only twenty-four years ago, which made him young for a vampire, and Christian was profoundly protective of his first and only child. But while he felt the Sire bond strongly, their relationship was not paternal the way it was among many other vampires and their Sires. Marc was Christian's best friend, the only real friend he'd had in centuries. He also happened to be an excellent tactician, and would someday be a powerful vampire in his own right. Christian trusted him, and felt lucky to have him at his side.

"At last! I was worried," Marc said answering the call. "Is it done?"

"Signed and sealed. I'm not anyone's favorite vampire around here, but they were happy enough to take what I offered."

"And the rest?"

"We're officially moving to Houston, *mon ami*. Though once I become Lord of the South, I may move us back to San Antonio. I like it there."

"You like the espresso at your favorite hangout," Marc said dryly. And he wasn't far off. That wasn't the only reason Christian preferred San Antonio, but he had grown fond of his River Walk café. "Are you flying back tonight?"

"I'll be on the plane within the hour. The time zones don't favor us, though, so I'll have to daylight at the fucking airport."

"I'll arrange for guards. Shall I pick you up after sunset?"

"Are you in Houston?"

"I don't know. Am I?"

Christian laughed. "As of now, you are. Though you only just arrived from Mexico."

"Good decision on my part. Mexico's getting crowded, if you know what I mean."

"All too well. I briefed Raphael's people on the situation down there . . . as much as I know. And I'm sure his next call will be to Vincent."

"It might be too late already. I think Hubert's on the move."

"I think you're right, and we need to prepare, because I suspect we're going to end up on the front lines of whatever's coming."

CHRISTIAN WOKE the next night, unhappy to find himself in the sleeping compartment of a private jet. It could be worse, he supposed. He was fortunate, and clever, in his investments, which made it possible to lease this private jet instead of sleeping it out in the back seat of a rental car deep in the bowels of the airport's public parking structure.

But that didn't make his present situation any more comfortable. He groaned as he climbed from the awkward sleeping berth. It wasn't a proper bed—more like what you'd find in a well-appointed RV, he supposed. He'd never been in an RV, so couldn't really say. A fellow vampire back in France had fantasized about renting one of those big American RVs and touring the continent. He'd been fascinated by the wide-open American plains. Unfortunately, Christian was pretty sure the vampire with the RV fetish had been among those recruited for Mathilde's power circle. Which meant he was now dead, along with everyone else.

What a waste.

Christian pushed aside the sad thought. When you lived as long as he had, you either learned to set aside common grief, or you drowned in it. Christian had lost friends, both vampire and human. He grieved for, and remembered them. But the constant parade of life and death would swallow you whole if you let it.

He stripped off the T-shirt and sweats he'd slept in, did his best to wash up and shave with the limited facilities provided, then donned a fresh button-down shirt along with jeans and boots. One thing he loved about Texas . . . everyone wore boots.

While he was gathering his things into a duffle, his phone rang.

"Good evening, Marc," he answered.

"It's a fine Texas night, and I'm two minutes away."

"Take your time. I'm comfortable enough here."

Marc laughed, and called his bluff. "Huh. Well, I'm pulling up outside the hangar now. You want me to lurk for a bit so you can enjoy your comfort a little longer?"

"I'm not *that* comfortable," Christian admitted. No vampire he'd ever met actually enjoyed daylighting in an airplane hangar. He shoved the last few things into his bag, and yanked the zipper closed, then opened the plane's hatch. The pilot had left the stairs deployed, so after a quick scan of the hangar, Christian took the stairs in two leaps and headed for the exit.

"You didn't stay at the house last night," he said, sliding into the passenger seat of Marc's sleek BMW sedan. There was no way Marc could have gotten to the airport so soon after sunset if he had. The house was more than an hour away.

"No. There's a crash pad for low-level vamps nearby. No questions asked. I didn't want you to wait in that hangar any longer than necessary. You hungry?" he asked. "Or should we go straight to the house?"

"I'm hoping to meet Anthony later tonight, so I'll need to change at the house. But I want to be at full strength for the meet, so let's hit a bar first. Someplace quiet and discreet. I don't want to announce our presence too loudly before I've had a chance to talk to Anthony."

"Quiet it is. There's a place in the new neighborhood."

"Good. I'll call Anthony en route and see what his availability is for later tonight."

"Think he'll take your call?"

"*Mais oui.* By now, Raphael will have contacted him and given him the happy news that I'm their new ally. He'll take the meet."

Marc snorted. "How'd Raphael and his people react?"

"Raphael is practical. It's part of what makes him so successful. He saw the value of what I offered, and that was it. His people were less sanguine about it, especially his mate. In her eyes, I'm not only one of the European invaders, but Mathilde's child, to boot. She's not even inclined to like, much less trust, me. Raphael doesn't trust me either, but I think he honestly wants the strongest candidate possible to win the South."

"As long as it's someone he approves of."

"Someone he can work with," Christian corrected. "I have no doubt that if Raphael didn't think I'd be good for the South, you and I wouldn't be having this conversation right now. I've heard stories of his power—it was all Mathilde talked about sometimes. But it's one thing to hear of it, and another to stand ten feet away from it."

"You've power enough to win the South on your own merits," Marc said loyally.

"I do, and I will. But I did the right thing in speaking to Raphael first. It's a matter of respect," Christian said, as he speed-dialed Anthony's office.

"Lord Anthony's office, how can I help you?" The woman's voice was creamy smooth, with just a hint of sexy purr beneath words that flowed with the musical drawl of someone born and raised in New Orleans. The sound of that voice struck Christian so hard that he pulled the phone away from his ear and stared at it for a moment, wondering if her physical reality could possibly match that wonderful voice.

"Christian Duvall here," he said finally. "I wish an audience with Lord Anthony and assume an appointment is required," he added, cursing himself for sounding stiff and humorless. He doubted that she of the lovely voice was even remotely as entranced by *his* voice as he'd been by hers.

"Well, Mr. Duvall," she said smartly, but with a touch of humor. Probably because he'd sounded like a stuffy old man. Okay, so he *was* an old man at 239, but he didn't look it and, despite all evidence to the contrary, he didn't normally act it either. Fuck!

"Excuse me?" he was forced to ask, since she'd been talking the whole time he was scolding himself, and he hadn't heard what she'd said. Even better. Now, she thought he was stuffy, old, and *stupid*.

But she only laughed, a sound that made his dick hard. *Mon dieu*, he was like a randy teenager. Had it been that long since he'd had sex? He'd fed regularly since arriving in Texas. It was always easy to find willing young women. He never took more than he needed, and always left the woman with sensuous memories, but he hadn't actually had sex with anyone in . . . he thought back . . . nearly two months. No wonder the mere sound of this woman's voice was doing him in.

"—not sure when his secretary will be back, but I can check with Lord Anthony for you, if you'd like?"

Christian blinked, aware that he'd drifted into his own thoughts again. "That would be kind, Miss . . ?" he said leadingly. He wanted this siren's name.

"Natalie," she provided. He'd have preferred the full name, but he would get that later. He might have failed miserably in this phone encounter, but when he and Natalie met, he would do better. He was, after all, French. And, say what you will about the French—and the Americans had plenty to say—they had perfected the art of seduction centuries ago.

"Natalie," he repeated, tasting the syllables. "Is Lord Anthony currently in his office?"

"He is. Would you like to hold?"

Christian didn't, in fact, want to hold. He hated being put on hold. But he wasn't going to tell Natalie that. So he said, "Of course."

"Be right back."

Christian nodded, even though she couldn't see it. Maybe she didn't think he was stuffy. After all, Natalie of the siren's voice worked in Anthony's office, which meant she was accustomed to dealing with vampires, many of whom reflected the manners of the age they'd grown up in. Which meant she might only think he was stupid. He frowned.

"Problem?" Marc asked, glancing over as he made the connection that would cross the beltway surrounding the city of Houston. Bush Intercontinental Airport was north of the city, while the house that Christian had purchased was just west of the city center, about thirty-five miles south of the airport, and all of it clogged with traffic.

Christian gave him a questioning look.

"You looked . . . pensive."

He smiled broadly. "Thinking of beautiful women, and all I can do with them."

Marc laughed. "The best kind of problem there is. You—"

Christian cut him off with a raised hand as Natalie's intriguing voice sounded in his ear.

"Lord Anthony's in a meeting right now, Mr. Duvall, but he did say you should come on by later tonight. How does 12:30 a.m. sound to you?"

"That sounds perfect." He didn't add that pretty much anything she said would sound perfect. That would have been too much, too fast, and the art of seduction, when done well, was slow and subtle.

"I'll put your name on his schedule. Do you need directions?"

"I don't, but thank you, Natalie. *À toute à l'heure.*"

"Oh!" she said, sounding flustered for the first time. "Well. Bye-bye then."

Christian was still smiling when he disconnected the call and looked around. Marc had gotten off the highway, but Christian didn't recognize the neighborhood. He'd visited Houston a handful of times in the last few months, mostly to look at houses. He'd been to Anthony's estate house once, too, and had known immediately that it wasn't what he wanted for himself when he became Lord of the South.

He hadn't been specifically invited that time. He hadn't even officially been living in the territory. But Anthony had held a loud, noisy party to celebrate the New Year—which was a big deal in vampire circles—and the guest list had been long and porous. Christian had shuffled down deep in order to avoid calling any attention to himself, and he and Marc had slipped in with a lively group of young vampires.

The house had been wide-open for the most part, and a few of them had taken the opportunity to visit Jabril Karim's infamous basement. Jabril had been Lord of the South for decades before he died, and the basement was where he'd imprisoned and tortured both his enemies and his stable of blood slaves. Anthony had walled off a portion of the space, and ordered a sleeping vault built for his people, but the rest of it had been stripped down to bare walls and left empty. Despite the intervening years, and several intensive cleanings, Christian had still been able to smell the blood that had been spilled so cruelly within those walls.

When he became Lord of the South, he'd give the damn house back to the Hawthorn heiresses, the two young women Jabril had tried to cheat of their inheritance. And if they didn't want it, he'd raze the building to the ground and sell the land.

No matter what happened, he would never live there.

"Christian?"

He was pulled out of his dark thoughts to see that Marc was parking in front of what appeared to be a very busy nightclub. There was a long line of people at the door, and the parking lot was nearly full.

"Have you been here before?" he asked.

"A couple of times last week, with some of Anthony's guys. It's not a blood house, but the owner sees the benefit of having vamps hanging around. The ladies do love us," he added with a grin.

"Dress code?" Christian asked, retrieving his black leather jacket from the back seat.

"You got your boots on?"

"Of course."

"Then you're dressed enough."

Christian laughed as he pushed the car door open. "You know," he said conversationally, as the two of them started for the front door, "it was pure serendipity that we ended up in the South, but I think I'm going to like it here."

"No argument from me," Marc said, and then turned to greet the doorman. "Hey, Wilson," he said. "Big crowd tonight."

"Big crowd every night since you all started coming around," the door-man agreed with a smile. "The ladies come to see *you*, and the guys come to see the ladies," he explained and unclipped the velvet rope to admit the two vampires. A group of twenty-something guys near the head of the line muttered in protest. But the women standing in front of them eyed the two vampires up and down, their stares bold and inviting.

Christian walked past with nothing but a polite smile. His only purpose in being here tonight was to feed, and he preferred the more anonymous encounters afforded by a dark and crowded dance floor.

Marc slipped a hundred dollar bill to the doorman as he and Christian entered the club, walking down a short, musty hallway to a pair of padded double doors that opened onto a landing directly above the club's main dance floor.

Christian stopped long enough to draw in a long, slow breath, taking in the scents of perfume and alcohol, along with the ever-present aroma of human sweat and a touch of marijuana. Cigarette smoking was prohibited in most restaurants and bars in the Houston area, but someone had appar-ently decided weed didn't count.

"This is what I call a target-rich environment," Marc said, flashing a grin worthy of Tom Cruise.

Christian gave his lieutenant an amused glance and shook his head. Marc loved American movies. He'd lived the last two and a half decades in France, but he'd been born in the U.S., and he was thrilled that Christian had decided to challenge for a territory here.

"Does this mean you're going to sing for your supper?" Christian asked him dryly. The movies might be Marc's obsession, but Christian had spent hours watching films with him. If nothing else, it was a good way to practice his American English.

"Nah, you won't sing with me, so it's just not the same."

Christian laughed. "I don't think you're going to have a problem," he commented, noticing the number of speculative looks he and Marc were getting.

It always surprised him how certain women in places like this seemed to recognize the vampires almost instantly. When Christian looked in the mirror, he saw a man like any other. Better looking than average, perhaps, certainly healthier, but that alone wasn't extraordinary. So how did these women identify them as vampires? Maybe he should ask one of them some-day. Before he sank fang and banished any semblance of rational thought from her mind, that is.

"Just a quick bite, Marc," he cautioned. "I want to stop at the house and change before my meeting with Anthony."

"In and out, it is. And I mean that in the most culinary sense."

"Go," Christian said, laughing. "Meet me back here in an hour, but don't leave the club. I have a feeling Houston is about to become a danger-ous place for us."

"You want to stay together, then? Double up?"

Christian weighed the idea, but rejected it almost right away. He and Marc had shared their women more than once, sometimes one woman between them, and sometimes a pair of women, whom they'd take back to their house or hotel, and then trade off partners during the night. But as enjoyable as that was, it was also time-consuming.

He shook his head. "There's not enough time to do it right."

"One hour then," Marc agreed and, taking the two steps down to the dance floor, quickly melted into the crowd.

Christian lost sight of him almost immediately, but he could still sense him nearby. Marc was his child. They had a connection that could only be broken by final death—the kind that ended in a pile of dust, a possibility too painful to contemplate.

Reminding himself that Marc was a strong vampire who was more than capable of defending himself, Christian turned to his own purpose in being here. And that was to feed, to gain strength before his meeting to-night with Anthony. A meeting that was important to both his and Marc's future on this continent.

He scanned the crowded room. Several women returned his assessing gaze, but most were too aggressive for his taste, too blatant in their invita-tion. Christian liked intelligent women, even bold women, but bold didn't mean brash. He preferred subtlety in all things.

His eye fell on a lovely young thing standing with a group of friends. The women were all casting glances his way, whispering among themselves. Most stared openly, their hunger for what he offered transparent. But the one who'd caught his attention dared only fleeting looks before lowering her eyes. It might have been an artifice, but he didn't think so. And, frankly, he didn't care. He wasn't going to mate the female, he only wanted to sink his fangs into her neck, and take what he needed. And, of course, leave her trembling in sexual ecstasy in return.

Christian captured her gaze the next time she ventured a look. It took only the smallest hint of his power. She wanted him; she was simply too shy, or too frightened, to demand it the way the others were doing. He descended to the dance floor, the crowd parting before him like a bow wave.

One of the club lights was shining almost directly down on his target, gleaming off her cap of short, dark hair, her big, brown eyes as round and startled as a doe's as she watched him approach. Her friends preened as he drew close, but their excitement gradually turned to disappointment, and in one case, anger, as they realized who his target was. The angry one, a bottle blonde with big hair and deep cleavage, tried to insert herself in front of him, but she withered before his cold stare.

He turned instead to his doe, drawing within a few inches of her. Close enough to see the tremble in her fingers as she clasped her hands to her chest, to hear the tripping beat of her heart and detect the sweet scent of her arousal.

"What's your name, *bichette?*" he asked, using the French term for the little doe she resembled.

"C-Carmen," she said nervously.

"Would you like to dance with me, Carmen?"

She looked confused for a moment, as if she'd expected him to grab her right there on the dance floor and sink fang. Was that how the local vampires behaved? If so, there were going to be some changes when he came to power.

Christian pulled her gently into his arms and began swaying to the music, as he moved them deeper into the crowd and away from her friends. The song was an upbeat tune, but he didn't care. He found a low, throbbing rhythm within the music, and moved gently from side to side, one hand holding Carmen's fingers against his heart, the other circling her slender waist, his fingers spread over her lower back. Slowly, her muscles relaxed, the tension leaving her body as the song continued. Before long, her head was resting against his shoulder and he tightened his hold, letting his fingers drift down farther, to just above the curve of her ass.

The song ended, fading out as another began, the DJ making the switch seamlessly. The new song was slower, something soft and bluesy, and the lights dimmed to reflect the new mood. Christian lowered his head to the curve of Carmen's jaw, drawing in the scent of her skin. And beneath that, the sweet perfume of her blood, rushing temptingly close to the surface, the big vein in the side of her neck plump and inviting.

He placed a kiss right beneath her ear. She shivered in anticipation and pressed her body closer to his, until he could feel the hard points of her breasts pushing against his chest. She gave a needy little moan, as Christian slow-danced her into a shadowy corner of the already dark club.

Carmen looked up at him with wide eyes when her back hit the wall. She blinked several times, as if waking from a dream, but then her pink tongue darted out to wet her lips. Christian's dick twitched. He wanted to push himself against her, to grip her tight, little ass and rub his cock against the heat he could feel pulsing from her pussy. Without warning, she raised up on her tiptoes and kissed his mouth. She was awkward and inexperienced, but Christian wasn't.

Suddenly impatient, he took over more than the kiss. He took command of her body, arms tight around her back as he lifted her higher, crushing his mouth against hers, his tongue thrusting, demanding she respond in kind. She moaned again, in surprise first, and then in hunger, her arms circling his neck as she mashed her mouth against his, tearing the delicate skin of her lip and flooding his senses with the taste of her.

Christian growled hungrily, his tongue sweeping out to take in every drop of her spilled blood, before he lowered his mouth to her neck. She gasped as he licked and sucked her velvet skin until her jugular was a swollen line, pushing beneath the surface, as if offering itself up to his bite.

His gums split as his fangs emerged. Sharp spikes of pain were quickly forgotten with the bounty of Carmen's hot blood so close that the rush of its passage was a faint vibration against his lips. He brushed the tip of one fang along her neck, and she groaned in need.

Gripping her short dark hair in one hand, he tipped her head to the side and struck, slicing through the warm silk of her skin, piercing the slight resistance of her vein. Her entire body shuddered in sexual frenzy, as her blood began to flow. It was hot and sweet, and tasted of innocence and sunshine, of a sexual need that was raw and unformed. And it flowed down his throat in a hot flood of life itself.

The darkest part of his vampire nature tried to rise up, to tighten his hold on her and drink until there was nothing left, until she went limp in his arms and her heart stuttered to a halt. There was a time he'd have done that. A time when he'd routinely left death in his wake, instead of sexual satiation. But that was a very long time ago, and doe-eyed Carmen did not deserve to die. She did not *need* to die. Not at his hand, and not tonight.

Taking a final, long draught of her blood, he withdrew his fangs, holding her against his chest as she trembled through the final throes of her orgasm, then licking the small wounds on her neck to be certain they closed properly.

Christian moved back enough to see her face, but she clutched his shirt, seeming unsteady on her feet. Sliding his fingers through her short hair, he tugged her head back gently. Her eyes weren't completely focused, but she smiled up at him, and Christian couldn't help but smile back. She was happy, and apparently it was contagious.

"Let's get you some sugar," he murmured. Donating to a vampire was the same, in all the critical aspects, as giving blood. This particular location wasn't likely to offer cookies—though he'd been to blood clubs that did— but orange juice was always available in a bar.

Holding Carmen steady with an arm around her waist, he started through the crowd, using just enough power to clear a path, without being obvious about it. When he was trying to attract women, he didn't mind making a grand entrance, but with a pale and trembling female on his arm who'd obviously just been bit . . . well, let's say there were some in the crowd who might object. And while there were some nights, and some clubs, where Christian would have welcomed the opportunity for a good brawl, this was not the night or the place.

All of the stools at the bar were taken, and the crowd was two people deep in most places. But Christian steered Carmen into a dark corner at the end, and *suggested* that the guy sitting on the last stool next to the wall might want to go elsewhere. The man vacated the seat just in time for Christian to slide Carmen onto the empty stool. She blew out a long breath, as if wearied by their hike across the dance floor, and Christian chuckled. He had a feeling he'd have liked shy Carmen if he'd met her under other circumstances. But as it was, he'd never see her again. Or if he did, she wouldn't remember him. He'd make sure of it.

While he waited for the bartender to make his way down the long, busy bar to them, he scanned the club, seeking Marc's familiar figure. Their hour was nearly up; it was time to leave. But while he knew Marc was near, he couldn't spot him in the crowd. Frowning, he tapped into their unbreakable link just as that link flared to life. Marc was outside the club, and he was pumping adrenaline like a guy getting ready to kick someone's ass. Shit. Only two minutes ago, Christian had been aiming for a subtle exit.

He signaled the bartender again, using a sharp push of power to make sure the man made a beeline to their end of the bar. Pulling out a hundred dollar bill, he gestured at Carmen and said, "Get her a Harvey Wallbanger, heavy on the juice. A second one if she wants it. Keep an eye on her after, and the rest is yours."

The bartender gave Carmen a knowing look. "Sure thing, boss."

Christian stroked a hand down Carmen's arm, and deposited a gentle kiss against her temple. "Have a good life, *bichette*." And then he was heading for the door.

He shoved the doors open with his power a moment before he reached them. A few of those waiting in line shouted in surprise—maybe because they'd been standing too close to the doors. He didn't care. The bouncer gave him a quick glance, but most of his attention was fixed on the scene unfolding on the far side of the parking lot.

"You going to need help?" the bouncer asked, without turning his head.

"No. I'll keep it quiet." Christian passed the man another hundred, his gaze locked on Marc who was facing down no fewer than six human males.

"Good man," the bouncer said. "Thanks."

Christian strode across the lot, not bothering to announce his presence. Marc would already know he was there. The Sire link went both ways. The six humans were backed up against a line of SUVs and trucks, and Christian could see two more men lurking between the vehicles. He didn't know if they were part of the gang, or had simply been caught in the wrong place when the confrontation went down.

Marc's shoulders relaxed when Christian walked up behind him. He was fully capable of taking on all six of the men facing him, and the two hiding among the trucks, too. But not without making a scene, and he knew that Christian wanted to avoid that.

"Is there a problem, gentlemen?" Christian asked mildly, stepping up to stand next to Marc.

"Who the hell are you?" one of the men sneered. Not the biggest one, but the one standing a half-step in front of the others. The leader.

Christian regarded him curiously. "I'm the guy evening out the odds here. Six against one. Not very sporting of you."

"It is when he's a vamper. So move along, asshole."

"How do you know he's a . . . *vamper*?"

"Saw him seduce Ben here's girl, that's how. Walked right up and whammied her, so she'd bend over for him."

Christian smiled, despite the seriousness of the situation. He strongly doubted Marc had bent the woman over anything. For that matter, he doubted Marc had *whammied* her either. Marc was *his* child, after all.

"I suspect the true source of your objection is that *Ben here's* girl willingly offered herself to my friend, without the need for *whammying*. And perhaps *Ben* is now feeling somewhat inadequate in the face of his girl's subsequent sexual satisfaction."

The leader blinked at him for a moment, as if his alcohol-fogged brain needed time to process what Christian had said. When it finally hit him, he scowled. "You're his buddy? Are you a vamper, too?"

Christian sighed. He looked over and exchanged a glance with Marc. "We don't have time for this."

Marc nodded. "I'm topped off, so if you want to conserve your energy for later . . ."

"No, I'll handle it." He raked his glance over the six men, noting the absence of the two who'd been idling among the vehicles. Apparently, they'd lingered to watch and had moved on when it became obvious that nothing exciting was about to happen. Unless one counted what Christian was about to do as exciting.

"Say good-night, Gracie," he murmured. He pushed a little of his power at the humans, and watched dispassionately as they all slumped to the ground. And if he took particular pleasure in the fact that the leader's head hit the ground a little harder than the others? Well, what did you expect from a vamper?

He smirked as the thought occurred to him, then turned at the sound of Marc's chuckle.

"If that's your idea of a brawl, we're going to need a place to work out. Either that, or build a gym into the house."

"We won't be at the house long enough. By the time it's built, we'll be gone. But there must be a good dojo or two in this city, preferably with someone who knows Krav Maga. Texas is full of military guys, and the Special Force types typically endorse the discipline."

"So we find a dojo, then."

"I'll probably be meeting Raphael's rep, Jaclyn, tomorrow. I can ask her about a place, and there's your friend Cibor. He'll probably know, too." Christian glanced around the parking lot, then down at the unconscious humans. "We should probably get out of here, before anyone notices these guys."

"The bouncer saw—"

"He's been taken care of. Let's go."

"ARE YOU SURE it was Christian Duvall who called?"

Natalie Gaudet rolled her eyes, thankful her back was turned so the other woman couldn't see it. Anthony's secretary, MariAnn, had asked this same question at least ten times in the last hour.

"All I can tell *you* is what the man told *me*. He said he was Christian Duvall, and he wanted an appointment. Lord Anthony was in his office, so I checked with him, and he said to schedule it for shortly after midnight."

"But Christian's never come to the office before. If I'd known he was—"

"Why the big fuss? They're all gorgeous—he's just one more in a long line."

"But Christian . . . he's, he's . . . tall, dark, and delicious. Like an ice cream cone that you just want to lick all over."

Natalie frowned. She liked ice cream as well as the next person, but comparing a vampire to an ice cream cone?

"Why don't you go on down the hall and freshen up before he gets here," she urged. "I'll hold down the fort." Anything to get the hysterical woman out of Natalie's air space for even a few minutes. The girl had been running around like a chicken without a head ever since she'd heard the name "Christian Duvall." Not in fear, mind you, but because she'd seen the vampire from across the room once and thought he was *so* handsome. As if every vampire who walked through that door wasn't just as fine to look at as the next one.

"Thanks," the overwrought MariAnn responded. "I'm going to run out to my car. I picked up my dry cleaning on the way in tonight, which must be fate, don't you think? I have to change my blouse, and maybe this skirt, too. And I think—"

Nat tuned out MariAnn's monologue on the wardrobe dilemma, something that had become a habit in the two months they'd worked together. The tuning out part, that is. Anthony had a tendency to hire secretaries more for their decorative properties than for their skills or experience. And with Natalie's office less than fifteen feet away from whatever pretty face Anthony positioned at the reception desk, tuning out had been critical to getting her own work done.

She admitted a certain curiosity about MariAnn's current hysterics, though. This Christian Duvall must really be something to drive the girl right up to the edge of hysteria like that. He hadn't sounded like much on the phone. Oh sure, he'd had a nice voice. But he'd also been rather stiff and formal. The attitude didn't exactly scream hunk-a-licious to her. It might have been a language barrier, though. English obviously wasn't his first language, and he had a fairly strong accent. But he hadn't seemed to mind when Nat joked with him about his formality. The very fact that he'd understood that she *was* joking told her he probably didn't have a stick up his ass. Not like some of the old ones did.

She looked up in time to catch the flash of MariAnn hurrying out of the office, her heels tapping down the hardwood floor of the hallway. She hoped the girl hadn't said anything important before she rushed out, but then she shrugged. Whatever. It wasn't her job to run this office. She was the accountant. Or more to point, the *forensic* accountant, brought in to unravel the twists and turns of old Jabril's sneaky finances. As an honest woman, she was appalled by the blatant theft the dead vampire lord had been perpetrating against the two young Hawthorn heiresses. But as an accountant, she had to admire the cleverness of it all. It took some real talent to manipulate books like that. Although a goodly amount of simple document forgery was involved, too.

In any event, it was her job to figure out what belonged to the Hawthorns and what was legally part of Jabril's estate, which was now Anthony's estate. Although, with Anthony having decided to give up the territory and return to New Orleans, it wouldn't be his estate much longer. Everything would be transferred to the new lord, whoever that was. She only hoped the new guy was honest, and didn't try to keep what wasn't his. Between Jabril making Mirabelle Hawthorn a vampire against her will when she was only eighteen, and sending the terrified Liz Hawthorn into hiding where she almost lost her life, the Hawthorn girls had suffered enough.

CHRISTIAN STRODE down the second floor hallway toward Anthony's office. He'd passed through checkpoints at the gate and front door, but security inside the building was remarkably light. Anthony ran his household as if he was still the Master of New Orleans, not Lord of the South. It was obvious that his heart was back in Louisiana. The only real question was why he'd taken on the South in the first place. Raphael must have been very persuasive, and Christian wondered what exactly had been promised.

But this empty hallway disturbed him on a level he couldn't quite pin down. It made the back of his neck itch, despite the absence of any apparent threat. Casting a faint probe behind the many closed doors, he found several humans, but only one or two vampires. Anthony's location was obvious, but he didn't have a single vampire with him. No lieutenant, no security. It was all very odd.

Christian sensed Marc's arrival downstairs. He'd stopped outside to answer a question from a vampire he knew from the previous week's socializing, and was just now entering the building. Christian hadn't protested the delay, because there had been no obvious danger. Despite his itching neck, he couldn't see Anthony scheming to ambush him in his office. It made no sense. It wasn't as if the vampire lord was being forced aside; he'd chosen to step down. And he'd never met Christian before, so there was no personal animosity between them. If anything, this total absence of security might be Anthony's way of delivering a subtle slap of insult, telling Christian that he was so insignificant that the Southern lord didn't even bother to guard against him. If so, he was in for a surprise.

Christian's steps were muffled on the hallway's wooden floor, but only because he was making an effort not to stomp like an elephant. He drew closer to the open double doors. There was no sign indicating this was

Anthony's office, but Christian didn't need one. Anthony wasn't the most powerful North American lord by far, but he *was* a powerful vampire, and by virtue of carrying the Southern mantle, his power and presence were enhanced. It was all the juice coming in from the hundreds, or even thousands, of vampires who called the South home. Christian didn't know for sure how many vampires lived in the territory. A decent briefing on the territory had been one of the things he was hoping for from tonight's meeting. It wasn't an ordinary request, but then, this wasn't exactly an ordinary situation. Vampire lords did not retire. They were assassinated and replaced.

He stepped inside the office, and glanced around. He could sense Anthony behind a second set of double doors, directly in front of him. But those were closed. There was a receptionist's desk, but no one was there. The computer screen was lit up, however, which suggested the occupant hadn't been gone long. A second office door stood open to the left, and he could hear the quiet sound of computer keys being typed from somewhere inside. Christian didn't bother to announce his presence. Anthony knew he was here, just as he knew Anthony was there. If the Southern lord wanted to play games by making Christian linger on the doorstep like a petitioner, he was welcome to it. But Christian wasn't going to participate in his games by seeking Anthony out either.

He strolled around the office casually, studying the numerous photographs and framed documents on the walls with some amazement. A vampire's near immortality was both a blessing and a curse. When one lived for centuries, one witnessed incredible, sometimes earth-shattering, events. Christian had fought in and survived more wars than he could easily remember, including two world wars, and several smaller conflicts that had encompassed his entire world at the time. And the technological leaps that had been made in the last hundred years still astounded him sometimes.

But the point was that every vampire who survived beyond his first century coped with the same problem of wanting to chronicle and remember one's history when that history encompassed centuries rather than decades. And each of them had ways of dealing with it. Some, like Raphael, gathered histories written by others—ancient books and texts—while still living very much in the modern age.

Others surrounded themselves with mementoes of a long life—photographs, art, letters.

But here in Anthony's office, there was no sense of history at all. Nothing in this office—not a photograph, a document, a memento—was older than twenty years. It could as easily have been the office of a human politician or CEO. Endless photographs of a smiling Anthony, shaking hands with what Christian could only guess were local politicians and businessmen. And scattered among them, framed documents commending Anthony for charitable donations, for work in the community, for building a fucking hospital wing.

All very admirable and up front, but . . . whom exactly did Anthony hope to impress with these credentials? Vampires wouldn't give a shit about any of this. Was it possible that this was only Anthony's public office? That somewhere in the bowels of the huge estate there was a private office more suited to a powerful vampire? If so, then greeting Christian here, in this very human office, was part and parcel with the subtle slap of Anthony's dismissal of him as a threat.

"You must be Mr. Tall, Dark, and Delicious."

The woman's comment wasn't a surprise. He'd known she was there, had detected her heartbeat from the hallway, heard the soft whisper of silk when she'd moved into the office doorway, and the snick of her heel catching on the deep pile carpet. But that didn't stop his gut from reacting to the sound of her voice. It was Natalie from the phone call. He smiled and spun to face her.

"SURELY NOT," THE vampire said, turning with the controlled grace of a dancer, his eyes flashing wickedly as he ran strong fingers through the loose length of his dark blond hair. "You're thinking of my lieutenant perhaps. His hair is much darker than mine."

Natalie had been watching him for a while, waiting for him to turn, wondering if this was the ice cream-lickable Christian Duvall that MariAnn had been going on about. Though she wouldn't have expected him to be blond, even it *was* a dark blond. She'd been admiring the breadth of his shoulders in the elegant suit, and his really nice butt. But despite MariAnn's gushing assessment still ringing in her ears, she wasn't prepared for the impact of that smile, or the spark of intellect in those deep blue eyes.

She blinked, trying not to let him see how he affected her, working so hard at it that it was a moment before she realized he hadn't disputed the tall and delicious part of her description. Vampire ego, there was nothing like it in the world. Although, in this case, she had to admit he had a point. The tall wasn't in any question. Christian Duvall—because who else could he be?—was three or four inches over six feet. And the delicious part was just as obvious.

But he wasn't the ice cream kind of delicious. He was too huge, too hard, with those big shoulders beneath a dark gray suit that had to be custom-tailored to fit his broad chest as well as it did. A square jaw, sensuous lips, and dark blond hair just long enough that it would hang in his navy blue eyes when he was on top of her, muscles flexing as he pumped . . . oh dear God.

Okay, so maybe MariAnn had a point.

Natalie whipped her computer glasses off and fought against the desire to put a hand to her hair, to make sure it was properly brushed. Nothing she could do about it, if it wasn't.

"I'm sorry, that was rude," she said, hoping he wouldn't notice the flush spreading down her neck and across her chest. Wishing she'd worn something with a higher neckline, but really, how could she have known? "Can I help you?"

The smile spread across his face, slow and easy, turning incredibly handsome into something . . . just fucking amazing.

"Christian Duvall," he said smoothly, and held out his hand, as if offering her a handshake.

Natalie responded automatically, and his huge hand dwarfed her slender fingers.

"We spoke on the phone," he added.

Natalie found her voice. "We did," she confirmed. "I'm Natalie Gaudet."

He shifted her hand in his grip, and lifted it to his mouth, touching the back of her hand to his lips, his eyes never leaving hers. "Natalie," he repeated, and her fragile wits scattered all over again. Okay, so he was uncommonly handsome, and she loved the way he said her name. NAH-tah-lee. And, yes, his accent was beautiful—even to someone brought up with the lyrical rhythms of Cajun country. Still, it wasn't as if good-looking men were hard to find around here. Maybe it was the way he was looking at her, as if he'd found an exotic treasure that he'd been searching for, and never expected to find sitting outside Anthony's office.

"Is Lord Anthony in his office, Natalie?" he asked, and she knew she'd been staring.

"Yes, of course. I'll just—"

She spun as a whoosh of sound announced the opening of Anthony's inner office doors.

"Leave her alone."

Natalie gasped at the abrupt warning in Anthony's rough voice, but Christian barely reacted. He straightened to his full height, his fingers slowly releasing their grip on hers, even as his thumb stroked the back of her hand. He gave her a quick wink, then swung easily around to face Anthony.

"Lord Anthony," he acknowledged, not seeming at all ruffled by the vampire lord's sudden appearance, or unfriendly tone.

"Your appointment is with me, Duvall, not my cousin," Anthony growled.

Natalie blinked in surprise. Cousin? What the hell? Sure, Anthony claimed some distant relationship to her family, but he'd never called her "cousin" before.

He was certainly hostile to Christian, though. She wondered about that, and whether Christian would take offense. Vamps were a volatile lot, and she'd seen them come to blows for less. But these two vampires were scary powerful, and she didn't relish being around if they got into it.

She needn't have worried, however. Christian took Anthony's mood in stride, quirking a quizzical eyebrow in her direction—maybe at the mood, or maybe because Anthony had called her "cousin." Christian's eyes posed the question he obviously didn't want to ask.

"Mr. Duvall just arrived, my lord," she said. Christian might be willing to ignore Anthony's bad mood, but she wasn't. "He's just—"

"I see what he's doing, Natalie. Come in, Duvall. Let's get this over with." Anthony spun on his heel and stomped back into his office, not even pretending to offer a welcome.

Natalie frowned after him, but Christian didn't seem to care. He offered her a half grin, and, placing one hand over his heart, he murmured, *"ma belle,"* before following Anthony. But then he turned at the last moment and said, "Oh, Natalie, my lieutenant was waylaid on the way in. I expect him to join us momentarily. Would you ask him to wait here for me?"

"Of course," she assured him.

"His name is Marc Forest," he told her, then got that wicked gleam in his eyes again. "Tall, dark, and delicious."

Natalie blushed hotly as he took two steps back in her direction, and produced a business card from the inside pocket of his jacket. She took the card and glanced at it, before looking up to find him regarding her intently.

"In case you need me. For any reason," he added, meeting her eyes with that intense gaze. Then he turned and continued into Anthony's office, closing the doors quietly behind him. It wasn't until she heard the firm click of the door closing, and the barely discernible rumble of the two vampires' voices that she was able to draw a full breath.

"Good lord," she muttered. *"That* should be illegal."

MariAnn hurried into the office at that moment, and Natalie stared. She'd obviously changed not just her blouse, but her entire outfit, right down to her shoes. The dry cleaning explained away the outfit, but where'd she get the shoes?

"What's illegal?" MariAnn asked. She rushed over to her desk, and pulled a mirror from her drawer the minute she sat down.

"Nothing," Natalie said. "Muttering to myself. If you're going to be here, I'm running down to the ladies' room."

"Sure."

"Oh, and there's a vampire by the name of Marc Forest, who should be showing up any minute. He's supposed to wait here for Christian Duvall."

MariAnn looked away from her mirror long enough to scowl attractively in Nat's direction. "Who is he?"

"I'm not sure. I think he works with Christian, though."

"Oh." She shrugged. "Okay."

"I'll be back in a few."

"Okay."

Natalie was smiling to herself as she hurried away from Anthony's office. MariAnn was going to be so pissed when she discovered that the target of her primping was already in with Anthony. Nat moved to one side of the hallway as yet another big, attractive vampire strolled by. About the same size as Christian, actually, but with short, dark hair and brown eyes. He grinned flirtatiously as he walked past, and she glanced back to see him turn at the door to Anthony's office. Tall, dark, and delicious. Christian was right.

She smiled privately, and continued down the hall, considering the unusual circumstance of Christian having a lieutenant. She wouldn't have thought regular vampires had lieutenants. But then, he was obviously European—his accent said he was French—so maybe he was a lord over there somewhere. And that was an unhappy thought, because the North American vampires were all banding together against the Europeans. She wasn't exactly in on the strategic planning sessions, but she wasn't deaf, dumb, and blind, either. She sat right outside Anthony's office, and conversations didn't always begin or end behind closed doors.

Fortunately, none of that was her concern. She was a lone human female. The doings of powerful vampires had nothing to do with her. She was only here because of Anthony, who'd blackmailed her into coming to Houston the same way he'd been blackmailing her family for generations. He claimed to be related on her mother's side, some distant ancestor who'd kept track of, and protected, his wide and branching descendants over the years.

The truth was that no one in her family knew if he was a relative or not. That he'd been around forever was definitely true, as was the fact that anyone who disappointed him tended to vanish without warning or trace.

Unfortunately, Anthony had somehow discovered Natalie's profession, and "offered" her a job. She hadn't wanted to move so far away from her family outside New Orleans, but she wasn't willing to risk their safety on Anthony's mood either. So, she accepted his offer. As it turned out, the work was fascinating, and, while she missed her family, moving away from them hadn't been all bad. For the first time in her life, she was truly on her own, without the interference of her father and two older brothers, all of whom considered it their sacred duty to scrutinize every aspect of her life.

Especially if that life involved contact with a male, no matter how innocent.

It was a pain in the ass and, Natalie was certain, the main reason she was still single and unattached at the ripe old age of twenty-five. Of course, the fact that she was an egghead with a genius IQ hadn't helped. Nor had living in the small Bayou town where she'd grown up, or the fact that she'd been skipped ahead a couple of years and so was younger than anyone in her high school class. College had been a little better, but her football star brother had been at Tulane at the same time, and he'd seemingly taken it as his personal mission to keep her a virgin forever. She loved both her brothers dearly, but they drove her to distraction sometimes. They were both big and dangerous men, just like her father, which meant she'd never had so much as a serious boyfriend. It wasn't until grad school that she'd even managed to lose her virginity, and that had been more a matter of determination than attraction.

Of course, she'd been in Houston on her own for nearly two years now, and she still hadn't met the man of her dreams. But what she did have was a level of freedom she'd never known before. And she *had* met plenty of dreamy men. Like Christian Duvall, with his beautiful eyes and wicked smile, and those broad shoulders that filled out a suit so very nicely.

Whoa. Full stop. She couldn't be attracted to a vampire. That wasn't anywhere in her life plan. Besides, vampires didn't *date*. Especially not the ones like Christian, who probably crooked his finger and women came running. And now he'd crooked his finger at *her*. And why not? She was pretty enough, and she looked especially good today in her dove gray skirt and black silk blouse, and especially her gray patent Louboutin pumps. French designer shoes. French vampire. He should appreciate those, right?

Damn it. She was turning into MariAnn. She had to stop thinking about Christian. Where were her brothers when she needed them?

THE SCENT OF Natalie's fragrance followed Christian as he strolled into Anthony's office. Subtle, feminine, but with just a touch of spice. Just like Natalie herself. She was a lovely temptation with her auburn hair falling loose over her shoulders, her silk blouse and figure-hugging skirt showing off her long, smooth legs. She'd been flustered by him, and he had a feeling Natalie didn't fluster easily. He wasn't in Houston to hook up with anyone, but that didn't meant he couldn't. He wouldn't mind a taste of Natalie. And he was a man who usually got what he wanted.

What he wanted most, however, was to rule the South. And tonight, he intended to start down that path. Unfortunately, the vampire lord now giving him a very unfriendly look from across the room was the necessary first step.

Anthony was old. Very, very old. Maybe even older than Raphael, which only proved that age wasn't everything when it came to a vampire's power. The years could build on a vampire's strength by enhancing his skills and teaching him new tricks. But his essential power, the thing that determined much of who he would be for the rest of his existence, was set in stone on the night he woke as a vampire for the very first time. And there was nothing he, or she, could do to change that.

So while Anthony was certainly powerful, he wasn't as powerful as Christian. And they both knew it. That probably accounted for some of the hostility the vampire lord was aiming his way, even though Christian was being very careful to contain his power, to avoid a direct challenge. He had no desire to fight Anthony; the Southern lord had already abdicated the territory and presented no threat.

But that didn't mean Christian was going to roll over for him either.

"Lord Anthony," he said politely. "Thank you for seeing me."

Anthony's expression never changed. He tugged on the vest of his three-piece suit, in what was probably a habitual gesture, then walked over behind his desk, as if trying to put a barrier between them. And a huge barrier it was, too. The desk was big enough to seat six, much less one average-sized vampire lord. But then, the entire office was as overdone as the reception area had been. The desk and visitors' chairs filled half of the room, with the other half containing a conversation grouping of a sofa and two chairs, all done in elegant fabrics and wooden curves, with colorful Tiffany-style lamps on delicate end tables. The walls were covered with the same kind of self-congratulatory photos of Anthony shaking hands with important people, and where there wasn't a photo, there was a certificate or award, all bearing Anthony's name.

"Have a seat," Anthony said in his unnaturally raspy voice. Christian knew this was the result of an injury from the vampire lord's human life, before he was turned. An injury that the vampire symbiote didn't see as important enough to fix, apparently.

Christian swung his gaze back to Anthony, then moved to stand in front of one of the visitors' chairs, where he waited politely for Anthony to sit first. The vampire lord scowled. He was as handsome as any other vampire—the symbiote had smoothed away any physical flaws long ago—but it couldn't make him taller. Age and ancestry combined to make the Southern lord around five feet, seven or eight inches, which was considerably shorter than Christian. The height difference wouldn't have mattered if Anthony had been the more powerful vampire of the two of them. But since he definitively was not, the height disparity only seemed to increase his dislike.

Anthony narrowed his eyes at Christian. There was nothing friendly in that look. "Raphael called about you. It's the only reason I agreed to see you," he said. His accent was not unlike Natalie's, but Anthony wasn't Cajun. Or at least, he hadn't started out that way. He was far too old. Christian suspected the lyrical accent was something adopted during the vampire lord's long association with the Cajuns of New Orleans. Maybe to fit in better, or maybe just because he liked the way it sounded.

Anthony sat abruptly, and Christian joined him, dropping onto one of the silk upholstered visitor chairs. He dipped his head in polite thanks, but didn't comment on Anthony's blunt statement. The situation was what it was. He couldn't change that.

"Raphael said the two of you reached a deal," Anthony continued, not even trying to mask his bitterness. "But no one asked me about any deal, and I'm not part of it."

Christian met the other vampire's flat stare with one of his own. He'd come here as a courtesy, to be civil. But fuck this.

"I think we both know, Anthony," he said conversationally, while intentionally leaving off the vampire's lofty title, "that I don't need your approval or your cooperation to get what I want. For that matter, I didn't need Raphael's agreement, either. But he, at least, was courteous enough to hear me out and, ultimately, wise enough to see the mutual benefit. Personal likes or dislikes don't come into it. My arrangement with Raphael will save vampire lives."

"Maybe. Or maybe the fact that you're barging in where you're not welcome will cost them instead. My people will fight you on this, Duvall. You've no right to this territory."

"I have the same right as any other vampire to enter the challenge. We keep what we can hold. It has always been thus."

"It has always been thus," Anthony mimicked, his voice a nasally whine. "Listen to yourself. You don't belong here, you pompous ass."

Christian wanted to jump across the desk, grab the scrawny little fucker, and show him exactly who belonged and who didn't. If he killed Anthony here and now, he wouldn't have to worry about any fucking challenge. He'd be Lord of the South by default. But then, he'd probably have to fight a slew of challenges anyway, since it was likely at least some of Anthony's people would want revenge. And Raphael wouldn't be pleased.

He rose to his feet and plastered a pleasant smile on his face, but he didn't bother to conceal his true feelings. Anthony reacted at once, jumping up and kicking the chair out of his way as he moved to put the wall at his back.

It was hardly the reaction of a vampire lord who was confident in his power. And Christian's smile turned smug. "I'll take my leave, Anthony, and wish you luck upon your return to New Orleans."

The vampire lord's dark eyes flared at the subtle warning in Christian's words. It was a reminder that when Anthony surrendered the territory, and went back to being Master of the city of New Orleans, he would owe fealty to the next Lord of the South, whoever that was. Even Christian.

If Anthony had disliked him before this little *tête-à-tête*, he thoroughly despised him now. And Christian knew he'd have to watch his back even more closely. He gave a mental shrug. It wasn't what he'd hoped for from tonight's meeting, but it wasn't a complete surprise either.

"*À bientôt,*" he said, then intentionally turned his back on the fuming vampire lord and walked out of the office, shoving the doors open with a wisp of his power.

Marc was waiting for him, already on his feet and alert by the time Christian slammed the doors open. He didn't need anyone to tell him how the meeting went. "Sire." He didn't go for the formal address often, but certain situations demanded it, and he understood.

"Let's go," Christian snapped. A quick glance told him beautiful Natalie was missing from the office, but that was probably for the best. He was in no mood to be charming.

"Lord Christian," the receptionist said breathily, calling his attention to her for the first time. She was a lovely young woman, but in her sheer blouse and cheek-hugging skirt, she was a typical vampire groupie, the kind he avoided in the clubs. He was surprised Anthony would have someone like her in his front office, no matter how decorative she was.

"What is it?" he asked impatiently.

She blinked rapidly at his tone. "I . . ." she stuttered, then shot a quick glance at Marc, and smiled instead. "Good luck."

Christian gentled his expression deliberately. "Thank you. Your name?"

"MariAnn, my lord."

He smiled. "Not a lord yet, MariAnn, but soon. Good evening."

Gathering Marc with a glance, he strode out of the office and into the hall, eager to leave Anthony and his hostility behind. No doubt, the vampire lord had already contacted his people to inform them of these latest developments. And he'd probably be on the phone whining to Raphael before long, too.

"I take it that didn't go well," Marc said in a voice meant for his ears alone.

"I didn't expect much, but got even less. It was necessary, though, and if nothing else, it gave me the lay of the land. We need to be doubly alert. Tony's playing sides, and I'm not exactly his favorite."

"No. As it happens, however, I can tell you who is. My buddy Cibor, the vamp who stopped me on our way in earlier—he's one of Raphael's people, part of the guard contingent sent to ensure Jaclyn's safety."

"Jaclyn," Christian repeated. "Raphael's supposed representative. I always knew the big guy was propping Anthony up, but having met him, I understand just how much Jaclyn must be helping him. No wonder she's sick of it. All the effort and none of the fun of being lord."

Their path took them down the hall and onto the open stairway landing above the front door. Christian shot a look downward, and found the entrance clogged with a large group of visitors going through security. He didn't want to wade through that, but, at the same time, instinct had him wondering if he and Marc were being herded.

"Back door," he said tightly.

Marc followed his glance. "Fuck."

"Tell me what Cibor said," Christian muttered as they retraced their steps to a side hallway that would take them to the back of the house.

"Okay, first, you were wondering who was behind Anthony's sudden retirement? It was Raphael. He didn't anticipate how totally ineffective Anthony would turn out to be when he put him in place after Jabril died, and he's tired of it. He told Anthony that he wants out, that he'll have to stand or fall on his own strength. Anthony is pissed as hell, and has complained bitterly to Jaclyn about the new arrangement, but she's not sympathetic either. She's the one who's been propping him up on a daily basis, and she's sick of it, too. She and Cibor, and her entire team, want to go home to California. They can hardly wait for this challenge to be settled, and they're not making a secret of it, which only adds to Anthony's list of grievances."

"Why would he share all of this with you? Raphael's people aren't usually so chatty."

"I'm your lieutenant, and Jaclyn got a call from Raphael. Apparently, you've picked up a backer."

Christian received that bit of information with more than a little interest. He'd wanted Raphael's so-called blessing, but hadn't anticipated that the Western lord would actively work on his behalf. Apparently, he'd been right when he'd told Marc earlier than Raphael wanted the strongest contender to win. He hadn't met any of the others yet, but he knew his own strength and after his visit to Malibu, so did Raphael.

"What else did Cibor have to say?"

"No surprises. He told me Anthony's really pushing for one of his own children to take over, and I think we all know why. Anthony will owe allegiance to whoever wins the challenge, and he'd rather it be someone who has a prior allegiance to him personally. Two of his guys are in the running— Noriega and Scoville. They've both been with him for centuries, which means their loyalty runs deep."

"Are there any other challengers? Anyone from outside the territory?"

"A few, but only two of them serious. Marcel Weiss is a fugitive from the Midwest, one of Klemens's people who's looking for a new home now that Klemens is dead, and Aden's in charge. And Stefano Barranza out of Mexico; he's unhappy with Vincent's rule. No one's sure who sired him, but he worked for Enrique."

"And let's not forget Hubert," Christian reminded him. "He's not going to sit back and politely wait his chance, while all of this shakes out up here. He'll take advantage instead."

Marc didn't say anything, because there was nothing to say. Hubert was roosting down in Mexico somewhere, building his army of unwilling vampires for only one purpose. He wanted the South. Christian hadn't talked to Hubert since Mathilde's death, and so he didn't know what Hubert's reaction had been to the news. But he suspected there hadn't been much in the way of grieving. Mathilde as Lord of the West would have been an uneasy neighbor, should Hubert win the South. Of course, an angry Raphael was far worse, but maybe Hubert was hoping that Raphael would value stability over personal vendettas, and ignore the fact that Hubert had helped Mathilde kidnap him. Or maybe he was banking on the fact that he'd left for Mexico right after Raphael had been taken, and that he'd never been a part of the power circle holding the Western lord captive. Or maybe he'd hoped that Raphael had sated his thirst for revenge when he'd killed every single vampire who *had* been part of that circle. Christian wouldn't have rolled those dice, but then, he never would have taken on Raphael in the first place.

"Are we going back to the house?" Marc asked, as they clambered down the staircase that would take them right to the door which exited onto the parking area in back.

Christian nodded. "It's late, and I need to think about our next move." He pulled the door open, and they both stepped out into the humid night air.

"Does that thinking include adding . . ." Marc's voice trailed off when they saw what was waiting for them in the parking lot.

"Looks like someone's eager to get started," Christian observed mildly. He took in the gang of vampires now closing in to form a half circle around him and Marc. Without saying a word, the two of them moved away from the door and put a solid wall at their backs, to avoid any surprises from that quarter.

"Noriega," Marc told Christian softly. "One of Anthony's fair-haired boys," he added loudly enough for the challenging vampire to hear.

"If I'd have known the company you keep, Marc, I'd have killed you the night we met," Noriega scoffed.

Marc laughed. "You'd have tried."

"Has the challenge officially commenced then?" Christian asked calmly. "I hadn't heard."

"You think something *official* will protect you when you lose?"

He smiled indulgently. "I was thinking, rather, that it would protect me when I *win*. I would like it to be a matter of record that you issued the early challenge. We don't want Anthony going to the Council and accusing me of an unsanctioned murder."

Noriega stared at him, blinking in seeming puzzlement.

"But I'm sure you considered that possibility already," Christian continued. "You know, when Anthony called you just now, and told you I was leaving."

Noriega's expression narrowed, and Christian could almost see the realization in his eyes that maybe he'd been played, and by his own Sire, too. But in almost the same moment, realization was replaced by determination. And Christian understood. The other vampire couldn't back down now, no matter what circumstances had brought him to this moment. There were too many witnesses.

"I don't care if the territorial challenge has officially begun or not," Noriega growled. "Your presence here offends me, and I'm challenging you. So defend yourself, traitor."

Christian's eyebrows shot up. "Traitor?" he questioned, as he shrugged off his jacket, and tossed it over a bush with a sigh. He really liked this suit.

"Do you think I don't know who you are?" Noriega asked. "You and your kind have destroyed your own continent, and now you want to take over ours."

"That hardly makes me a traitor," Christian commented, rolling up his sleeves. "As for what I want . . . if I have the strength to take the South, then by every law and tradition of vampire society, it is and should be mine. Now, are we going to fight, or are you going to bore me to death?"

Noriega swelled with outrage. "Fuck you," he swore.

"Marc," Christian said in warning, as the vampire behind Noriega drew a sword, the sound rasping through the warm night. At least it wasn't a gun.

"Got it," Marc assured him. "You worry about Noriega."

Christian rolled his shoulders and shook out his arms.

"What the fuck are you doing?" Noriega demanded.

"You said you wanted to fight."

"I said I challenged you. This isn't a fistfight. We're vampires, dick-head."

"Oh," Christian replied, feigning surprise. "You mean like this." He released his power with a smug smile, taking far too much satisfaction in the look of shock on Noriega's face. "Do you really think I walk around spilling power for everyone to gauge? Or that I'm stupid enough to challenge for a territory I have no hope of winning? You're going to die, Noriega. I hope your death is worth it to Anthony."

Noriega struck without warning. Christian didn't hold it against him; it was, frankly, his only chance. It didn't *work*. But it was the smart move.

Christian's shields snapped into place faster than thought, almost as if they'd detected Noriega's attack before the action was fully executed. His shields deflected the attack, buying time, as his mind went into analytical mode. His opponent had raw power, no doubt of that. But not as much as Christian, and he had no technique at all. Fortunately, Christian had both, and to spare.

His first volley was a wash of power that knocked out most of Noriega's followers. He heard Marc muttering at his side, and knew his lieutenant thought he was taking on too much, that he should be concentrating on Noriega. But this was only the first skirmish of the challenge, a bare taste of what would ultimately be a full-out war, and he didn't want to lose Marc to a well-placed blade over something this foolish. Noriega was outclassed, his gang nothing but a distraction. But fate was a capricious bitch, and Christian wasn't in the mood to take chances. So he knocked Noriega's gang out of the fight—they were unconscious, not dead. Yet.

Noriega struck while Christian was dealing with the others, taking advantage of his brief distraction with a powerful blow that drove him back a half-step. His shields bowed inward with the force of it, and he heard the buzzing noise that meant his shields were stressed. Noriega grinned, thinking he had Christian at a disadvantage, and stalked closer, throwing volley after volley of concentrated power, hoping to shatter his shields before he could rally a defense.

But this wasn't Christian's first fight, nor would it be his last. Aware of Marc at his back, he bolstered his shields to the front, and then he attacked. Like a soldier tossing grenades, he lobbed clusters of power against the other vampire. One after the other, the sticky balls of energy clung to Noriega's shields before exploding inward, hammering away at his strength, forcing him to divert power to his shields or risk a collapse. And with every cluster he threw, Christian took a step forward in the physical realm, moving closer and closer to Noriega, as the other vampire reeled under the relentless assault.

Noriega stumbled and fell to one knee, but jumped up almost immediately, roaring his defiance. Swinging his arms wide, he slammed them together, crushing Christian's shields between them, the power of his blow enhanced by the physical strength of his vampiric nature.

It was a significant blow, but Christian saw it coming, and bumped up his shields in anticipation of the strike. The smell of ozone filled the air, as his shields sizzled, working to absorb and deflect the energy. But Noriega had put too much of his remaining power into the attack, and his shields were weakened. He'd also made the mistake of coming far too close to an enemy who was much stronger than he was.

Bracing his feet, Christian punched through Noriega's weakened shields, pushing even closer until they were only inches apart. He reached out and gripped Noriega by the throat, watching as shock replaced the anger in his opponent's eyes. He saw the moment that Noriega discovered the true nature of Christian's power, a power so dangerous that every vampire who knew of it was dead. Except for Marc.

Christian flexed his fingers around Noriega's throat, squeezing the breath from him. But the true death, the death that no vampire could survive, was the one delivered by his unique talent. Christian held Noriega's stare as he drained the vampire of his power, sucking him dry like the vampire he was, and feeding his own power at the same time.

Noriega's eyes were wide with disbelief, with the knowledge of his own imminent death. There was anger, too. Anger that he'd been used by Anthony, that he'd been deceived by Christian. But that was life, and death, among powerful vampires. A territorial challenge was not a game played lightly, and death was always the result.

Christian waited until Noriega's power was a mere trickle, and then he leaned close and whispered, "I'll give your regards to Anthony." Before the spark of life left Noriega's body, he snapped his neck, punched into his chest with his other hand, and ripped out his heart. A moment later, the vampire turned to dust in his hands.

Christian's heart was racing with the overload of energy that was always the result of using his gift. It was as if his enemy's power was too much on top of his own. For the first few minutes, it always seemed impossible for his body to hold so much. He stared unseeing, hands flexing at his sides, as the cloud of dust that had been Noriega settled over the still-unconscious forms of his followers.

A muffled feminine gasp drew his attention upward, and he caught a glimpse of Natalie's face as she backed quickly away from the upstairs window. *So she'd seen him fight, seen him kill*, he thought, as he slapped his hands together, loosening the muscles and getting rid of the clinging remains of Noriega. He wondered what she made of it, whether she'd ever seen a true vampire confrontation before, and whether it would drive her home to the safety of her family in New Orleans.

He frowned at the blood staining his hands and shirt, then rolled his sleeves down and buttoned them anyway. Taking the jacket Marc offered, he slipped it back on, shooting his cuffs as he shrugged his shoulders and settled the jacket in place. He didn't like the idea of Natalie going back to

New Orleans. He couldn't have said why exactly, but he hoped she would stay.

"Let's go," he growled to Marc, quite honestly furious with himself. "Noriega's ambush was a surprise. And it shouldn't have been."

"I didn't think Anthony would risk one of his own so early in the game," Marc said quietly. "If he was going to sacrifice someone, I'd have expected it to be one of the outsiders."

"Maybe he tried. Maybe they were too smart to trust him."

"Fucking Noriega," Marc muttered.

"Fucking Anthony," Christian corrected. "Sending one of his own children to die. He had to know Noriega couldn't best me. You know—" he said thoughtfully. "I was prepared to let Anthony retire to New Orleans when I become Lord of the South. But now . . . I think I'll have to kill him."

HIDDEN BEHIND the heavy fold of drapery, Natalie peered down at the yard behind the house under the yellow gleam of pole lights in the parking area. She'd seen Christian and his lieutenant striding away from Anthony's office earlier, had seen him turn toward the back of the house. She'd been unable to hear what they'd been saying, but it had been obvious the meeting with Anthony hadn't gone well. She didn't know why she'd followed him after that, why she'd hurried down the outside hallway to the tall window where she could watch him and Marc Forest leave. But there was something about him that drew her, something more than his good looks and charming smile. Something that told her she'd like to get to know him better. And that was a first for her. She'd been working in Anthony's office for nearly two years now, surrounded every day by gorgeous males, and she'd never once been tempted to do anything more than say *hello*. So why Christian Duvall?

She didn't have an answer, but she sure as hell had more questions. She'd seen Noriega and his gang waiting when Christian emerged into the parking area, and she'd almost called Anthony for help. But something had held her back, a nagging suspicion that the timing was simply too fortuitous. That Noriega seemed to have known not only when Christian would be leaving, but which door he'd be leaving through. And she remembered Anthony's blatant hostility toward Christian earlier, when he'd come out of his office to find them talking to one another.

She didn't know Christian that well, but she knew Anthony. And she didn't trust him. He'd been blackmailing generations of her family into working with him. She'd wracked her brain for something she could do to help Christian, as she'd watched him toss his jacket aside and roll up his shirtsleeves to bare powerful forearms. She'd taken a moment to sigh in girlish pleasure at the sight, but then her next thought had been to call Jaclyn. They worked together, and if nothing else, Jaclyn would know what to do. But hard on that thought the fight had begun, and she'd been too terrified to move.

It had all happened so quickly. Noriega's followers all falling like flies, and then Noriega raging hot as he advanced, while Christian only got colder and colder, ice to Noriega's fire. And then, in a blur of movement too fast for her to follow, Christian's fingers were wrapped around Noriega's throat, and he was literally reaching into Noriega's chest and ripping out his heart. She hadn't been able to stop her gasp of surprise when Noriega had turned to dust, but hoped she'd backed away quickly enough that no one would realize she'd been watching. She didn't even know if humans were permitted to see such things.

She knew she should be horrified by what she'd witnessed. It had been violent and bloody, and Christian had been a brutally efficient executioner. But as she stood in the dark hallway, hiding from discovery, it wasn't horror making her heart pound, her breath come short. It was desire, pure and simple. She'd always been attracted to big, powerful men, but she'd never *wanted* someone the way she did Christian Duvall. She tried to imagine all of that power and heat and brutal intensity channeled into sex, and felt her cheeks heat with embarrassment, surprising herself at the strength of arousal that just thinking about it conjured up. She didn't usually react to men like this.

She watched from her hiding place as he picked up his fine suit jacket, and shrugged it on, then shot his cuffs like some James Bond hero, before strolling off into the night.

Why him? Why did he hold such a powerful appeal to her, instead of one of the perfectly nice and eligible men she'd met since moving to Houston, or even one of Anthony's many vampire minions? Christian was a killer. And she wanted him. If she could just figure out why, maybe she could make the feeling go away before it was too late.

Chapter Three

MARIANN WAS unusually quiet when Natalie finally returned to the office. She'd been gone longer than planned, but she'd needed some time to come to grips with what she'd seen, and what she suspected. She never made the mistake of underestimating Anthony. And she didn't know if she could face him without him reading the truth on her face, or in her thoughts.

MariAnn looked up when Natalie walked in from the hallway. She didn't say anything, but stared intently at Natalie, her gaze shifting sideways and back a couple of times, as if to indicate the closed door to Anthony's office. Natalie frowned, but didn't hear or see anything amiss. His door was almost always closed, whether he was alone or not.

She paused, then leaned over MariAnn's desk, and under the guise of writing a note, murmured, "Is someone in there?"

"He's alone," MariAnn whispered. "But a few minutes ago, he threw a fit. And I mean *threw*. Stuff was crashing all over the place in there." All of this was said with many furtive glances at the closed office door, her fingers clenched around her pen as if it was a lifeline. "He called Noriega earlier, but no one's called or anything since then, so I don't know what set him off."

Natalie's stomach clenched. She knew what had set him off. Anthony was Noriega's Sire. From what she knew, that meant he'd have felt Noriega's death, and now she knew, for sure, that he'd talked to Noriega just before the fight with Christian. She'd suspected as much, but . . . had he ordered Noriega to confront Christian? Or had he been trying to talk him out of it instead? Maybe that's why he was so upset.

The door to Anthony's office opened and both women jumped in surprise. MariAnn was suddenly intent on her keyboard, typing away like a madwoman, while Natalie jolted upright and started for her own desk. But Anthony's next words stopped her.

"I've received some bad news," he said, without preamble. "Terrible news." He looked away, as if fortifying himself to say it. "Noriega is dead."

MariAnn stared at him, her eyes filling with tears. "But I just spoke to him," she whispered.

Anthony nodded. "He was murdered."

Natalie gasped, not having to pretend her shock, since she knew he was lying.

"It was that new vampire, Duvall, who was here earlier," Anthony explained, with a convincing show of grief. "He must have found out that Noriega was joining the challenge, and decided to take him out rather than face him in a fair fight. They ambushed Noriega—Duvall and that lieutenant of his—caught him completely unaware and all alone. He was dead before he knew what was happening."

Natalie blinked, trying to figure out what to say. She didn't know why Anthony was bothering to lie to them, but she *did* know that she couldn't let him realize she knew the truth. He might pretend to be her benevolent ancestor, even call her "cousin" apparently. But he wasn't. She had lots of uncles and aunts, and cousins, too. She knew what family felt like, and Anthony wasn't one of them. His goodwill was a fragile thing and it came with a price. As long as you did what he wanted, as long as you were helpful, he was a great guy. But if you crossed the line, he never forgave you. And Noriega's death might just be the line she shouldn't cross.

"I'm very sorry, my lord," she said finally. "Is there anything we can do?"

Anthony drew a deep breath through his nose, visibly gathering his strength. It was a masterful performance, and it made Natalie rethink everything she thought knew about him.

"Not right now. In fact, MariAnn, why don't you go on home? I won't be seeing anyone else tonight. I need some time alone to deal with this loss."

"Of course, my lord," MariAnn murmured. She stood and gathered her things, but made no move to leave. "Are you coming, Natalie?" she asked timidly.

Natalie was so tense that she jerked at the sound of her name, her gaze shooting from MariAnn to Anthony in time to see an irritated expression cross his face before he smoothed it back to a mask of grief.

"I need a moment of Natalie's time first," he told the girl. "You go on home." He gave Natalie a slight nod, as if to confirm his request that she remain, and then walked back into his office, leaving the door open in invitation.

MariAnn gave her a panicked look, but Natalie smiled, warmed by the girl's concern. It made her reconsider all the bad things she'd ever thought about her. "It's okay," she said. "I'll see you tomorrow."

MariAnn nodded gratefully, then hurried out into the hallway, closing the hallway doors behind her, and leaving Natalie shut inside with Anthony.

This was about the last place she wanted to be in this moment, but there was no way she could refuse. Especially since doing so would only create suspicion where there was none. Anthony didn't know she'd seen the fight between Christian and Noriega, one thing she definitely had going for her.

She followed him into his office, and managed not to jump when he closed the doors behind her with a flick of his hand. She couldn't control her reaction to the total catastrophe of the once-orderly office, however. The huge desk was still standing—probably because it was too big to lift, even for a vampire—but its top was bare, the wood gouged and grooved with deep scratches. Everything that had been on the desk was scattered on the floor, and the guest chairs, with their gold embroidered silk, were now no more than kindling, the fabric nothing but twisted shreds. A few photographs or mementos still clung to the walls, their frames broken and glass shattered. But most were part of the twisted pile of wreckage on the floor. As she stood there, something crashed behind her and she spun around to stare, only to find Anthony standing right in front of her when she turned back, his dark eyes studying her closely.

"Forgive the mess," he said dismissively, then gestured at the lone, remaining piece of furniture, a velvet-upholstered love seat that had been shoved against a wall.

Natalie glanced at the seat, but remained standing, keeping her gaze on Anthony as he walked over to stand behind the desk. His chair still looked serviceable, but it, too, had been savaged.

"How close are you to finishing your work here?" he asked.

She frowned at the unexpected question. "I've made good progress, but this is a lengthy project. Our latest update was just last week, and it still stands. I estimate another three to four months to completion."

He sighed. "Natalie, I think you should come back home with me when I leave. To New Orleans."

"But we discussed this last week also. You and I and Jaclyn. And you all decided I would finish up the project, working under the new vampire lord."

"Yes, but last week I thought one of my own would succeed me in a peaceful transition. But now, with this murder . . . I'll have to report Duvall to the Council. I don't know if they'll take action against him or not, but either way, this could get very ugly. And I don't want you caught up in it. You're a woman of refinement, and unaccustomed to such violence."

A raggedy beep came from over in the corner, where the desk phone was hidden beneath a pile of broken photographs. "Ibarra here, my lord. Front door security."

"What is it?" Anthony responded with forced patience.

"MariAnn just passed through, my lord. She said you're shut down for the night, but Jake Baudin is here, and he says you're expecting him."

Anthony's scowl at the interruption disappeared, his expression returning to its usual blank mask. "Send him up." He turned his attention back to Natalie. "We'll talk again. You should go home."

She dipped her head in agreement, then reached for the door. It opened before her hand touched it, and she was confronted by a vampire she'd never seen before. Jake Baudin, she assumed. And he was obviously a vampire, or he couldn't have gotten up here this fast. He was tall and rangy, with a trim beard and dark hair. She didn't know what he did for Anthony, but that very fact made her suspect it was something nefarious. She had access to every aspect of the estate's finance and files, including data on both human and vampire personnel. And *that* included the so-called free agents, which was nothing but a pretty name for spies, who lived in other territories. And she'd still never heard of Jake Baudin. Add to that the fact that Anthony suddenly couldn't get rid of her fast enough, and she realized Baudin was someone Anthony had never wanted her to know, and now wanted her to forget.

Given the night's already suspicious events, however, and now this unknown vamp's sudden arrival, she wasn't about to ask questions.

Baudin nodded courteously and stood back to let her leave Anthony's office. She kept her eyes down as she walked by, and waited until he'd disappeared behind the closed double doors, then she all but ran to her office, wanting only to get out of the building and into her car. She needed to go somewhere where she could think, needed to decide what to do about all of this. She could bug out immediately, of course. Just pack up and go home to New Orleans, just as Anthony had suggested. Of course, he probably hadn't intended for her to leave *tonight*, but he probably wouldn't question it either.

On the other hand, she could go along with what Anthony wanted, and agree to leave with him. Or at least pretend to. With the challenge about to get underway, and all of the other vampire lords arriving in just a few days, Anthony couldn't afford to leave before then. Which would give her plenty of time to get a discreet word to Christian about what Anthony had said about Noriega's death, and that he was planning to go to the Council with it. There had to be a reason he was calling it murder, rather than what it had been—a fair fight that Noriega had lost. Vamps were aggressive and cranky in general. They challenged and fought each other all the time, and death wasn't an unusual outcome. So why was this one significant?

Anthony *hated* Christian for some reason, so if he was bothering to lie about what had happened, then it had to be bad for Christian. And even though she'd convinced herself that Christian was bad for *her*, and that she wanted nothing to do with him—or at least she didn't *want* to want anything to do with him—she knew she couldn't leave him in the dark about Anthony's machinations either.

She sighed, knowing this didn't make sense. She'd barely met him. So why this sudden need to protect him? But . . . a phone call couldn't hurt, right? And then she could go home to New Orleans, with Anthony none the wiser.

She shoved her laptop into her tote. Normally, she locked it up here in the office, because it contained all of her records and research on the estate's finances, which she called the Hawthorn project. But tonight, she wanted it with her. There was too much weirdness going on, and she'd spent way too much time on this project to have all her work disappear because of some twisted vampire politics.

She glanced once at the closed doors as she hurried through the outer office, hearing the rumble of deep voices. If she hadn't had such a well-honed survival instinct, she might have snuck over to the doors and tried to listen. But there was no such thing as sneaking up on a vampire, and she wasn't even the tiniest bit suicidal.

She locked and closed the hallway door behind her, then hurried down the corridor. She needed to talk to someone who would listen. And she knew just where to find her.

ANTHONY LISTENED as Natalie moved about the office, gathering her things. He caught the slide of a desk drawer, the shuffle of papers, the click of her heels. She was always the perfect lady when she came to the office, always dressed femininely, gracefully, in skirts and high heels. No low-cut necklines or thigh-baring outfits. Anthony was the first one to admit that MariAnn was guilty of both of those things, but she played a different role in the dynamic of the office. She was a vampire groupie and, as such, intentionally enticing to his vampires. They enjoyed flirting with her and, if rumors were correct, many of them had done far more than mere flirting.

But his Natalie was *not* intended to entice. She was a professional—an intelligent and refined young woman doing an important job. A Southern woman who knew how a proper young lady conducted herself in the workplace. She'd avoided the various parties that were so much a part of life on the estate, and had never even dated one of his vampires. Which was as it should be. Natalie was meant for better things than groping in the corner of a blood house. She deserved a powerful vampire who could protect her, and provide for her. A vampire like Anthony. And he'd be damned if he was going to stand back now, and watch while that French bastard slid in there in his place. He'd seen the way Natalie had looked at Duvall, with his slick ways and good looks. She was an innocent. Of course she'd been charmed by him. As for Duvall, she'd be nothing more than his latest conquest, another notch on the bedpost.

Anthony wasn't about to let that happen. Natalie was his, and it was time she realized that. Perhaps he'd been too patient, too considerate of her modern sensibilities. It was time he stepped up and showed her where she belonged.

The solid sound of the outer door closing and the snick of the lock told him she'd finally left the office. He glanced at Baudin to find him eyeing the rubble of Anthony's once-elegant office. His already simmering rage threatened to boil over. This office had been his refuge, proof that he deserved to be where he was, that he was more than Raphael's puppet. Every picture on the wall had been carefully chosen, every piece of memorabilia had marked a significant moment in his long life, a history of one triumph after the next. And now it was nothing but shards of glass and wood, crumpled paper with fancy writing and golden seals. And it was all Raphael's fault. He was the one who'd inflicted that bastard Duvall on him, as if Raphael had any rightful say in who succeeded Anthony as Lord of the South.

Anthony knew what everyone said, that he was too weak to rule by himself, that without Raphael and his lackey, Jaclyn, he would have fallen long ago. He'd been furious when Raphael had informed him that he was bowing out of their arrangement—*informed him,* as if he had no say in the matter! What they'd had was a partnership, damn it. Raphael might have supplied the raw power behind the scenes, but it was Anthony who'd done the work, who'd taken a territory that had been falling apart under Jabril's heavy-handed rule, and made it a cohesive whole once again. But had that black-eyed bastard so much as mentioned his contribution? Hell, no. He'd simply made the decision that worked best for him, and given Anthony an ultimatum.

Well, Raphael was about to discover he wasn't the only game in town. Anthony would return to New Orleans all right, but he would do it on his own terms. And once there, he would rule absolutely, with no one to question his abilities or dictate his actions.

Baudin shoved some rubble around as he walked over and sank onto the velvet loveseat. He appeared completely relaxed, unfazed by the destruction all around him. It was part of what made him such a good spy, the ability to adapt with ease. Well, that, and enough power to deceive almost any vampire, short of an actual vampire lord. And since he was one of Anthony's own children, his loyalty was as reliable as it could be. His assignment this time around had been to check on Hubert and his secret army down in Mexico. Anthony had been briefed by Raphael's lieutenant, Jared, about the predicament in Hawaii while it was still going on. He didn't know all of it, because he wasn't part of the Western lord's inner circle, despite the fact that *he* was Lord of the South. Lucas had been there, naturally. It was disgustingly obvious the way Raphael favored the Plains lord. But Anthony had been shut out, left with whatever tidbits of information Jared chose to share.

He *had* been warned, along with all of the other North American lords, that a European invasion might be imminent. No one thought Mathilde's attack on Raphael was the sum total of the Europeans' effort to take the continent. And with the revelations still coming out of Mexico regarding the late Enrique's collaboration with their European enemies, Anthony had assumed his territory would be next on the invaders' list. Especially since Vincent was still busy cleaning up the mess Enrique had left behind. But had *Raphael* considered that before announcing his plans for the South? No, he'd rushed ahead, leaving Anthony to make his own arrangements. And that's what he'd done, too. Fuck Raphael.

Pretending a calm he didn't feel, he settled back in his desk chair, ignoring the unpleasant roughness caused by several deep tears in the expensive leather.

"What's Hubert up to these days?" he asked Baudin.

"War, my lord," Baudin said bluntly. "Ever since Mathilde died, he's been preparing frantically, dead set on taking the South. It's almost as if he thinks someone—most likely Raphael—is going to show up at any minute, and he needs to finish his personal invasion first. He seems to believe that once he's pre-empted the challenge by launching a successful bid for the territory, all will be forgiven, that Raphael will simply accept him as a *fait accompli*. As Lord of the South." Baudin aimed a questioning look in Anthony's direction. "He won't, will he? I mean, if Hubert manages to take over, Raphael will step in and slap him down, right?"

Anthony's gaze narrowed on the spy. It didn't escape his notice that Baudin assumed it was *Raphael* whom Hubert feared, and *Raphael* who would be the one doling out punishment. Hell, it didn't even seem to bother Baudin that if he was right, and Hubert took the South by force, he'd probably kill Anthony in order to be sure the mantle of the South fell to him. He wouldn't want to trust that Anthony would willingly surrender outside of the formal challenge. After all, Hubert would still be viewed as an invader, not a challenger.

"You could always leave the territory," Anthony said mildly. He needed Baudin too much right now to kill him.

"Nah, I like it here. And I don't like that bastard Hubert. I especially don't trust his self-made army. Most of those vamps should be put down. They're more like animals than humans."

That caught Anthony's attention. "There's something wrong with them?"

"Nothing enough time and attention couldn't heal. But Hubert's turning too many, too fast, and he's not being selective. Most of them can't even read, much less understand the tactics of war. And they've all been turned without consent. He's going to remote villages and taking anyone he can get his fangs into. Anyone male, that is. He wants fighters, and he's old enough to think women can't get the job done."

"There must be a few of them who have potential."

Baudin shook his head. "Yeah, but he doesn't let them live. He offs those before their first night is over. He doesn't want independent thinkers, he wants an army of zombies."

"It can't be that bad," Anthony scoffed.

"Wait until you see them; you'll understand."

"You say that as if I'll be seeing them soon."

The spy nodded. "It's why I'm here. Hubert's accelerating his plans. I expect him to move on your territory within the week."

Anthony straightened in surprise. "One week? Your last report said we had a couple of months."

"That was before Mathilde died, and before your plans to resign went public. I told you, he wants to take the South before the challenge is settled, thinking Raphael will go along with it."

"Raphael isn't the only one Hubert needs to worry about," Anthony snapped.

"As you say," Baudin replied, unperturbed by Anthony's fit of temper. "But that's not how Hubert sees it. Raphael's like his personal nightmare. He was plainly terrified when he heard the big guy had escaped, and then had killed Mathilde. He was so scared that he didn't, or couldn't, even control his reaction. Not great for morale among the troops, by the way. Especially not those of us who've retained the ability to think."

"Raphael will be here this weekend," Anthony said thoughtfully.

"For the challenge kick-off," Baudin agreed. "Hubert had hoped to be sitting in your place before then, but he's given up on that." His lips twisted in a wry smile as he took in the battered condition of Anthony's chair, but he didn't say anything out loud. Apparently, his survival sense had finally kicked in, and he'd realized he'd been less than flattering toward his own Sire.

But Anthony had much bigger problems. If Baudin was right—and he trusted the spy's judgment on this, at least—then Anthony would be forced to put his plan into motion this week. He'd counted on being long gone by the time Hubert made his move, had assumed his successor—preferably one of his chosen candidates—would face Hubert and his vampire army.

"We'll have to deploy closer to the border," he said thoughtfully, thinking out loud. "The outpost near Laredo is well-positioned to cover wide stretches."

Baudin nodded. "You don't want to let him get too deep into Texas before you hit him."

Anthony pursed his lips, staring blindly at the destruction of what had been an antique sideboard. Baudin was right again. Hubert would have to be met at the border.

But Anthony couldn't risk himself so early in the conflict, which meant someone else would have to lead the forces against Hubert. He tapped a finger thoughtfully on the desktop. He could send one of his own children, but that could destroy his larger plan for New Orleans. On the other hand . . . *Duvall* wanted to rule the South, didn't he? And what better chance to prove his fitness than by championing her defense? He wouldn't be able to refuse either. What kind of message would that send to the vampires who might someday look to him for protection?

Anthony smiled slowly at his own cleverness. Sending Duvall to the front would solve more than one problem for him. And if Hubert happened to kill him . . . so much the better.

Chapter Four

Mexico City, Mexico

"DUVALL'S IN HOUSTON already?" Vincent Kuxim spoke in the general direction of the speakerphone, as he paced restlessly in front of his desk. Conference calls like this weren't the norm in the world of vampires. Hearing was too acute and eavesdropping too common. But tonight, the party in the next room—a party he'd much rather be enjoying—nullified even the best vampire hearing, and it was more efficient this way.

"In Houston, and already fighting challenges, according to Jaclyn." That was Juro, Raphael's security chief. If anyone knew the comings and goings in Raphael's territory, it was Juro, especially when it involved an unexpectedly powerful vampire, even if the South wasn't precisely Raphael's territory.

"Jaclyn," Vincent repeated. "Why isn't she going after the South herself?"

"No interest," Raphael said simply. He and his people were on speakerphone, too. "She and her staff want to come home."

Vincent glanced at his lieutenant, Michael, who shrugged back at him. Some vampires were wired to be ambitious, and some weren't. It was a good thing. Kept the bloodshed to a minimum. But he still didn't understand it.

"Is the challenge open already? Then why am I dragging my ass to Houston this weekend?"

"Because it's not officially open yet. Anthony claims Duvall ambushed one of his vampires and took him out preemptively."

"Which vamp?"

"Noriega." That was Jared speaking this time. He'd spent a lot of time in the South, and probably knew the players better than any of them.

Vincent frowned. "I don't know him. Guess I never will now. But it doesn't sound like you believe Anthony's story."

"It's becoming obvious that Anthony wants one of his own to succeed him," Jared replied. "Noriega would have fit the bill, except for one thing. He didn't have the power to win the challenge."

"And Duvall?" Vincent asked, knowing he was missing something in this conversation.

"He would have flicked Noriega aside like a bug," Jared said flatly. "Anthony's claiming Duvall saw Noriega as a threat. That just doesn't fit."

Vincent paced back and forth a couple more times. "You think Anthony set his own child up to take the fall. If Noriega managed to succeed, then Duvall's dead and out of Anthony's hair. If not, then Anthony files a claim with the Council, and gets rid of him that way." He walked over to join Michael who was now busy on the computer, searching incoming files. Michael looked up and shook his head.

"I don't have a formal complaint from Anthony yet. Do you?"

"I received a courtesy phone call from him," Raphael provided in his deep voice. "The formal claim will arrive tomorrow."

"Anthony has to know this won't stand up to scrutiny. So what game is he playing?" Vincent asked.

"He's delaying," Raphael said. "The question is why."

"Shit. I don't need this. I've got those European fuckers lurking in every corner of my territory, thanks to Enrique. Can I at least trust the intel that Duvall provided on Hubert?"

"We're still checking it out, but as far as we can tell, it's good," Juro replied. "The biggest question is whether most of it is still relevant. Mathilde had intended for Duvall to work with Hubert, and he did go to Mexico to meet with him initially, but he'd already blown Hubert off by the time Mathilde died. If I were Hubert, I'd have changed things up by now, just in case."

"Send it to me anyway. I'll see what we can make of it."

"On its way," Juro confirmed.

"Fantastic. Now I've got a party to get back to."

"If you've got time to party, things can't be too bad, *mi amigo*," Jared joked. He and Vincent had known each other long before Vincent became Lord of Mexico.

"It's Lana's birthday," Vincent told him. "And it's almost time for presents."

"Tell her happy birthday!" Cynthia Leighton spoke up for the first time, although Vincent wasn't surprised to discover she was there. Raphael's mate was a fighter in every sense of the word. Just like his own Lana.

"I will," Vincent told her. "And, Raphael, I'll tap my sources in Texas, and let you know if anything interesting crawls out. See you in Houston." He punched the disconnect button, then turned to Michael. "Or maybe not. It sounds like the challenge might be over before it gets started. You know anything about Christian Duvall?"

Michael closed the computer and stood. "Not a thing. But that'll change by morning. I've set up some searches."

"Excellent. Party time."

The noise level swelled as Michael opened the heavy door to a combination of music and laughter, and multiple conversations all going at the same time. But as Vincent stepped into the room, his gaze tracked unerringly to the birthday girl. Lana Arnold, human, bounty hunter, the love of his life. She was wearing a dress tonight. The short, playful skirt made her legs look even longer than they were, and the killer high heels made his dick hurt. The dress was red, a color his Lana had been born to wear. It added a warm glow to her gorgeous mocha skin, and contrasted with the black silk of her hair. He thought about ripping the dress off her later on. Thought about all that long, silky hair sliding over his belly as she—

"Does she know?"

Vincent turned to find his "sister" Camille standing next to him. They'd been nest mates for decades under Enrique's tutelage, and had believed themselves to be vampire siblings. Until Vincent had discovered, just recently, that Enrique was not, in fact, his Sire. But that hadn't changed anything about his relationship with Camille. She was his sister in every way that counted, and he loved her. She was one of the very few vampires he trusted absolutely.

"Does who know what?" he asked her.

Camille smiled. "You look at Lana with such hunger in your eyes, *man-ito*. Does she know you love her?"

"Of course, she does," he scoffed, bristling a little at the question. "You were there the day I fought Enrique. I crawled through a soup of my own blood and bones to get to her after I dusted that bastard. I gave her my wrist, even though I was gushing so much blood, she could have lapped it up with a spoon instead."

Camille shook her head, then reached up to cup his cheek. "Idiot. Tell the woman you love her."

Vincent smiled confidently. Covering Camille's hand with his, he brought it over to his lips and kissed her fingers. "Have a little faith."

He made his way across the room, the partygoers clearing a path ahead of him automatically. He could have cleared the room with a touch of his power, but that wasn't necessary here. These were his people, his friends. Lana turned to watch him approach, eyes bright with excitement, her mouth turned up in a smile that was just for him.

Hell, yes, he loved her.

"Dance with me, *querida*," he said, lowering his head to brush his mouth against hers.

"The music is—" She started to protest that the music was too fast.

Lana was a graceful woman, but she'd never learned to dance, and didn't believe she could. But at that moment, the music changed to something slow and sexy. She rolled her eyes at his smug look. "Lord of all he surveys," she muttered.

"Not all," he murmured, pulling her into his arms. "Just the playlist."

She laughed and wrapped her arms around his neck. "Sexy beast."

"That's me."

Their bodies fit together perfectly as they swayed to the music, her breasts warm and soft against his chest, his cock swelling where it rubbed against her belly. Lana closed her eyes and rested her cheek against his, as other couples moved onto the dance floor around them.

"This is perfect," she whispered, lifting the fingers of one hand to trail through his hair and around to caress his bearded jaw.

"You are," he agreed.

She smiled and kissed his neck.

"Lana."

"Mmm?"

"Will you marry me?"

Her heartbeat stuttered, and she froze for an instant against his chest.

"What?" she asked, sounding breathless.

"Will you marry me, *querida*?"

She leaned back enough to stare up at him, her eyes wide. "Really?"

Vincent laughed, then taking her left hand in his right, he dropped to one knee. The music faded away. So did the crowds, the talk, the laughter. Only Lana remained.

Sliding his hand into one pocket, he produced the ring he'd had custom-made, and held it out to her.

Her eyes went impossibly wider, and filled with tears, as she dropped to her knees next to him and threw herself into his embrace, wrapping her arms around his neck. "Oh my God, oh my God, oh my God," she was whispering.

Vincent snugged an arm around her back and pulled her close. "No god, *mi amor*. Only me."

"Only . . . I love you," she choked out.

"And?"

Lana blinked in a moment's confusion, then laughed happily. "Yes! Of course, yes!"

Vincent slipped the ring on her left hand, then stood, helping her to her feet along with him, as everyone around them started cheering. Resting a hand on Lana's hip, he pulled her close, then leaned down and whispered in her ear. "You know I love you, right?"

She *tsk*ed loudly, and elbowed him in the side. "Of course I know that."

It was Vincent's turn to laugh as he met Camille's eyes over the crowd, and winked. She grinned back at him, and shook her head. *Bastard*, she mouthed at him.

"MAYBE IF WE GET married here, your dad won't come," Vincent muttered two hours later. The party was over, the congratulations rung, and the sun was looming.

"Vincent," she chided, slapping his arm. "Of course, he'll be here. I'm his only child."

"And you're marrying a vampire."

"He likes you."

"He's afraid of me. And for good reason. If he hurts you—"

"He won't hurt me. When should we do this? And can we invite Cyn? Will Raphael let her come?"

Vincent snorted. "Right, like Raphael dictates where Cyn goes."

"You know what I mean. Vampire politics. You're a lord, he's a lord . . . it's all very twisted."

"Haven't you heard? We're all buds now."

"Uh huh. What was that phone call you got earlier?"

Vincent watched as she stepped out of the red dress, leaving her in nothing but a matching bra and a pair of barely-there silk panties. And those shoes.

"Vincent?"

His attention snapped back to her face. "Sexy," he commented. "Come here, wife."

She made another *tsk*ing sound. "Not yet," she said, coming into his arms. "Tell me about the phone call."

"Not sexy," he grumbled. "It was Raphael. There's a new player on the board for the South, and it sounds like he's throwing a wrench into Anthony's plans for the succession."

"I thought it was kind of a winner-takes-all thing."

"It is, but it's beginning to look like Anthony had a winner in mind, and it isn't the new guy."

"Does it matter to us?"

Vincent shrugged. "Not really. According to Raphael, this new player—Christian Duvall's his name—is pretty damn powerful, and he wants to join the alliance, so . . ."

"But you're worried about something."

"I'd like it a lot better if the South was settled once and for all. We've got problems of our own, and I don't need their shit bleeding into mine."

"Lovely imagery."

Vincent slapped her firm ass. "You asked."

"Uh huh. You have too many clothes on." Pushing his jacket off his shoulders, she started working on the buttons of his shirt.

"About the wedding," he said, sliding his hands around her hips and cupping the round globes of her ass beneath the silk of her panties. "As soon as possible."

Lana gave him a quizzical look.

"Anything you want works for me, as long as it's here in Mexico City, and we get married sooner, not later. A month is too long."

She grew very still, staring up at him. "Vincent, is there something you're not telling me?"

"It's war, Lana. Things happen. And I want you to be mine."

She met his eyes for a long time, searching. "Okay," she said finally. "One month. I need you, a dress, and my dad. Maybe a few friends. And my mom if she wants to come. One month."

"It's a date."

Chapter Five

Houston, Texas

NATALIE CHECKED her posture, straightening her back where she sat near the wall, watching the Krav Maga class on the other side of the dojo. It was an advanced class, which meant she had trouble following all of their moves, despite her familiarity with the discipline. Krav Maga wasn't beautiful; it wasn't meant to be. It was functional and deadly, and it got the job done. Natalie had picked up the basic moves from Alon Riese, her best friend and the instructor for the current class, but despite his encouragement, she'd never pursued it further.

Joining a dojo had been at the top of her list after she moved to Houston, but judo was her discipline. Her father had introduced her to the martial art as a child . . . "just in case." That would be just in case she was in a situation where neither he, nor either of her giant brothers, were around to pulp any horny boys into submission.

She sighed and slumped back against the wall. She'd never had to deal with any of those horny boys, because her brothers always got to them first. And they hadn't been much of a danger anyway. But at least the training was excellent exercise. She could say, with perfect modesty, that she'd always been in great shape.

These days, her work at the dojo still helped her keep fit, but it also burned off the stress of a job that involved staring at numbers all day long, trying to translate the story they told of crooked vampire lords and unscrupulous bankers. She loved her job. It was challenging, but also sometimes exhausting. Which was why she often ended her nights with an early morning visit to the dojo, before heading home for a hot shower and a few hours of sleep.

"I don't know how you do it." Her friend Janette Baldwin was sitting next to her, and punctuated her words with a jaw-breaking yawn, which told Natalie what the *it* was. Janette was a night person forced to live the life of an early bird. She ran a very successful daycare and preschool in downtown Houston, which meant she had to be there to greet all the earliest moms and dads when they dropped off their children. Natalie had met her at the first gym she'd joined in the city, and then Janette had followed her to the dojo when she decided the gym wasn't what she needed.

"And I don't know how *you* chase a bunch of rugrats around all day and still have the energy to get up an hour early to come here," Natalie told her. "Don't you get enough exercise at the prison?"

"Nat! Stop calling my school a prison! Someone will hear you and think I'm a screw at the big house or something."

Natalie laughed. "A screw at the big house? You've been watching too much reality TV."

"Besides, I like coming here," Janette said quietly, her gaze riveted on Alon's muscular form as he efficiently put every single member of the advanced class on the mat. Krav Maga might not be elegant, but Alon sure was. Natalie could appreciate his beauty, even though he didn't ring her particular bell. They'd tried dating once, early on. But there was no heat between them; they were better as friends.

Janette, on the other hand, had a major crush on Alon, but was too shy to do anything about it. Unfortunately, Alon seemed blissfully unaware. He was always friendly, always respectful, but that was it. Much to Janette's continued dismay.

"Stop ogling Alon, and talk to me."

"I can't talk to you until you tell me what's going on."

"I'm not sure . . . I don't know how much I can say."

"Okay, so it's vampire stuff."

"Janette—"

"Come on, Nat. I know where you work, that's no secret. And there's no other reason for you to be so stressed about it. Tell me what's up. Pinky-swear I won't tell anyone else."

Natalie bit her lip, thinking hard. She had to talk to someone, or she'd go nuts. And Janette was one of only two people in her life she could really talk to, especially about the vampire stuff. She didn't even tell her family how she felt about working for Anthony, because (a) she didn't want to upset them, and (b) she didn't want to get them on Anthony's shit list. So there was Janette, and there was Alon. And that was it.

"Okay, but not a word to anyone. I don't give a shit about Anthony, but I don't want you to get hurt."

"Those vamps probably don't even know I exist."

Natalie snorted. "You'd be surprised, so not a word."

"Fine, fine, what's going on?"

"Okay, so there's this new guy—"

"Oh, my God," Janette exclaimed, clutching Natalie's arm. "A new guy? An actual guy with a penis and everything?" she said, pretending to be tearing up with emotion. "I'm so proud."

"Shut up," Natalie said, trying not to laugh. "And keep your voice down. Yes, there's an actual guy, but not like you think."

"Is he gorgeous?"

Natalie groaned in exasperation. "Of course, he's gorgeous. They all are. But . . ."

Janette studied her, eyes wide. "Oh, my God," she said again. "I'm right. You like this one."

"He's different," Natalie admitted.

"Different how?"

She blew out a long sigh. She didn't know what to say, how to make Janette understand. It wasn't any *one* thing, it was . . . "It's the whole package," she admitted slowly. "It's not just his looks, although God knows he's handsome. But he's smart and charming and nice." Her inner voice scoffed, *Nice, Nat? Really?*

Janette stared at her like she'd grown a second head.

"Okay, so not *nice*. That's the wrong word. But he was sweet and polite."

"Sweet and *nice*? Does he want a job at the preschool? 'Cuz you make him sound like somebody's dog."

Natalie gaped at her in disbelief. "He's not like that at all! He's huge and built, with shoulders out to there, and the most amazing blue eyes, and his smile—" She snapped her mouth shut when she realized she'd been had.

Janette covered her mouth against a laugh.

"Okay, so call me shallow," Natalie sniffed. "He's beautiful. Fine. But you know how you meet some people, and there's this spark of intellect in their eyes, an awareness or something that tells you this person is smarter than the average bear. Well, I love that, and he has that spark, whatever it is. And . . ."

"And you want him," Janette said knowingly.

Nat puffed out a breath. "I do," she admitted. "But that's not the problem."

"Of course not. This is you, after all."

Natalie switched her gaze to the Krav Maga class for a bit, then turned back to Janette. "I saw something I wasn't supposed to see. Something involving Christian."

"That's the new hunk's name? Christian?"

"Christian Duvall, yeah. Anyway, I saw this thing, and then I heard Anthony talking about it, and . . . he lied," she finished with a whisper. "Anthony, I mean. He lied about what happened, and I think it's going to get Christian in trouble. And I don't know if I should tell him about Anthony, or let it go. It's all vampire business, and they have their own rules, and

I'm . . . an accountant."

"Forensic accountant," Janette clarified loyally. "And *you're* smarter than the average bear, too. If you think there's a problem, tell the guy. It's not as if you owe Anthony anything. He's like the creepy family stalker, the one who nobody knows, but who shows up every Thanksgiving, and never brings pie."

"He gave me his card," Natalie said suddenly.

"Ew. Anthony?"

"No! *Christian.*"

"Which means he wants you, too," Janette decided.

"I didn't say—"

"Oh, please. You want him, and I say it's about time. If you don't use it as God intended, pretty soon, your vagina's—"

Natalie hissed at her to shut up. "Can you say that any louder?"

Janette laughed. "Call him, Nat. You don't have to come right out and lay it on him. Just feel him out first, and then if it flows, it flows. And you can warn him about the other thing, too."

"You're right. I need to warn him."

"But wait until after you've had sex to tell him, because—"

"We are *not* going to have sex. I'm going to call—"

"Fifty bucks says you're bumping nasties within the week."

"Bumping nasties. Charming. And I'll take that bet."

"Yippee! Momma needs a new pair of shoes."

"You're ridiculous."

"And you're about to get laid," Janette whispered. "Do you have decent underwear, or is it all granny panties?"

"Not that it matters, but my lingerie is perfectly presentable."

"So, granny time, huh?"

"No! Stop it."

Janette leaned against her, laughing. "I want pictures."

"Of my underwear?"

"No, silly. Of the hunk-a-licious who finally broke your fast." She checked her watch, then pushed to her feet with a sigh, using the wall as a brace. "I have to go home and shower. Will I see you tomorrow?"

"Probably."

"Well, if I don't, I'll know why. So, don't forget the fifty bucks. And the pictures."

Natalie watched Janette walk along the wall toward the door. She also saw her wave good-bye to Alon, and get a friendly nod in return. Maybe Natalie *was* in a dry spell, but she wasn't the only one. And she wasn't about to break it with a certain sexy vampire either. Not because he wasn't attractive, but because he was far *too* attractive. And she had a feeling that once she got sucked into the raging river that was Christian Duvall, she might just drown.

Chapter Six

CHRISTIAN WOKE to two messages the next night. The first wasn't altogether unexpected. Unofficially, Jaclyn was using her power to boost Anthony's position as Lord of the South, but officially, she was Raphael's representative. Kind of an ambassador to Anthony's court. So it wasn't a total surprise that she'd want to meet with Christian, and maybe even debrief him on what he knew about Hubert and Mexico. He was sure she'd been updated on the intel he'd shared with Raphael and the others, but she might want her own in-person briefing.

It was the second message that surprised him. His cell phone was sitting on the bedside table, playing the messages on speaker while he dressed. The sound of Natalie's sexy Cajun drawl snapped his head around, and had him dashing over to pick up the phone and listen more closely. But what he heard was more troubling than exciting. It wasn't what she said, so much as an undercurrent to her words, a slight tremor in her voice.

"Christian, it's Natalie. We met earlier . . . well, by the time you get this, it will have been last night that we met." There was a pause, as if she didn't know how to continue, but then she did. "I wonder if we could meet for coffee . . . or something. Somewhere away from the estate. I'm probably making too much of—" She drew a deep breath. "Anyway, if you could, call me when you get this. This is my cell phone, so anytime."

Christian frowned at the number, then played the message one more time.

"Marc!" he yelled, and heard his lieutenant's door open down the short hall, followed by rapid footsteps.

Marc appeared in the open doorway. "What happened?"

"Nothing yet, but listen to this."

He played both messages for Marc, whose reaction to Natalie's voice was much the same as his. "Jaclyn's business as usual, but this Natalie . . . who is she?"

"I forgot you didn't meet her. She works in Anthony's office, an accountant, I think. Sexy as hell, by the way."

"Damsel in distress. Go get her, bro."

Christian smiled slightly, but shook his head. "There's a complication, which makes this interesting, and more than a little troubling. Anthony calls her his cousin, but I don't think that's really the way he thinks of her."

"You think she's setting you up?"

Christian considered the possibility. She'd be the perfect weapon against him. Sexy, beautiful, and smart, with just enough vulnerability to appeal to his protective streak. Anthony would have noticed the appeal she had for him last night. But, there was the other half of the equation. The fact that Natalie didn't seem to like Anthony any more than he did. She'd been visibly startled when he'd called her "cousin," and, damn it, she really did sound scared on that message.

"I don't think so," he said, answering Marc's question. "I think she knows something. Something Anthony doesn't know she knows, or at least doesn't want her to share."

"Why share with you, though? She barely knows you."

"Yeah, but I'm charming as hell when I set my mind to it."

Marc coughed obnoxiously. "So call her back, and take her up on the coffee. That's a first date thing, you know. When a woman's not sure she wants to commit to a *real* date."

Christian gave him a dry look. "Thanks for the confidence. I'll call Jaclyn first, then Natalie. Sounds like I'm heading back to the estate either way, and you're coming with me."

"You better believe it. After last night, neither one of us should venture into that viper's pit alone."

NATALIE DOCKED her phone, and snapped on her seatbelt, then backed hurriedly from the carport attached to her townhouse. Anthony had wanted her to live on the estate, but she'd declined. The main house was reserved during the day for vampires, but there was what used to be servants' quarters in a building some distance away from the main residence, which was reserved for the various human staff. She could have bunked there, but it would have been too much like a college dorm, and she'd had her fill of that after her second year at Tulane. Besides, she hadn't been that happy about being essentially blackmailed into working for Anthony, and didn't want him any closer than necessary.

Instead, she'd rented this very nice, furnished, two-bedroom, two-story townhouse with no personality whatsoever. It was well located and functional, but with the bland décor, it had no soul. She'd managed to add a little bit of her own personality, sprinkling the rooms with family pictures, and the occasional knickknack. But it still didn't look like a place where anyone *lived*. Maybe because she'd never intended it to be her home.

Right now, however, all she cared about was that it was close to the estate, with very little traffic between here and there at this time of night. And tonight that mattered, because she was tragically late. She'd tossed and turned most of the day, stressing over the message she'd left for Christian, worried that Anthony would somehow discover what she'd done, whether because he was tapping her phone, or reading her mind. Neither of which made sense. First, she was pretty sure he *couldn't* read her mind. If he could have, she'd have been out of a job long ago, since she didn't, for one minute, buy into his benevolent distant ancestor routine.

But that was logic. And there'd been no logic in her bed last night, as she'd rolled from one position to the next, trying to find a comfortable spot, and rehearsing in her head what she'd say to Christian.

And then there was Christian himself. She knew she should stay away from him. Hadn't she convinced herself of that last night? He wasn't good for her health or her heart. But she couldn't stand back and watch him be murdered. She was convinced that's what Anthony was plotting. He'd tried with poor, dumb Noriega. That had failed, but she had a feeling his next ploy would be a lot less spontaneous, and a lot more deadly.

Pulling up behind a line of cars at the red light, she called up her messages. There was only one . . . from Christian. Heart beating a thousand miles a minute, she hit play and listened to his deep voice as he assured her that he'd be happy to meet at her convenience, and asked her to call him back. But her heart almost stopped when he said he'd be at the estate tonight, in another meeting. Whom was he meeting? Was she already too late? She'd specifically asked him to meet her somewhere else, because she didn't want him near Anthony until he understood the danger he was in.

She tapped the call back, listening to it ring as the line of cars started moving again. Christian's phone answered almost immediately, but it was his voicemail.

"It's Natalie," she said simply. "Call me. Before you get to the estate, if you can. I'd really like to meet somewhere less crowded."

Well, that was great. That sounded like she wanted a romantic assignation or something. She might as well have suggested they meet at the local motel. She groaned out loud, and kept driving. She had to get to the office. Anthony would wonder if she didn't show up soon, and maybe even go looking for her. He might not be able to read her mind, but he probably could track her phone easily enough. If Christian had called, she'd have detoured to meet with him first, but now he was at the one place he shouldn't be.

Feeling the weight of her decision, wondering how she'd gotten involved so deeply, so fast, she made the turn that would take her to the estate.

CHRISTIAN LEFT MARC with Cibor, and settled into one of the big, cushy chairs around the conference table, eyeing Jaclyn as she closed the door and sat on the other side of the table. The conference room was part of a suite of offices that Jaclyn had to herself, along with what appeared to be a sizeable staff. If anything, her offices were more palatial than Anthony's, although it could be argued that the entire house was his, while only these few rooms were Jaclyn's. It was worth noting, though, that Jaclyn had only one human on her staff, and that was her secretary. And he'd bet that all of her vampires owed allegiance to Raphael, just as Jaclyn did.

And that made him wonder again about the relationship between Anthony and Raphael. Cibor had said Anthony was bitter about Raphael's decision to pull out of the South. But the resentment must have been building before that. Any way you looked at it, Anthony was beholden to Raphael, and he must hate it. He could never be truly his own man, and would always feel Raphael looking over his shoulder. And what about the other lords? They all had to know the true situation. Did they consider Anthony less than themselves? Not a full member of the Council? That would grate on Anthony's every nerve, wouldn't it?

"Christian Duvall," Jaclyn said, scooting her chair back and crossing her legs. She was an attractive female. Dark-haired, sharp-featured. Intelligent, but with an edge that Christian admired in an opponent, but found off-putting in a woman. At least a woman who wasn't an opponent.

"Jaclyn," he responded, pronouncing her name in the French way. *Zhak-LEEN.* She wasn't French, but her people were. Christian didn't know her entire story, but he knew she'd been born in Quebec, and that the Québecois version of the French language was her native tongue.

Jaclyn smiled warmly. "Raphael asked me to convey his regards, and to tell you he spoke with Vincent, who is understandably interested in whatever you might know about Hubert and any others. You'll probably hear from him directly in the next day or two."

Christian tilted his head in acknowledgment. "I'll be happy to share whatever I know," he said, and waited for her to get to the point. She hadn't called him here to tell him about Vincent.

Leaning forward, her arms on the table, and her body language shifting to that of a confidante, she said, "Raphael also heard about the ambush last night."

And there it was. The real reason for this meeting. "Ambush," Christian repeated. "And did Raphael hear who ambushed whom?"

Jaclyn barked out a surprised laugh. "Direct and to the point. I like it. Anthony is claiming you murdered Noriega in order to get a jump on the challenge, that you feared the competition."

Christian managed to confine his scorn to a raised eyebrow. He feared

Noriega? That was hilarious. "And what does Raphael think?" he asked, since she seemed to be waiting for the question.

"Raphael has met you," she said simply. "And his lieutenant, Jared, has met both you and Noriega. Let's just say that the facts are in question."

Christian tipped his head again. "Please convey my appreciation to Raphael for the update," he said, and meant it. The Western lord hadn't needed to let him know what Anthony was doing, or even that he doubted Anthony's version of events. That he had done so indicated yet another level of support that Christian hadn't counted on.

"Be careful, Christian," Jaclyn said solemnly. "Anthony might be lacking in power, but he's very shrewd, and doesn't care who pays for what he wants. He's also remarkably egotistical, even for one of us."

"I lived a quarter century in Mathilde's court. I understand what motivates a sociopath."

She nodded her head silently. "You may not believe this, but Raphael is a neutral observer in the challenge. He wants the strongest champion to prevail. The South needs a strong leader."

"I do believe that," he said, with a confident grin. "Which is why *I* will be the one who prevails."

Jaclyn smiled back at him. "I tend to agree with you. Unofficially, of course."

"Of course."

"You're new to Houston, aren't you?"

"More or less. We visited a few times to look at real estate."

"So what can I help you with? Information on the city? The best blood houses?"

"We're well set on those fronts. Marc is an excellent scout. There is one thing, however. I need a good dojo, preferably one with a master who embraces the discipline of Krav Maga."

"Now, *that* I don't know anything about, but I know someone who does," Jaclyn said, and reached for the phone. She hit a speed dial button, then listened for a moment, before Christian heard the faint sound of a woman answering.

"Natalie," Jaclyn said, sharpening Christian's attention. "Could you come to my office for a moment?"

Listening intently, Christian could distinguish Natalie's lyrical accent and sexy purr, even when all she said was, "Of course. I'll be right there."

Jaclyn hung up and said, "Natalie is our forensic accountant. I'm a financial analyst, which is why Raphael chose me for this assignment in the first place, but Jabril's underhanded accounting schemes are well beyond my accounting abilities."

"She arrived with Anthony?" Christian asked, wanting to learn whatever he could of the curious relationship between the vampire lord and Natalie.

"A few months after. Apparently, he knows her family or something. I don't think she's thrilled to be working here, but she's quite brilliant at her job, and I'm grateful to have her."

"And the dojo?" he asked.

"Oh, of course. Natalie is a fan of . . . judo, I think. 'Fan' isn't the right word, I know. She has a belt of some sort. She'll probably know what you're looking for."

"Excellent," Christian said, and settled back to wait for Natalie's appearance. He was feeling very smug about this night so far. Raphael's tacit endorsement, Jaclyn's more than tacit support, and now Natalie was being delivered right into his presence. He couldn't have planned it better.

NATALIE WAS RELIEVED when Jaclyn called and asked her to come down to the office. She'd been sitting at her desk, staring at the same set of numbers for two hours, waiting for Christian to return her call. Why hadn't he phoned her yet? Had Anthony gotten to him already? Had the Council moved against him, based on Anthony's lies?

She shut down her files and snapped her laptop shut. Standing, she ran a nervous hand through her hair, smoothed her skirt, and pulled on her jacket, then slipped her glasses into her pocket and the computer under her arm. She knew she was developing a real paranoia about her work when she wasn't even willing to leave the laptop while she walked to the other end of the house. But she couldn't bring herself to leave it. And besides, she might need the information on it when she talked with Jaclyn.

She walked out to where MariAnn was searching beauty product sites on the Internet, and said, "I'll be in Jaclyn's office. I'm not sure how long. She has some questions."

"Okay," the receptionist said, without glancing up.

Jaclyn's office was as far away from Anthony's as you could get, while remaining in the same building. Anthony's offices on the second floor overlooked the front of the property, and were to the left of the main doors.

Jaclyn's offices were in the opposite corner, overlooking the back of the house, and separated from the main stairway by an intervening hallway. Her offices had been bedrooms originally, but no one slept aboveground anymore.

Natalie checked her phone as she walked, tempted to call Christian again. "Right, like he didn't get the first message, or the two hang-ups after that," she muttered to herself. One of Anthony's guards walked past, and smiled. Maybe he was just being friendly, but she suspected he was amused by her muttering. That was okay. Let them think she was nothing but an absent-minded number-cruncher.

She swung down the back hallway, and pushed open the door to Jaclyn's office. Her human assistant, Lisa, was typing away—no Internet surfing for her. And Cibor was lingering in an open doorway down the hall, talking to someone Nat couldn't see. She waved her fingers hello, then gave a questioning look in the direction of the closed conference room door. Cibor did that chin lift thing that guys did, the one that could mean all sorts of things, but in this case meant, *"Why, yes, Natalie, go on in."* Becoming a vampire didn't change everything.

Natalie opened the conference room door and froze in her tracks, overwhelmed by dueling emotions. On the one hand, she was so relieved to find Christian sitting there, looking perfectly healthy in black jeans and a sweater, that she drew what felt like her first full breath of the night. On the other hand . . . why the fuck couldn't he have called her if he was sitting in the same damn building?

Christian was on his feet and in front of her before she could say a word, his eyes searching her face, probably seeing the dark circles and the frazzled hair. If his expression was anything to go by, he wasn't liking what he was seeing. He cupped her cheek in one big hand, his fingers spearing back into her hair, as he stepped even closer. "Are you in trouble, *chére?*"

Natalie shook her head, horrified to discover her eyes filling with tears of relief that he was alive. But Christian took them the wrong way.

"Merde!" Christian cursed. "I knew I should have called sooner." Putting his arm around her, he guided her over to a chair, as if afraid she'd lose her way, or maybe fall over, if he left her on her own.

"I'm fine," she said, completely embarrassed. She didn't cry, she didn't faint, and she sure as hell didn't break down like a hormonal teenager because a handsome boy gave her a soulful look. "Really," she insisted. "I just didn't sleep well, and—"

"Why not?" he asked, turning to take a bottle of water from Jaclyn. He held the cold bottle against her neck briefly, then twisted the cap off and handed her the bottle, wrapping her fingers around it next to his, and urging her to take a drink.

"Stop." She took a small sip, then put the water on the table. "Thank you, but stop treating me like an invalid. I'm fine," she added firmly, speaking to Jaclyn, who was standing behind Christian with a worried look on her face.

"Tell me why you didn't sleep," Christian demanded, his handsome face going all macho badass, as if he could compel her to answer by force of personality.

"I called you," Natalie said accusingly, avoiding the question by turning it back on him.

"You two know each other?" Jaclyn asked.

"We met yesterday," Christian replied without looking, and gave Natalie a hard stare. "I should have called," he conceded. "I was going to stop by your office on my way out of here."

"I told you we needed to meet somewhere else. It's not safe here."

"Not safe?" Jaclyn repeated. "Natalie, what—"

"What did you see?" Christian asked, narrowing in on her concerns with remarkable clarity.

"What did she see? See when?" Jaclyn insisted, her voice betraying more than a little impatience at being kept out of the loop.

"I saw Noriega waiting for you," Natalie blurted out. "And I saw—" She sucked in a breath, staring at Christian, wondering if she should admit everything, even to him.

"You saw me kill him." Christian was whispering, but she could tell by Jaclyn's sucked-in breath that she'd heard.

"But that's good news," Jaclyn said excitedly. "She can tell the Council—"

"She tells the Council nothing," Christian snarled, standing and spinning to face Jaclyn, putting himself in front of Natalie.

"But her testimony—"

"Would paint a target on her back. I'll take care of Anthony, and whatever idiot he sends next. Natalie stays out of it."

Jaclyn gave him an appraising look, a smile playing around her lips. "It's your decision. But, you understand that Raphael will be told the truth."

Christian didn't look happy about that, but he nodded once, sharply. "I understand."

"Well, I don't," Natalie snapped, jumping up from her seat. "Anthony lied about what happened, and there's—"

Christian spun to face her again, the clear warning on his face enough to cut her off. Either he was being an ass and refusing to discuss it, or he didn't want to talk about it in front of Jaclyn. She decided to play along for now, but he was going to have to tone down the alpha male crap if they were going to get along. *Which apparently we are*, she thought resignedly.

He grinned as if he knew what she was thinking. "Jaclyn tells me you know a good dojo," he said, taking her hand. "Let's go get coffee. We can talk about it."

Natalie blinked at the sudden change of subject. A second blink and they were out of the conference room and on their way down the back hallway with Christian on one side, and Marc on the other.

"Let me carry that for you," Marc said, sliding the laptop from beneath her arm. She didn't even remember picking it up. Or maybe she'd never set it down. Natalie went to grab it back from Marc, but Christian touched her arm with a grin.

"My lieutenant is perfectly trustworthy."

"I'm sorry," she muttered, blushing hotly. "I'm becoming paranoid."

"Paranoia is a survival instinct. You should listen to it."

"But not in this case," she noted dryly.

Christian chuckled. "No."

They didn't go for the main staircase, but hurried down the back stairs instead. Marc took the last several steps quickly, pausing to check the window in the door before opening it slowly and looking around. He nodded to Christian, and the three of them hustled out to a big, black BMW sedan as Marc beeped the locks open.

Christian slid into the back with Natalie, while Marc slid behind the wheel. He passed the laptop over the seat to Christian, then turned the key and accelerated smoothly out from behind the big house.

The guards barely glanced at them when they passed through the gate, far more concerned with who was coming *in*, rather than going out. And before long, they were speeding back toward the city.

"Where are we going?" Marc asked, meeting Christian's gaze in the mirror.

"The house," Christian said, raising an eyebrow in her direction, when she shot him a questioning look. "You wanted coffee. We have excellent coffee. And something you won't find elsewhere. Complete privacy."

Natalie swallowed, her throat suddenly dry. Privacy? With Christian? She could imagine all sorts of ways *that* wasn't a good idea. "You have a house?" she asked weakly.

"We have to stay somewhere, and as you saw for yourself, it's not exactly safe for us on the estate."

She nodded. "Okay. But just for coffee. My car is—"

"We'll get you back to your car," Christian said, settling back in his seat. "Now tell me why Jaclyn says you know a good dojo."

"ARE YOU LISTENING at all?" Natalie asked irritably. They'd been on the road a little while, heading for the house he and Marc called home. Natalie had been telling him about the dojo she frequented, and her eyes were now flashing with an anger that made Christian smile. He much preferred her anger to the fear that had been clouding her face earlier, and the tears had nearly undone him, no matter that she tried to hide them.

He had a weakness for women, a need to protect them. Though he'd learned the hard lesson that not all women were worthy of protection.

Especially not in the world of vampires.

It was his father's fault, Christian considered. His father had taught him to always look after his mother and sisters. Christian had understood the admonishment when it came to his mother; she was his *mother,* after all. But his sisters had been older than he was by several years, and had seemed to devote most of their energy to tormenting him. That fact had brought him to the reluctant conclusion that he was supposed to protect all women, regardless of their disposition.

But his feelings for Natalie went beyond that. When she'd walked into the room tonight, every cell in his body had been screaming at him to go to her, that she was *his* to protect. He'd acted without thought—the need to touch her had overwhelmed everything else in that moment.

He'd never had a reaction like that to any woman before, and wasn't sure what it meant. Did he want Natalie in his bed? Hell, yes. Hearing her sexy voice cry his name as she shattered around his cock would be reason enough. But did she have the potential to be more to him? He frowned, not knowing the answer to that question. Or maybe not liking the answer that kept trying to push its way past his doubts.

"Are you really interested in this?"

His attention snapped to Natalie's narrowed gaze. He was interested, but he hadn't been listening. He wasn't going to tell her *that.*

"Of course," he lied smoothly. "What can you tell me about the dojo master?" Whoops. Her eyes narrowed even further. Had she already told him about that?

"Other than the fact that he's my best friend?" she said pointedly.

"Of course. Friendship is all well and good, but where did he get his training?"

"Maybe you should meet him instead. Him having a penis and all, you'll probably listen better."

Marc's bark of laughter told Christian everything he needed to know about what he'd missed.

"My apologies, *chére.* I admit to a certain distraction this evening. I'm puzzled by Anthony's hostility. I never met him before yesterday, so I don't know where it comes from. And I can't help wondering what he hopes to gain from it."

Natalie's expression lost its anger, becoming thoughtful as she considered what he'd said. "I don't know that much about vampires," she said. "I mean, yeah, I've been working for Anthony for almost two years now, but I haven't had that much interaction with anyone outside his office. Except for Jaclyn, but she's different."

Christian tilted his head curiously. "Different?"

"More . . . human."

His smile broadened into a grin. "Jaclyn is both powerful and well-connected. She's probably more deadly than most of the vampires on the estate, not to mention the vampires on her own staff, and *their* job is to protect her. You're making assumptions because she's female. That's sexist."

"Oh, that's rich coming from you."

"For the record, I find most women generally more interesting than men. I was distracted earlier, but it had nothing to do with your lack of a penis. I'm actually delighted you don't have one."

"How do you know?" she demanded, then immediately blushed so fiercely that he could feel the heat from her skin. "Okay, forget I said that. You bring out the worst in me."

Christian inched closer until his lips were against her ear. "I like it when you lose control, when the schoolmarm glasses come off, and the real you comes out to play."

"That's not the real me," she muttered. "The real me is the one who sits in front of a computer all day, wearing those glasses, and following boring numbers from place to place."

Christian didn't believe that. The tidy accountant was the woman she'd been raised to be—a proper, Southern woman. But the real Natalie was the one whose heart had been in her eyes when he'd touched her earlier, who'd been frantic to warn him about Anthony, even though they'd barely exchanged ten words before that. The Natalie who held a black belt in judo. And, yes, he *had* been listening when she'd talked about the dojo earlier. It had simply taken his brain a minute to catch up with everything he'd heard.

"The real you is many things, Natalie, but none of them is boring."

"I don't know what—" she started to whisper, then turned to look out the window as they pulled into the driveway of a large ranch-style house. "Is this where you live?"

The garage door opened, and Marc drove inside, hitting the visor button to close the door behind them.

"For the time being," Christian told her. "Once I'm Lord of the South, we'll need something bigger." He opened the door and slid out of the car, holding a hand out for her to exit on his side. He saw the indecision in her eyes, the urge to open her own door, to put distance between them. He didn't say anything to persuade her either way. But he knew a fierce satisfaction when her slender fingers gripped his, and she emerged from the car to stand so close that their bodies were nearly touching.

She seemed startled by that closeness, as if she'd expected him to step back. Her gaze snapped up to meet his eyes, then traveled down to linger at his mouth, her tongue coming out to lick her lips. His cock grew heavy, and he nearly groaned out loud. Could she be that innocent? Did she truly not know the effect she had on him?

"Coffee?" he managed to ask. It was either that, or grab her and disappear into his basement bedroom for several hours of ravaging.

"You really do have coffee here?" she asked.

Marc laughed at her question, as he unlocked the door between the garage and the kitchen, drawing Natalie's surprised attention.

"Don't mind Marc," Christian told her. "And, yes, we really do have coffee."

"I didn't . . . that is, I've never seen a vampire eat or drink anything before."

"Except blood," Christian corrected.

"Not even that," Natalie admitted. "I mean, obviously I know that's what you all do. But I've never seen it."

Christian guided her through the open doorway with a hand pressed against her lower back. "Never?"

"I told you, I worked in Anthony's office, but that's it. I have my own place. I come to work, I'm in the office all night, and I go home."

"No going to blood bars, no clubs?" Christian found that hard to believe. The humans in Mathilde's court, and the few other courts he'd visited, all embraced the vampire life style, seeking out vampires as lovers, which meant offering themselves as blood donors.

"None. Anthony quietly discouraged it, but that's not why I didn't do it. I was just never interested."

"But you knew Anthony from New Orleans, yes? He called you *cousin.*"

"I don't know why he did that. He's never called me that before last night."

Christian knew why, and it had nothing to do with any *cousin-like* feelings on Anthony's part.

"So you're not related, then?" he asked her.

She shrugged. "He does claim a kinship with my family, but none of us knows where he really comes from, and privately, we don't consider him family."

"And yet you're working for him."

"When Anthony wants something, he doesn't give you much choice. I don't know how he heard about me and what I do. I have a reputation in the field, but it's a rather obscure field and a tight-knit group. But he found out somehow, and while he was discreet, the message to me was clear. If I didn't take this job, my family would suffer. I'll admit that the work is fascinating, but all I've wanted was to finish the job and go back home."

Christian noticed that she'd said "wanted" not "want." As if her goals had changed recently. "And now?" he murmured, sliding his fingers around the curve of her hip, drawing her in until their bodies touched.

She jumped at the contact, giving him a look that was both startled and confused. "Now?" she repeated, staring at him wide-eyed. She swallowed hard, and said, "Now, I think I'd like a cup of coffee."

Christian gave her a half smile, and leaned over to touch his lips to the top of her warm hair. "Then, that's what you shall have. I must warn you however, that you might fall in love with my brewing skills."

MARC FLICKED ON the lights in the kitchen, and Natalie caught sight of the gleaming machine taking up half the counter space on one side.

"I can make you anything you'd like," Christian said with unabashed pride.

"Wow. That's a serious espresso maker."

"Christian takes his coffee seriously," Marc said, biting back a smile.

Christian pushed up the sleeves of his black sweater, and went directly to the machine. He opened a cupboard next to it, and began setting out ingredients, his hand poised over the row of syrup bottles lined up against the tile backsplash. "The usual, Marc?"

Marc opened the fridge and pulled out an old-fashioned glass bottle of milk, and an über-professional looking stainless steel whipped cream dispenser that made her hope Christian never saw the imitation stuff sitting in a tub in her freezer. These guys were *really* serious about their coffee. The unreality of the moment struck her—here she was, sitting in a house in the suburbs, watching two big, buff vampires putter around the kitchen, making fancy coffee. Or maybe not *just* coffee. She frowned when Marc returned to the cupboard for . . . caramel sauce?

She stared at the drink Christian was constructing. "Is that a caramel macchiato?"

"Best drink ever invented," Marc said.

"He's a farm boy at heart. Loves his sweets," Christian said at the same time. "He's mine, but I can only do so much."

Marc didn't seem bothered by the description. In fact, he seemed rather pleased. But what Christian had said only confused Natalie. This was one of those vampire things that she didn't fully understand. Vampires were humans who'd been "turned" by another vampire. She knew that much, and she knew that not just any old vampire could create a new one. There was a definite rank structure among vampires, based on power, and only the top few could make a new vampire.

"Does that mean Marc is your vampire child?" she asked Christian, then caught her breath, hoping she hadn't asked something taboo.

"Of course, he is," Christian said agreeably, as he whacked the filter to dislodge the spent grounds. He winked at her. "I do good work, don't I?" He aimed a fond look at Marc, and asked. "How's that macchiato?"

"Perfect, as always."

"So what will it be, Natalie?" Christian asked her, as twin streams of espresso poured into matching cups, and the rich scent of a dark brew wafted through the air.

Natalie shrugged, figuring she might as well go for it. "Can you do a pumpkin spice latte?"

Christian slid his gaze sideways in a glance that she couldn't interpret. Was he insulted that she'd asked? Or appalled at her taste in drinks? But he didn't say anything, just opened the same cupboard, and pulled down a shaker of something that sure smelled like pumpkin spice. Was there anything he didn't have in that cupboard?

Minutes later, the unmistakable scent of autumn baking joined the delicious aroma of real coffee beans, and Christian slid a grande-sized ceramic cup onto the counter in front of her. She took a cautious sip, and . . .

"You really did it. This is delicious!"

"I told you," Marc said, taking a stool at the end of the kitchen's island counter with his macchiato. "He takes his coffee seriously."

Christian joined them a moment later, sitting next to Natalie with a double espresso in a brilliant blue ceramic cup. As she watched, he plucked two sugar cubes from a dish sitting on the counter, then picked up a small, golden spoon and began stirring.

"So, Natalie," he said casually. "What happened in Anthony's office after I left last night?"

"What makes you think something happened?"

Christian gave her a chiding look. "I am an uncommonly powerful vampire, *ma chére*. I can hear the racing of your heart, the shallowness of your breath. And I pay attention to things that matter. You were both surprised and relieved to see me when you walked into Jaclyn's office tonight. You suspect Anthony of plotting against me, and were afraid he'd already succeeded when I didn't return your call."

"Why *didn't* you call me back?" she demanded, deflecting like crazy. Because she *had* been convinced Anthony had done something to him, and she didn't want to deal with the way it had made her feel. Not with him sitting so close that she could smell the citrusy scent of his aftershave, could actually *feel* his presence as if he disrupted the laws of physics by being there. She wanted to reach out and stroke the smooth skin of his jaw. Wanted to squeeze his forearm to see if the muscles there were as solid as they'd looked when he was banging that damn espresso filter around.

Christian's sexy mouth curved slightly, as if he knew what she was thinking. "Jaclyn had already asked to meet with me. I planned on coming by your office afterward."

"But I warned you to avoid the estate. Couldn't Jaclyn have met you somewhere else? Here, maybe, for a cup of coffee?"

"You didn't warn me, you only said that you wanted to meet elsewhere. And while I could have asked Jaclyn to meet me away from the estate, in this instance, she was speaking for Raphael, and him, I do not set aside lightly. In any event, I'm not afraid of Anthony or anyone else. And as for the other . . . only Marc and I know about this house. And now, you."

Natalie gave him a confused look. "But where do people think you sleep?"

"I own a condominium in the Huntingdon tower."

Natalie was amazed. The Huntingdon was some of the priciest real estate in Houston. "You own a condo at the Huntingdon, as a *cover*?"

Christian shrugged. "An investment. But I prefer this house."

"Are you leasing this one?"

"No. Making a residence vampire-safe requires modifications that most landlords would not welcome. I purchased this house as soon as I decided to compete in the challenge."

"But if you win the challenge and rule the territory, won't you own the Hawthorn estate along with everything else? Isn't that how it works?"

He nodded, and sipped his espresso. "But I won't keep it. I don't like the estate house or its memories. I can still smell the blood that was spilled there."

Natalie made a face. She'd never be able to walk those halls again, without sniffing for blood.

"But you're avoiding my question," Christian persisted. "What happened in Anthony's office after I left?"

"It wasn't what happened in his office. Or not only," Natalie said reluctantly. "I told you I saw the fight, so I know Anthony's lying. And you're right, he doesn't want you here, but I don't know why either."

"I suspect he had a successor already picked out from among his own children. Someone who would retain their allegiance to him, giving him all the perks of the lordship without the responsibilities."

"And then you showed up."

"I not only showed up, I outclass every one of his children, as well as Anthony himself. He can't defeat me in a straight-up challenge, and he knows it."

"And that's why I wanted you to avoid the estate. He's planning something sinister, I know it."

Christian stroked the backs of his fingers along her cheek. "I cannot hide out like a coward. If I am to rule this territory, I must show that I can hold it."

"And what about Jake Baudin?"

He raised his eyebrows in question. "I don't know who that is. You?" he asked Marc, who thought for a moment, then shook his head.

"After you left, Anthony got a phone call from someone telling him about Noriega. At least, I think that's what they told him, because he had a major temper tantrum. Tore up his whole office."

"The call was probably from one of Noriega's buddies, the ones who backed him when he confronted me. They're all quite alive, *ma belle*, despite what you think you saw. I knocked them out to even the odds, but only Noriega died last night."

"Oh." Natalie felt like she should apologize. "I'm sorry."

"*Ce n'est rien.* You couldn't have known."

She'd thought he killed all those people, and he said it was nothing. Natalie didn't forgive herself so easily, but she continued with her story. "After Anthony trashed his office, he came out, all serious and sad, and told us that Noriega was dead, and that you were the one who'd murdered him. And then, totally out of the blue, he told me I needed to go back to New Orleans with him. And not like on the same plane, more like, with *him*, if you get my drift."

"You cannot go anywhere with him, Natalie, much less back to New Orleans. I won't—"

"Don't finish that sentence, big guy. Believe me, I have no intention of going anywhere with him. But if I *wanted* to, you'd have nothing to say about it."

YOU'D HAVE NOTHING to say about it. Her words replayed in Christian's head while he fought to control his reaction. He sure as hell *did* have something to say about whether or not Natalie went off with another male, especially if that male was Anthony. But did she really believe what she'd said? Was she going to ignore the obvious chemistry between them? Why the hell did she think he couldn't stop touching her? And why did she think he'd insisted on bringing her here? For a cup of coffee? Hell, no. As fine as his coffee was, that wasn't the reason. It was because this house was *his* territory. He could protect her here.

And while *she* might be confused about why Anthony had a sudden urge to drag her back to New Orleans, *he* sure as hell wasn't. Anthony wasn't the most powerful vampire around, but he was stronger than most. And he wouldn't have missed the sizzling attraction between the two of them last night. That kind of chemistry crackled in the air to a vampire's senses. And it must have infuriated Anthony. Christian had seen the covetous look in Anthony's eye when he'd looked at Natalie. Who knew how long he'd been lusting after her, playing her along by pretending to be some distant relative, the benevolent uncle. Natalie might have fallen for it, but Christian wasn't buying it.

The obvious attraction between him and Natalie--the one that she seemed determined to ignore—had obviously pushed Anthony to make his move. Hence, the sudden invitation to New Orleans. And if Natalie rebuffed him . . . well, let's just say that Anthony struck Christian as the kind of vampire who wouldn't hesitate to use his power to get what he wanted.

Christian glanced at Marc, who was already finishing off his macchiato, and placing his cup in the dishwasher.

"I'll see what I can dig up on Baudin," Marc said. "He's probably one of Anthony's spies, but in whose camp?"

"Hubert's down in Mexico," Christian suggested. "That's the next conflict, and Anthony knows it."

Marc nodded his agreement, and left the kitchen. Christian followed the light sound of his footsteps down the hall to the basement stairs, and heard the basement door close behind him. That was one of the renovations Christian had mentioned to Natalie. They'd upgraded and finished the basement to include an office and sleeping quarters for the two of them, all secured within the confines of a first-class vault, which had been built by the best vampire construction team in the country. It hadn't been easy or cheap to secure their services, but they'd been worth the cost, *and* the wait.

Christian switched his attention back to Natalie, who was gazing at the empty doorway where Marc had left the kitchen, like a child waiting for her mother to reappear.

"He'll be fine," he told her, intentionally misunderstanding the look on her face.

"What?" she said absently, blinking her awareness back to him.

"Marc. He'll be fine. The office is downstairs."

"Okay," she said, suddenly nervous. "Should I, um . . ."

Christian gave her a questioning look.

"Are *you* going to drive me back to get my car?" she asked, as if doubting he could actually drive.

"No," he told her, standing.

"I can call a taxi—"

"No," Christian repeated, moving into her space until his thighs were pressed against her hip where she sat on the bar stool. He speared his fingers through her hair, then gripped the nape of her neck in a blatantly possessive hold. "You won't be going home tonight."

"But I have to—"

Christian bent his head and took her mouth, a soft brushing of lips at first, enough to give him the scent of her, and to feel her lean into his kiss.

He smiled inwardly and ran his tongue along the crease of her lips. Her lips opened in a gasp, and he took it as an invitation. Fingers twisting in her silky hair, he tipped her head back, and slid his tongue inside, exploring, tasting. Wanting more, he closed his teeth over her plump lower lip, and was rewarded by a hungry little sound as she strained upward, trying to get closer to him.

He growled softly, one arm sliding around her back and pulling her halfway off the seat, crushing her breasts against his chest. She was a slender woman, but her breasts were full and lush, the nipples poking through her blouse to rub against his chest.

He inhaled deeply, drawing in the warm scent of woman, the delicate musk of her arousal. He could have her right now, if he wanted. He could lift her up onto the counter and spread her out for his pleasure. And her pleasure, too. But Christian knew women. And while the lovely Natalie would welcome him between her thighs, and would no doubt come screaming around his cock more than once . . . she'd regret it—as they say—in the morning.

And he didn't want Natalie for one night, or two. He didn't know exactly how much he *did* want. But he knew he wanted more than that.

He broke the kiss gently, touching his lips to the corners of her mouth, to her cheeks, her eyes. She made that hungry sound again, and the way her hands were gripping his waist made him want to devour her, but he pulled back.

She blinked up at him in confusion.

"It's late," he said quietly. "And you should stay here. You'll be safer." He made it her choice, but he had no intention of letting her go home.

Her mouth tightened briefly, and he thought she'd argue, but she didn't. "Fine. But only because I'm tired."

Christian bit back his grin. "Come on, I'll show you the guest room."

NATALIE WAS CONFUSED. She'd heard so much about the seduction skills of vampires, how everything for them was about blood and sex. And here she was, in Christian's house, not even sure exactly where in the city she was, totally at his mercy . . . and he was turning on the lights of his guest room. His *guest room*! What the fuck?

After that kiss. . . . And, hell, that wasn't just a kiss. That was a seduction. He'd made love to her mouth, kissing her more thoroughly than she'd ever been kissed before. And she'd assumed that was only the beginning. She'd expected to feel the scrape of his fangs at any moment, had braced herself for the overwhelming tide of sexual need that was featured in every story she'd ever heard about vampires.

But instead, he was leaving her alone in this very nicely furnished bedroom. He was being the perfect host, pointing out the fresh towels, the toothbrush still in the package, the terrycloth robe that would have been right at home in the most expensive spa. She checked surreptitiously to see if it had a monogrammed "C" on the pocket. Maybe he had so many female guests that he was always prepared.

But if that was true, then why was he leaving her here alone? Because it sure seemed like he was. He'd gotten her all stirred up with that kiss, and now he was going to wish her sweet dreams?

He started for the door, and she thought that was it, but then he grabbed her hand and pulled her close, twisting her arm behind her back and holding her body flush against his.

"There are shades behind the curtains, so you can sleep during the day tomorrow," he murmured, still in that seductive voice.

"What about you?" she asked. "Where do you sleep?"

"We have quite comfortable accommodations in the basement. Part of those renovations I mentioned."

She studied his handsome face, trying to read the expression in those deep blue eyes, and finding she couldn't. She had no idea what he was thinking. Damn.

"Aren't you—?" she started to say, then hesitated before drawing a deep breath and taking the plunge. "Are you going to invite me downstairs?"

Christian's eyes heated briefly, then shuttered with regret. Or maybe that was just her wishful thinking. He twisted a lock of her hair around his fingers, and used it to pull her even closer. "You're not ready yet."

Natalie felt a stab of disappointment, and something that felt an awful lot like hurt feelings. And a little bit of anger. "You don't trust me," she said flatly.

He smiled. *"Non, ma belle* Natalie,*"* he whispered. "You don't trust *me.*" He pressed his hand against her lower back, pulling her against his groin where she could feel a very obvious and very hard erection. She gasped, and his mouth came down on hers with a hard, hungry growl, crushing her lips against his, his tongue stabbing between her teeth as she strained upward, wanting more.

Christian broke away, leaving her breathless, her mouth raw, her body thrumming with desire. He kissed her again, lightly this time. "Sleep well. There's food in the kitchen, and the house is yours for the day. Sunset tomorrow is after eight; we'll join you by nine, and take you wherever you want to go."

His arm tightened around her back again, and she could still feel his body's reaction to her. He was still hard, his cock a thick length against her belly. She wanted to rub herself against it, to drown herself in the sensation. It shocked her how much she wanted that. How much she wanted *him*.

Christian was wrong. It wasn't that she didn't trust him. She was simply afraid that she'd never be able to walk away from him once she'd surrendered.

"Will you be here when I wake?" he asked, as if sensing her doubts.

Natalie was torn. It had been too long since she'd dated anyone seriously. Hell, it had been even longer since she'd had sex with anyone. And she'd never encountered anyone with Christian's raw sexuality. It called to her. But it also terrified her. Her brain was urging her to tell him whatever he needed to hear, and then call a cab the minute the sun was up. Go home, maybe have a morning coffee with Janette, get her friend's take on all of this.

But looking into his eyes, seeing the question there, she knew she couldn't do that. If she left now, they'd be over before they started. And while he scared her, it was a very different kind of fear. He would never hurt her, but he could very easily break her heart. And still she wanted him like she wanted her next breath. Wanted the heat, the intensity, the sheer presence that was Christian Duvall.

"I'll be here," she promised.

"*Bon. À demain.*"

Natalie would have lingered in the doorway to watch him walk down the hall. Christian in motion was a beautiful sight. But he spared her that humiliation. He gave her a final squeeze, then released her, setting her two feet away, and closing the door behind him when he left.

"Well, harrumph," she muttered, truly understanding what the word meant for the first time. She walked over to the elegantly appointed bathroom, and noticed that the shower included a handheld nozzle.

Perfect. Christian might have abandoned her to her sexual frustrations, but that didn't mean he couldn't still star in her fantasies.

IT TOOK EVERY ounce of Christian's self-control to leave Natalie standing there, all flushed and aroused. He'd been tempted to taste her, to slide his hand up the silky length of her leg and dip his fingers into the wetness he could scent between her thighs.

But he'd meant what he said to her. She wanted him, but she didn't trust him. Not yet. So, he'd forced himself to focus on what needed to be done, rather than what he'd rather be doing.

He stepped into the unadorned stairwell leading to the basement, pausing long enough to secure the door behind him before continuing downward. The door was triple locked with a thick steel bolt that was doubly anchored into steel girders on both sides, backed up by a biometric lock that was keyed to his and Marc's thumbprints. And that was just the first line of defense.

Continuing down the stairs, he entered the vault and closed the heavy door for the night. Summer was nearly upon them. The days were growing longer, the sun rising earlier every morning. He and Marc still had some work to do tonight, but the day would be on them soon enough.

"Natalie get settled?" Marc asked, sounding neutral enough, but Christian knew what he was really asking.

"She's in the guest suite."

Marc arched a brow in his direction, but didn't pursue the subject any further. "We received an interesting message from Anthony," Marc said instead.

"When?"

"Ten minutes ago. He wants a meet tomorrow night. He claims an invasion by Hubert out of Mexico is imminent, and he wants to share the intel he has with all of the challengers, so we can—and this is a direct quote—join together to fight this foreign menace."

Christian snorted his opinion of that. "You think he was talking about me?"

Marc laughed. "Not this time, but that doesn't mean he's on the up and up, either."

Christian sat on the chair next to Marc, sliding down until his tailbone was nearly off the seat. "I'll have to be at the meeting, even if it's just all part of his game."

"The trick will be figuring out the rules in time to win."

"Oh, I'll win. Anthony isn't half as shrewd as he thinks he is."

"What about Natalie?"

"Natalie's mine."

"I got that, but Anthony won't. He seems attached."

"Then I'll have to unattach him."

Chapter Seven

NATALIE WAS EATING toast and eggs the next night when Christian walked into the kitchen, looking fresh and rested in a black cashmere sweater, and black slacks that emphasized his narrow hips and flat belly. He looked good enough to eat. Way better than the eggs she'd made, which had started out fried and ended up as some sort of sad hybrid between fried and scrambled. Her momma was a terrific cook; so was her daddy. Natalie? Not so much.

"You want coffee to go with your . . ." Christian gave her plate a doubtful look, and didn't finish the sentence, as he headed for the espresso machine.

"I used all your eggs," she informed him, then glanced down at the mishmash on her plate. "I don't usually cook."

"And the world thanks you," he murmured with a small smile, then stopped and stared. "Did you make coffee?" He was frowning at his precious machine in a way that made Natalie think he didn't like anyone else touching it.

"I did," she said casually, trying not to laugh, as she sipped her delicious latte. "Do you want some?"

He gave her a horrified look, and she lost the battle, laughing so hard she was afraid the latte was going to come out her nose.

He glared at her, looking a bit insulted. "Do you have a machine at home?"

"Of course, I do. But it's an ordinary Mr. Coffee. It was fun figuring out the Einstein version, though," she added, lifting her chin in the direction of his machine.

Christian didn't say a word, just turned and began inspecting his baby. She'd swear she caught him stroking it and murmuring things to it under his breath at one point, but she wisely kept that observation to herself.

"Most people couldn't figure her out so quickly," he said rather sourly.

So the machine was a *her*. Interesting. "I'm a fast learner."

"You slept?"

"Several hours," she lied. She'd slept, all right, but her dreams had been filled with erotic images that weren't exactly restful. "I woke early, and figured I'd work until you all got up. But then I got hungry."

"Work?"

"My laptop," she said, nodding at the computer sitting on the island.

"You have Jabril's original financials on there?" he asked, his gaze suddenly intent.

"Yeah," she said slowly, dragging the word out. "Why?"

"Who else has them?"

"No one. Not the latest results anyway. Jaclyn has the original docs, and I usually update her files on the first of the month. But that's not for a week yet."

"Does Anthony have access?"

"No. He's in the monthly meeting I have with Jaclyn, so he gets the verbal report, but not the actual files."

"And he's okay with that?"

Natalie shrugged. "He always seemed to be." She inhaled the delicious aroma of brewing coffee that was filling the kitchen. "Can I have a refill?"

"Latte?" he asked, steaming a metal pitcher of milk.

"Please."

He added the milk to the big cup he'd poured the espresso into, then spooned on some foam, and set it on the countertop in front of her. But he didn't stop there. Placing one arm on the seat behind her, and bracing the other in front of her, he enclosed her in the scent and strength of his powerful body.

Natalie turned her face up to his and kissed him. She hadn't meant to do it. It was as if her body knew what it wanted and didn't consult her brain. Even then, she'd meant to leave it at that—a good-evening peck on the lips. But Christian had plans of his own. Moving closer, he dropped his arm from the bar stool to her back, lifting her halfway out of the seat as he kissed her thoroughly. As if he was a starving man, and she was his favorite food.

Somewhere in her brain, she registered that she was, in fact, his favorite food. But her gut knew it wasn't like that. This wasn't a taste test; this was a man who wanted to fuck the woman he was kissing.

She gripped the taut skin of his waist beneath his sweater, and moaned softly. He wanted her; she wanted him. So why had he left her alone with the shower attachment and her fantasies this morning?

Christian broke the kiss with a lick of her lips, lowering her back onto her seat and making sure she was secure before letting go. "Drink your latte," he said, smiling. "You're going to need it."

Natalie blinked back into the real world. Those kisses of his were addictive. She took a sip of her latte and moaned again, earning a half-lidded look from Christian.

"It's delicious," she explained. She wanted to add that the barista was delicious, too, but the second half of his sentence abruptly registered. "What do you mean I'm going to need it?"

"Anthony e-mailed last night," Christian said, sliding the filter into place and starting a fresh espresso. "He's calling a meeting of all the challengers to discuss the threat from Hubert."

The kitchen door swung open and Marc walked in, going directly over to Christian who was holding out a frothy latte in a big, pretty cup that was completely at odds with the powerful male now wrapping his big hands around it like it was the golden nectar of the gods.

"Thank you," Marc whispered fervently.

Natalie couldn't help it. She started laughing, and only laughed harder when the two vampires both turned to stare at her.

"You guys are hooked on that stuff," she managed to say finally.

"This is not *stuff*," Christian said, taking a sip of his espresso. "It is ritual and culture. An experience that involves all the senses."

Natalie opened her eyes wide to avoid laughing again. "Okay," she agreed.

"If you'd rather, I can leave you to your Mr. Coffee swill, and your . . . *eggs*," Christian said, somewhat snottily.

"No, no," she said quickly, putting both hands around her latte, just in case he tried to steal it back. "So what's this about a meeting with Anthony?"

Christian gave her a knowing look, but went with the topic shift. "We assume Anthony has spies in Mexico, and that he's had news. Maybe from the mysterious Jake Baudin. But that's not the curious part. What's curious is that he's decided to include me in his briefing."

"But you're one of the challengers. He has to include you."

Christian grunted his opinion of that.

"Or maybe the intel came from Raphael, and Anthony knows Jaclyn will tell you anyway."

"I'd probably have heard from Raphael's people directly, if that was the case. I think Anthony probably does have new intel from his own sources, but he doesn't strike me as someone who shares easily. And I don't think he'd feel compelled to invite me out of fairness, either. He's inviting me for reasons of his own, but I'd bet anything it involves getting me out of way."

"So, why go to the meeting?"

"Because I want to know what he's doing, and I want whatever intel he has. And because hiding out isn't my style."

A phone rang somewhere deep in the house. "The bat phone," Marc said, and raced out of the kitchen. And when a vampire *raced*, he really moved. Marc was gone before Natalie fully registered his first step.

"Bat phone?" she asked, turning to Christian.

"A land line. Only a very few have the number."

Marc reappeared at that moment, phone in hand. It was a regular, cordless phone, the kind that could have multiple, wireless handsets. Marc held it out to Christian, giving him a significant look. "It's Mexico," he said.

Christian's eyebrows shot up in surprise, but he set down his cup, took the phone, and left the kitchen. Natalie heard his soft footsteps fade down the hall, and then nothing.

CHRISTIAN WAITED until he was safely in the basement, with the door closed behind him. He didn't care about Marc overhearing this conversation; he'd tell him everything anyway. But he wasn't completely confident about Natalie. He'd let her believe last night that the lack of trust went one way. That he trusted her, even though she didn't trust him. But that wasn't quite true. He trusted her enough to want her in his bed, but he didn't trust her with his life, or Marc's. A single wrong word to Anthony or one of his vampires, and they could both be dead. Even bringing her to this house had been a risk, but the need to get her into his own territory had been too strong to ignore.

Settling into one of the big chairs in front of the house's security console, he tapped the button to open the phone line, and said, "Christian Duvall here."

"One moment," an unidentified male voice said.

It was less than a minute before he heard the soft scrape of the phone being transferred, and then a deep, heavily accented voice said, "This is Vincent."

"Lord Vincent," Christian acknowledged. "An honor."

Vincent snorted a dismissive laugh. "Let's dispense with the bullshit, Christian. I talked to Raphael; he says you know about what's going on in my territory."

"I gave Raphael and his people everything I know, my lord. But I'm happy to answer any questions you have, or to brief you personally."

"Look, I'm not going to bullshit you. I only trust you because Raphael says you're okay."

"I am gratified by his trust." Christian realized he was being his typical stick-up-the-ass formal self, but it seemed warranted this time. Vincent was a territorial lord, and one whom Christian didn't know at all. Vincent said he trusted Christian, but Christian had no reason to trust in return.

"So, who's set up camp in my territory, and what is he planning?" Vincent asked.

"As far as I know, the who is Hubert. As for the what . . . his specialty is creating large numbers of throwaway vampires. They're barely sentient when he finishes with them. He turns them at need, and burns through them almost as fast. They're completely disposable to him. His usual mode is to overwhelm his opponent with sheer numbers, and then move in for the kill."

"And where is he?"

Christian was taken aback by the question, revealing, as it did, Vincent's ignorance about his own territory. The Mexican lord must truly trust Raphael's judgment to reveal something so damning. He understood the conundrum, though. Vincent was newly installed as Lord of Mexico, while Hubert and his hidden army had been there for months and months, working with Enrique. Vincent would have to travel every square mile of his entire territory—something that would take months more—in order to figure out who belonged there and who didn't. It was possible that the only vampire Vincent knew he could rely on, outside his immediate circle, was Raphael.

"My last meeting with Hubert was four months ago," he told Vincent. "I had declined Mathilde's offer to join her in the plot against Raphael in Hawaii, and flew instead into San Antonio. Hubert and I met in a camp he had set up on the border. He was alone, except for his lieutenant Quentin. We discussed strategy briefly, but once he realized I wasn't there to support his efforts, he became considerably less forthcoming. It was obvious to me, however, that his camp near San Antonio was not his main base of operations.

"If I had to guess," Christian continued, "knowing what I do about how Hubert works, and the type of victim he prefers, I'd look for his main contingent to be somewhere far away from where we met. Not so far that he couldn't travel easily, but far enough away that he'd assume we couldn't find it without really looking. Somewhere that would supply him with a large number of uneducated, superstitious peasants to work with."

"You just described half of Mexico."

"It has to be somewhere remote, where no one would remark on a sudden surge in the vampire population."

"But the families would notice, no matter how remote. I'd expect refugees, some sign of the violence."

"Precisely. And that is why Hubert takes the whole family when he makes his vampires, sometimes even children. Though he's just as likely to kill the children as turn them. Or use them for blood."

"Jesus, why hasn't someone eliminated this monster before now?"

Christian laughed without humor. "In Europe, *mon ami,* one such as Hubert would be applauded for his brutality."

"Fuck. You still have any contact with those people?"

Christian understood that "those people" were his former European brethren, and he was gratified not to be included in their number. "I've heard nothing from Europe since Mathilde died, but I'm not surprised by that. Mathilde's failure would have rattled Hubert, and once he learned that I wasn't going to ally myself with him, he probably withdrew to wherever his stronghold is, and is now making vampires as fast as he can."

"This is not good news."

"Regrettably, no."

"Fuck me. All right. Is your agreement with Raphael still in play?"

"If by that, you mean are we still allies, then the answer is yes."

"Will you let me know if you learn anything more?"

"*Mais oui*, and I assume you will do the same?"

"I thought Anthony was regularly briefing the challengers," Vincent commented curiously.

"More or less. But I find his intel difficult to trust. He seems to have a favorite to be the next lord, and I am *not* that person."

"He can favor anyone he wants, but that's not the way this works. Whoever wins it, rules it."

"So I keep telling everyone," Christian said dryly. He heard voices on Vincent's end of the line, and then the Mexican lord telling someone he'd be right there.

"I've got to deal with this," Vincent said. "I'll keep looking, and let you know what I find."

He hung up without bothering to say good-bye. Christian shrugged, more than satisfied with the conversation. Vincent was nearly the same age as he was, old enough to have honed his strength, but young enough to have retained the flexibility of the modern age. He would be a good neighbor and ally once Christian became Lord of the South.

Assuming Vincent could be trusted to mean what he'd said. Unfortunately there was only one way to be sure of that, and by then, it might be too late.

"I NEED TO GO home and change clothes," Natalie said, as the two vampires prepared to leave for the night, and take her with them. "Anthony pays attention to appearances. He'll notice if I show up in the same clothes I wore yesterday. Plus, you know . . . ick. You should just drop me at the estate. My car's there, so I can drive home, change clothes, and come back."

"No, we'll stop at your place on the way," Christian disagreed, as the three of them trooped into the garage. "While you're there, you should pack enough to see you through a few days. It's no longer safe for you to be on your own."

Natalie bristled. "I've been on my own for years. I don't need—"

"Ordinarily, I'd agree with you. But these are hardly ordinary circumstances. Anthony doesn't strike me as the most even-tempered vampire when he doesn't get his way, and he won't like you spending time with me." He held open the back door of a big, black Suburban for her, while Marc climbed in behind the wheel.

"I'm aware of that," Natalie snapped, carefully hiking her skirt in order to climb into the back seat without flashing Christian. She didn't like the way he was moving in and dictating her life. But she disliked Anthony's newfound attentions more, not to mention what might happen if he discovered that she'd witnessed Noriega's death. She wasn't shortsighted enough to forego the protection Christian offered. And then there were those kisses. She wanted more of those, and whatever went with them. But that didn't mean she had to cave to his every whim. At least not without a fight.

Unfortunately, Christian didn't fight back. He didn't get angry, or snap back at her. He simply stood in the SUV's open door, eyeing her patiently, as if he had all the time in the world to wait for the crazy lady to see reason. Fucker. He wasn't any fun to argue with.

"Fine," she told him finally. "I'm not completely self-destructive, you know."

Christian smiled suddenly, and it was like the sun coming out. "Can you work in Jaclyn's office today?" he asked, as he climbed in after her.

"Sure, but what will I tell her?" She slid across the leather seat to make room for him. Which took some doing, because Christian was a very big guy.

"You don't have to tell her anything. She understands more than you think, and she's not fond of Anthony."

Natalie nodded. She knew that. It was one of Anthony's pet peeves that he'd never managed to co-opt Jaclyn. She started to give Marc her address, but he was already punching it into the navigation system. At some point, Christian had checked her out enough to know where she lived. She wasn't even surprised. Vampires, especially powerful vampires, didn't respect any boundaries but their own. Christian had wanted the information on her, so he'd gotten it. Something as prosaic as *asking* her for it had probably never occurred to him. She liked confidence in a man, even arrogance, as long as it was deserved. But if she and Christian were going to have a relationship, he'd have to remember that she wasn't one of his minions.

She frowned as the thought occurred to her. *If they were going to have a relationship?* Good lord, when had her thoughts taken that particular detour? Okay, yeah, she wanted him, but a *relationship?* She turned and studied him in the dark interior of the SUV—his chiseled profile broken up by the single lock of hair hanging over his forehead, the coiled power of his big body, and his confident posture as he sat with one arm flung across the back of the seat behind her.

Oh, who was she kidding? Hell, yes, she wanted a relationship. One night, or even three, with this beautiful man would never be enough.

He turned suddenly, his mouth curved in a sly smile, and winked at her. Natalie blushed, thankful for the shadows that hid her reaction. Needing to look somewhere else, she glanced out the window, and saw they were nearly at her address. She leaned forward. "It's on the left," she told Marc. "The kind of grayish building."

"Got it," Marc said. "Do you have a garage?"

"Carport in the back. You can pull in, since my car's not there. Assuming this beast will fit. I drive a Prius."

"I didn't think those were legal in Texas," Marc joked.

"I get looks, believe me. There it is, number three," she said, directing him.

Marc slid the big Suburban right into the tight parking space, slick as could be, though Natalie had to close her eyes, certain they were going to crash into the wall. Next to her, Christian laughed.

"For a woman who works with vampires, you have very little faith in our abilities."

"I mostly work with numbers," she said tartly. "Those I have faith in. Which is why I know that *that* was a tight fit."

She climbed out of the SUV, with her keys in one hand. The Suburban took up so much space that there was only room for them to get out on the driver's side, so Christian came out right behind her. She'd showered at his house while he'd still slept, and so she only needed to put on fresh clothes and a little makeup. "Give me twenty minutes to change and pack a few things," she said, sliding her keys into the lock. "The Mr. Coffee's right over there, if you want something to drink," she added.

"And the nightmare continues," Christian muttered.

Natalie laughed as she hurried into her bedroom, stripping off her clothes on the way. She took five minutes for a swipe of mascara and some blush, then stood in her walk-in closet, trying to decide what to wear to the office tonight. Normally, she wore skirts. Anthony liked a businesslike appearance, and skirts and heels made her feel good about herself, pretty and sexy. But tonight, she wanted to be invisible. So she pulled on a cream silk blouse and tank, and some black slacks, finishing off with a pair of spike-heeled ankle boots.

"I like the boots."

Natalie spun around to find Christian leaning against her open doorway, one foot angled over the other, looking very comfortable and scrumptious, his arms crossed over his muscled chest.

"You startled me," she said accusingly. "I didn't hear you come up-stairs."

He freed a hand to point a thumb at his chest. "Vampire. We move quietly."

She knew that. She might have been able to pretend before that hers was an ordinary job, and that the people she worked with were just as ordinary. But they weren't. The death she'd witnessed two nights ago had made that perfectly clear.

"I'm almost ready," she told him, reaching for a jacket.

"You need to pack a bag. And bring your dress for Saturday night."

"Right," she muttered, staring at her clothes and considering how much she'd need to pack, and how long she'd be gone. She frowned abruptly, then turned to give him a puzzled look. "Saturday night?"

"The challenge gala," he explained.

"But I'm not invited to that."

"You are now. I'm inviting you."

"I don't know if I have anything appropriate for . . . What are you doing?"

Christian was digging around in her closet. "This is perfect," he said, holding up a dress that she'd bought on a whim, but never worn. It was short and sexy. A little too sexy, which was why she'd never worn it. It was a dark emerald green that did wonders for her coloring, with silk layered over satin, and a bodice that scooped low. But it wasn't the revealing bodice that had kept it hidden in her closet. The back of the dress was a graceful drape of silk that bared her skin almost to the curve of her butt. It looked great—she'd put it on more than once in front of her mirror—but she'd never managed to dig up the courage to wear it in public.

"Oh, I don't know if—" she started to say, but he cut her off.

"I do; you'll be the most beautiful woman at the gala." He grinned. "Don't worry, I'll fight off any unwanted suitors."

"What about wanted ones?" she asked saucily.

His gaze narrowed. "Them, too."

She chuckled at the success of her jab, then eyed the dress. It was gorgeous. And, really, how could she say "no" when he said she'd look beautiful?

"Okay," she agreed. "I need to grab the shoes."

"Don't forget to pack enough for a few days. It's too dangerous for you to stay here until the challenge is decided."

Natalie's unease at what he was saying overrode her irritation at his tendency to give orders. "Dangerous? Do you really think—?"

"That Anthony would hurt you?" He studied her for a moment, as if trying to decide if he should tell her the truth, as if wondering whether she could handle it.

"Tell me the truth," she demanded.

His lips tightened briefly, and he said, "Yes."

"But he's never done anything like that before."

"And he'd probably regret it. But in the final analysis, only one person matters to Anthony, and that's *Anthony*. I don't believe for a minute that he plans to retire quietly to New Orleans. He has a game in play that will maximize his own power and wealth after the succession. We just don't know what it is yet. But *whatever* it is, I've spoiled it for him, and he'll do what it takes to get rid of me. He wants you for himself—"

She opened her mouth to protest, but he continued.

"—I can see it in the way he looks at you. He covets you, as if you're already his. He may even have convinced himself he loves you, or that you love him. But if he gets angry enough, he'll hurt you. Either to claim you for himself, or to get to me." He stepped closer in the confined space, cupping her cheek in his big hand. "You matter to me. Anthony knows that."

Natalie looked up at him, unable to stop herself from leaning in until her breasts nearly touched him. Her chest felt constricted, her heart too big for the space, pounding in her ears until it was all she could hear. Christian tightened the fingers of his other hand around her hip, pulling her in until there was no space between them, and the tips of her breasts scraped the thick muscles of his chest. His gaze traveled over her face, lingering on her lips, and she knew he was going to kiss her.

When his mouth met hers, her lips were already open in welcome. She expected to be ravished, but was enticed instead, his lips caressing hers with delicate, sliding kisses, his tongue quick and teasing, until she went up on her toes, and pressed her mouth to his to demand more. She felt his smile against her lips, felt him shift the angle of her head as he sank deeper into her, as his tongue swept forcefully into her mouth, stroking, tasting. Natalie wrapped her arms around his neck with a pleasured sigh. She couldn't remember wanting *anyone* the way she did Christian. She was *hungry* for him. Every inch of her longed for him, from the ache between her thighs to the swell of her breasts, and everything above and below.

But he was being so careful with her. As if she were something fragile, as if he had to hold himself back. She wasn't terribly experienced. Hell, she'd *never* experienced a man like Christian. But she wasn't going to break, either. And she didn't want him to hold back.

She boldly closed her teeth over his lower lip, stopping just short of drawing blood, shivering as his growled response rolled down her throat, trembling deep between her thighs, and knotting her nipples into hard peaks. His arm tightened around her back as he jerked her even closer.

"Careful, *ma chère,* or you'll get what you ask for."

"Good," she whispered fiercely. Or at least, she meant it to be fierce.

Christian twisted his fingers in her hair and tugged her head back, forcing her to look at him as he searched her face. And then he stepped away.

"We both need to get to the estate," he said.

Natalie scowled at the sudden shift in mood, and would have snapped at him, but he wasn't finished.

"This isn't the time," he said patiently, trailing his fingers down her cheek and over her lips. "The first time I make love to you will not be up against a wall with my lieutenant waiting only a few feet away."

Her face heated with embarrassment. She'd forgotten about Marc and his vampire hearing. What had she been thinking? That he'd throw her on the bed right then and there?

"I'm sorry," she whispered, and tried to step away from him, but he didn't let her go.

"Don't be sorry," he said, taking her hand and pressing it against his very hard erection. "I want you, Natalie. But not here, not now. Tonight . . . in my bed, where you belong."

Natalie's heart was pounding so hard, it felt like her entire body was shaking with it. He released her and stepped back. "Finish packing. You're staying with us for now."

"How come you're in charge?" she muttered, mostly for form, and to prove to herself that she could still speak despite the desire rocking her bones. But Christian didn't see it that way. She sucked in a breath as he hooked an arm around her neck, and placed his lips against her ear.

"I am always in charge, Natalie. Remember that in a few hours, when you're screaming my name."

NATALIE WAS STILL shivering at the memory of that seductive whisper as they drove the several miles back to Anthony's estate. Christian hadn't said anything else, but his eyes gleamed as he stretched an arm over the seat behind her, his fingers playing in her hair, and dropping teasing strokes against her neck.

"So, tell me more about Alon and his dojo," he said after several silent miles.

It took Natalie a moment to concentrate enough to parse the meaning of his words.

"Natalie?" Christian said.

"Right. Alon. I started there initially because he offers late night and early morning classes. The timing works really well with my schedule."

"What's his discipline?"

"A little of everything, I think. But he's *rokudan* in judo."

"*Rokudan. S*ixth level, black belt," Christian commented. "And *your* ranking?"

Natalie admitted to herself that she was surprised he knew what *rokudan* meant, and also that he'd remembered that she practiced judo. "I made *shodan*, first level, just before I left New Orleans."

"How long have you been studying?"

"Since I was a child. My older brothers both took classes, and I insisted on going, too."

"Your father permitted it?"

She snorted softly. "Daddy talks a tough game, but I'm his baby girl. I get what I want. Is judo your discipline?"

"Among others," he said absently. "Alon . . . that's an Israeli name."

"You're right. He'll say only that he's former Israeli military, but I suspect he was more than that. He started a Krav Maga class right after he opened the dojo. It draws a lot of guys to the late night classes."

"Excellent."

Natalie couldn't see his face in the dark SUV, but his excitement was evident in his voice. "You know Krav Maga?" she asked curiously.

Marc snorted a laugh from his seat up front, and she saw Christian grin in response.

"I'll take that as a 'yes,'" she said dryly.

"Marc and I picked it up from a mutual friend in Europe. I'd be interested in meeting your Alon," Christian said casually.

"Alon's not mine. He's a friend."

Christian leveled a smug look in her direction, and she cursed under her breath. Why had she felt the need to tell him Alon was only a friend?

"When are the next Krav Maga classes?"

Natalie thought for a moment. She'd been staying up all night for nearly two years, working with the vamps, and yet, she still lost track of the date sometimes. "Today's Friday, right?"

Christian nodded. "And the gala is tomorrow," he reminded her.

"That's okay. The advanced Krav Maga classes are Sunday and Wednesday nights."

"We'll go on Sunday, then. "Did you bring your gear?"

"I have a locker at the dojo, but the Sunday class is too heavy for me anyway. I'll watch you guys, instead."

"We'll do our best not to embarrass you," he said, but he didn't sound all that worried about the possibility. And why would he? He made walking down the hallway look like an exercise in athletic grace. She could only imagine what he'd look like on the mats.

She glanced up when the lights of the estate came into view, and her hands tightened into fists in her lap. As if sensing her unease, Christian covered her fists with his much larger hand, tugging her fingers open as he linked their hands together.

"You'll go directly to Jaclyn's office. I spoke to her before we left the house, and she's contacted Anthony to let him know you'll be meeting with her. So he'll be expecting it."

Natalie almost groaned. He'd rearranged her schedule without consulting her, before he'd even discussed the possibility with her. But she didn't see the point in saying anything to him about it. He was who he was. She wasn't going to change that. She wasn't even sure she wanted to. And besides, in this case, she was glad to avoid seeing Anthony.

"Jaclyn's guards will be there, naturally," Christian continued, obviously trying to reassure her. "And once my meeting with Anthony and the others gets started, Marc will join you."

"I'm not worried," she said, trying to reassure him back. "How long do you think—?"

"I won't know until I see what Anthony has planned. If it's the straight briefing he claims it is, no more than an hour."

"And if it's something more?" she asked, suddenly worried more about Christian's safety than her own. "What if it's another set-up, like before?"

"Then I'll fight. But I don't think Anthony will come out into the open like that again. Not tonight, anyway. And I am not without resources of my own, *chère.*"

Marc pulled the SUV around to the side of the big estate house, stopping in the same lot where her own car was parked, between the main house and the former servants' quarters. The lot was a yellow-lit blot on the otherwise elegant estate, something Anthony had added after he took over the territory. It was practical, but ugly.

"Your cell phone," Christian demanded, and she turned it over automatically, scowling as an afterthought. She really had to stop doing everything he ordered.

She watched as he tapped in first his cell number, then Marc's, then added her number to his phone. Marc passed his phone back, and her number was typed in there, too. When Christian handed her phone back, she checked the directory, and laughed out loud at what he'd typed under his own number.

"Lord and Master?" she read, quickly deleting the entry and typing his name instead.

"It seemed apt."

"You are *so* deluded."

"Or prescient. Take your pick."

Natalie let her unladylike snort tell him exactly what she thought of that.

CHRISTIAN HELD the door as they entered the building the same way he'd left it the other night, when Noriega had been waiting for him. Bypassing the kitchen, they took the back stairs up to the long corridor outside Jaclyn's office. He saw Cibor waiting at the end of the hall, and nodded when the bodyguard raised a hand in greeting.

Turning to face Natalie, he rubbed his hands lightly over her upper arms. "Remember," he said. "Don't leave Jaclyn's office unless someone's with you. Preferably Marc or Cibor."

"Yes, Master," she said softly, gazing up at him from beneath her long lashes.

Christian gave her a narrow look. She was a bit of a smart ass. He liked that about her, but that didn't mean he didn't occasionally want to take her over his knee. He thought about her nicely rounded ass sticking up over his lap, rosy with heat from his hand, and shifted his stance slightly to relieve the sudden pressure in his groin.

Something of his thoughts must have shown on his face, because Natalie's pupils suddenly widened until only a small rim of chocolate brown iris showed around the edges. Her heartbeat kicked a little faster, and he lifted her hand to kiss her fingers. "*A bientôt, ma chère.*"

She blushed prettily, then reclaimed her hand, and headed for Cibor. Christian enjoyed the sway of her hips as she walked down the hall. He grinned briefly when she turned to wave good-bye just before disappearing into Jaclyn's office. Cibor nodded again in Christian's direction, then followed her inside.

Knowing he'd made her as safe as she could be, at least in this place, he and Marc turned back for the stairs.

NATALIE WENT directly to the conference room. She felt a little silly holing up here in Jaclyn's office, and wondered if maybe they were making far too much of this whole situation. After all, she'd worked right outside Anthony's office for almost two years, and been perfectly safe. On the other hand, he *had* gotten a little weird since Christian showed up, and she didn't want Christian worrying about her. He had to be at the top of his game to deal with Anthony and the other challengers. So she'd stay where she was, safely tucked away. She rolled her eyes at the idea, even though there was no one to see it. Walking over to the big table, she set up her laptop, then went to the small fridge in the corner to grab a bottle of water.

On a whim, she checked all the bins for blood, figuring there must be some for vampire guests, right? She found only water. Feeling slightly disappointed, she took the icy cold bottle back to her station for the day, and pulled out her chair, but then stopped. She had to pee. The bathroom was right across the hall. Surely, she could cross the hall safely, she reasoned. But remembering her vow, and determined not to be one of those too-stupid-to-live chicks, she sighed, and went in search of Cibor.

He was standing at the small security station near the front desk, and looked up with a smile. "Need something, sweetness?"

Natalie smiled. Cibor was such a flirt, but his heart belonged to Jaclyn. "Just the restroom," she said, fighting embarrassment. This was quite literally a *natural* need. Nothing embarrassing about asking the big vampire to escort you to take a pee.

"Right across the hall," he told her.

Natalie nodded. "I know. Can I just—"

"I'll stand in the office doorway."

She swallowed a groan, and led the way. As promised, Cibor halted in the office doorway, and she could feel his eyes on her until the restroom door closed behind her.

Ignoring the mirrors, which would only confirm the effects of her restless night, she went to the stall and took care of necessities, then came out and washed her hands. Still drying her hands with the paper towel, she headed for the exit.

Her first thought when she opened the door was to look for Cibor. But he wasn't there. And the door to the office was closed, which was odd, too. She looked left and found an empty hallway, to the right and . . . Anthony stood there, backed by two of his bodyguards. He hurried over to her, a surprised look on his face, as if this was nothing but a wonderful, chance encounter.

He eyed her slacks with a quick moue of distaste, but was smiling when he lifted his gaze to her face. "You look lovely as always, my Natalie," he lied smoothly. She *knew* he didn't like it when she wore pants, which was rarely.

He reached for her hand, and brought it to his lips. All she could think of was Christian doing the same thing that morning, and how much she'd loved it. And now her hand felt contaminated, and she wanted to rush back into the restroom and wash all over again.

"Unfortunately, I'm on my way to a meeting right now, but you and I need to talk," Anthony continued, unaware of her reaction. "We should have dinner together later tonight. Just the two of us. Somewhere nice," he said slowly, then snapped his fingers, making her jump. "Ah. I know the perfect place. I'll pick you up at your townhouse at midnight."

Natalie was too stunned to speak, but she had to. Where was Cibor? And what was this? Anthony had never socialized with her before. They'd never exchanged so much as a word outside the office, and now he wanted to take her to dinner? And what was with the *my Natalie?* He'd never said *that* before. One thing she knew for sure. She didn't want to have dinner with him tonight, or any other night. But she couldn't tell him that. He wouldn't take it well.

"Jaclyn and I will be working—" she started to say, but he didn't let her finish.

"Jaclyn can spare you for a few hours. And don't worry about changing clothes. What you're wearing will be fine for tonight," he said.

As if she'd been worried about dress codes for their big date. *Right.* She had to stop this before it went any further.

"Anthony, I don't think that's appropriate. You're my boss, *and* my cousin." What the hell, might as well use his fabricated kinship to her advantage. "And besides—"

"Don't worry about what others think. We both know the truth."

Was that supposed to make her feel better? She had a feeling *her* truth was vastly different from *his*.

"You're still my boss," she said, shooting a desperate glance at the closed door to Jaclyn's office, and wondering where Cibor was.

"But not for much longer. The challenge will be over soon, which is why I must leave you now. Duvall will be in the meeting, by the way. He's a powerful vampire, but not invincible. And all sorts of things can happen during a challenge. A wise woman would understand that."

Natalie couldn't believe it. Had he just threatened Christian if she didn't agree to . . . what? Become his girlfriend? Run away with him to New Orleans? When the hell had Anthony lost his fucking mind? She stared at him in disbelief, but his eyes said it all. They were hard and glittering, daring her to call his bluff. If she'd been the only one on the line, she'd have told him where he could shove his midnight dinner, and his *relationship*. But Christian was about to walk into a trap, and with no way to warn him, she was the only one who could keep the jaws from closing.

She swallowed her anger, and said, "I'll be ready at midnight."

He smiled broadly. "Excellent. I shall look forward to it, but now I must run."

Natalie didn't linger to watch him scurry down the hall like the rat he was. She raced across the hallway to Jaclyn's office and opened the door to find Cibor sitting at his station, perfectly at ease. He glanced up when she entered. "Hey, Natalie," he said. "You meeting with Jaclyn tonight?"

Every muscle in her body froze. Anthony had done something to Cibor, manipulated his mind to make him forget the last half hour or so of time. He didn't remember that she'd already spoken to him, or that he'd been standing in the doorway, guarding her while she used the restroom. Anthony had stolen that from him. She wouldn't have thought it possible, but then, she'd never thought of Anthony as anything but a fussy, self-important man. She'd never really considered the power he had at his fingertips, the power he could draw upon as a vampire lord. She'd been a fool, and now others were paying for her blindness.

"No," she said faintly to Cibor. "I'm just working up here for a while. There's too much going on in Anthony's office, and I need the peace and quiet."

"Good deal."

"Is Jaclyn in, though?"

He nodded cheerfully. "She's is her office. Go ahead. She's always glad to see you."

Maybe not for long, she thought woefully. Not once Jaclyn discovered Anthony had been screwing with her favorite bodyguard's head, and it was all because of her.

"Thanks," she said, trying to seem normal, and failing miserably from the puzzled look on Cibor's face. She walked down the hall in a daze. This was all unreal. How had she gone from being the unnoticed forensic accountant, to becoming the center of a conflict between two powerful vampires? She wanted to go back to when Anthony was nothing but a family legend, to when her life was quiet and uneventful, instead of this whirlwind of emotions and fears.

She approached Jaclyn's office, prepared to tell her just that. She was going to go home. Jabril and his twisty accounting could wait, so could Anthony and his stupid dinner date, and especially the territorial challenge, which she didn't give two fucks about. Fuck Christian, too, and . . . Her thoughts trailed off, and she sighed. She didn't want to fuck Christian. Well, she *did*, but not like that.

She knocked on Jaclyn's door, then pushed it open. "Jaclyn, you in here?"

The female vamp looked up with a smile. "Natalie. Are you all set up in the conference room? Is there anything—" She broke off with a frown as she studied Natalie's face. "What's wrong?"

Natalie had to force her legs to keep moving, to walk over to a chair where she could sit down. She didn't want to tell Jaclyn what had happened. She'd be furious. But Jaclyn had to know about Cibor and what Anthony had done. As for the rest of it? Like Anthony blackmailing Natalie into going out with him, because he had this delusional idea that they were going to run away together? That was her problem, and she'd deal with it. But Cibor was Jaclyn's, and Jaclyn was Raphael's. Natalie didn't understand everything about vampire politics, but she understood that much. Anthony had crossed a line.

"Natalie," Jaclyn said sternly. "You're scaring me. What happened?"

"It's my fault," Natalie said faintly.

"What is?"

"I don't know anything for sure, but—"

"Just spit it out," Jaclyn demanded, clearly worried now.

"I think Anthony messed with Cibor's head. I think he—" She looked away, not sure how to say it, but Jaclyn was already on her feet, storming around her desk.

"Tell me what the hell happened," she snarled, getting closer.

Natalie stood in alarm, and explained quickly. "Cibor was standing in the doorway, watching while I went to the restroom. But when I came out, he was gone, and Anthony was waiting for me. He said—" She stopped. She didn't want to tell Jaclyn about the supposed date, because she'd tell Christian and he'd go nuts. "Anthony wanted to talk to me, but when he finished, and I came back to your office . . . Cibor was there, and he was acting as if he was just seeing me for the first time tonight."

Jaclyn's expression, which had been getting darker with every word Natalie spoke, now turned positively terrifying. She spun for the door, fangs bared, eyes glittering, as she yanked it open. "I'll kill him," she hissed.

Natalie cringed. "I'm sorry," she whispered, but Jaclyn was already gone.

Natalie followed more slowly. She didn't have a hope of keeping up with the vampire's speed, even if she'd wanted to. Which she didn't. It might be better if she simply avoided Jaclyn and Cibor for the time being. Neither one of them would be eager to see *her*. Not after she'd brought all of this down on their heads, even if it hadn't been deliberate. It wasn't her fault Anthony had suddenly become obsessed with her, but she shouldn't have let Christian talk her into involving Jaclyn and Cibor.

She went directly to the conference room, determined to gather her things and go home. She should have stayed there anyway, should never have let Christian persuade her to come into the office. She didn't need to be here. She could work anywhere. A part of her recognized she was trying to find a way to avoid seeing Christian, to avoid telling him about her "date" with Anthony. He wouldn't even begin to *listen* to her argument for why she should just go out with him, and get it over with. It was just one evening. She would go along with Anthony as he made his pitch, and then let him know gently that she wasn't interested. Maybe his pride would be pricked, but he'd be back in New Orleans soon, and there were plenty of women there who would welcome his attention.

Christian would insist she was in danger from Anthony, but she couldn't really buy into that. He'd waited two *years* to make his play for her, and probably would have waited longer if he hadn't seen her flirting with Christian in his office. She absolutely believed he'd hurt Christian, however. Anthony hated him for reasons that went way beyond her. She was attractive enough, but she was no Helen of Troy, for God's sake.

On the other hand, Christian had messed up Anthony's plan for the outcome of the challenge. *That* was what had really pissed him off. In fact, she thought his sudden interest in her might be motivated by a desire to win her away from Christian. *That* idea held merit. She wasn't the great passion of his life, she was a thing. A thing that Christian wanted, and, therefore, Anthony was going to take her away from him. It would be even richer when Christian discovered she'd gone out with Anthony in order to protect *him*.

Natalie almost groaned out loud at the thought of telling Christian just that. She didn't know him all that well yet, but she knew he'd be furious. Not only at Anthony, but at *her* for going along with such a scheme. But while she might be reluctant to tell him, she was more certain with every minute that she was doing the right thing. Which meant she had to get out of there before Christian returned. If Anthony was keeping an eye on her, she wanted him to see that she'd gone home, and that she hadn't gone to Christian looking for help.

She walked down the hall to the conference room, where she'd left her things, and caught sight of Jaclyn and Cibor standing near his desk. Jaclyn had her arms around the much bigger vampire, and his head was lowered to touch hers. Cibor's eyes were closed, and Jaclyn was murmuring something, her cheeks wet with pink tears. Natalie's heart ached with guilt. This wouldn't have happened if Anthony hadn't come looking for *her*. She lowered her head and went over to gather her purse and laptop. Stepping back to the open doorway, she glanced over at the two vampires. But they were totally wrapped up in each other, and not paying her any attention.

She headed for the hall door, not looking left or right, not calling any attention to herself. Once out in the hallway, she went directly to the back stairs, and down to the kitchen, then out to the parking lot, and over to her little car.

She shivered when she climbed inside and closed the door, her fingers trembling as she inserted the key and started the quiet engine. She told herself it was just the cold night temperature making her shake. That her car had been sitting in the lot for too long, and the chill had settled in. She reached over and turned on the heat, but it didn't seem to help. Nothing did. But she kept going, driving past the estate guards, waving at their cheerful greetings, and then turning onto the highway toward her townhouse.

She knew what she had to do. Christian would be upset, but he'd understand, she told herself. Once she had a chance to explain. He'd understand.

"AS SOON AS THE meeting's underway, I want you back with Natalie," Christian said, as he and Marc clambered down the stairs to Anthony's office.

"I'd rather stay with you," Marc said, when they started down the long hallway.

"Anthony probably won't let you in the meeting, and having you sit on your ass in his waiting room would be useless."

"But I'd be closer if you needed me."

"I can hold them off until you reach me."

"And if they gang up on you? What if this is Anthony's final play?"

"I believe what I told Natalie earlier. First, Anthony's style isn't direct confrontation. When he comes after me himself, it'll be from the shadows. And second, I need to be in this meeting, to hear whatever intel he claims to have, and to try and figure out his next move."

"Yes, Master."

"Not you, too," he sighed, thinking of Natalie's smartass response.

Marc laughed. "Nah, you really *are* my lord and master."

They swung through the open doors of Anthony's office to the sound of his receptionist's trilled greeting.

"Good evening, Marc," she all but sang. Her breasts were thrust out as she straightened to attention, and her eyes were only for Marc.

Christian swallowed a laugh, but Marc didn't seem to mind. He smiled broadly at the admittedly pretty young woman. "MariAnn," Marc said warmly. "You're a gorgeous sight this evening."

"Oh," she said, blushing, as she brushed away his words. "Aren't you sweet?"

Christian rolled a glance in his lieutenant's direction, before addressing the girl. "Are the others inside?"

She swung her gaze to him for the first time, a look of surprise on her face, as if she hadn't noticed he was there before. "Oh! Yes, my lord, I think you're the last one."

"Excellent. Marc?" he said, reminding his lieutenant what his orders were.

"I'll be waiting, Sire," Marc said, flirtation forgotten.

Christian gave a single, short nod, then pulled open the door to Anthony's office. The remaining three challengers were all there, and they turned, as one, to regard him with very unfriendly looks. It was in the nature of vampires to be generally hostile to one another, particularly in a situation like this, with the challenge afoot. But Christian couldn't help feeling that he was the common enemy here, the unifying force. It shouldn't have been that way. After all, two of the remaining challengers were from outside the South. But somehow, he'd been transformed into the focal point of their dislike.

He looked around the office. And found no Anthony. *What the fuck?*

"Where's Anthony?" he demanded.

A bulky vamp with pale hair, one whom Christian had never met before, shrugged negligently. "Taking a shit? Said he'd be right back."

Christian spun for the exit, suspicion blooming into certainty. But as he reached for the edge of the half-open door, it was pushed wide, and Anthony was there.

"You're finally here, Duvall," Anthony said, his scratchy voice grating on Christian's ears. "Sit. And have your lieutenant join us."

Christian didn't bother to hide his surprise. But he did conceal his suspicion. Anthony wanted Marc in the meeting? Why would he do that? None of the others had any backers with them.

"Well?" Anthony demanded. "Get him in here and sit down."

Christian bristled automatically at the order. Anthony might be Lord of the South—for now, but Christian was *not now* and would never *be* his to command. He swallowed his irritation. It was important that he find out what Anthony was up to, and the only way they could do that was by sitting here and listening to the fucker talk. If he wanted Marc in the meeting, if that's what it took to get this thing started, then it looked like he was staying. He'd have preferred to have Marc guarding Natalie, but Cibor was more than capable, and Jaclyn was, too.

Marc was still standing in the outer office, his eyes on Christian. He'd have heard the whole conversation, and was waiting to see what he should do. Christian gestured him inside, and the two of them sat together, taking chairs around the small conference table. The furniture was obviously new. Probably replacements for whatever Anthony had destroyed during his tirade. Glancing around, Christian noticed there were a few blank spaces on the wall, but if you didn't know better, you'd believe the place had always looked this way, never guessing that it had been a wreck only two days earlier.

Anthony walked around and sat behind his desk, giving everyone else a sour look, as if they were intruding on his time, and *he* hadn't been the one to call the damn meeting.

"So, we're all here. I'd like to know why." That same pale-haired vamp pushed his chair back from the table, and shifted his unfriendly look in Anthony's direction. Christian found it rather refreshing.

Anthony glared at the vampire's disrespectful tone. "I already told you, Weiss. I've received intel on the Hubert situation. I'm doing this as a courtesy, so shut the fuck up and listen."

So this was Marcel Weiss, Christian thought. The challenger from the Midwest. He was one of Klemens's people who'd fled Chicago after Aden took over. On the surface, he didn't seem powerful enough to rule the South, but then, *on the surface,* neither did Christian. They were both hiding their true strength, knowing that they could end up facing any one of the others in this room during the challenge. And a smart vampire learned to shield what he brought to a fight.

Weiss's only reply was to snarl in Anthony's direction, after which he leaned back in his chair and feigned boredom.

"All right, then," Anthony grated. "Scoville," he said, addressing the only vampire in the room who was one of his own children. The only one of his own left in the challenge, now that Noriega was gone. "Why don't you set out what we've learned, and then I'll answer any questions."

"Yes, my lord," Scoville agreed meekly. The subservient response wasn't completely unexpected. Anthony was Scoville's Sire, and that sort of obedience was hardwired into a vampire's brain. But it spoke to Anthony's insecurities that he demanded such meekness from his people. So different from the relationship Christian enjoyed with Marc.

"For obvious reasons, Lord Anthony has spies throughout Mexico," Scoville stated. "Most of them have been in place since long before Vincent took over. But with this new European invasion, their reports have taken on an even greater urgency. Vincent is intent on uncovering any of Enrique's European allies who might still be lurking in Mexico, but he doesn't have the luxury of focusing all of his attention in that direction. Some of Enrique's hold-outs still question Vincent's newly won rule of the territory, and he has to put down those challenges, as well.

"We, on the other hand, can't afford to ignore what the Europeans might be doing, and Lord Anthony's network within Mexico has proven invaluable."

Christian couldn't believe the amount of blatant flattery in Scoville's recitation. Did Anthony require that much ego stroking all the time? Or was this performance aimed only at this particular audience.

"In particular," Scoville continued, "we have a spy placed very close to Hubert, and he tells us that Hubert will attack sooner rather than later. Hubert thinks to take advantage of Vincent's distraction, as well as the pervasive confusion on the continent about what really happened in Hawaii with Lord Raphael."

"Raphael should share the details of what happened. After all, he defeated his enemies. There's no reason—" Weiss started to say, but Anthony interrupted.

"Give it up, Weiss. That's never going to happen. Raphael makes up his own mind, and to hell with the rest of us."

Christian exchanged a glance with Marc at Anthony's vitriolic tone. He didn't think the assessment of Raphael was quite fair. But he found it intriguing that the more time he spent in Anthony's company, the more he realized how much the Southern lord disliked Raphael. Maybe even more than disliked. Had their relationship always been this way? He wasn't alone in assuming that Raphael and Anthony were, if not friends, then at least friendly with one another. Why else would Raphael have supported Anthony's rule over the South?

It was beginning to look as though Raphael had chosen Anthony not because he respected him, but because he didn't. He'd wanted someone he could control on his Southwestern border, and Anthony was weak enough to fit the bill. Christian didn't like Anthony, but he had to admit that the vampire lord's resentment of Raphael was beginning to make sense.

The vampire sitting at Christian's left blew out an impatient breath. "I'd like to know why Hubert's moving on the South at all," he said, in heavily accented English. "Why not take advantage of the mess Vincent created in Mexico when he killed Enrique, and seize that territory instead?"

This had to be Stefano Barranza. Marc's info put him as a close associate of the now-dead Enrique, so it made sense that he'd be unhappy with Vincent's rule. It was just stupid, however, for him to pretend Vincent wasn't powerful enough to defend his territory, or that Enrique hadn't deserved to die. In Christian's view, Vincent had done the world, and vampires in particular, a huge favor by taking the corrupt lord out.

"Hubert is targeting what he sees as the most vulnerable territory," Christian said quietly. "Mathilde was supposed to have eliminated Raphael, which would have weakened Anthony."

Anthony bristled at this dismissal of his power, but he didn't dispute Christian's reasoning. And Christian didn't give a fuck about insulting Anthony, so he continued. "As for Vincent, he was Enrique's lieutenant for more than a century—a position he won by virtue of his superior strength. And let's not forget that Vincent won the territory by defeating Enrique in an open challenge. He's a much tougher opponent, and Hubert likes to win."

"Well I for one would like to see an independent South," Weiss snapped predictably. "Raphael has far too much power already." Coming from a vampire on the run from Aden, this wasn't surprising. After all, Aden was a staunch Raphael ally.

What amazed Christian was that, hatreds and resentments aside, he seemed to be the only vampire in this room who appreciated the genius of Raphael's North American alliance. From what little he'd been able to piece together, it was precisely that alliance which had thwarted Mathilde long enough for Raphael to break free and defend his territory. Christian was also the only one here who truly comprehended what life would be like if Hubert succeeded in establishing himself on this continent. Mathilde was gone, but there were others who would follow in Hubert's footsteps if he succeeded, and every vampire in North America would pay the price. This was a huge continent. The wars would never end.

"Hubert is only one vampire," Anthony rasped. "He can be defeated like any other, which is why we're here."

"You propose all of us working together then?" Christian asked. It was the last thing he'd have expected.

Weiss snorted his opinion of that. "We're vampires, and this is a competition, not a support group."

Anthony dipped his head in agreement. "I'm not proposing anything. I'm simply doing my duty as Lord of the South to facilitate the challenge and ensure the best result."

Christian managed not to roll his eyes in disgust. What a waste of time. He needed to move this meeting along, and get back to Natalie. "Do you have any specific knowledge of Hubert's whereabouts? After all, it's no news to any of us that Hubert has designs on this territory."

Anthony's mouth pinched in irritation. "Not everyone is privy to the plottings of our European cousins," he said pointedly. "Perhaps *you* have information to share?"

Christian's mouth turned up in a bare smile. "I know this much. When Hubert comes, he'll come in force, with an army at his back. If you hope to hold the territory against him, we would do better to coordinate our efforts."

Scoville seemed to nod his agreement, and opened his mouth to say something, but a sharp glare from Anthony stifled whatever it was.

"I'll keep that in mind," Anthony sneered. "And I will, of course, continue to share whatever intel I receive. Are there any questions?"

Christian couldn't imagine what questions there could possibly be since nothing new had been discovered. It made him wonder again what the true purpose of the meeting had been. He stood to leave, but Anthony detained him with a raised hand.

"Stay a moment, Duvall," he said, making it sound more like an order than a request.

Christian considered telling him to shove it up his ass, but it occurred to him that Anthony's motive in inviting him to this meeting might finally be revealed. He gestured for Marc to go with the others, then lingered until Scoville, who was the last to leave, closed the door behind him.

"I don't like you," Anthony said plainly, taking a stance behind his desk with both hands on his hips.

Christian tilted his head sideways dismissively. Was he supposed to care whether Anthony liked him or not?

"You're bad for the South, and bad for the continent."

Christian kept his gaze on Anthony and waited.

"As Lord of the South, I'm asking you to leave my territory."

Christian almost laughed out loud. Really? Did he think that would work? "Regrettably, Anthony—" he said, intentionally omitting the lord's title, "—you surrendered that authority when you announced your resignation. Once the challenge was live, you granted territorial access to any and all challengers, until it's resolved."

"The challenge isn't live yet," Anthony snarled. "Not until this weekend."

"I beg to differ," Christian replied, noting the obvious signs of Anthony's growing rage. "You unofficially opened the challenge when you sent poor Noriega out to ambush me. Tell me," he continued, taking a step closer to the angry lord. "Did you honestly believe he could defeat me? Are you that blind? Or was he only a sacrifice to rally the troops? To gain support for whichever one of your children you *really* want to succeed you?"

"You don't know what you're talking about," Anthony snapped. "That was Noriega's decision, I didn't—"

Christian tilted his head in sudden understanding. "It's not Scoville either, is it? He's the only one of your children left in the open competition, but he's merely the next stalking horse. So who is it, Anthony? And how do you expect him to triumph, if he's too weak to even compete openly?"

"Get out of my office, you foreign guttersnipe. We'll see who triumphs, and who doesn't," he growled.

Christian would have dismissed his words as empty posturing, but there was a gleam in the old vampire's eye, a hint of victory in the sneer he aimed Christian's way. It gave him a very bad feeling, and when he examined the source of that badness, he could find only one cause.

Natalie.

He turned and walked out of the office without another word, gathering Marc on his way. He waited until he was out in the hallway, then pulled up his cell phone and called Natalie's number.

"Straight to voicemail," he said tightly, heading for the stairs and Jaclyn's office. Marc followed, his own cell phone in hand.

"Cibor's not answering either," he said, and Christian had to force himself not to race to Jaclyn's office, not to give Anthony that satisfaction. But the four vampires who tried to block his path were another matter entirely.

Christian slowed to a stop. He didn't recognize any of them, until a fifth vampire pushed his way to the front.

"Wait," Christian ordered Marc quietly, then acknowledged the fifth vampire. "Scoville," he said. "I really don't have time for this."

Scoville didn't say anything, just placed himself at the head of the group, taking a position a step removed from the others to make it clear that he stood on his own.

"Are you tonight's sacrifice then?" Christian asked him. He was outwardly calm, but inside, he was raging at this delay. It had to be more of Anthony's scheming, except that Christian couldn't believe he had managed to subdue Cibor, much less Jaclyn. He couldn't believe Anthony would even have had the balls to try, given that Jaclyn and all of her people belonged to Raphael.

He forced these thoughts aside. Right now, it didn't matter what was happening in Jaclyn's office. What mattered was the vampire in front of him who didn't have a hope in hell of defeating Christian. That was, unless Christian permitted himself to be so distracted that he got in a lucky hit. And that wouldn't do Natalie any good either.

"Sacrifice?" Scoville repeated, with a puzzled frown.

Christian shrugged. "Noriega was the first. Anthony sent him against me knowing he'd die. Tonight, it's you."

"Lord Anthony didn't send Noriega anywhere; you murdered him."

Christian shook his head impatiently. "You know better than that. Or you should." He released a fraction of his true power, enough for the other vampire to get a good taste of him. "Why would I waste my time challenging someone like Noriega?" he asked.

Scoville's eyes widened briefly, an automatic response that was beyond his control.

"Noriega had no business entering the challenge," Christian continued. "You knew him. You know I'm right."

"Noriega was smart, and he had friends. He wouldn't have faced you alone."

"He didn't. But none of them had the power to back him up, either. He was out of his league."

"Lord Anthony—"

"Anthony wound him up and sent him out to fight me," Christian snapped. It was time to end this. "Don't you wonder why? Don't you think you should *know* that, before you become the latest dead pawn in his game?"

Scoville frowned, doubt written on his face. "Why are you telling me this?"

"Because someday soon I will rule this territory, and I will *not* throw vampire lives away for nothing."

The other vampire stared at him, clearly wavering, but not yet willing to go against his Sire's wishes.

"I'll kill you," Christian warned him. "Not even these others will be enough to stop me. So, ask yourself . . . who will benefit from your death? Anthony obviously wants one of his own to succeed him. But who is it? Not you. You'll be dead."

Christian saw the unwelcome knowledge hit Scoville's expression, followed quickly by betrayal, and then anger. He scowled at Christian, blaming the messenger. But in the end, he was smarter than Noriega. "Damn you," Scoville whispered sharply. Then he spun on his heel, ordering his backers to follow with a jerk of his chin.

Christian didn't waste any time watching them leave. With a silent command to Marc, he ran the final distance to Jaclyn's office, shoved open the door, and stared around frantically. The phone was ringing in an empty office. Where the hell was everyone?

He ran to the conference room where Natalie should have been sitting, but it was empty.

"*À la fin,*" he muttered. *Enough!* He gathered his powers, closed his eyes, and concentrated, scanning every room, searching for . . . anyone. There had to be someone left here, someone who knew what the fuck was going on.

"Christian," Marc said, but Christian shushed him with a hand gesture, then opened his eyes and started forward.

"Two vampires, corner office," he said and strode down the hall. The office belonged to Jaclyn, and the image he'd gotten had been strong enough that he knew she was there.

Christian reached the closed door of Jaclyn's office and shoved it open, not bothering to knock. She was inside, and she wasn't happy. She raced over from where she'd been sitting with Cibor, fangs bared, hands curled into claws, ready to defend her bodyguard who sat on the couch, eyes closed, head back against the cushions.

Christian stepped back, hands raised in a placating gesture. "Jaclyn," he said quietly. "It's Christian Duvall."

She stared at him for a long moment, her eyes gleaming a gold-tinged red, a low growl rumbling in her chest, as she clenched and unclenched her fists in rhythm. And then like a light switching off, her fangs retracted, reason returned to her eyes, and she drew herself up to suck in a deep breath.

"Christian." She sounded far more exhausted than she should have. Jaclyn had significant power.

"What the hell happened?" He forced himself to be quiet and calm, when what he wanted was to shake the truth out of her. "Where's Natalie?" he asked, voicing his deepest concern.

"Anthony," she said, the growl returning to her voice. "He *dared . . .*" She drew a deep breath, making a visible effort to think rationally and answer his question. "He planted a compulsion in Cibor's head, in order to get time alone with Natalie."

"He has Natalie?" Christian experienced an emotion that was nearly foreign to him. Genuine fear.

Jaclyn shook her head, seeming confused. "She left," she said slowly, as if forcing her brain to recall what she'd seen. "I was with Cibor, but . . . I remember her saying she was sorry, and then gathering her things." She looked up at Christian. "Sorry for what?"

"I'm going to find out. Did you call Raphael?"

"*He* called *me*. He's already on his way here for the challenge, and says he'll deal with it when he gets here."

"He'll have to stand in line." Christian spun away, but Jaclyn's voice stopped him.

"Raphael wants Anthony for this, Christian. If he's done something to Natalie, you can't kill him."

Christian turned and met Jaclyn's worried gaze. "If he's done something," he repeated, but he couldn't finish the thought. He respected the hell out of Raphael, but if Anthony had so much as *touched* Natalie, he'd be dead before morning. "Tell Raphael I'll try to leave Anthony alive for him. But no guarantees."

She nodded. "She's blaming herself for all of this, Christian. She needs to understand it wasn't her fault."

"Oh, I'll make sure of that," he said grimly. "I'll make sure she understands a lot of things."

NATALIE PUT THE last of her dinner dishes into the dishwasher, and closed the door. She didn't know why she'd bothered to fix anything. Her stomach was so knotted, she hadn't been able to eat. And she doubted it was going to get any better. She'd tried to distract herself with work, but her mind kept blinking over to the coming confrontation with Anthony. Their *date*. He hadn't said where they were going, or what this *perfect place* of his was, but she didn't think she'd be able to swallow more than a cup of tea, or a glass of wine. Or maybe she'd just throw up in his face, and they'd call the whole thing off. The way she was feeling now, projectile vomiting was definitely a possibility.

She forced herself to climb the stairs to her bedroom. She had no intention of primping for the date, but she needed to get dressed. She walked into her bedroom and looked around aimlessly, then crossed to the bathroom, and stood staring at her reflection in the mirror. She looked awful. Stress did that to a person. She hated the idea of spending even an hour with Anthony, but hated even more what he might do if she refused. He'd already hurt Cibor, and, by extension, Jaclyn. And what about her family? Anthony was just petty enough to take it out on them because she wouldn't go out with him.

Which reminded her. She needed to call her parents, just to be safe. She picked up the phone and hit the appropriate speed dial, then listened to it ring. Part of her wanted to get their answering machine. It would be so much easier to leave a message. But another part wanted to hear their voices.

"Hey, baby girl." Her father's words rolled with a Cajun accent that was much deeper than hers, and the more time she spent with him, the stronger her own accent became.

"Hey, Daddy."

"What's wrong?"

She forced a laugh. "Why would you ask that?"

"Because I know my Natalie. Come on, talk to your daddy."

She blew out a long breath. "I just wanted to warn you . . . about Anthony."

"If that bloody bastard's giving you any trouble, you just come on home. Don't you worry about anything else."

"It's not that bad. Honestly. But you know how he likes to play games. Well, he's playing one now. There's this guy I'm dating—"

"Who?" her father demanded, forgetting all about Anthony.

"Now, Daddy. Don't go getting all protective on me."

"As if there's any other way for me to be with my own baby girl."

Natalie smiled, and it felt good. If there was one thing she was sure of, one thing that would never change, it was that her parents loved her.

"That means more than you know," she murmured, then stiffened her resolve. "His name's Christian . . . the guy I'm dating. And he reminds me of you." She thought she might have heard a light sniff from her father's side of the phone line. "Anyway, Anthony and Christian don't get along, so Anthony's pretending he and I are . . . involved, as a way to get back at Christian."

"As if."

Those two words issued in her father's deep voice with its Cajun accent were so perfect that she laughed out loud.

"That's what I said, too," she told him. "But you know how Anthony gets. So if he calls you or anything, just ignore him. And, you know, you and Momma be careful."

"That old bloodsucker doesn't scare me. Don't you worry about us. And if your new beau is worth your time, he'll tell you the same thing."

"You're right about that," she muttered, then said. "I've got to go, Daddy. I expect Christian any minute now."

"You tell him what I said."

"I will."

"And you come visit us. Your momma misses you."

Natalie smiled. Translation . . . her *father* missed her.

"I'll come soon. Now I've got to go. Give my love to Momma."

"I'll do that. You take care, baby girl. I love you."

"I love you, too, Daddy. Bye-bye."

When she hung up, she felt both better and worse. Better because she always felt better after talking to her father. And worse, because talking to him made her so homesick.

Her phone beeped with a new voicemail. She'd ignored the incoming beep when she'd been talking to her father. And she ignored the voicemail, too. She'd left Christian a message earlier, but ignored all of his calls and messages since then. She wasn't going to debate this on the phone. He was just going to have to wait until she could talk to him in person. Besides, she already knew what he'd say. He wouldn't want her to go tonight, would insist he could handle Anthony. But he didn't know Anthony like she did. She wasn't going to risk Christian's life just to avoid one crummy date.

Pushing away from the mirror, she leaned into the shower and turned on the water, waiting until it was hot before stepping under the spray. While she showered, she obsessed about how angry Christian was going to be. Her stomach churned, and she wondered how she'd gotten involved so deeply, so fast. And when he'd become so important to her.

Once out of the shower, she did a quick blow dry of her hair, and pulled on some underwear, then wrapped her robe around herself, and was crossing into her bedroom when the ringing doorbell made her jump. Her gaze shot to the clock on her bedside. A little early, but not unexpected.

Doing a quick finger-comb of her hair as she went past the mirror, she hurried down the stairs and over to the door, doing a quick check through the peephole. Her already knotted stomach twisted harder.

Time to face the music.

She looked again. He did not seem happy.

"Open the fucking door, Natalie," Christian growled. "I can hear you breathing."

Damn vampire hearing. She yanked the door open. "You're early."

Christian's back had been to the door while he'd been saying something to Marc, but when the door opened, he did a graceful spin, and now he was glowering down at her. "It's lovely to see you, too, *chère*. Invite us in."

Natalie stared at him. She'd been so set on her course when she left the estate earlier, so certain she was doing the right thing. But now . . . now she was beginning to think she'd acted rashly, that her much vaunted intellect had been overtaken by fear, and she'd let it rule her decisions. That wasn't like her. She usually overthought everything, so what had happened? She suddenly realized she didn't know what she wanted anymore. And Christian was waiting.

"Of course," she said finally. "Come in, both of you. But you have to listen to me," she added, as first Marc and then Christian slipped past her.

Turning, Christian moved her out of the way, and closed the door, only to loom over her, his deep blue eyes glittering with anger. "So talk, *mon ange*. Tell me why you left Jaclyn's office, left the estate, without a word of explanation. Why you ignored my repeated calls to ascertain that you were, *at the very least,* alive and well."

"I called you," she snapped. "And I told you to come over here. There was no point in arguing over the phone when it's so much more satisfying in person!"

Christian grinned. "Are we going to argue, *chére*? What about?"

Natalie licked her lips nervously. This was it. Doomsday. "About me going out with Anthony tonight." She didn't even finish her sentence before Christian's eyes filled with blue fire and she braced herself for his roar.

"Have you lost your fucking mind?" he growled, in a voice so deep it made the floors tremble.

"No, I have not," she said, standing firm in the face of his anger. It was nothing she hadn't expected. "He'll be here at midnight, and—"

"*Merde!* Do you have any idea what a vampire like Anthony can do? You were there at Jaclyn's. Did you see what he did to Cibor? And believe me he's much—"

"He threatened you!" she shouted, abruptly tired of being treated like an idiot. "Yes, I know what he can do, and, yes, God damn it, I know what he did to Cibor. Why do you think I'm doing this?" She snapped her lips shut, having said far more than she'd planned.

Christian stared at her a long time, while she waited for him to explode. Maybe shoot fire out of his eyes or something this time. But he didn't do any of those things.

"Do you trust me, Natalie?"

She blinked at the sudden question, but there was only one answer. "Of course I do."

The corner of his mouth ticked up in a smile at her quick response, but his next words were deadly serious. "I want to check your head, to see if your mind's been tampered with. Because I can't think of any reason why you'd think that I need *your protection.*"

Ah, yes. There was the roar she'd been waiting for. "Well, pardon me, great one," she drawled sarcastically, "for believing you might need me for anything. And, no, I will not let you tap into my brain."

His eyebrows shot up. "Afraid I'll discover you think I'm brilliant and handsome?"

She puffed out a dismissive breath. "Hardly. Now sit down and listen to me."

Christian cupped her cheek in one hand, his thumb moving in slow, soothing circles over her chin. "No, *chére*. You listen to me. I need you for many things, but I do not need you to protect me against Anthony, or any other vampire. That's my business, and I'm very good at my business."

"But—"

"No," he said, that one word saying it all.

He was completely unwilling to discuss it. Why had she ever thought they could have a rational conversation?

"He thinks if he gets you away from me, he can win you over. And if not, then he'll force your mind to his way of thinking. Never mistake Anthony's pettiness for stupidity. He has no morals, no limits when it comes to—"

"Christian," she said patiently.

"—getting what he wants. And he wants—"

"Christian," she said again.

"—you. There is no way I'm letting you spend five minutes with him, much less an entire—"

"I agree with you," she said flatly, giving him her version of the blue fire stare.

"—evening. What?"

"Geez, how stupid do you think I am? I'm not going anywhere with Anthony. Why the hell do you think I called you over here?"

Christian was frowning at her, but she could hear Marc laughing softly.

"I assumed—" he started to argue, but she stopped him.

"You know what they say about assuming."

His frown deepened, while Marc laughed harder. Christian glanced over at his lieutenant, and then back to her. "I don't think I want to know. Okay, I'm listening. Tell me why I'm here."

She reached up and stroked Christian's face, so smooth over the curve of his cheekbones, slightly rough where his beard was a dark gold shadow. He leaned into her hand, rubbing like a cat. It made her smile. "Can we sit down first?"

He pulled her toward the sofa.

"You want some coffee?" she asked innocently.

He gave her a narrow look as he sat down, taking her with him. "Very funny," he said. "Now tell me why I'm here."

"Don't you want to be?"

"Natalie," he growled in warning.

"Fine. First of all, do you think you *should* check my head, just to be sure Anthony didn't do something to me? He was waiting for me in the hallway outside Jaclyn's office. That's why he messed with Cibor, to get him to go back inside and leave me alone."

"I can check, but I don't think so. You wouldn't have called me here otherwise."

Her eyes widened. "What if *that's* the compulsion? What if he wants you here?"

"Then I'll be Lord of the South before the night is over. What's your plan?"

"Simple. I knew I couldn't deal with Anthony on my own, and I knew I'd never talk him out of coming here tonight. So I called in the big guns. You."

Christian laughed, putting his arm around her and pulling her against his side. "Just for that, I'd kill him for you tonight. Unfortunately, Raphael wants him, because of what he did to Cibor. I promised I'd wait until he arrives tomorrow to discuss it."

"The challenge," she said, surprised she'd forgotten. Raphael and the others were still coming for the challenge *tomorrow night.*

Christian nodded. "Nothing will stop that, but Raphael would have come anyway. Anthony's a fool to mess with you on my watch, but he's many times a fool for trying to compromise one of Raphael's people. If Raphael's known for one thing, it's loyalty to his own."

Natalie swallowed her sigh of relief. She didn't want to prick Christian's alpha ego, but she was happy to let Raphael take on Anthony. She didn't need Christian to prove anything to her, and she didn't want him risking his life. Anthony wasn't worth it.

"Oh my God, how's Cibor?" she asked, ashamed she hadn't asked already.

"He's fine. Jaclyn's with him."

"Jaclyn probably hates me. I never should have tried to hide up there. None of this would have happened."

He tightened his arm, squeezing her close. "Of course she doesn't. She's worried about you."

Natalie shrugged, not sure she believed that. She glanced away, wanting to change the subject, and caught sight of the clock in her kitchen. "I need to get dressed!" she said urgently, pushing away from Christian, and standing up. "Anthony will be here any minute, and we need to be gone."

Christian stood next to her, but he clearly didn't share her urgency. "But that would be rude, *ma chére*. To make Anthony drive all this way for nothing? I wouldn't dream of it."

She gripped his hand tightly. "I thought maybe we'd go somewhere, be gone when he gets here."

Christian gave her a disbelieving scowl. "You want me to run? From *Anthony?* I know you can't judge this for yourself, *mon ange*, but he does not have the power to kill me, even if he was inclined to try. Which he won't, because he's too afraid of dying, himself."

Natalie rubbed her eyes, thankful she hadn't put her makeup on yet. She wanted this night to be over. She wanted Anthony out of her hair, and Christian in it. In that order. "But you said you can't kill him, because of Raphael."

"I can't kill him tonight, but I can sure as hell make sure he understands what's mine. And what will never be his."

Natalie gave him an exasperated look. What was with the *mine* bullshit? She didn't belong to anyone. Although, in her deepest, non-feminist heart, she had to admit it gave her a little thrill to hear him say it.

"I need to get dressed," she repeated abruptly. It was the one thing that made absolute sense right now. Clothes. "Make yourselves at home. I know you don't like my coffee, but there's vodka in the freezer, and scotch in the cupboard next to the sink. Glasses are in the same—"

The doorbell rang, stopping her in mid-sentence, replacing exasperation with . . . not fear exactly, but trepidation. She believed Christian when he said he could defeat Anthony. But best-laid plans and all that. Accidents happened. People got lucky.

She couldn't think of any other trite sayings. She turned to Christian who cupped her cheek in one big hand, his fingers spearing back into her hair, as he moved even closer. "Don't worry," he assured her. "We won't let anything happen to you."

Natalie noticed that Marc had come to his feet, and now stood just behind Christian, his arms crossed over his chest.

"I'm not worried about me," she confessed.

"Then you've nothing to worry about. Answer the door, but don't invite him in."

"Should I get dressed first?"

Christian tilted his head, taking in her finger-combed hair, her makeup-free face, and the big robe which left it unclear how much, or how little, she had on underneath. Natalie felt a blush heat her cheeks. He smiled.

"No, you're perfect, just as you are."

She didn't believe *that*, but figured he knew what he was doing. She tightened the sash on her robe, still wishing she'd used the time spent arguing with Christian to go upstairs and put on some clothes. A quick check of the peephole confirmed it was too late for that now. Anthony stood out there. Sucking a deep breath of courage, she opened the door, and was shocked to see that he was all alone. Other than when he was in his office, she couldn't remember a time when she'd seen him without a bodyguard or two lurking close by. Maybe they were waiting in the big limo idling at the curb.

Or maybe Christian had been right, and Anthony's intentions this evening had been something less than honorable, or even legal.

"Lord Anthony," she said, sticking to formalities, as she dug down and managed a weak smile.

"Natalie," he said warmly, but then he got a good look at her, with her makeup-free face, her barely brushed hair, and her robe. "Am I too early?"

"Anthony!" Christian's voice came from behind her, and his arm dropped over her shoulders in a blatantly possessive gesture.

She hid her surprised reaction, just barely, but didn't even try to stop the instinct that had her pushing back into Christian's strength as rage lit up Anthony's face.

"Duvall," he growled. "What are you doing here?"

Christian didn't answer Anthony's question, turning his attention to Natalie instead. "*Ma chére,* go keep Marc company, would you?"

Natalie wanted to insist on being there for whatever was about to happen. After all, she'd been the one who'd set this whole thing up. The one who Anthony had no doubt revolting plans for tonight. Standing this close to him, she imagined she could feel tendrils of his thoughts trying to reach out and grab her, the way he'd attacked Cibor. But her mind had always been her strongest attribute, and there was no way he was getting in there. She pictured a wall around it, starting with stone blocks and reinforcing it with steel. And maybe those tendrils hadn't been all in her imagination, because she thought she detected a flash of surprise in Anthony's eyes, a moment before Christian's arm tightened around her. He pulled her out of the doorway, then shifted to stand between her and Anthony. "Stay with Marc, *chére,* please."

Natalie moved back. She had no argument with getting farther away from Anthony. But she wasn't going to hide behind Marc either. This was her fight as much as Christian's, and she wanted to be there for it.

Anthony had observed the whole exchange, his face darkening with rage. "Come here, Natalie," he said harshly, with a whip of command in his voice that she could hear, even if she wasn't inclined to obey. To Natalie, Anthony's attempt to compel her was an interesting curiosity. Something she filed away to be researched later.

Christian's reaction was completely different. It was like a match sparking tinder. His entire posture changed, as if he'd been holding back, and now all bets were off. Every muscle in his body tensed, and all traces of affability disappeared in an instant. Setting her firmly behind him, he faced down Anthony, his hands curled into fists at his sides. Behind her, Marc had come to attention at the same time, and he took her arm now, and carefully put himself between her and the two angry vampires.

"Stay the hell away from her, you sick fucker," Christian growled, "or I'll kill you where you stand."

Anthony made a scoffing noise. "Kill me? Empty words, Duvall. You don't have what it takes."

Christian stepped out of the townhouse and onto the porch, forcing Anthony to back up or be crushed. And he must have seen something more in Christian's face, some vampire quality that she didn't yet understand, because shock abruptly erased all traces of scorn from Anthony's expression, and he nearly stumbled when he took an urgent step backward, away from Christian.

"The only reason you're still breathing, *Lord* Anthony," Christian snarled, "is because Raphael has claimed your death for himself. But push me a little harder, and I'll forget all about the promise I made."

Anthony paled even further as he backed down the walkway. "This isn't over, Duvall," he hissed. "Not for any of you. You have no idea what's coming."

Natalie pushed into the open doorway, shaking off Christian's hand when he tried to stop her, and refusing to budge until Anthony's limo was out of sight. She was shaking inside, coming down from the cascade of fight-or-flight hormones triggered by the confrontation. Christian pulled her out of the way and closed the door, and she locked down her emotions, refusing to wimp out and cry or, God forbid, start trembling like a leaf.

Christian put an arm over her shoulders, and she waited for him to give her an encouraging hug, and tell her it would all be okay, that he'd protect her. But instead, he used his arm to turn her in the direction of the stairs, and said, "Go get dressed."

Natalie scowled. Bossy fucking vampire. But since she had no argument with putting on some clothes, she didn't call him on it. This time.

"Are we going somewhere?" she asked.

"Home."

CHRISTIAN CONFERRED briefly with Marc once they arrived at the house. There was work to be done, but most of it involved Marc's talents, not his. They needed to find out as much as they could about the real situation in Mexico. Anthony's parting shot might have been bluster, but it had held a ring of truth that he couldn't ignore. Something more was coming, and they needed to figure out what it was. Christian considered calling

Vincent to discuss the problem. They'd established something of a rapport in their previous brief conversation. But before he did that, he needed more information.

"I cracked Anthony's system, but there's nothing there," Marc said, shaking his head. "Ten years ago, I could've walked right through his firewalls. But now everyone has security experts and closed networks, with no Internet access. Get me in the building, and I'll have full access in no time."

Christian snorted dismissively. "I don't think Anthony's going to be inviting us back anytime soon."

"I'm not giving up yet. There are still a couple of trails I want to follow."

"Better you than me," Christian said, and slapped Marc on the shoulder before leaving him at the basement door and heading back to the kitchen, where he could hear Natalie moving around.

He was relieved to be able to turn the research over to Marc. He wasn't in the mood to sit down at a desk and stare at a computer screen. He was altogether too energized, almost as if his skin would split from the pressure building inside him. It could have been the challenge, the fact that things were finally moving forward, but that wasn't the real reason and he knew it. It was Natalie. He'd wanted her from the moment he'd heard her voice on the phone. Meeting her had only sharpened his desire. But even worse was the knowledge that he wouldn't be satisfied with a quick night or two buried in her body. He wanted to keep her.

"I'm going for a swim," he announced, ignoring Natalie's look of surprise as he strode through the kitchen, yanking his sweater off as he walked. The pool had been one of the big selling points of this house for him. Swimming was the ultimate relaxation. Well, that and sex.

He glanced back as he slid the glass door open and flicked on the pool lights. "Are you coming?" he asked Natalie. She was standing on the other side of the kitchen, still wearing the hoodie she'd pulled on before leaving the townhouse, and looking confused.

"I don't have a suit," she protested.

Christian laughed. "Neither do I," he said, and started to strip.

NATALIE FOLLOWED Christian outside just in time to catch his dive into the pool. Steam formed a translucent fog over the turquoise water, and a bare ripple of movement marked his progression across the pool. She took a few tentative steps closer to the pool's edge, eager and yet reluctant to see Christian in all his naked glory. Even clothes couldn't conceal the athletic perfection of his body, the breadth of his shoulders and chest, his strong legs and tight ass. She was desperate to see him in nothing but skin, but she was also terrified. She wasn't used to feeling anything this intense for a man. She had a grinding need for him that would only be satisfied with sex. Sweaty, throbbing, groaning sex. Something she was pretty sure she'd never had before. Sure, she'd had sex a few times, but it had never been like this. Not like she was sure it would be with Christian.

He surfaced long enough to execute a perfect racing turn at the end of the pool, then disappeared again as he started his return lap. Natalie blinked in confusion. He was actually going to swim? She'd assumed it was just a way to get the two of them naked in a pool, but he was doing laps? She didn't know whether to be relieved or insulted.

Blowing out a disgruntled breath, she figured she should at least take off some of her clothes. She was beginning to feel foolish standing there, clutching her hoodie around her like a terrified virgin.

She dropped the sweatshirt on the same chair where Christian had tossed his pants. Toeing off her Nikes and socks at the same time, she considered whether to go further. Unfortunately—or maybe fortunately, she wasn't sure yet—she was still wearing her most unsexy underwear.

"Don't be such a prude, Nat," she muttered to herself. She turned her back to the pool—okay, maybe a little prudish—and pulled off her T-shirt and jeans, adding them to the pile of clothes. She shivered in the cool night air, and turned to eye the steam coming off the pool longingly. Even if she didn't go in the water, it would be warmer at the pool's edge. She glanced down at the boy shorts and sports bra she was wearing, and rolled her eyes. She was being stupid. Her underwear was less revealing than the bikini she normally wore to go swimming.

Moving over to the pool, she sat on the edge and lowered her legs into the water. It felt good, and the steam was just as warm as she'd thought it would be. In the middle of the pool, she could make out Christian's blurry form as he continued his damned laps. For all the attention he was paying her, she might as well strip naked and dance under the stars. Laughing at herself, she braced her arms behind her and leaned back, but the sky was far too saturated with city lights to reveal any stars for her to dance under. She closed her eyes instead, and enjoyed the silky feeling of warm water against her legs, the faint heat of the steam on her face, feeling completely relaxed for the first time in days.

Which was why she screamed when two big hands slid up her calves a moment before Christian emerged on a warm wave that splashed half of her body and left her sitting in a puddle of cooling water.

She was still gasping, her heart racing, when he braced his forearms on either side of her thighs and grinned up at her.

"Aren't you coming in?" he asked, his legs treading slowly, keeping himself above the water with effortless ease.

Natalie stared. He was just as beautiful as she'd known he would be. Water sheeted off powerful shoulders and slid down the planes of his chest. His arms, next to her thighs, were corded with muscle, his hands a hair's breadth away from her bare skin.

"Natalie?" he asked, amusement dancing in his eyes as they reflected the underwater lights.

"I'm not sure," she admitted, fingering the wide strap of her bra nervously. "I've never . . ."

His eyebrows shot up. "Never been skinny dipping? Come on, *chére*, let's expand your horizons."

"Isn't it cold?"

He moved closer, his fingers grazing her thighs for a moment before resting against her skin in a blaze of heat. "I won't let you get cold," he said quietly

Natalie's gaze shot up to meet his eyes. There was no glint of humor anymore. There was nothing but naked desire. "Take it off," he said, his dark voice a caress of sound in the steamy air.

Nerveless fingers struggled with the tight hooks on the front closure of her sports bra. He didn't try to help her, didn't move at all, except for his eyes, which followed her fumbling fingers with an intensity that made her hands shake even worse.

She felt a warm brush of something hot and wet, and looked down to see Christian kissing his way up her thigh, those strong fingers sliding to the inside of her knees to spread her legs. He lifted his eyes to hers again, as he insinuated himself between her thighs, powerful arms levering his body out the water as he kissed her fumbling fingers, first one hand, then the next, before sliding back into the water, and draping her legs over his shoulders.

Natalie blushed when he kissed the inside of her thigh, his mouth only inches away from her sex. She wondered if he could smell the arousal throbbing between her legs, the desire slicking her pussy.

"Natalie," he growled, giving her fingers a meaningful glance where they'd frozen over the hooks of her bra clasp. His hands slid around to cup the curve of her ass, and a helpless noise escaped her throat when his fingers slipped beneath her underwear to dig into her bare cheeks, tugging her closer to the edge of the pool, bringing her eager pussy closer to his mouth. She closed her eyes against the sight of him. He was the very image of temptation whispering against her thighs, and she was abruptly driven by a desperate need to free herself from the confining bra. Her breasts felt suddenly too big, her nipples aching pearls of exquisite sensation that scraped against the tight cotton fabric with every breath.

Christian's fingers gripped the back of her underwear and tugged, his eyes meeting hers, almost daring her to say "no."

Natalie's body had become a single, throbbing, pulse of desire, every beat of her heart sending scorching need pulsing through her arteries. She ripped the last hook away, and her chest expanded with a deep breath of relief as the confining bra fell away from her breasts, her nipples so hard and swollen that the fabric hung up briefly before she dragged it down.

A rumble of sound came from deep in Christian's chest as he eyed her bare breasts. He yanked her underwear over her hips, under her ass, and down her legs in a single, smooth motion, and tossed them to one side.

"Do you want this, Natalie?" he asked, his expression deadly serious as he stared up at her.

She swallowed, her voice scratchy on a dry throat. "Yes," she said, and knew it was true. She wanted Christian with a yearning that wouldn't ease, but this was more than that, more than simple sexual desire. She wanted *Christian*, not just the beautiful vampire, but the man. "I want *you*," she told him.

His smile was the one mothers warned their daughters about, what fathers guarded their daughters against. He was sin and temptation, and the promise of a sexual ecstasy that few ever experienced.

Natalie closed her eyes against the overwhelming ache of longing that flooded her soul with that smile. But her eyes flashed open at the feel of Christian's hot breath on the tender skin of her inner thigh. She looked down to see him kissing his way closer to her core, pushing her legs wide until she was completely bare to him, her pussy only inches from his mouth. She flushed with embarrassment and would have closed her legs, but his shoulders held her knees wide, his fingers sliding up her thighs, stroking ahead of his lips until his thumbs grazed the lips of her pussy, already slick with her juices and puffy with arousal.

"Christian," she gasped as she felt the edge of his teeth on the tender skin of her thigh.

He kissed the spot he'd just bitten, even though she'd barely felt it. It wasn't his fangs, but his human teeth that he'd bitten her with. Her eyes opened blearily, and she watched as he licked and sucked her inner thigh, her breath catching when she realized his mouth was lingering just above the big femoral vein.

"Have you ever been bitten by a vampire?" Christian murmured, his words a cool brush against her wet skin.

Natalie shook her head, then realized he was facing her thigh, and couldn't see her. "No," she rasped.

He looked up at that, his smile one of amused disbelief. "No? All of those beautiful vampires walking the halls, and you've never indulged?"

She shook her head again.

He lowered his mouth to her thigh and hummed wordlessly, sending a shiver of lust straight between her legs. "I like that," he murmured. "I like being the one to pop your cherry."

"Christian!" she breathed, shocked and turned on at the same time.

He chuckled softly, before licking his way to the very edge of her pussy, then pulling back again, to blow on her wet flesh.

Natalie's hips thrust upward, almost unwillingly, eager for the touch of his mouth. He smiled against her skin, then suddenly slipped his tongue between her folds and licked, his tongue rough against sensitive flesh, as he tasted her from the swollen opening of her pussy to her throbbing clit. She moaned and pushed against his mouth, but he only circled that engorged nub, making her keen with need.

"Tell me again," he demanded, then moved his mouth back to suck gently at the skin of her thigh.

"I want you," she gasped, barely able to get the words out for the pounding of her heart.

His soft growl vibrated against her thigh a moment before she caught the flash of his fangs, and then the sharp pain of his bite stabbed into her thigh, and a shocking wave of carnal greed rolled through her, shivering over her clit and prickling her skin, making her womb ache beneath the clenched muscles of her abdomen, and tightening her nipples into hard peaks above the swollen flesh of her breasts. Natalie cried out, as the sensation crashed over her, thinking *this* was what everyone had told her about, this incredible feeling of erotic pleasure.

But that was only the beginning. Unfettered lust suddenly raced through her veins like fire, lighting up every nerve, every muscle. Her back bowed from the force of it, her legs spreading wide as if she could somehow free herself from the pressure of this consuming need. Her head fell back, her desperate cries impossible to contain. She didn't think about anyone hearing her scream, didn't consider the neighbors, or even Marc in the house behind her. Her only thought was to let it go before it destroyed her. Christian snarled as he lifted his mouth from her thigh, his fangs sliding out and his tongue lapping up the remaining blood, soothing the wound that didn't hurt, but *ached* as though she could never have enough of it.

Natalie sobbed in relief, thinking it was over, that her body would be hers once again. But her sobs turned to renewed cries as Christian's sinful mouth moved up her thigh, his kisses wet on her overheated skin, his thumbs spreading her wide a moment before his mouth closed over her clit and sucked.

She choked on a sharp intake of air, and would have fallen back to the concrete, but Christian's arms shot out, wrapping around her back, sliding her down his body as he pulled her into the water. His hands were everywhere, stroking her back, her legs, pressing her trembling body against his hard length, anchoring her. She clung to his shoulders, feeling as if she'd fly into pieces and disappear if she let go. Her legs tangled with his as he kissed her, his mouth moving over her neck, her shoulders. He lifted her effortlessly to get to her breasts, closing his teeth over her nipple, taking her right to the edge of pain, before caressing the swollen tip with his tongue as he made soothing noises.

Natalie didn't know what was happening to her, didn't know what to do with this raging need, this hunger that was tearing her apart. She wanted to scrape her nails down his back, to dig furrows into his powerful shoulders, to see red blood mingle with the turquoise water. She was shocked at the strength of her own desires, at the sheer lust driving her. She wasn't like this. She was quiet, conventional, and always in control.

As if he'd heard her thoughts, Christian dug his fingers into her ass, grinding her against the marble-hard length of his erection. Her breath caught as his fingers caressed the crease between her butt cheeks, and then released in a keening moan when one thick finger slid into the tight little hole. She opened her mouth to say something, anything, but then he wrapped her leg around his hip and slammed his cock deep into her body, claiming her more completely than any man had ever done, more, she suspected, than anyone else would ever do again. She despaired even as she exalted, dreamily wondering how she could go on knowing that she might never again experience the piercing joy of making love to Christian Duvall.

He pulled his cock out in a long, slow stroke of sensuousness, only to slam back into her with a snarled oath. "Stay with me," he demanded, and began fucking her hard and fast. His cock was big, and she was tight, but so wet. So very wet and slick and ready for him.

Her cries rippled over the water as he fucked her with fingers and cock, his mouth swallowing her pleas for release, or maybe she was begging for more. She didn't know anymore, couldn't distinguish where she ended and he began. She could only hold on to the unrelenting strength of him, crying out helplessly when a fresh orgasm tore her apart and put her back together in one glorious explosion of ecstasy. She laughed crazily when Christian kept driving into her, wondering how much more pleasure her body could take. But then without warning, he shuddered hard. His mouth slammed down on hers in a passionate kiss, his cock bucked inside her, and she felt the warm rush of his release.

CHRISTIAN HUGGED Natalie close, holding her upright and murmuring meaningless words against her ear as she hung limply against him. He needed to get her out of the water before she became chilled. The water was warm, but it would soon drain what little reserves she had left after her multiple orgasms. He couldn't stop his satisfied grin at the thought, any more than he could stifle the smug confidence that he was feeling as she trembled in his arms. His Natalie wasn't a virgin, but she wasn't experienced either. She'd never been bitten, and her shock when he'd slid his finger into her tight little hole hadn't been feigned. His drained cock twitched at the thought of dipping more than his finger into that sweet ass.

Natalie moaned softly, as if she'd sensed the reaction of his cock. But he didn't know if the moan meant she was too exhausted for more, or if she was anticipating even greater pleasures. Whichever it was didn't matter, because she was practically unconscious, and he wanted her fully able to enjoy everything they did together.

Swinging her up into his arms, he walked to the stairs and climbed out of the pool. Natalie moaned again, but her shivers made the meaning obvious this time. The night air had hit her after the warm water, and she was cold. Putting on a burst of vampire speed, he dashed into the house with her in his arms, snagging his sweater from the kitchen barstool as he strode through the house and down the hall to the guest room where she'd slept last night. She clung to him tightly when he went to put her down, so he pulled back the covers with one hand and slid into bed with her until she was breathing evenly. He would have liked to sleep next to her, and had a flash of how delightful it would be to roll over at sunset and pull Natalie into his arms. He'd tug her beneath him and sink his fangs into her neck, before spreading her legs and fucking her awake. He could still feel the pulsing of her sheath around his cock from when she'd come earlier, the way her tight pussy had squeezed him nearly dry.

And if he didn't stop thinking about that, he was going to fuck her again right now.

Releasing her gently, he snagged his sweater and slid it over her head, kissing her thigh as he rolled it over her hips and under her ass. Then he climbed out of bed, pulled the covers up, and left her with a final kiss on her warm lips.

She didn't stir when he slipped out into the hallway and closed the bedroom door. He was at the basement stairs when it occurred to him that she would very probably wake during the day tomorrow, and wonder where he was, or when she'd see him. After all, he was her first vampire lover, and while she had to know the basics of a vampire's sleep cycle, her first morning-after in a near empty house might be confusing. So he left her a note near the espresso machine, and went downstairs to find Marc still hard at work.

"Any luck?" he asked, passing through the computer room on his way to their personal quarters.

Marc glanced over his shoulder, one eyebrow raised at Christian's lack of clothing. "No," he said dryly. "Unlike you, apparently."

Christian grinned, but didn't say anything as he ducked into his bedroom and grabbed a pair of sweats. He and Marc had shared lovers in the past, and had certainly compared stories, but he didn't want to talk about Natalie. He wasn't sure what he felt for her, but he knew it was something different, something unique.

He reappeared in the doorway, rubbing a towel over his wet hair. "So you think Anthony's running a closed network on the estate?"

"Sure looks that way. Even if I couldn't break the security on his network, I should at least have been able to *find* it if he was connected to the Internet."

Christian frowned. "I wonder if Jaclyn could help."

"I wonder if she *will*. Wouldn't that be the same as Raphael taking sides in the challenge?"

Christian shrugged dismissively. "It's done all the time. The lords aren't supposed to, but everyone plays favorites. Besides, Jaclyn is her own person, not just Raphael's mouthpiece. And after what Anthony did earlier, I think she'd welcome the chance to fuck him over."

"I think there's probably a long line for the privilege."

Christian laughed. "His children seem loyal enough." But then he recalled Scoville's easy acceptance of his argument about Noriega. Maybe Anthony didn't have the loyal following he thought he did.

"Give it up for tonight," he told Marc. It's nearly sunrise. You need blood?"

Marc pushed away from the computer, spinning his chair around as he stood. "Nah, I'm good. But you must be drained." He snickered, and Christian reached out and slapped the back of his head as he went by.

He walked over and pulled the interior vault door closed, sealing off the bedrooms from the rest of the basement. His thumbprint and a second code threw the bolts on the heavy door, just as the first rays of the sun burst over the horizon, igniting a warning fire in his brain. And by the time the yellow ball of flame crested the horizon, he was sound asleep in his big bed, with the rich taste of Natalie's blood lingering on his tongue.

Chapter Eight

NATALIE WOKE WITH a start. The room was dark and empty, and, for a moment, she couldn't remember where she was. And then the night came crashing back, and she remembered everything. She covered her eyes with a groan. Had she really been that wanton, needy creature? For sure, *that* had never happened before. This was all Christian's doing, some vampire magic he'd worked on her. Her sex pulsed in remembered heat, flooding her pussy with wet need, and her breasts felt swollen and sensitive beneath the soft fabric of . . . Christian's sweater. He must have put it on her after carrying her to bed. His scent surrounded her, and she couldn't stop the soft moan that trembled from her throat. God, she wanted him. He was like a drug. Every inch of her was on fire, replaying the touch of his mouth, the sharp sting of his fangs, the hard thrust of his shaft.

Her hand slid beneath the sweater, her fingers finding the slick moisture between her thighs. Her clit throbbed to her touch, her sex wide open and aching as she slipped two fingers inside herself. She added a third, but it didn't come close to the thickness of Christian's cock, the way he'd stretched her wide, her inner muscles clenching around him as he'd fucked her slowly, deliberately. His fingers gripping her ass as he—

She came with a muffled cry, her pussy contracting hard, squeezing her fingers as her thumb stroked her clit. She lay there for a moment, her chest beaded with sweat, her heart pounding beneath her breasts. And then she rolled to her side, and curled in on herself as if to contain the pleasure, wishing Christian was there to hold her instead.

She must have drifted back to sleep then, because the next time she woke, she had the definite sense that it was later. The little bit of light leaking around the dark blinds was just pale enough that she knew it was afternoon, not morning. And a quick glance at her cell phone told her she was right. Rolling to her back, she smoothed the soft fabric over her breasts, feeling her nipples harden. She toyed with them briefly, then snapped upright. Something was happening to her. Despite the long, dry spell of celibacy that had been her time in Houston, she usually didn't masturbate more than a couple of times a week, and she rarely woke up wet. That she was even thinking about coming on her own fingers for the second time in one day was unheard-of.

This was Christian's fault, too. Although, with her pussy still twitching pleasurably from the previous night, she was having a difficult time convincing herself that this new development was a bad thing.

But enough was enough. She had work to do, and tonight was the gala that Christian had to attend, despite the confrontation with Anthony. And she was going with him. She had her dress and shoes, and the underwear to go with them. But if she was going to do the dress, and Christian, justice, she'd need some serious prep time. And some food. She didn't care if it was breakfast or something else, but she needed sustenance.

The idea of food finally got her out of bed, and as if to make sure she didn't backslide, her stomach grumbled loudly. Remembering the pitiful state of Christian's refrigerator—at least when it came to real food—she decided to make a run to the grocery store. She didn't know this neighborhood, but there had to be something nearby, and she'd seen Marc drop the SUV keys on the table next to the door.

But she wasn't going anywhere all sweaty and stinking of sex, with her thighs still sticky from last night. She needed to shower, and it made no sense to do it twice, which meant washing her hair, and shaving her legs. Her stomach grumbled again, but it would just have to wait.

By the time she'd cleaned up, found the grocery story, and driven back, there were less than two hours left until sunset. She didn't know exactly what time the gala started, since she hadn't been formally invited, and hadn't been part of the planning either. Anthony had never involved her in any of the vampire activities, which now struck her as somewhat odd. It was as if he'd been intentionally keeping her from meeting any of the many vampires who hung around the estate. She didn't want to think too much about his reasons for that, even though it was pretty clear by now that he'd been saving her for himself. And that idea still had too high of an *ick* factor to contemplate.

Intentionally setting it aside, she unwrapped the sandwich she'd picked up at the grocery deli, added some chips, then settled down in front of her laptop. She still had a job to do, and besides, she loved her work. Loved finding clues in the numbers, following the trails.

She was deep in her own head, seeing nothing but what was on the computer screen, when a warm hand caressed the bare skin of her lower back. She shrieked and nearly fell off the kitchen stool, only to be caught by a laughing Christian.

"That's not funny," she protested, slapping away his hands.

"It sort of is," he said, ignoring her efforts and pulling her into his arms. He gave her a smacking kiss on the lips, then glanced at her computer. "You're working?"

She nodded. "It relaxes me."

"I could relax you," he crooned, his big body surrounding her as he leaned forward to trap her in his arms. "Unfortunately, we leave in an hour," he added.

"What?" Natalie straightened abruptly, her head nearly cracking Christian on the chin when she swung around to stare at him. "You're dressed," she said stupidly. But he was. His white tuxedo shirt wasn't fully buttoned, and his tie hung open, but everything else was in place. Black pants, black leather belt and shoes, and now that she was paying attention, she saw the elegant black jacket draped over the back of a chair. "Fuck!" she swore and pushed at his chest, trying to force him back. The effort was totally futile, of course. Christian would move when he wanted to, and not before. "Christian," she said exasperatedly, "I have to get ready."

"I sort of like this look," he said lazily, his hand sliding beneath her T-shirt and around her ribs to cup her braless breast.

"Christian," she breathed. It was meant to be a protest, but it didn't come out that way.

He kissed her. Not the brief smack of a hello kiss he'd given her earlier. This was heat and desire and sex. He pulled her into his arms, his hand clenched in her hair, a hungry edge adding urgency, his lips almost rough as he explored every inch of her mouth before pulling back. Natalie was lost in sensation, her head back and eyes closed. Her fingers gripped his waist, crushing the fine cotton shirt as she held on for dear life. He licked the corner of her mouth, then tightened his hands on her arms.

"You need to get dressed," he murmured.

Her eyes opened lazily, and she groaned. "Not fair," she muttered.

"Go on," he said, turning her toward the doorway and slapping her butt. "I'll rinse your dishes."

"Ass," she muttered, too soft for him to hear. Or maybe not.

"You'll be paying for that later," he called cheerfully, and was still laughing when she slammed the bedroom door.

CHRISTIAN STROLLED through the gathering of beautiful people with the most gorgeous woman in the room on his arm. He closed Natalie's fingers over the crook of his elbow, and held them there. It was either that or explore the enticing expanse of bare back exposed by her sexy dress. He'd been fighting an erection ever since she'd hurried out of her bedroom earlier, her hair a sensuous pile of curls that looked like she'd just been well fucked, her legs smooth and silky beneath the short dress, with a pair of black stiletto heels making them look even longer. He couldn't blame any- one but himself for her tempting appearance. He'd selected the dress, after all. But damn, she looked good. And despite the tension they were both feeling about Anthony—wondering if he'd be stupid enough to show up tonight when Raphael was gunning for him—Natalie was charmingly excited about the gala.

He scanned the room slowly, without being obvious about it. Scoville was in attendance, though he'd all but dropped out of the race after his chat with Christian the other night. And Marcel Weiss was across the room, sending hate-filled glares from within his circle of supporters. But there were notable absences. Noriega was missing, of course—that's what happened when you jumped the gun; you missed the big party—but Stefano Barranza was also nowhere to be seen, and Christian found that suspicious. It wasn't mandatory for challengers to show up at the gala kick-off, but it was customary. It was a chance to measure opponents' power, to flaunt your own, and, if you were lucky, to come to the attention of the current vampire lords who were in attendance. Barranza's absence made Christian wonder if the Mexican vampire had decided to drop out altogether, or worse, if he was down in Mexico seeking a new alliance with Hubert.

But while the challengers had a central role to play, they weren't the indispensable attendees at this party. That honor went to the vampire lords, and Christian had to admit that it wasn't often one saw so many of them in one room. The current batch of lords got along with each other in a very un-vampire-like way, which made getting together a lot easier. That was Raphael's doing. And it would be the *un*doing of the Europeans, unless they changed their tactics. But he wasn't going to be the one to warn them.

The lords stood apart from the crowd, their mates by their sides. Mates were almost always in attendance for challenge launches. The lords were there to contain the aggression-fueled violence that could erupt at these things, while their human mates were on hand to help contain the aggression of the lords themselves.

Christian was keeping a close eye out, but there'd been no sign of Anthony, which only reaffirmed his assessment of the Southern lord's survival instincts. Raphael and his mate, Cynthia, had arrived early on, along with both Duncan and his woman. Vincent wouldn't be attending, but that wasn't a surprise. He could hardly leave his territory when there were known infiltrators actively working to bring him down. And thus far, Christian hadn't spotted any of the others—Sophia, Lucas, Rajmund or Aden—but the night was still young, and the lords tended to arrive singly rather than all at once, to avoid a sudden crush of power in the room. Nerves were strung tightly enough. By now, everyone had heard about what had happened to Cibor, and Raphael's anger because of it. And when a vampire as powerful as Raphael got angry, no one in the vicinity was spared the effects.

Next to him, Natalie tensed, and her fingers twisted to grip his nervously. Christian followed her line of sight and found Jaclyn and Cibor, deep in conversation. Jaclyn's hand was hooked around Cibor's elbow, her breast was pressed against his arm, and their lips were almost touching.

"Look at Cibor, *chére*. He's fully recovered. Raphael will have made sure of it by now."

She nodded, and Christian bent to kiss her artfully tousled head. "He and Jaclyn look awfully cozy, though. Maybe the crisis brought some deeper feelings to the surface," he mused.

He was surprised, but relieved, when Natalie laughed. She hugged his arm against her soft breast, and leaned in to whisper conspiratorially, "They've been lovers for years. Didn't you know that?"

He reconsidered the last few days. The signs had all been there, but he'd missed the obvious, because it wasn't commonplace for two vampires to become lovers. "That's rather unusual."

She tilted her head, gazing up at him curiously. "Why? I'd think it's a natural fit. Shared interests and all that."

"But no food, no blood source. Is it just the two of them, or is there a third?"

"You mean . . ." Her cheeks were stained such a delicious pink, that he was tempted to take a small bite, just to taste.

"That's exactly what I mean," he whispered, settling for a slow brush of his lips over her cheek, feeling the heat. "They must be hunting and feeding together. Seducing together. I wonder if they hunt men or women."

"But I thought blood and sex went together . . ." Her words trailed off on an indrawn breath. "Are you saying that they, um, that they both . . ."

"Oh, yes."

"Oooh." She studied the couple with an assessing and entirely unexpected gleam in her eye. "Did you and Marc ever . . . you know."

Christian put his lips against her ear, exploring the soft shell with his tongue before murmuring, "Yes, we did. Many times."

Her chest flushed with arousal above the tight bodice of her dress, her nipples creating slight bumps where they were trying to push through the fabric.

"Would you like to do that with us, Natalie?" he murmured. "Does it excite you?"

She licked her lips, and he wanted to snap his teeth at the sweet, rosy tip of her tongue. "I've . . . that is, I've never—"

Christian wrapped both arms around her, hugging her close to his chest. "It would be delicious, *mon ange*. But only if you want it."

Natalie's fingers clenched in his shirt a moment before he detected a powerful presence to his left.

"Christian Duvall. I don't believe we've met," drawled a deceptively relaxed voice with a deliberate flavor of the deep South.

Christian kept an arm around Natalie's waist as he turned to greet the newcomer. And what a newcomer he was. Duncan Milford, Lord of the Capital Territory. They'd never met, but Christian knew of him. Everyone knew of Raphael's longtime lieutenant.

"My lord," Christian said with a respectful nod of his head. "My companion, Natalie Vivant Gaudet."

"Charmed, my lady," Duncan said smoothly. "And intrigued. Cajun and Creole, if I'm not mistaken."

Natalie gave him a wide smile. "You are not, my lord," she said, her own lilting accent in full force. "A Cajun father and Creole mother, both back several proud generations."

"And beauty, as well, surely."

Christian was beginning to suspect that Duncan was laying on the Southern accent a little heavily. He'd spent more than a century in California with Raphael; it was unlikely he'd managed to hold on to his accent for all that time. Maybe he was trying to relax Natalie, or maybe to disarm Christian himself, with what the Americans called "good ol' boy" charm.

Christian gave him a bemused look, to let him know it wasn't working. No disrespect, but no dice, to coin another American phrase.

"Anthony seems to be missing tonight," Duncan said, his accent all but disappearing as quickly as he'd shifted subjects.

Christian huffed a breath. "You can say many things about Anthony, none of them good, but he has a highly developed sense of self-preservation."

"Ah, yes, that business with Cibor," he said disingenuously. Christian had no doubt at all that Duncan and Raphael had thoroughly discussed the previous day's events. "Jaclyn must have been in a fine temper over that," he added.

Which provoked Natalie's sharp elbow in his side. Apparently everyone knew about Jaclyn and Cibor except him.

"She was understandably furious," Christian agreed, wondering where all of this small talk was leading. "As was I."

Duncan nodded knowingly. "I feel the need to apologize on Anthony's behalf, Ms. Gaudet. He is a member of our Council."

"There's no reason to apologize, my lord. Christian took care of Anthony just fine," she said with a loyalty that warmed his cold heart.

"Did he?" Duncan eyed Christian speculatively. "I would guess then that you are not exactly Anthony's favorite person."

Christian gave Duncan a flat stare. "If not for Raphael's prior claim, Anthony would be dead by now."

"And you would be Lord of the South."

"I'll be that anyway. But I'd have killed him for what he tried to do to Natalie."

Duncan gave a sideways tilt of his head in acknowledgment. "Are the challengers all here tonight?"

Christian didn't need to scan the room again. He could place every one of his competitors without looking, and, curiously, Barranza had still not shown. "Not all of them," he told Duncan. "One is mysteriously absent, while another made the bad decision not to wait for the formal challenge. It wouldn't have changed the outcome, but he might have lived long enough to enjoy the party."

"I'm betting the dead one was one of Anthony's?"

Christian studied Duncan, surprised that the Capital lord was aware of Anthony's scheming. And what Duncan knew, Raphael knew. He nodded in agreement. "Noriega. He should never have been in the challenge, and Anthony had to know that." Christian didn't bother to hide the anger in his voice. Noriega hadn't had to die.

A sudden ruffle of power from the dais had them both turning to look as a big, blond vampire joined the crowd, going immediately over to shake hands with Raphael. His woman went with him, a pretty, buxom little thing who was quickly enveloped in a hug by Cynthia Leighton. The two women couldn't have looked less alike, but they clearly knew each other well, and immediately moved off to the side for a private conversation.

"Rajmund," Duncan commented, confirming Christian's guess. "And his mated wife, Sarah. And I believe that's all of us for this gathering. Lucas and Aden chose to remain home to cover any surprises from our European friends." His brow wrinkled in concern. "And we're a little concerned about Sophia. No one's heard from her in the last week. And Cynthia's attempts to contact her mate, Colin, have been unsuccessful, which I understand is unusual."

Christian was sorry Sophia hadn't made it. He'd been curious about her. Female master vamps weren't that uncommon, but female lords were rare. Even more rare, now that Mathilde was gone.

Up on the dais, Raphael turned, his black gaze resting on Christian for a long moment, before settling on Duncan.

Duncan frowned briefly, then smiled and said, "Raphael would have a word with you, Duvall. Come say 'hello.'"

Jaclyn and Cibor appeared out of the crowd at that moment to surround Natalie, pulling her gently out from Christian's grasp. Christian trailed his fingers along her back as she moved away, but he let her go, because he understood that Duncan wasn't the only one who'd been communing with Raphael. And apparently the Western lord wanted his conversation with Christian to be private.

Besides, Natalie looked so happily relieved when she was enveloped in a group hug by the two vampires, that he didn't have the heart to stop her. Although, he did make one thing very clear to them.

"Just remember," he said, catching Jaclyn's eye. "She's mine." He said it lightly enough, but they knew he was serious. He gripped Natalie's chin, turning her face to his for a kiss, before saying, "I'll be right back, *chére*. You stay with Jaclyn, *oui?*"

She nodded, but just to be safe, he caught Marc's eye, where he stood chatting up a blond human a few feet away. Raphael wasn't the only vampire who could issue telepathic requests to his children. Marc whispered something in his companion's ear, then came over to stand on the other side of the group hug.

With Natalie securely under Marc's care, Christian walked alongside Duncan as they made their way to the dais. They moved through the crowd steadily, but casually, not wanting to call too much attention to what was happening. Anyone seeing Raphael speak directly to Christian would presume it was a tacit endorsement of his challenge; that was unavoidable. But there was no need to shine a spotlight on it.

Raphael and Rajmund both turned when Christian and Duncan stepped up onto the dais, with Rajmund greeting Duncan like an old friend, which he probably was. They'd both been lieutenants to North American lords for many decades, before becoming lords in their own right.

But Rajmund's next move was unexpected—he offered his hand to Christian. "Rajmund Gregor," he said. "Call me Raj."

Christian shook his hand. "Christian Duvall."

Raj grinned. "Looks like you'll be joining us soon."

Christian's smile was more cautious. He'd never doubted he would succeed in winning the South, but he'd expected his eventual reception on the Council to be more in line with Anthony's intense dislike, or at best, Juro's reluctant respect. This wide-open acceptance from both Duncan and Raj was not at all what he'd anticipated. But he'd sure as hell take it.

"One way or the other," he told Raj, agreeing with his assessment, but alluding to Anthony's continued existence at the same time. There were two ways to gain the lordship. He could fight and defeat all of the remaining challengers, or he could simply kill Anthony and have done with it. He knew which one he'd pick, if given a choice. He wanted Anthony to die for what he'd done to Natalie.

"Come on, Raj," Duncan said suddenly, his worried gaze on the other side of the dais, where the three mates were deep in conversation. "I don't like the looks of that."

Raj glanced over his shoulder and swore softly. "Fuck. We'll talk later,

Duvall. Congratulations." And he and Duncan were gone, hurrying to join their respective mates.

"My Cyn gets bored at these things. She gets . . . creative," Raphael offered, with more than a touch of amusement in his voice.

Christian didn't know what to say to that, so he simply nodded, as he regarded the three women.

"Do you think you can kill Anthony?"

Raphael's abrupt question swung Christian's attention back to where it belonged, on the most powerful vampire in the room. He studied the Western lord's face, looking for clues as to what he wanted him to say, and wasn't exactly surprised to find nothing there. So he went with the truth.

"I *know* I can kill him. And with all respect to you, my lord, given what happened to Cibor, his death should be *mine*."

"Because of the territory?" Raphael asked.

Christian shook his head. "Because of my Natalie. Because Anthony had plans to take her out for an evening, and use his power to compel her consent. He would have forced her to agree to her own rape, and that would have destroyed her."

Raphael's black eyes went cold, and Christian thought for sure he'd gone too far. But Raphael's next words proved him wrong.

"You're right. His offense against your woman is far greater. I relinquish my claim. His death is yours."

Christian experienced a moment of disbelief, followed by the exquisite rush of pure vengeance. He could already taste Anthony's blood on his tongue, could already hear his screams. *Soon*, he promised himself.

"Thank you, my lord," he said fervently. "His death will be as painful as I can make it."

Raphael bared his teeth in a terrifying grin that made Christian glad they were on the same side. "Give my regards to your woman," he said. "And enjoy the rest of the evening."

Christian bowed slightly from the waist. He'd been dismissed, and he didn't mind. He'd been away from Natalie for too long, and there were too many vampires on the hunt in this room.

He strode across the room, loosing just enough of his power that the crowd gave way before him. Natalie was exactly where he'd left her, still in between Jaclyn and Cibor, with both their arms around her. They might not be actively trying to seduce her, but it was obvious they wouldn't mind, either. The wonder was that they hadn't done so before now.

Christian growled softly, then reached in and slipped an arm around Natalie's waist, neatly extracting her from the group hug. Cibor stiffened slightly, but Jaclyn only laughed.

"We were taking care of her for you," she teased.

Christian gave her a knowing look. "Much appreciated, but I'll take it from here."

"*It* is just fine on her own," Natalie said, with a growl of her own. "Stop talking about me like I'm not here."

"You're right, *chère*. I apologize."

She rolled her eyes, but turned in the circle of his arm and brought her lips to his ear. "Is that Raphael's mate?" she asked.

He could feel the press of her soft breast and, combined with the lingering adrenaline rush of his promised vengeance against Anthony, it made his dick harden. He wanted to scoop her off to somewhere private, where he could push her skirt up her silky thighs and fuck her until she begged him to stop.

She must have caught some of that in the look he was giving her, because she blushed furiously, and said, "Stop that."

He grinned at the way her words mirrored his thoughts. "Stop what?"

"You know perfectly well what. So, is that Cynthia Leighton?"

Christian turned his reluctant attention back to the dais where Leighton and Raphael now stood with the other lords and their mates. "It is."

"Hmmm," she said, with enough of an undercurrent that Christian gave her a curious look. "Aren't we a few lords short?" she asked quickly, almost as if she wanted to deflect his attention.

Christian had a moment's worry, remembering what Raphael had said about Leighton causing mischief, but decided not to pursue it further. At least not tonight. "Three, to be exact. Well, not counting Anthony, who didn't have the balls to show up."

"Isn't one of the lords actually a woman? Is she up there?"

"You mean Sophia. No. She's missing in action, and the others are actually worried about her. Which, if you knew anything about how powerful vampires interact, is remarkable."

"Do they think she's dead?"

He shook his head. "If she was dead, we'd all know it. When a vampire lord dies, the power backlash is strong enough to be felt all over the continent, but especially by the lords. We'd all feel it."

"Well, that's good," she murmured.

Christian smiled bemusedly. "If you say so. I've never met the woman." He lowered his head enough to kiss her lightly. "I think we've fulfilled our obligation here, don't you?" He straightened, and glanced over at Marc. "You ready to blow this pop stand, *mon ami*?"

Marc laughed at his use of the American colloquialism. "Ready to get out of this tux," he agreed.

"Time to go home," Christian decided, then put his lips to Natalie's ear and purred, "Someone still has a lesson to learn."

CHRISTIAN DIDN'T waste any time once they returned home. While Marc went directly to the basement quarters, Christian followed Natalie into her bedroom and closed the door behind him, leaning against it as he watched her undress. She started to step out of her heels, but he stopped her.

"Keep the heels."

She gave him a little smile, then reached up and pulled some pins out of her hair, allowing it to tumble to her shoulders, before turning to the dresser where she slowly removed her jewelry—long, dangly earrings and a bracelet to match. Rubies, he thought, with small diamonds. He'd buy her something better, something to mark her as his.

She pulled at the zipper under her arm, turning to face him as the dress slid down to pool at her feet, leaving her in nothing but a barely-there black lace bra and a tiny pair of matching panties. She stood, and stared at him boldly, despite the blush heating her pretty cheeks.

Christian did a lazy scan of her body, head to toe, and back up again, lingering at all the intriguing places covered by those bits of lace. When he met her eyes, he let her see the hunger that was burning his throat, and creating a heaviness in his groin.

He crossed the room slowly, holding her gaze, watching her pupils dilate with emotion. There was fear there, but also desire, excitement. Was she afraid of *him*? Or of her own response to him? She licked her lips, a deliberate provocation that answered his question.

Reaching out, Christian hooked his fingers in the center of her bra and tugged her closer. Flicking the clasp open, he pushed the delicate cups aside. Her breasts were heavy against his palms, large on her delicate frame, their tips a deep rose against the golden hue of her smooth skin. He molded the soft globes with his fingers, coaxing her nipples into hard nubs as she leaned into his caress. She rolled her head on her shoulders, humming her pleasure with eyes closed as she savored the sensation. Her silky hair brushed against the backs of his hands, as her fingers gripped his belt, holding on as if she needed his strength to remain standing.

Christian freed one hand to twist in her thick hair, pulling her head back and holding her still for his kiss. His tongue traced the outline of her lips, before dipping into her warm mouth. Natalie went up on her toes with a soft moan, pushing for more, crushing her mouth against his in demand.

He only smiled. Breaking the kiss, he lifted his hand from her breast to glide it down over her ribs, past her waist, gripping her hip briefly before slipping his fingers beneath the slender band of her panties. He snapped it with a quick movement, and she jumped, eyes flashing wide open.

He met her surprise with a lazy grin as the lacy bits fell down the length of her legs to hit the floor, and she stood before him naked, except for her shoes. Dipping a hand between her thighs, he found her slick with arousal. She shuddered when he pushed a single finger into her opening, and her hands came up to grip his arms as she widened her stance, giving him better access.

Christian touched his lips to her forehead, whispering down over her eyes, to her cheeks, the corner of her mouth.

"You're still dressed," she fretted.

"Yes, I am."

She looked up at the unapologetic confidence of his words, then gasped as he slipped a second finger into her pussy, and began stroking her, in and out, their gazes locked. A haze of desire clouded the rich brown of her eyes.

"Christian," she whispered, pleading.

He held her stare, fingers pumping, gliding through the rich cream of her desire. He could feel the slight tremor of her thighs, the quivering of her inner muscles, as her body responded to the constant thrust and release of his fingers. Her nipples were hard pearls digging into his chest through the fine fabric of his shirt as she lifted her face to his, desperate for a kiss. He caressed her lips, his tongue stabbing between her teeth to taste the delicate flavor that was Natalie, matching the rhythm of his fingers into her sodden pussy.

With a small, needy noise, she thrust her hips forward, pushing hard, trying to force her clit against the pressure of his hand.

Christian growled, and slid his other hand around her hip, his fingers digging into the curve of her ass, before slapping her butt cheek in warning. "Behave."

Natalie gasped her protest, and slapped his chest. A slap he barely felt. He chuckled and felt the heat as her skin warmed with a feverish flush that rolled over her cheeks and neck, before bringing a lovely, pink tinge to the tops of her breasts. Scraping his fingers up her smooth back, he wrapped her hair around his hand again, and gently tugged her head back.

"Onto the bed, *chére*."

Her eyes flashed open in an instant of confusion, and he curled his fingers around the nape of her neck. "Crawl onto the bed, *mon ange*, I want to see that pretty ass in the air."

Her entire body seemed to heat with embarrassment this time, and she made a little noise of wordless distress. His Natalie wasn't wildly experienced. In fact, he imagined most of her previous sexual encounters had been conducted in the missionary position, in the dark. But, for all her shy blushing, she wasn't unwilling. Even if he hadn't had his fingers buried in the evidence of her soaking wet pussy, he could smell her arousal.

She glanced toward the big bed, then back to meet his eyes once more, as if to be sure he really wanted her to do this. And then she walked over and climbed onto it, crawling all the way up to nearly the headboard before she stopped and looked at him over her shoulder.

Christian nearly had a heart attack. Did she know how she looked? What she did to him? She was the very image of temptation. Her lips were puffy from his kisses, her big brown eyes gazing at him in perfect submission, asking what she should do next. Long, auburn hair swept over her back and shoulders, and her position provided only tantalizing glimpses of her breasts, which swayed beneath her with every breath. But it was her ass that called to him. The perfect heart shape, the firm and rounded cheeks.

He started across the room, intent on taking her, but then paused. Hadn't he just observed to himself that Natalie was, if not an innocent, then at least inexperienced? He needed to gentle her, to introduce her to the variety of sexual experiences in a slow, sensuous way. She probably didn't even realize the temptation she presented, offering her ass to him like that. At least he hoped she didn't. Because slowing the fuck down, literally, was one of the hardest things he'd ever done.

"Put your head on the bed, *chére,*" he said quietly, as he began stripping off his clothes, tossing his jacket and shirt onto a chair, toeing off shoes and socks as he unbuckled his belt. "But keep that sweet ass in the air," he added, in case she didn't understand what he wanted.

Her eyes widened, but she did as he asked, which immediately made him wonder *why* he'd asked for that. The position didn't exactly make it easier to resist her. Her glistening pussy was on full display, arousal slicking the swollen lips.

"Fuck me," he swore, then unzipped his tux pants and let them drop to the floor, stepping out of them and directly onto the bed behind her. His cock was so rigid it hurt. He stroked himself with one hand, while caressing her ass with the other, squeezing one of her exquisitely rounded cheeks.

He could fuck her like this. She was more than ready for him. He could follow that inviting trail right into her pussy. It was difficult not to, but his *plan,* which he'd only concocted in the last few minutes, was to seduce her. To show her all the ways he could make her body sing.

Bending low, he swept his tongue the full length of her slit, savoring her sweet flavor. Natalie squirmed, unintentionally taunting him even further. "Christian," she whispered.

He bent over and kissed the cheeks of her ass, biting gently. "Do you want me to stop?" he asked, while he was privately begging her to say "no." The gods must have heard his prayers, because she shook her head, which caused her ass to wiggle and did nothing for his self-control.

Nearly moaning in relief, he gripped her hips and flipped her over. Natalie cried out in surprise, but then smiled, spreading her thighs, and lifting her hips off the bed in welcome. He moved between her legs, letting his cock settle in the slick heat of her pussy, but he didn't enter her yet. He was going to teach his angel all the ways he could make her feel wonderful.

He lowered his head to the curve of her neck, nibbling and sucking hard enough to leave his mark on her. He licked away the small pain, then continued over the delicate curve of her jaw, kissing her eyes closed, brushing his lips over her mouth, before licking his way downward. His teeth closed over her collarbone, and he was struck by how fragile it was, so breakable. All of her was like that. It made him want to lock her in his basement and never let her out. He growled softly, but then Natalie's fingers moved through his hair, digging in his scalp, and he was reminded that she was strong, too.

He transferred his attention to her breasts—beautiful and round, with large nipples that begged to be sucked. He took one in his mouth and did just that, closing his teeth over it until she moaned hungrily, her hips lifting off the bed to brush against his cock. He groaned and flexed his hips to coat his cock in her wetness, as he switched his attention to her other breast, sucking her nipple into plump eagerness. But this time, Natalie's fingers lingered in his hair, holding on tight enough that it hurt as she pulled him against her chest, forcing him to continue worshiping her breasts.

The pain from her grip was a jolt of lust straight to his already hard cock, and he wondered how much more he could take. He'd wanted to pleasure her, to make her come with nothing but his mouth and his fingers before finally fucking her until she shattered around him. But his Natalie was no ethereal creature. She was a woman who knew what she wanted, and demanded it. He grinned against her breast, delighted at her responsiveness. But she needed to learn that he was *always* in charge.

His fangs split his gums, and he bit down on her nipple, drawing only a drop of blood. But it was enough to trigger the euphoric in his blood, enough to send Natalie soaring into orgasm with no warning but the heat of his bite. She arched beneath him, her back leaving the bed as she screamed, her strong fingers sliding down to his back where her nails dug furrows into his skin.

Christian groaned at the pain, and nearly came on the soft skin of her thighs. He cursed under his breath. He wasn't finished with her, but if he wasn't careful, his balls weren't going to give him a choice. Sliding down her body, he kissed her flat belly, the neat patch of curls over her pubis, and then dipped his tongue into her pussy. He groaned again. She tasted so sweet, as if her innocence was pooled between her thighs, just waiting to be savored. He used his mouth, mimicking the sex act, feeling her sheath contract around his tongue as her body twitched in the final throes of her bite-induced climax.

"Christian," she whispered, her voice hitching with emotion.

"*Natalie*," he murmured back, and blew softly over her swollen clit.

Her hips flexed, and she moaned. "Oh, God."

Using his thumbs to bare her pussy completely, he drew her clit into his mouth, gripping her ass with both hands when she bucked so hard that he nearly lost his grip. She was crying out continuously now, little pleading noises in time with the thrust of her hips. Freeing one hand from her ass, he slid two fingers into her pussy, driving them in and out as he sucked her clit until it was a ripe fruit begging to be bitten.

He bit down, piercing the exquisitely aroused nub with one fang, snarling at the sweet blood that coated his tongue, as Natalie went wild, writhing beneath him, her fingers digging into the cover of the bed, her thighs closing around his head so hard that his ears rang. Rasping his tongue over her clit one last time, he lifted himself over her body, then reached between them and positioned his cock at her entrance. He hissed with pleasure when he finally plunged deep into her welcoming heat. The walls of her sheath gripped him hard, trembling around his cock, becoming a sensuous ripple when he started to move, her body caressing him, urging him to climax with her. He kept thrusting, unwilling to end this yet. With a demanding growl of his own, he twisted her hair around his fist, holding her in place as he kissed her, only to be reminded once again that Natalie was no delicate, passive thing. She met his mouth with a demand of her own, crushing her lips against his until both their mouths were bleeding, their teeth clashing, tongues twisting.

With a final hard kiss, he abandoned her mouth for her neck. He wanted blood. The tiny taste he'd gotten from her clit, and now her lips, had only whetted his hunger. His balls grew heavy between his legs, drawing tighter as his orgasm roared close. He lowered his mouth to her neck, right over the mark he'd left earlier and drew hard on the vein until it was plump and begging. And then, he sank his fangs into her flesh.

NATALIE SUCKED IN a shocked breath, whispering Christian's name on a choked sob, as the climax soared through her. She was helpless against it, as if her body was no longer hers to control, just this throbbing, thrashing thing that knew only pleasure. Christian's mouth was still at her neck, her body so exquisitely sensitive that she'd have sworn she could feel the irresistible draw of his mouth as he fed on the hot flow of her blood. Every place his mouth had touched blazed with fresh desire, as if his lips were everywhere, kissing her all over again and all at once. She dug her fingers into the thick muscle of his shoulders, desperate for something to hang on to, something to anchor her to earth.

A spear of resentment stabbed through her that he could remain so in control, while she could only hold on and hope to survive. But then he lifted his head with a groan, and his hips began thrusting so fast that she could barely distinguish in from out, so fast that her pussy seemed to burn with it. And then he climaxed, and joined her in surrendering to sensation. His eyes were closed, his jaw clenched, his cock flexing inside her as his release shot deep into her body, leaving him helpless to resist. He moaned, almost as if pain, and she stroked a soothing hand down his back, until finally he collapsed on top of her, his breath hot on her damp skin, his face buried against her neck.

They lay together for a silent moment. Panting, sweaty. Natalie was stunned at the sheer power of their lovemaking. She'd never known it could be like this. Christian lifted his head abruptly, hissed a soft curse, and then quickly licked away the warm trickle of blood from her neck, and sealed her wound. She'd been aware of the blood, but hadn't had the strength to say anything. She wasn't sure her tongue was working yet.

Christian turned his gaze to her, and she noticed his eyes were gleaming blue with power in the darkness. She'd never realized before—she hadn't had the opportunity to know—that vampires' eyes glowed with strong emotion, not just when they were using their power.

He smiled down at her, so handsome. She reached up to brush away that one lock of hair from his forehead.

"You taste so very sweet, *chére*," he purred.

She blushed automatically, but managed an answering grin. "It's the blood," she quipped, and then cursed herself for feeding him the straight line, when his smiled widened.

"And everything else, too," he said wickedly. "Your pussy is every bit as sweet as your vein. Your clit even better."

Natalie nearly groaned with embarrassment, but her body didn't. Her body loved the idea that he found her pussy sweet. She would have sworn that she had nothing left to give, that she was climaxed out, but at the look in his eye, and the dirty words from his mouth, she felt a gush of warmth between her thighs, and her pussy pulsed with fresh hunger.

Christian chuckled, low and masculine and she suddenly realized his cock was still buried inside her. He'd felt her body's reaction. She turned her head away from him, wanting to cover her face in shame, but he wouldn't let her. His strong fingers turned her back to look at him.

"I love the way your body reacts to me," he said solemnly. "I love that you're so exquisitely sensitive to every touch, and yet so demanding in what you want. Your body was meant to be worshipped, *mon ange*. And I thank the gods that I'm the one who gets to do it."

She felt tears stinging the back of her eyes, and blinked them away. He wouldn't find her so great if she devolved into a sobbing mess.

"Me, too," she whispered. "I mean . . . your body. I like it, too." She groaned inwardly. *Smooth, Nat. Real smooth.*

But he only grinned and dropped a quick kiss on her lips. She winced in anticipation, remembering the blood they'd both shed, tearing their mouths in their hunger to get to each other. But there was nothing. She ran her tongue over her lips, and found a slight tenderness, but not the shredded flesh she'd expected.

His eyes followed her tongue. "It's the blood we shared," he told her, and she frowned in confusion. "When you kissed me so hard that you shredded our lips," he explained.

She gasped in outrage. "I recall you kissing me first, big guy."

"Naturally," he agreed. "You"—he kissed her slowly, sensuously—"are extremely kissable."

"What about the blood?" she asked, still confused.

"When my blood mixed with yours, it healed your lip, or at least enough that it's no longer bleeding."

Natalie blinked in surprise. She knew vampires healed quickly, but had no idea that their blood could heal others, too. She was still absorbing this piece of information when he said, "You should sleep now. You must be tired."

She *was* tired. But it was a sated sort of exhaustion, the kind that made her want to stretch with contentment. It was also the sort that made her want to curl up next to Christian, and sleep it off *together*. And then she wanted to wake up in his arms, and do it all over again. But that wasn't going to happen. She wondered when he'd trust her enough to sleep with her. It made her a little sad that he still didn't.

She felt her eyes closing in spite of her thoughts, felt the soft brush of his lips on her forehead, and then he was pulling the covers back and lifting her beneath them.

The last thing she remembered was the sound of his deep voice. "Sleep, *mon amour.*"

CHRISTIAN WAITED until he was sure Natalie was deep in her dreams, then climbed out of the bed, and headed for the basement and his secure sleeping vault. He hated leaving her, hated knowing that she would wake up alone, as would he. But he wasn't sure she was ready for the reality of a vampire lover, or that *he* was ready to drag her into the hazards of his life.

She was already in danger because of him, and it would only get worse once he became Lord of the South.

ANTHONY STARED out the window at the Houston skyline, seething with so much anger that his fangs were pressed against his lips and blood dripped from his palms where his nails had pierced the skin. Fucking Christian Duvall. Why couldn't he have stayed where he belonged? Or better yet, why hadn't Hubert killed him the moment he made it clear that he was no longer playing the European's game? That had been the moment of Duvall's greatest vulnerability, the perfect moment to strike. But had Hubert recognized it? Had he seized that moment and rid them all of the danger that was Christian Duvall? No, that idiot European had been too busy turning peasants into mindless soldiers. If you could call those things soldiers. They had not an ounce of independent will, and were a bit too fervent in their worship of Hubert, even for *his* taste.

It was too late for that now. No point in moaning over the past. The fact was that Duvall was still alive and ruining all of Anthony's carefully laid plans. Because of Duvall, he was forced to hide away in this condo, while waiting on Hubert to make his move. But far more egregious was the way that French bastard had moved in and stolen Natalie right from under his thumb. He'd had her there for nearly two years, while he plotted and planned for their future together. And maybe he'd been foolish not to have made his move sooner. She was, after all, a young woman. And like all women, she wanted a man to love and protect her, to provide a home that she could turn into a gracious reflection of their lives. And he'd planned to give that to her, he still would. But he hadn't wanted to begin their lives together under Raphael's thumb. She was to be part of his *new* life, a life where he was in full command of his destiny, of *their* destiny together.

He knew for a fact that she hadn't taken a lover the whole time she'd been in Houston. And she'd never fallen for the easy seduction of his vampires, despite her many opportunities. She'd been waiting for him, but perhaps he'd made her wait too long.

He slammed a hand down onto the thick arm of his chair. He couldn't believe she'd fallen for Duvall, of all people. He was a player, anyone could see that. It was all a game to him, one woman after the next. And now *his* Natalie had become the fucker's next target. Assuming he hadn't already bedded her. But Anthony couldn't believe that. He *knew* his woman. She was meant for *him*. She would see that, once he got her away from Duvall. But he'd have to move fast, before it was too late.

Unfortunately, he couldn't be the one to rescue her, because Raphael was making a big fucking deal about Jaclyn's bodyguard. Or lover, or whatever he was to her. Who cared? He'd needed a few moments alone with Natalie, and the vamp was in the way. So he'd blanked a bit of the vamp's memories. It wasn't anything the great Raphael hadn't done a thousand times. If Natalie hadn't noticed the change and innocently pointed it out, no one would have been wiser. In retrospect, he should have told Natalie what he'd done, and asked her not to mention it. But again, that was the past.

If he was going to get what he deserved, what he'd been working toward since he'd taken over the South, he needed to look forward, to the next move in his plan.

He'd already spoken to his allies, and Duvall would soon be nothing but a memory. But first, he had to get his Natalie to safety. He couldn't risk something happening to her by accident, just because she'd been taken in by that Frenchman. Which brought him full circle. He had to get her away from Duvall, and for that, he'd require help.

The doorbell rang, sounding loud in the nearly empty condominium. No one but his closest children knew about this place, and he'd taken only a handful of those with him when he'd decided a tactical retreat from the estate was necessary. He wasn't in *hiding*, though he knew some would call it that. But that was because they didn't know his strategy, they didn't have his *vision*. He wasn't hiding, he was avoiding unnecessary risk, while biding his time.

One of his guards stepped into the doorway behind him. "Marcel Weiss, my lord," he said.

Anthony didn't look back, but simply raised a hand, indicating the guard should let Weiss in.

A moment later, Weiss's cynical voice said, "Rather a cliché, isn't it, old man? Lurking in the dark and staring through the big picture window? All you need is rain and a bat signal, and you're set."

Anthony's lip curled. He didn't like Weiss. Under other circumstances, he'd have happily killed him, just for being an asshole. For the time being, however, their goals dovetailed neatly. Weiss wanted to rule the South—which meant getting rid of Duvall. And Anthony wanted Natalie back.

"No priceless scotch to share?" Weiss persisted, as he plopped himself into the chair next to Anthony's.

"You got my message," Anthony said, not bothering to reply to the foolish comments.

"Obviously. I'm here. The question remains, however, *why* am I here? Your message was rather short on specifics."

"We share an enemy."

He caught the curious tilt of Weiss's head in his peripheral vision.

"Duvall," Weiss said. He might be an asshole, but he was a smart asshole.

"Duvall," Anthony confirmed. "I can't do any hunting right now, for obvious reasons."

"Is Raphael still in town? I thought he'd left already."

"He did leave, but Jaclyn is still around, and Raphael left additional guards with her. Not to mention Duvall, who, I understand, has been given *permission* by Raphael to kill me himself." He snorted dismissively. "Duvall has an inflated opinion of himself. I still rule the South. He's only one, while I am many."

"And yet, you're giving it all up," Weiss reminded him. "Before we talk any kind of joint venture, I'd like to know why."

"My reasons are my own. Suffice it to say I miss New Orleans. I only came here because of Katrina and the destruction it caused. The properties I lost were worth millions. But that wasn't what drove me away. It was the voices of my children who died in their sleep, drowning, while I could do nothing to help them." Anthony shook himself out of the memory. He hadn't meant to reveal so much. "I want to go home now. But I want it on my terms. Whatever vampire rules the South behind me can make that possible. And I can make *you* that vampire."

"Why me?"

"Why not? You obviously hate Duvall, and I think we both know he's your strongest opponent. I had hoped one of my own would succeed, but Noriega failed, and Scoville has turned coward and bowed out. That leaves you or Barranza, and *he* seems to have disappeared. No one will even admit to knowing his whereabouts, unless you . . ."

Weiss laughed. "I didn't off the Mexican. So, I'm your *only* option, is that it?"

Anthony pretended to think about it. "I guess you're right," he said, as if it had never occurred to him.

"So what's the plan?"

"Duvall has my woman. I want her back. I have people in place to tell me if he goes out tomorrow night, and where he'll be. I'll pass that intel on to you, and you grab my Natalie. Gently. I don't want her injured."

Weiss scowled. "The woman's easy. But what about Duvall? Why can't I just kill him, and take her at the same time?"

"You believe you can defeat him?"

"With the right tools, yeah. I'll need guns."

"This is Texas," Anthony said dismissively. "That's not a problem."

"It is when you don't have an ID."

"Also not a problem. Leave a list with my guard, and one of my staff will handle it. Tell him where you want them delivered, and when."

Anthony sent a telepathic message to his guard. The vampire appeared a moment later, and lingered in the doorway waiting.

Weiss laughed and stood up. "That's it, huh? Still no scotch, I guess. I'll expect a call from you tomorrow, old man. And I want those weapons. I'm not going up against him unprepared."

"You'll have what you need. But, remember, Weiss. Natalie Gaudet is your target, your *only* target. Duvall is a bonus, but only once my woman is secure."

Weiss grunted his agreement, then followed the guard from the room.

Anthony listened to Weiss's departing footsteps, nearly lost beneath the heavy tread of his guard's boots. And then he resumed his contemplation of the Houston skyline. He hadn't planned on Weiss killing Duvall, had thought the vamp would be too cowardly to go against him. He didn't *need* him to kill Duvall. There were plans in place that would cover that quite nicely. But if Weiss wanted to try, Anthony was more than happy to give him that chance. As long as he got Natalie to safety first.

He exhaled on a long breath, feeling hopeful for the first time since Raphael had painted a target on his back. By this time tomorrow, Natalie would be his again, and if he was very lucky, Duvall would be dead.

Chapter Nine

NATALIE WOKE ALONE . . . again, which bothered her more than it should have. It wasn't as if she and Christian were going to do morning cuddles, or sex before breakfast, or even lunch. What troubled her was the subject Christian had raised the first night she'd spent in his house . . . trust. It was obvious to her that he didn't trust her to be around him during the day when he was at his most vulnerable. Actually, daylight might be the only time a vampire as powerful as Christian was *truly* vulnerable.

She told herself she should be glad that she didn't have to deal with seeing whatever state a vampire entered into when the sun was in the sky. Was it like human sleep? Did he breathe? Did his heart beat? She frowned. Well, of course those things must happen. He'd been human once, which meant he still had the same circulatory system, still needed oxygen and especially blood. So how was a vampire's sleep different?

An unwanted thought intruded, suggesting that Christian's decision to sleep alone might not be a matter of trust at all. Maybe he was uncertain how she'd react, and was sparing her delicate sensibilities. If that was it, then he needed a dose of reality. Admittedly, she hadn't lived a hard life, but that didn't mean she needed to be coddled. One of the main reasons she'd accepted the move to Houston was because it broke her out of the protective cocoon her father and brothers had woven around her.

If she and Christian were going to have a real relationship, he needed to know that she could handle the reality of a vampire's life. She didn't even have to think about whether she wanted a relationship with him. The answer was hell, yes. She wasn't ready to marry the guy tomorrow, but she sure as hell wanted more than a few nights of sex. Mind-blowing, knock-your-socks-off sex. But there was more to him than sex. Yes, she'd experienced more orgasms in two nights with Christian than she had in her entire adult life before him. And, yes, he'd done things and made her *feel* things that no other man had even come close to.

But he was also smart, charming, and compassionate. And let's not forget that all of that was wrapped up in one incredibly gorgeous package of hunk-a-licious male. She'd have to be crazy not to want more of him, more of what they might have.

So, then, how could she prove to him that she was as tough as he needed her to be? She'd heard the stories of Cynthia Leighton. You couldn't live around Houston vampires without hearing the rumors of what a badass she was. But Natalie knew her own limitations. She was no pushover, but she wasn't a badass. She'd fired lots of guns, but never at a person. And she'd never contemplated killing an actual vampire lord the way Leighton had. But that didn't mean she was weak. There were all kinds of strength in this world, and hers happened to be in her head. She was smart as hell, and knew how to use what she had. So how could she use that fabulous brain of hers to demonstrate her toughness to Christian?

She glanced at the clock, and saw it was nearly noon. Christian and Marc would be trapped downstairs fast asleep until sunset. But that didn't mean their investigation had to sleep, too. She'd overheard Marc talking to Christian about not being able to access Anthony's internal network, and had known immediately what they were trying to do. They needed something from Anthony that he wasn't willing to give up. That was no surprise, since Anthony took paranoia to an entirely new level.

But she knew Anthony's network better than almost anyone on the estate. She worked as a forensic accountant, but she could just as easily have been a forensic computer analyst instead. Almost all financial data was stored on computers these days, and she couldn't figure out the *where* of hidden data if she didn't first understand the *how*. She'd chosen the accounting career path simply because she liked numbers, but she still kept up on new developments on the programming side.

She knew that Marc would never succeed in tapping into Anthony's inner files, because the network where that data lived wasn't connected to the Internet at all. It was a matter of both security and practicality. There was no need for anyone outside the estate to access that information. Hell, most of the people *on* the estate couldn't access that private network. But *Natalie* could. Her job required that she have access to everything, including the most sensitive data of all. Every financial transaction in or out of Anthony's accounts as Lord of the South, every transaction regarding the estate for the last twenty years, was at her fingertips. She'd never explored beyond the financial data, but that didn't mean it wasn't there. Or that she couldn't get to it.

Filled with purpose, Natalie rolled out of bed, groaning only a little when what felt like every muscle in her body protested. Sex with Christian wasn't for pussies. She choked on her own laughter at the thought, then felt her face flush with heat. She had to get over this reaction to him. If she was going to go back to the estate, she'd need to be at the top of her game. And she sure as hell couldn't be pulsing on the edge of orgasm all day.

She forced herself to her feet and headed for the bathroom. A cold shower would be a good start.

TWO HOURS LATER, Natalie was sitting at her laptop in Anthony's estate kitchen. She checked the clock for about the tenth time in ten minutes. She knew Christian wouldn't be happy that she was here, but he needed to realize that she knew what she was doing. After all, she wasn't an idiot. Anthony employed human guards during the day, but he'd never really trusted them, and had no close associates among them. They manned the gate and perimeter, but had no duties in the main house.

Plus, she was working in the kitchen, which was all but deserted during the daytime. There was no human food stored or prepared here, since the human staff had their own kitchen in the adjacent building on the other side of the parking lot. The kitchen also had the benefit of a door directly to the back parking lot. And yet it was close enough to give her access to Anthony's private network.

Additionally, today was Sunday, and even vampires took the weekend off. Which meant there were even fewer people around. On the other hand, the few who were there had been buzzing with rumors of Anthony's whereabouts. They all knew she worked closely with Anthony, and so seemed to think she knew where he was. They'd shared what they knew in hopes of getting her to share what *she* knew. Details had varied from person to person, but the one thing they all agreed on was that he was long gone from Houston. The most popular theory was that he'd fled to New Orleans, although some versions had softened it to him "visiting" his former city, rather than cowering there in fear. Natalie wasn't sure she bought the idea of him fleeing Houston altogether, but she'd filed it all away to tell Christian later.

Even with few interruptions, though, it had taken her longer than expected to accomplish what she'd set out to do today. First, there'd been a delay in getting back to the estate. She'd forgotten that her car wasn't at Christian's house, since they'd taken the SUV back home after the confrontation with Anthony. Deciding she wanted her own wheels back, she'd called a cab to pick her up at Christian's and take her back to her house. From there, she'd driven her car to the estate. And then it had taken a long time to locate Anthony's personal files on the private server. It wasn't as if the data was tagged and labeled "Anthony's Secret Files—Do Not Read." No, the vampire lord was way sneakier than that, and, again, totally paranoid. Fortunately, her entire job consisted of digging out the secrets of people just like Anthony, people who thought they were the smartest people in the room, and far too clever to get caught.

Unfortunately for them, *Natalie* was usually much smarter than they were, and had a real talent for following data trails. It was what had made her so much in demand back home, and, unfortunately, what had drawn Anthony's attention to her in the first place. She knew all the tricks people used to hide information, and had developed her own algorithms to quickly sift through data and identify patterns. But knowing how to do it wasn't the whole game. It took time, which was something she was quickly running out of.

A nervous glance at the window told her that the sun had maybe an hour left in the sky. She turned her back on the blindingly bright ball of sunlight, determined to get her work done. She didn't want to risk coming back here tomorrow, even assuming Christian didn't blow a gasket after today's adventure. Another thirty minutes would be enough. The sun would be touching the horizon by then, but even vampires needed some time to shower and dress, and she'd be gone before they ventured up from the basement.

When she finally slapped her laptop shut, her stomach was roiling with nerves. If Anthony found out what she'd done . . . Actually, she didn't know what he'd do. He'd always been careful with her, but that was before Christian, and before he'd made an enemy of Raphael. She'd never seen Anthony as furious as he'd been yesterday at her townhouse, but she'd never forgotten her family's history with him, either. Never forgotten how he treated people who "disappointed" him. If he discovered she was stealing his files to help Christian, she had no doubt that she'd fall into that "disappointed" category, and all bets would be off. She was glad again that she'd called and warned her family. But the best way to protect them was to be sure Anthony never discovered what she was doing.

She glanced at the window again. Time to get the hell out of Dodge. She stood and slipped the laptop into her bag, just as she heard a door slam down the hall. A moment later, the kitchen door opened.

"Hey, Natalie!" Jaclyn's human assistant, Lisa, greeted her as she walked in and set a medium-sized shipping box on the counter. "I heard you were working here today, but I thought I'd missed you," she said, as if it was perfectly normal for Natalie to be spending the day working in the kitchen.

"You almost did," Natalie said, striving for casual. "I'm on my way out."

"Good. This is for you. It actually came yesterday, but I didn't see you, what with the big gala and all." She pushed the brown box across the counter to Natalie.

"Me? Why would someone send me a package to your office?"

"It's from Cynthia Leighton. She included it with the usual courier stuff. Do you two know each other?"

Natalie shook her head. "I saw her at the gala last night, but I've never even spoken to her."

"Well, she sent you a present. Open it."

Natalie glanced at the window, where the sun was almost gone. "I don't know, I'm supposed to meet Christian." It wasn't exactly a lie. She *had* left him a note saying she'd meet him at the dojo.

"Aw, come on, Natalie. Aren't you curious?" Lisa slid a pair of scissors across the counter to rest next to the box. The woman had come prepared.

"You're sure it's not going to explode?" Natalie asked jokingly, trying to ease her own tension as she used the scissors to split the tape over the seam, then pulled the box open. She looked down at the contents and blinked in surprise. "It's a gun. Why would Leighton send me a gun?"

Lisa moved closer, and peered into the open box. "And ammunition, too," she said, lifting out one of four smaller boxes. "Fifty rounds in each of these. Something called . . . Hydra-Shok? I've never heard of it, but, then, I don't know that much about guns. How about you?"

Natalie picked up the pistol and pulled it from its holster. "Glock 23, Gen 4," she said absently. "Forty caliber."

Lisa gave her a surprised look. "You know guns?"

"My granddaddy owns a gun store. I worked there part-time during high school and college. He and my father made sure I knew what I was doing."

"Do you have your own guns?"

Natalie shook her head. "Not here. I have a couple that I left home in New Orleans."

Lisa laughed. "You might be the only person who comes to Texas and leaves her guns *behind*."

"I didn't think I'd need them. Even back home, I used them mostly for target shooting. You know, just in case."

"Well, you've got one now."

"Yeah, but why?" Natalie rooted around in the packing material until she found a small envelope with a simple note card. The card had the initials "CL" embossed on the top, and was filled with neat handwriting.

"What does it say?"

Natalie read the message, and scowled. "She says every woman should be able to defend herself," she lied. She wasn't about to tell Lisa that Leighton had specifically mentioned that the ammo was great against vampires, and that it might come in handy with Christian hanging around. What the fuck was that supposed to mean? Why would Leighton want Christian dead? And why would she ever think Natalie would do the deed?

"She might be right, what with Anthony going nuts the way he did. I think a long vacation is in order," Lisa was saying, and it took a minute for Natalie to register what she was talking about.

"Sounds like a good idea," she said, putting everything back into the box and tucking the flap into the end as securely as she could. "Thanks for bringing this down, Lisa, but I've got to run."

"To meet the scrumptious Christian," Lisa said knowingly.

Natalie couldn't stop her grin, but she kept moving. The vampires would already be stirring downstairs, and while Anthony might be on the run, not all of his allies were. They'd probably be more than happy to deliver her wrapped in a bow.

And then there was Christian, who wasn't going to be happy when he got her note. The sooner he saw her in the flesh, the more wind it would take out of his pissed-off sails.

"Could you tell Jaclyn I'm working from home for the next couple of days? She can reach me on my cell, if something comes up."

"Sure thing," Lisa agreed. "And say 'hi' to Christian for me."

Natalie responded with the expected chuckle, but didn't slow down. Her instincts were beginning to itch, and she couldn't get out of there fast enough.

CHRISTIAN KNEW as soon as he woke that Natalie wasn't in the house. This didn't make him happy, but he wasn't immediately worried. There were all sorts of reasons why she might have left, including a new run for groceries. Now that she'd be staying with him, she'd need to stock up.

He stopped first in the bedroom she was using, the one where he'd made her come multiple times last night, before leaving her limp and asleep. The bed had been made, and her things were still hanging in the closet and scattered on the bathroom counter. The room smelled of her perfume and . . . arousal. *Bad girl,* mon ange, he thought with a smile. He scanned the room, but saw no note. He headed for the kitchen next, and found what he was looking for, next to the coffeemaker. His smile disappeared.

"Merde! Marc, we're leaving!" he shouted, then called Natalie's cell phone. It went straight to voicemail. Muttering every curse in every language he could think of, he disconnected and tried to think reasonably. If she was still at the estate, she probably had her phone off, either to minimize distraction or to avoid a ringing phone calling attention to her presence there. She hadn't done as he'd asked and stayed away altogether, but she was a very smart woman. Smart enough to take precautions and avoid running into anyone. But if she lingered after sunset, she was at risk. There were enough vampires who'd tied their futures to Anthony's, that even with him on the run, there would be some who'd grab her just to curry favor with him.

Think, he ordered himself. There must be someone he could call, someone he could trust. The proverbial light bulb went off in his head. Of course. There was only one person in that house that he trusted. He brought up Jaclyn's number and called her.

"Jaclyn Martel's office," a pleasant female voice answered.

Christian was struck by the use of Jaclyn's last name. He'd known it, but didn't think he'd ever heard it spoken before. "Christian Duvall, here," he said snapping back to attention.

"Oh hi, Christian. This is Lisa, Jaclyn's assistant. She's not in yet, probably still sleeping off the big party last night. But if you're looking for Natalie, you just missed her."

Christian played along. "Damn. She must have her cell off. Did she say where she was heading?"

"It sounded like she was going directly to the dojo to meet you. Maybe she hit traffic or something."

"That's probably it. Thanks, Lisa."

"Do you want Jaclyn to call when she gets in?"

"No, that's okay. I'll catch her later."

He disconnected, then grabbed Natalie's note, which he'd tossed aside after reading the first two lines. Sure enough, it said she would meet him at the dojo. That didn't explain why she wasn't answering her phone, but it did tell him where he could find her.

"What's up?" Marc asked, pulling his shirt down as he stepped into the doorway.

"Natalie, bless her cute little ass, decided to work at the estate office today." He handed the note to Marc who read it quickly.

"So we're heading to the estate?"

"No. According to Jaclyn's girl, she's on her way to the dojo already."

"Should I bring our gear?"

"Sure, why not? A little exercise will keep the violence level down once I find her."

NATALIE HAD FINISHED her warm-up, and stepped off the floor to check her cell phone for messages, when the back door opened with its customary metal creak. She looked over, and saw Christian and Marc step inside. They drew attention just by walking down the hall. Not only because they were beautiful, which they were, but because the two of them turned a simple walk into a lethal prowl. And she wasn't the only one who noticed. Two women were just emerging from the locker room, and their lively conversation turned off like a spigot when they caught sight of the vampires. Marc glanced over and smiled at them, and they stumbled so hard that Natalie winced, expecting them to go down in a pile of hormonal confusion.

Christian wasn't paying attention to their erstwhile admirers, however.

His eyes were locked on her, and she smiled at him, feeling happy and a little stupid for getting so excited that he was there. Was she making too much of what they had? So they'd had sex, and okay, so it had been more than just once, and more than just sex. It had been life-altering, mind-blowing, burn-up-the-sheets sex. But that didn't mean she should be getting all jittery when he walked into a room. She wasn't that pathetic, was she?

Christian's gaze never left her as he stood by the locker room door, and waited for her to come to him. He looked good in his black jeans and crew neck sweater, a gear bag slung over his shoulder. But would it have killed him to walk a few steps down the hall to meet her halfway? It was as if she was the peon, and he was royalty, waiting for her to come to him. And could he at least *smile* like he was glad to see her?

She opened her mouth to tell him all of this, but as soon as she was within reach, he took her hand and pulled her toward the back door. "Talk to Alon," he told Marc, and then hustled her out into the parking lot behind the dojo.

"Talk to Alon about what?" she asked, having to hurry to keep up with his long strides. "And hello to you, too. *Rude.*"

Christian glanced down at her, and she realized he wasn't being rude. He was angry.

Natalie felt her own temper rising up to meet his, but told herself to stay cool. She'd expected this. And maybe he wasn't angry at *her*. There were all sorts of things going on, lots of plans and conspiracies afoot. Maybe his anger had nothing to do with—

"Why'd you go there?" he demanded, as soon as they were outside.

So much for the idea that he wasn't angry at *her*. The temper she'd banked while trying to be *reasonable*, flared hotter than ever. She shook her hand loose from his. "I had stuff to do. Didn't you get my note?"

"What good is a fucking note if I'm dead to the world while you're skipping right into the heart of the enemy?"

"Dramatic much? I was hardly *skipping*, because I'm not an idiot. And I left before sunset." Although some of the fight went out of her, because she believed that he really had been worried. And, given recent events, he probably had a reason to be. But that didn't change the fact that he was being a bully. "I don't owe you an accounting of my time," she said defiantly.

Christian moved closer, taking outrageous advantage of his greater size and strength to loom over her. Natalie backed up until she hit the brick wall next to the door. This was apparently exactly what he wanted, because he leaned down to put his face right in front of hers.

"Did it occur to you that I might have been worried?" he asked. He sounded so sincere, his deep voice filled with real concern, that Natalie felt guilty.

For all of two seconds. Then she remembered that vampires were masters of manipulation. And there was something just a little bit sly sparkling in his eyes.

"I left a *note,*" she reminded him. "And I had my cell phone with me. You could have called." She squawked in surprise when he grabbed her cell phone from her hand, and held it up to her face.

"Your ringer is turned off," he said, glaring down at her.

Uh oh. Busted. "I turned it off so no one would hear it ring," she said stubbornly. "I was being stealthy."

Christian's luscious mouth twitched slightly. Natalie was pretty sure he almost smiled.

"I'm sorry," she said placing her hands on his chest and leaning in. "But if you'll just listen—"

"Promise you won't do it again," he demanded, doing an excellent imitation of the brick wall at her back.

Her eyes narrowed in irritation. "I'm trying to—"

"Promise."

Natalie had never wanted to be a vampire, but right at this moment, she really wished she could growl like one. "Fine," she said, willing to be the adult. "I won't . . ." She frowned. "Wait. What am I promising?"

"Not to go waltzing into the lion's den with no idea of the danger—"

Fuck that. "First I'm skipping, and now I'm waltzing? I'm not a child, Christian. I'm a *reasonably* intelligent adult, and I know how to protect myself. I know that estate inside and out, and it was *daylight.* I was trying to help you, damn it."

That shut him up. But not for long. "Help me do what?" he asked, scowling down at her.

"I have access to Anthony's private files. I knew I could—"

"Jesus, Natalie. Are you *trying* to get yourself killed?"

"It's my *job,*" she insisted. "I know what I'm doing, and I'm a damn sight better at it than you are!"

"You're an accountant, for fuck's sake."

"I'm a *forensic* accountant, you ass. What do you think I do all day? I work on computers, identifying patterns, establishing trails, and following them to the truth. I dig out information that other people hide! And I don't need your permission to do a favor for a friend!"

Christian's expression changed abruptly, becoming darker, his eyes gleaming slightly in the mostly unlit alley. "Is that what I am?" he asked in a rough whisper, closing her in with his body, one arm braced on the wall next to her head. "Am I your *friend, chére?*"

Her body reacted instantly, his voice and overwhelming presence bringing back the weight of him on top of her, the delicious stroke of his cock between her thighs. She shivered at the memory, and saw the knowledge in his eyes. He knew what she was thinking, knew what he was doing to her. But even knowing that, she couldn't help her reaction.

"No," she said, then gulped nervously. "I mean, yes, but—"

"But what, sweet Natalie?"

"I don't know. Stop looming over me!"

He chuckled softly, and she sucked in a breath to yell at him some more, but then he was kissing her, his tongue stroking her lips into opening for him, and then probing further until she could feel the hard points of his fangs pushing against her upper lip. His arm swept around her waist, tugging her against him, and Natalie rose onto her toes. She knew he was seducing her, knew she should resist. But she didn't want to. She'd missed him, damn it. Ever since sunset, she'd been waiting for his call, wanting to hear his voice, to see him again. Hoping he felt the same way, that he wanted her again, too.

They kissed until they were both breathless, until their bodies were hot and aroused, his cock hard against her belly, her pussy trembling and wet. She stared up at him, her heart racing.

"I didn't mean to worry you," she whispered, brushing his hair off his forehead.

"I know," he said, his fingers were tender against her cheek. "And I do trust you. You're familiar with the estate, and smart enough to know how far to push it. But I still worry."

She nodded. "And I was right about what to look for. It was worth it."

His mouth tightened, and she knew he was on the verge of disagreeing, and starting the argument all over again. So she changed the subject. "What did you mean when you told Marc to talk to Alon? Talk to him about what?"

His scowl took on a different note. "Is there something between you and Alon?"

Natalie had to fight not to laugh. He was jealous. The idea made her happy, even if there was no cause for it. "I told you. Alon's my best friend in Houston."

"You two never dated?"

"Once, when we first met. But we didn't click that way. So, what's up?"

He eyed her thoughtfully, as if wondering how much to tell her. And Natalie stared right back at him, challenging him to tell the truth. He shrugged.

"Alon is curious," he said. Which told her exactly nothing.

"Curious about what?"

Christian gave her a patient look, as if she was being dense. "About becoming a vampire," he explained slowly. "He's a strong man, and a natural warrior, at the height of his power."

Natalie was stricken. "But wouldn't he have to die first?"

He doubled down on the look that said she was being dense. "Am I dead, Natalie?" he asked, cupping her ass and grinding his still stiff cock against her.

She blinked in confusion, trying to think past the sexual hunger that always seemed to swamp her around him. "No, of course not," she insisted. "But I always thought—"

"What? That we haunted hospitals and battlefields looking for potential vampires? Helpless victims to bring over to become our minions?"

Natalie opened her mouth to protest, but he continued.

"Actually, you wouldn't be far wrong. Many of us were turned under exactly those conditions as recently as a hundred years ago. But not anymore. Not with vampires more out in the world than ever before. We have people coming to *us* now, *asking* to be turned."

"Why?"

He shrugged. "Some see our evolution as an opportunity, a chance to live forever. Always young, always strong. Of course, there are others who think it's the work of the devil." He smirked, his feelings on that subject obvious. "The truth is, however, that only a relative few of us are strong enough to bring someone over, and we tend to be selective in whom we choose. After all, immortality *for* them is immortality *with* them. And even then, not everyone survives the process. Nor can you choose what the transition will do to a particular individual. A corporate tyrant today could find himself the lowest vampire minion tomorrow, with no measurable power of his own. And then every vampire is beholden to his Sire, no matter who he was before, or how much money he has."

"What about Alon?" she asked.

"No matter what vampiric powers he ends up with, he will always be a warrior, and an asset to his Sire. But it's still not a decision to be made lightly."

"Will you tell me what you decide?"

"No. That is for Alon to share."

Natalie pursed her lips unhappily, but he only grinned and kissed away her unhappiness. "Come on, Marc wants a workout."

NATALIE SAT ON the floor, legs crossed in front of her, her back against the wall. Christian and Marc had just emerged from the locker room in identical black gis, with plain black rank belts. They crossed the room on bare feet and exchanged a few words with Alon, who made a sweeping motion with his hand, giving them the floor. There was only one class scheduled, an advanced judo class taught by Alon. But, like everyone else in the dojo, the five men and one woman saw what was happening, and faded back against the wall to the watch the show. It was rare that Alon surrendered the mats to anyone, so the class members knew something was up.

Alon himself came over and sat next to Natalie, close enough that his shoulder was touching hers, close enough that it drew Christian's attention. He caught her gaze, his own shifting downward to the point where their shoulders met, and then back up again to meet her eyes, with one eyebrow raised in question. Natalie would have laughed, but there wasn't any humor in Christian's expression. They were barely a couple, and already he was going all super possessive on her. She'd heard that about vampires, especially the powerful ones. They were instinctively territorial, and that instinct didn't end with control over real estate. It extended to everything and, especially, every*one* in their lives.

She returned Christian's stare, opening her eyes wide, and giving him a silent "What?"

He grinned finally, which elicited a gasp from the lone woman in the judo class, and from one of the men, too. Christian simply returned his attention to Marc. They exchanged a couple of words, then bowed briefly to Alon, as the dojo master, and more deeply to each other. Natalie held her breath when they started to move, circling slowly, hands and feet in constant motion. She didn't know what to expect from this encounter. She'd seen Christian fight Noriega, had seen him kill with impunity. But this was completely different. It was a purely physical match, no vampire magic involved. And Marc wasn't his enemy. Still, vampires were so much stronger than humans. Could they pull their punches to avoid damaging each other? And would they bother to appear human since they had an audience?

Christian said something in French, too low for her to pick up. And in the blink of an eye, the fight was on. Everyone in the dojo was leaning forward, focusing hard, trying to follow the blur of hands and feet that was the two vampires fighting. They were using Krav Maga; she knew that much. But she'd never seen anything like this. The flow from one attack to the next was seamless, their every move graceful and deadly. And, no, they weren't bothering to pull their punches. The sound of fists and feet hitting flesh was so loud that Natalie could almost feel the impact, so loud that it reverberated over the floor and off the walls. The two vampires shook off blows that would have snapped human bones, bounced up from throws that would have left a human writhing and crippled on the floor.

They were beautiful in their brutality. Two wild and powerful creatures engaged in a fight for survival. And having the time of their lives. Both were grinning like crazy people, moving back and forth across the mat, deftly shifting direction whenever they came too close to the observers, demonstrating a situational awareness that was amazingly acute, given the speed and violence of their encounter.

"Whoa," Alon whispered, next to her. "That is *kick* ass."

"Gorgeous," she murmured.

"Which one?" he asked, his amusement obvious.

"Both of them," she said quickly.

"Yeah, but you've got your eye on Blondie. You in love at last, Nat?"

Natalie shot him an annoyed glance. "Of course not. I barely know him."

"That's how it starts, babe," he said, tossing a friendly arm around her shoulders. "And it's overdue. You've been hiding behind that computer for too long."

"Ssshh," she hissed. "Pay attention."

He chuckled softly, but she could feel his arm tightening around her as he strained to follow the action. He was barely blinking for fear of missing something.

With no warning that Natalie could discern, the action abruptly stopped. The two vampires each took a step back and bowed formally, but then grins split their faces and they embraced, pounding each other on the back. Alon jumped to his feet, and raced over to join them. The men and woman from the night class shuffled closer, but didn't intrude, though whether it was out of respect *for*, or fear *of*, the combatants, Natalie didn't know. Maybe a little of both, because she sure as hell was intimidated by the demonstration she'd just witnessed.

Intimidated, yeah, and maybe just a little turned on. Maybe even more than a little.

"Natalie," Alon called. She jumped to her feet, and crossed the dojo floor, joining the three of them just off the mat. Alon put an arm around her, tugging her into their group, and she saw Christian's jaw tighten as he focused on that touch.

Only his eyes moved as he met her gaze in a silent question. She was either his, or she wasn't. But if she was, she didn't belong in Alon's embrace.

Natalie wanted to protest. Alon was her friend, and the embrace meant nothing else. But this was one of those fragile turning points in a relationship, where it could go either way. An unexpected bolt of desire shivered over her skin, and she knew which way she wanted it to go. Christian couldn't have missed her reaction, but his expression never changed. The next move was hers.

Patting Alon's hand where it rested on her shoulder, she ducked out from under his arm and crossed to Christian's side. He stretched out a hand and pulled her in tightly, his arm circling her waist, his hand resting possessively on her hip. Natalie looked up and blushed at the amusement in Alon's eyes. But then Christian touched his lips to her temple, and everything inside her relaxed, as if her body had known all along where she belonged. It was only her brain that had needed to catch up.

"I was telling Christian that he and Marc are welcome anytime," Alon was saying. "Maybe he can convince you to take up the discipline."

Christian glanced down at her. "You're not in the class?"

She shook her head. "It's a little beyond me."

"We're starting a beginner's class in two weeks," Alon informed her with a wicked smile. He'd been after her to take up the Israeli discipline ever since they'd met.

"I'll think about it," she said, although she didn't mean it. Especially not after seeing what it looked like when practiced by vampires.

Alon's grin turned knowing a moment before his assistant called to him from across the room, holding up the phone. "I'll be right back."

Meanwhile, Marc, who had slipped away to the locker room while Christian spoke with Alon, emerged wearing a T-shirt with his gi pants, and carrying two duffel bags. He stopped long enough to exchange a few words with the lone female in the advanced judo class, then walked over, dug out a T-shirt from one of the duffels, and held it out to Christian. The two of them exchanged an intent look that made Natalie suspect they were communicating silently. Christian's next words confirmed it.

"We're going home," he informed Marc. He slipped out of his gi jacket and quickly pulled the offered T-shirt over his head, but not before giving Natalie, and everyone else, a view of his deliciously muscled shoulders and perfect abs. She smiled smugly, knowing she'd be up close and personal with that body before the night was over.

Christian was bent over, shoving his jacket into the duffel, but he caught her smile when he straightened, and grinned back, as if he was thinking the same thing. He draped a heavy arm over her shoulders. "Are you ready?" he asked, his tone making it clear that he was talking about a lot more than just driving home.

She tried to ignore the way her entire body had tightened in response to his innuendo. "I have to change first," she said, indicating the gi she was still wearing. She ducked out from under his arm, and started for the locker room, but he pulled her back for a quick kiss.

"Make it fast," he told her. "I'm not happy having you out in the open like this."

She patted his cheek. "You worry too much. I'll be twenty feet away in a closed room."

Christian gave her a look that promised payback for the cheek pat, and she was smiling as she pushed through the swinging door.

CHRISTIAN WAITED until the door closed behind Natalie, then gave Marc a questioning look. "You talked to Alon?"

"I did. And he's done his homework," Marc told him. "I think he might know more about vamp stuff than I do at this point."

"Does he have family?"

"On a kibbutz in Israel. Parents and two brothers, some toddler nieces and a nephew. His only sister was killed during a bombing in Jerusalem."

Christian frowned. Family could be a problem, especially if they were religious. "What do they think about this?"

"He says they're fine with it. They're socialist for the most part, and not particularly religious."

"He talked to them about it specifically?"

Marc nodded. "Apparently, he's been considering this ever since he met Natalie. He knew about vampires before that, but she was the first person he'd come across with any personal knowledge. Frankly, I'm surprised meeting her would make him *more* interested rather than less. I don't think your woman was all that fond of vampires before meeting *you*."

Christian shrugged. "I'm a charming guy."

Marc scoffed loudly.

"Show some respect, asshole. I'm your Sire."

"Right," Marc said, his expression shifting to one of mocking attention. "Don't want to give the newbie the wrong impression."

"Where did I go wrong?" Christian muttered. "Okay, I'll ask Alon to come by the house later. We'll talk, and I'll make a final decision. In the meantime—"

"I'm back! And look! All in one piece, too!" Natalie bounced out of the locker room, with a huge smile.

Marc nearly choked to death trying not to laugh, while Christian could only scowl. Obviously, it wasn't only with Marc that he'd gone wrong.

"Let's go," he growled, indicating the door to the back parking lot.

"My car's there, too," Natalie said, jiggling the keys in her hand.

"Leave it, we'll—"

"I'm not leaving my car again," she said stubbornly, planting her feet.

Christ, was he a powerful vampire or not? Shouldn't *somebody* be cowed by him? "Fine," he snapped, and turned to Marc with a jerk of his head. "You drive her car. Natalie and I will take the SUV. Natalie, give him your keys."

"I don't like the idea of—" Marc started to protest, but, wonder of wonders, he caught the impatient look Christian was sending him and changed his mind. "Go north down the alley," he said, pointing. "You lead, I'll follow."

Alon came up to say good-bye. He shook Marc's hand, then reached out to hug Natalie, pulling her away from Christian and into his arms. It took every ounce of control Christian possessed not to tear the man's arms off, but he told himself that Alon didn't know what he was doing, that the human and Natalie were friends, nothing more. That didn't stop the low growl of warning that rumbled up from his chest.

Natalie shivered a little at the sound, but she quickly kissed Alon's cheek and broke away from his embrace. "I probably won't see you tomorrow," she told him, "but—"

"I think Alon should come home with us," Christian interrupted, shifting his attention to the Israeli. "If you're available, that is. We have things to discuss."

"Sure thing," he said firmly. "I'm finished for the night, and my assistant can close up."

Christian hadn't told Natalie, but he'd already decided to turn Alon, if that's what the man truly wanted. He was going to need soldiers, loyal soldiers, when he became Lord of the South, and the best way to ensure that was to make an army of his own. He couldn't do it all in a day, or even a year, but Alon was a good beginning, and he'd make a great security chief. Natalie had said he was former Israeli military, but Christian knew there was much more to it than that. He'd known, even before talking to Alon, that he'd been Special Forces, and almost certainly one of the covert branches. There was a coiled readiness to such men, a constant awareness of everything around them, even when they were pretending not to pay attention.

But first, Christian had to be certain that the human knew what he was asking for, that he understood deep in his gut that there could be no return from this decision, other than death.

When Alon rejoined them, Christian took Natalie's hand, and walked out to the parking lot, with Alon leading the way. Unlocking the SUV with the remote, he opened the front passenger door and nudged Natalie in that direction, while Alon reached for the back door. Either Marc would bring Alon back to the dojo later tonight, or, if it got to be too late, he could always borrow Natalie's car and drive himself. The thought struck him that at least that way, Natalie might remain safely at home during the day tomorrow.

She turned as she climbed up and settled on the passenger seat. "I never told you what I discovered today in Anthony's files." She started to say more, but he'd already stopped listening, one hand held up in warning.

Instinct had him turning toward the mouth of the alley a moment before the surrounding walls pulsed to the sound of a powerful engine ramping up. Christian shoved Natalie flat onto the front seat as gunfire erupted from behind them, shattering the SUV's rear windows, and punching through metal. Marc had already started Natalie's small car, and he now zoomed forward, slamming it into position next to the SUV, before shoving the door open and racing to Christian's side. The smaller vehicle provided some additional cover from the hail of bullets, but it was too late for Alon. The warrior had followed his instincts, turning to face their attackers, protecting his friends with the only weapon he had—himself. He'd been hit badly, his body dancing wildly under the hail of gunfire.

Natalie screamed Alon's name, and tried to crawl out of the vehicle, but Christian slammed the door, keeping her inside. He started forward, intent on catching the assailants before they could escape, but Natalie didn't stay where he'd put her. She jumped out of the vehicle and went to her knees next to Alon, leaving them both completely unprotected.

"Marc!" Christian roared, and caught the weapon his lieutenant threw at him from the back seat of the SUV. He preferred to fight as a vampire, but as a wise man once said, you don't bring a vampire mind trick to a gunfight. At least, not until you've gotten rid of all the fucking guns.

He and Marc took up position in the angle between the two vehicles, hoping to draw fire away from Natalie and the injured Alon where he lay on the other side next to the building. One of their attackers fell, and the others were suddenly more intent on maintaining cover than on shooting anyone. Christian lowered his gun, letting Marc keep their enemies busy, while he took stock of the situation. Their assailants were both human and vampire, and their white SUV—an irony he would appreciate later—appeared to be heavily reinforced. The man on the ground—injured but not yet dead—was vampire, while the remaining two gunmen were one of each. They were braced behind what were obviously bullet-resistant doors, and seemed mostly concerned with keeping their heads down. At the same time, Christian could detect a fourth, definitely vampire, presence sitting in the back seat of the vehicle.

He fired off a quick telepathic warning to Marc, then dropped out of the present, and into the expanded consciousness where powerful vampires could go. Using all of his considerable power, he probed past the hidden vampire's shields and tried to identify him. The lurker was powerful enough to resist the intrusion, but not powerful enough to stop it. Christian had just slipped into the other vampire's awareness, which told him all he needed to know, when he was jolted back to the alley by the sound of Natalie's angry scream.

He nearly jumped to his feet to go to her, but Marc held him down, pulling open the SUV's driver-side door instead. Christian slid across the seats to the other side of the vehicle, where Natalie was fighting off her attacker. The remaining human assailant had used Christian's distraction with their master to slip past their defenses, probably crawling on his belly along the wall to get to her. But even as Christian was rushing to save her, he saw that he'd underestimated her ability to save herself. So had her attacker, who was handicapped by an obvious desire not to hurt her, and to take her alive. This was a kidnapping, not a murder—at least, not for Natalie. But she wasn't going easily. She was a whirlwind of defense, her feet and hands flying as she beat back her very human attacker, until he was forced to drop his useless gun in a desperate bid to fight her off without shooting her.

It was a turnabout that Christian would have appreciated under other circumstances, but not with Alon's life on the line, and not when their enemy could change his mind at any moment, and decide he didn't need Natalie alive after all.

"Natalie, down!" Christian yelled, and she dropped like a rock, stunning her attacker into immobility for no more than a second or two. But that was all Christian needed. With a thought, he sent a focused blast of power burrowing into the human's brain. The man's mouth opened in a scream he never got to voice, before he collapsed to the ground like a bag of bones.

Christian popped the door open above where Natalie was still working on Alon's motionless body, using her shirt in a fruitless attempt to stop the bleeding. "Stay down," he ordered her, then gathered a second, focused blast of power. This one was for Alon, to keep his heart beating until he could get back to him.

He slid back to Marc's side again. Only one gunman remained, a vampire whose resistance suffered from his desire to keep living in the face of Marc's superior skills. That made two dead enemies, and one badly injured but still alive, lying on the ground next to the white SUV. And the leader of them all, who was still hiding in the back seat.

"Marcel Weiss," Christian muttered, telling Marc the name of the master vampire lurking in the shadows while his people died.

Marc nodded, and sent a withering volley of fire at the lone defender's position.

Marcel wasn't making an appearance, but Christian knew they had to wrap this up. It had been no more than three minutes since he'd first heard the screech of the white SUV's tires, but there were screams coming from the dojo, and he could sense more than one human huddling near the back door. He reminded himself that many of the people inside were trained professionals, either police or military, and while they were too smart to walk into the middle of a gunfight, he had no doubt that more than one call to 911 had already been made. In fact, he could hear distant sirens that might well be the human police responding to their calls.

He thought about Alon, lying in a pool of his own blood, and about Natalie, and how close she'd come to being kidnapped. Fuck that. Natalie was his, and Alon was, too. Forgetting reason, dismissing concerns for his own safety, he slammed into the remaining vampire gunman's brain—bulletproof was no guard against his kind of assault—and turned it to mush, then snapped a shield of power around himself and stepped out into the open.

"Marcel Weiss," he called, augmenting his voice so that it dug right into his enemy's ear. "If you would be Lord of the South, come out and face me."

The back door of the white SUV opened silently, and Marcel Weiss—the Midwestern vampire who'd decided he couldn't live under Aden's rule—stepped out of the vehicle and into the open. He was carrying an HK MP5 submachine gun hanging down at his side.

"Let me have the woman, and we'll call it a draw," Weiss called.

Christian laughed. "There will be no draw tonight, Weiss. *You* challenged *me*, remember?"

Weiss lifted one shoulder. "All I really wanted was the girl," he said casually, but in a flash of movement only a vampire could follow, he raised the gun and aimed at Christian, his finger tightening on the trigger.

As fast as Weiss was, however, Christian was faster. Weiss screamed as the gun exploded in his hand. He belatedly attempted to gather his shields, but Christian wouldn't let him. He didn't know what Weiss had been thinking to stage a challenge in such a public place—and with guns of all things—but the sirens were getting closer, definitely heading their way, and it was time to end this.

He advanced upon Weiss, lobbing grenade-like bits of power at the other vampire, disrupting his every attempt to structure some shields. Weiss's right hand was shattered, bone gleaming whitely beneath the gushing blood. His inability to stop the bleeding spoke to how weak he was, or at least how rattled by Christian's unceasing attacks.

"Stop," Weiss ground out, holding out his one good hand, palm forward, as if to build a wall to hide behind. Except, there was no power to back it up. "I yield," he rasped, staggering.

"There is no *yield* in this contest, Weiss," Christian informed him, still maintaining his own shields lest Weiss be pretending more weakness than was real. "You should have checked the rules before you started."

"It wasn't supposed to come to this. Anthony wanted the girl, that's all."

Christian laughed in disbelief. "And you thought I'd just let that happen?"

Weiss shook his head in confusion, his concentration clearly fraying. "Fine. You win. I'll be gone by—"

Christian gathered himself for a final strike. "You still don't get it, Weiss. I don't win until you're dead." He shaped his power into a burning spear and sent it flying through the air. Weiss screamed, and tried to bat it away, but the weapon wasn't a physical thing to be knocked from the air. And Weiss no longer had the power, or the control, to deflect it any other way.

The weapon stabbed through his nonexistent shields and pierced his heart, where it flamed hotter than the hottest forge, turning that vital organ into dust. He died as silently as his human minion, his mouth open in an empty scream for a fraction of a second before his body joined his heart in turning to dust.

There was no sound for an instant, and then Natalie's sobs broke through Christian's awareness. "Alon," he whispered, and raced around the SUV to where Natalie still knelt over her friend's motionless form, her blood-soaked shirt still pressed to his chest, struggling to stanch too many wounds. It was pointless. She might stop one hole from bleeding, but there were too many others. The only thing keeping Alon alive right now was Christian, and even he couldn't stave off death forever.

"Let me have him, *chére*," he said gently, trying to pull her away.

She fought him, her hands and arms covered with so much blood that Christian worried he was wrong, and she'd been shot after all. "I have to help him," she cried over and over, while Christian ran his hands roughly over every inch of her, ignoring her attempts to push him away.

"Natalie, stop," he snarled finally. "I can't help him if you won't let me!" He shook her slightly, trying to get her attention, until at last her vision seemed to clear, and she raised her eyes to his.

"Is he dead?" Her voice was shaking, terror lurking on the edges.

"No," Christian said, the word hard and determined. "And he won't be, either." He turned to his lieutenant. "Marc, get our gear, but leave the Suburban. We'll take Natalie's car. Natalie?"

She was still shaking, but her voice was strong. "Yes?"

"Get in the car with Marc. Alon and I will be in the back."

Marc jumped to obey him, understanding, without being told, that they needed to be gone before the police arrived. They'd want to take everyone in for endless questioning, and that never went well for vampires. And then there was Alon. If they stayed here, an ambulance would be called and he'd die before they reached the hospital. If he was to survive the night, it would not be as a human. And Christian didn't want any witnesses to what some would see as a miraculous resurrection.

Natalie, too, seemed to recognize the necessity of a clean getaway. She leaned into her Prius and speedily flattened the back seats, then opened the rear hatch, so that Christian could climb inside. It wouldn't be comfortable, but comfort wasn't among his priorities right now. Marc helped him get Alon into the car, holding the bleeding human while Christian climbed into the tiny space, then easing him into Christian's arms.

Closing the hatch, Marc quickly settled behind the wheel, next to Natalie, then drove away at top speed. Bystanders would assume they were rushing someone to a hospital. And in a way, they were. By the time the police discovered Alon was missing, he'd either be dead, or he'd be a vampire and beyond human authority.

NATALIE WATCHED numbly as Christian carried Alon into the house and disappeared down to the basement. Marc started to follow, but paused at the head of the stairs, his dark eyes full of compassion. "You should go ahead and clean up, then try to sleep," he said kindly. "You won't see either of them again tonight."

"Is there *anything* I can do?" she asked, desperately needing to be useful.

"Not tonight, sweetheart. It's all up to Christian now. But you know . . . he's damn powerful. If anyone can save your friend, it's him."

She nodded, believing him, not only because he said it with such conviction, but because she knew Christian. Vampire or not, he was an honorable man. He'd do everything he could to save Alon. "Okay," she said faintly. Marc turned and was gone.

Natalie stared at the empty space where he'd been and frowned unhappily. She had to accept that there was nothing for her to do. Not with Alon, at least. She had the files she'd copied from Anthony's server, and she was way too wired from the night's excitement to sleep. But it wasn't the kind of wired that would lend itself to analytical thinking.

She made her way to the bedroom that she thought of as hers, wondering again how long it would be before Christian trusted her enough to admit her to the inner sanctum in the basement. What would it be like to sleep next to a vampire all day long? And what if she wasn't tired? Would she be trapped down there anyway?

Thoughts chased each other around in her head until she turned on the light in the bathroom and got a look at herself for the first time since the attack. She closed her eyes, and fought the urge to gag. She was *covered* in blood, and none of it was hers. That fact nearly drove her to her knees. She began tearing at her clothes, wanting them *off*. There wasn't enough cleaning product in the city of Houston to get all of that blood out. And even if she could, she'd never be able to wear any of them again.

Stripping down to skin, she left the clothes in a pile, and climbed into the shower. The events of this evening kept playing back in her head, and it wasn't a flattering picture. She'd been scared out of her mind, and there was no denying it. Sure, she'd managed to fight off her attacker, but she'd been useless when it came to Alon. There'd just been so much *blood!* She'd never seen anything like it before.

Maybe that's why Christian hadn't even bothered to tell her "good night." Or why he hadn't spoken to her since they'd piled into her car. But what did he expect? She'd never even been close to anything like that before. The noise alone had been terrifying—roaring engines and screeching tires, the guns and the screams! It wasn't anything like the movies. It was just unrelenting noise. A barrage of sound that had hurt her ears, and scraped every nerve raw until she could barely think. And then there'd been Alon, lying on the ground, surrounded by a growing pool of blood . . . and her brain had simply gone blank.

She sank to the floor of the shower, knees hugged to her chest, wishing for Christian's powerful arms, for the strength of his big body wrapped around her, keeping her warm, keeping her safe. She tightened her jaw and drew a deep breath. "Suck it up, Nat," she said. Christian had no time to hold her fucking hand. He was too busy saving Alon's life.

She climbed to her feet, and finished washing away the blood, then shampooed and rinsed her hair twice before she was satisfied it was clean. She dried herself off and pulled on her sweats to sleep in. Her usual little nightgown made her feel too vulnerable today. She slid under the covers and lay there, listening to every creak and crack in the big house. She wondered if they had any alcohol in the kitchen. A glass of wine might help relax her enough to sleep. Otherwise she didn't see how . . .

Sleep took her between one breath and the next.

Chapter Ten

ALON WAS LYING next to him when Christian woke the next night. As a new vampire, he wouldn't wake for a while yet, but that first awakening would be hard. This was true for every new vampire, but it would be especially traumatic for Alon, given the violence of his near death, and the abrupt nature of his transition. He would need blood, and not just any blood either. Only Christian's blood would suffice tonight. First, because it cemented the bond between vampire and Sire. But in this case, there was a more important reason; Alon would need the healing strength that only a powerful vampire like Christian could give him.

Christian had some time before that happened, though. Younger vampires rose from their enforced sleep much later than their elders. Strength was a factor in that, too, but there was no way of knowing how powerful Alon would be, this early in his new life. As a vampire lord—or at least as a vampire powerful enough to *be* a lord—Christian woke as soon as the fireball of the sun dropped below the horizon, despite the light still burning across the sky. That gave him at least two hours before Alon would wake enough to need him.

Swinging his legs off the bed, he sat up and searched the house with his vampire-enhanced senses. Marc was just beginning to wake; another fifteen minutes and he'd be fully alert. Upstairs, Natalie slept, but not well. Her mind was restless, and he suspected if he went to her, he'd find her emotions in turmoil, as well. It didn't exactly surprise him. Last night had been troubling by anyone's standards. What *did* surprise him was that she was still here at all. She hadn't lived the kind of life that exposed her to this level of violence, and he'd half expected her to be on a plane back to the bayou, where she'd never again have to deal with vampires, and most especially not with *him*.

Of course, there was Alon to consider. Maybe she'd only hung around to make sure he was okay.

Christian took a quick shower and pulled on a T-shirt and jeans, going commando, and leaving his feet bare. There was no need to dress more formally, he'd be back here soon enough. He checked to be sure Alon was still resting peacefully, then opened his bedroom door. Marc emerged into the hallway a moment later, still wrapped in a towel from his own shower.

"Keep an eye on him," he told Marc, hooking a thumb over his shoulder. "I'm going to check on Natalie." He started for the closed vault door. It wouldn't open until he entered the security code.

"You think she heard what Weiss said about Anthony?" Marc asked "About him wanting her alive?"

Christian frowned. "If she didn't, she'll figure it out. It'll be better if I tell her up front. She'll be pissed otherwise."

"Fucking Anthony. What happens now?"

"Now I stop dicking around and take the damn territory. Fuck the challenge. I need to find Anthony and kill him."

"What about Stefano Barranza? You think he's dropped out?"

Christian shook his head. "I think he's down in Mexico causing mischief that's going to bite us in the ass when we're not looking. It would be easy to forget about him, but that might be just what he's hoping for."

"I'll check around, see if there's any word on his whereabouts."

"And I'm going to talk to Natalie."

"Better you than me."

"*Only* me," Christian said, feeling his possessive instincts flaring bright and hard.

Marc grinned. "I'll keep an ear out for Alon."

"I won't be long."

Christian entered the twelve-digit security code. The heavy door popped open an inch, and he shoved it the rest of the way. The computer console where Marc worked was silent, no alarms, no flashing message notifications. Nothing had happened during the day that their programming considered worth telling him about. But then, most everyone he'd expect to hear from after last night had been asleep all day, just like him.

He took the stairs two at a time, emerging into the quiet of the upstairs hallway. Natalie's door was closed, but he could hear the sheets rustling as she tossed and turned, trying to sleep. He knocked, but didn't wait before opening it. He felt her heartbeat kick up in alarm, and she rolled to the far side of the bed, dragging the covers with her, her eyes wide and staring.

"Natalie."

"Christian," she breathed. She dropped face-first into the sheets for a moment, then lifted her head with a relieved smile. "I didn't think to check the time. The sun's down?" she asked, then scolded herself. "Well, obviously the sun is down. Duh."

"Get dressed, *chére*. We need to talk."

"Alon?" she asked, and her face lost all of its usual color.

"Alon is fine," he assured her.

"Then what—"

"Get dressed. I'll make coffee." He didn't wait for her to answer. He closed the door and headed for the kitchen, where he found peace in the routine of using his machine, and was soon enjoying his first espresso. He had no doubt there would be more cups of the dark brew, because this was promising to be that kind of a night. Natalie showed up just a few minutes later. Her face was clean of makeup, her long hair pulled into a neat pony-tail, and she wore a pair of loose sweat pants, with a cardigan sweater pulled over a belly-baring T-shirt.

He tried not to stare, as he imagined what was under the sweater. It was obvious that she wasn't wearing a bra, and even that glimpse of flat belly was making him want her. His cock felt heavy, and his fangs ached with the desire for her blood. This wasn't hunger. He was powerful enough to go days without feeding. This was something else. This was the need to claim his woman. He didn't want blood; he wanted *Natalie's* blood. And then he wanted to fuck her brains out.

Whatever happened next was up to her, however. She was the vulnerable one. If she decided she wanted to go home, he'd do his best to get her there safely, and make sure she stayed that way with no interference from him.

He leaned against the counter, sipping his espresso, and watching over the rim of his cup as she walked into the kitchen. She shuffled right up to him and put her hands on either side of his waist, her eyes big and shadowed with doubt, as if uncertain of her reception. Going up on her toes, she pressed her mouth to his and demanded a kiss.

Christian's lips curved with satisfaction. Setting his cup on the counter, he wrapped his arms around her back, yanked her against him, and surrendered to the need that had been tightening his chest from the moment he'd opened her bedroom door. Her lips opened willingly beneath his, her tongue warm and delicate as he captured it and sucked hard, before stroking his own tongue over every inch of her luscious mouth.

"Did you sleep well?" he asked, because if he didn't say something, he was going to fuck her right there in the kitchen.

Natalie's eyes were blurry with desire, which did nothing to ease his straining erection. She smiled sweetly in response to his question, and said, "No, I didn't. I was worried about Alon, and then you—"

"Alon is no longer your concern." Christian knew he was overreacting, but he couldn't stop the hot stab of possessiveness that turned his words into an angry snarl.

She blinked in surprise, then scowled right back at him. "Look," she snapped. "I know you're all big macho vampire and everything, but Alon is still my best friend. If he needs anything, I have the right to help him."

"Really? And what would that be, Natalie? This *anything* that only you can give him?"

She narrowed her eyes in irritation, lips pursed, thinking hard. "Blood," she said suddenly, nearly spitting out the single word. But almost as soon as she said it, she slid her gaze away from his nervously. "I mean, if he needs blood, I could—"

Christian shifted his grip to her arms. "You don't go near him right now," he growled. "Do you know what happens when a vampire wakes for the first time? There is no thought, no reason, there is only *hunger*. He would rip out your throat and never blink an eye."

"Alon would never—"

"He's not your fucking Alon any longer. He's *mine*."

"I don't under—"

"You know what else you don't understand? *You're* mine, Natalie. Your *blood* is mine. No one feeds from you but me, and I'll kill anyone who tries."

She seemed to stop breathing for a moment. He watched the meaning of what he'd said fill her eyes, saw her understand for the first time what was really happening when he drank from her. That fire in her veins when he bit her, the electric jolt that went right to her clit . . . it wasn't just sex. It was nutrition, and she was his food. Knowing that he was vampire, and confronting what it really meant, were two different things.

He saw the shock of realization in her eyes, and he was suddenly cold. He set her away from his body, then opened his hands and let go of her arms. She wasn't the first woman who'd rejected what he was, but she was the first one who'd mattered.

He felt his own eyes shutter, concealing whatever emotion she might read there. "I have to check on Alon," he said quietly, and moved toward the door, but Natalie grabbed him, her grip surprisingly strong on his forearm.

"Stop that," she demanded.

He gave her a cool look. "Stop what?"

"Stop pushing me away. You keep looking for a reason for us not to get closer. I don't trust *you*, you don't trust *me*, it's too dangerous, and now this bullshit. So I didn't understand about Alon. Okay, I'll learn. But that has nothing to do with you and me."

"No? What were you thinking just now? I saw it in your face. You were horrified at the very idea of what I am, and what *you* are to *me*."

"Oh, fuck that! So I reacted, so what? I'm not as good as you at controlling every little goddamned tic on my face. I'm not a machine like you are, I *want* to feel—"

He grabbed her again, holding her roughly against him. "You want to *feel*?" he growled against her cheek, his tongue following his words as he licked her skin. "Is that you want from me, *chére*?" He reached between their bodies and slid his hand into her sweatpants, finding nothing but bare skin.

Stroking over her smooth belly, his fingers dipped between her thighs and found her naked and wet, her soft folds welcoming as he pushed two fingers deep into her pussy. "Do you feel that?" he whispered.

She shuddered, her entire body trembling against his as the sweet fragrance of her arousal filled his senses. He began pumping his fingers in and out, his thumb playing circles around the swollen nub of her clit, teasing, never touching. He didn't want her to climax yet. He wanted her on the edge, begging to come. She wanted to *feel?* He'd make her fucking feel until she was screaming for release.

"Christian." Her voice was a needy whisper as she moved against his hand, spreading her legs wider. "I want—" She broke off with a moan, a soft sound that ended in a sobbing breath.

"What do you want?" he murmured, kissing her eyes, her cheeks, licking the salty flavor of the tears leaking from beneath her eyelids.

"I want," she started to say again, hesitating briefly before her eyes flashed open to stare into his. "I want you to bite me," she said with a hiccupping breath. Her tears were rolling freely down her cheeks. "I want *you.*"

Christian stilled, his fingers buried deep inside her, his own heartbeat pounding in his ears as he stared at her.

"Christian," she whispered. "Please."

His fangs slid from his gums, aching for the thick, warm taste of her blood coating his throat. "Natalie," he said. Just her name, but so much more. It was a question, and more than one. Was she sure that she wanted this? That she wanted *him?* Did she know what she was asking?

"Yes," she said, seeming to understand. "I want you, just as you are."

Christian bent his head, his mouth going to the taut curve of her neck, sucking at the thick roll of her vein until it was plump and ready, bursting with the rich bounty of her blood. His fangs grazed over her tender skin—once, twice. And then he bit her, groaning with pleasure as the warm honey of her blood filled his mouth and slid down his throat.

Natalie buried her face against his shoulder as he bit her, sinking her teeth into the thick muscle, muffling cries of pain that quickly changed to desire, as his bite sent waves of raw need cutting through her veins. Her belly clenched under his hand, and she gasped when he stroked his thumb directly over her clit, softly at first, then pressing down until she bucked against him, her pussy squeezing his fingers as she bit back her moans, clinging to him in order to remain upright in the throes of her orgasm.

Christian's fangs were anchored to her throat, his arm banded around her back, the fingers of one hand digging into her hip. He waited until she was nearly limp in his arms, until there was nothing but the occasional jolt as her body recovered from her orgasm. Then, holding her still, he withdrew his fangs, relishing the last few drops of her sweet blood as he licked the wounds shut. With a final teasing stroke over her sensitive clit, he pulled his fingers from her pussy. They were coated in the cream of her orgasm.

"Natalie," he murmured. He waited until her eyes opened in a hazy focus, and then he brought his fingers up to his mouth and deliberately licked them clean, savoring every bit of her juices.

She blushed furiously, and buried her face against his chest. "You're horrible," she said.

"That's not the impression I got," he replied smugly. "Perhaps I need to try again." He slid his hand teasingly over her belly again, but she stopped him, pressing her body tightly against his and wrapping her arms around his neck.

"I don't think I'd survive it," she muttered, then noticed the bloody mark of her teeth where his neck met his shoulder, just visible above his T-shirt. She touched it carefully. "I'm sorry," she said, but he shook his head and covered her fingers with his, rubbing the injured spot.

"Don't be sorry. It marks me as yours, just as my bite marks you. Vampires are a possessive lot, *chére*. You should know that before we take this any further. I'm a vampire lord, whether I have a territory yet or not, and you're mine. If that's not what you want, then—"

She put her fingers over his lips. "Stop. I told you. You're what I want. And, don't forget, it goes both ways. You're mine, too."

"Always," he said, and was surprised to discover he meant it.

Natalie's smile was beautiful, her feelings written on her face and in her eyes. "I have to shower," she told him. "You want to join me?"

He shook his head. "I'd love to, but I can't. I wasn't being mean earlier. Alon really does need me tonight, and he'll be waking soon."

"You were being a little mean," she said gently, "but that's okay. I'm going to get dressed, and go through those files that I—"

"We need to talk about that," he interrupted. "And about last night."

She frowned. "You think last night had something to do with the files?"

"Maybe," he said. He wasn't convinced the two things were connected, but he didn't believe in coincidence either. Not when it came to vampire politics. "You go ahead and shower, and after I get Alon settled, you and I and Marc will talk."

"Okay." She went up on tiptoes and kissed him. "Give Alon a kiss for me," she said saucily. She spun away and headed out of the kitchen, but not before Christian slapped her pretty little ass and growled a wordless warning.

She was clearly terrified. Or at least, that's what Christian told himself as she laughed all the way to her bedroom.

Mexico City, Mexico

Vincent stared down at the contract sitting before him. The paragraphs of constipated words went on and on, saying things that any moron would have known without being told. Why did lawyers feel the need to spell out every insignificant detail, covering their asses against the most unlikely outcomes, including possibilities that simple common sense should have argued against?

And why the hell did he have to sit here reading this crap when his territory was in turmoil, with new rebellions seeming to spring up almost daily? It was like that game of whack-a-mole. Every time he put down one rebellion, a new one sprang up. And while he had a good team of people, the ones he could trust absolutely were still few in number. In time, that would change, but for now, he could only rely on those who'd been with him for years. The ones who'd been secretly sworn to *him* rather than Enrique. And as if all of that wasn't enough, now he had this European bullshit to deal with.

Logically, he knew it would get better, that this instability was typical of any transition in the vampire world. But sometimes his gut rebelled against logic, and it felt as if the crises would never end, that this would be his life from here on out. And when that happened, he had trouble remembering why he'd ever wanted this fucking job in the first place.

Throwing down the pen he'd been using to annotate the contract, he picked up his cell phone and called Lana.

"Hey, baby," she answered, sounding perfectly happy to hear from him, but a little distracted.

"You want to go for a run? Or a swim?" he asked her.

"Um, can you give me half an hour?"

"What are you doing?" he demanded rather grumpily.

"Aw, is his lordship bored?"

"Just answer the question, smartass."

"Well, you know that wedding dress I told you I needed for the big day? It turns out those things need to be fitted, and if I move right now, I'm going to get skewered by about a thousand tiny pins."

Vincent frowned. He'd have time to finish the contract. Damn. "Okay, thirty minutes. I'll meet you—" He was interrupted when his lieutenant, Michael, opened the door, his knuckles rapping on the wood as he entered. One look at his face, and Vincent knew it was bad.

"Something's going on, *querida*. I'll call you right back."

"Vincent?" Lana's voice sounded concerned, and Vincent had a feeling she was right to be.

"Finish your dress," he told her. "And don't worry."

"Vincent—" she started to say, but he hung up, reaching for the paper Michael was holding out to him.

He read through it quickly, then looked up. "What the fuck is this?"

"It looks like an intel report from Anthony."

Vincent read it again, paying closer attention to the small details that made the report seem credible. "Anthony's supposed to be in hiding. And who the fuck faxes something this urgent? Hell, I didn't even know we had a fax machine."

"Maybe this is all he has access to wherever he's hiding. The bigger question is how the hell he knows what's going on, and can we trust anything he says."

"I'm not moving troops without more credibility than *this*. Close the door," he said, then spun in his chair and picked up the receiver on a slim, silver landline phone sitting on his credenza. Pulling up the speed-dial list, he selected Anthony's number and waited. This might be the age of modern technology, but international calls still endured a lot of clicking and dead air before finally going through. He was more than half-surprised when Anthony answered himself.

"Vincent." Anthony's rough voice was made more so by an unusually bad connection.

"Anthony," Vincent greeted him in like fashion. "I just received your report." He didn't go into any details, waiting to see what the Southern lord would say. If this intel really had come from him, then he'd know what Vincent was talking about.

"My apologies. I intended to call before you received it, but the situation here is . . . difficult."

Vincent figured that was one way to describe it. But he still wasn't sure Anthony could be trusted. "Where does this information come from? I was under the impression that you were . . . lying low."

"Hiding, you mean," Anthony snapped. "I know what's being said. But I know the truth of it. Christian Duvall wants my territory, and he doesn't mind playing dirty to get it."

"That's not what I heard from Raphael."

"Oh, yes, the bodyguard," he sneered dismissively. "I altered five minutes of his memory, something we've all done a thousand times. It's hardly a killing offense. Raphael's being manipulated by Duvall and refuses to see it. But why are we wasting time on this bullshit? You got the intel. So what are you going to do about it?"

Vincent contemplated his reply, reluctant to admit that Anthony was right. Twisting Cibor's mind wouldn't usually be a killing offense. Except that Cibor was one of Raphael's children, and he was in Houston on Raphael's business. Even so, Vincent suspected Raphael's wrath was motivated at least partially by his dislike of Anthony. He would never have ceded the matter to Christian otherwise. Now, Christian's vengeance . . . *that* was quite justified. Anthony had tried to get his woman alone, with every intention of capturing her mind, and then raping her. If someone had done that to Lana, if they'd even contemplated such an outrage, he'd have ripped them to shreds.

And none of that had anything to do with this latest intel from Hubert's camp. Assuming it was valid.

"Let's say we put personal vengeance aside for the purpose of this discussion," he told Anthony. "Where'd this intel come from, and how do I know it's any good? For that matter, how're you still getting reports at all?"

"I'm in hiding, not living in a cave. And I'm still Lord of the South, no matter what Raphael thinks. My people remain loyal to me, and I to them. More importantly, I don't want my territory compromised by a war in Mexico. If Hubert gains strength down there, it endangers all of us up here. As for the intel, it comes from my man in Hubert's camp. That's why I faxed. I wanted you to see the full text of his report, and fax was the easiest way to get it to you, given my current circumstances."

Vincent relaxed slightly. That actually made sense. "So the confidence level on this info is high?"

"One hundred percent. My agent is deeply imbedded, and well within the inner circle."

He frowned. Anthony's agent must be one hell of a liar, then, because it wouldn't be easy to fool a vampire as old and powerful as Hubert was reputed to be. Still, he couldn't afford to simply ignore this.

"Thank you for the warning, then. We'll handle it." As he hung up, he heard Anthony wish him good luck. He stared at the phone. *Good luck?* What the fuck was that? He looked up at Michael, whose vampire hearing would have picked up both sides of the conversation.

"My lord?" he asked.

Vincent glanced again at the intel report, then stood, reading off the name of the city where Anthony's agent claimed Hubert was planning a takeover. "Patrizia," he said, picturing the map of Mexico. "Ever heard of it?"

Michael shook his head. "No, but I Googled it, and I checked for landline phone listings as soon as this came in. There were several, and I called them all. No one answered. Not one."

"Not a good sign, but it *is* the middle of the night. Where is this place anyhow, and how big is it?"

"About fifty miles south of Ciudad del Carmen. That's the closest airport. It's a fishing village of about 1200 people."

"That ties in with what Christian said about Hubert, that he likes isolated villages as raw material for his zombie armies. That's his word for them, but it fits. Raphael has reports from Europe. Hubert doesn't make half-feral slaves like some of the old-timers used to create to feed their own power. He wants his creatures able to follow orders, to fight and kill for him."

"They'll still die like any other vampire," Michael growled.

"Probably easier. They have to be low on the power scale in order for Hubert to control them. But if I can take out Hubert, they should fall like flies. The shock will kill them."

Vincent stood, having made his decision. "I'm not taking any chances. If there's nothing there, we'll have wasted a few hours, and some helicopter fuel. But if Anthony's right, then Hubert might have turned half the town by now. I want every warrior we can spare without degrading our security here, and I want all of my own security team. I need people I can trust at my back. Have the jet prepped for departure, and get someone working on transport at the other end. I want those helicopters waiting for us when we arrive." He came around the desk. "I need to talk to Lana."

"I'M COMING WITH you," Lana said, yanking a black, long-sleeved T-shirt over her head and tucking it into the black combat pants that she favored. There was no sign of a wedding dress or the seamstress who'd been sticking her with pins.

"This is war, *querida*. You should remain—"

She was suddenly up in his face, snarling like a wildcat. "If you like your balls, you won't finish that sentence."

Vincent was stunned wordless for a long moment, but then he grinned down at her. "You'd never do that. You like my balls too much right where they are."

"Maybe," she admitted. "But the sentiment holds. I'm going with you."

"There's no maybe about it, and, yes, of course, you're going with me. What was I thinking?"

"Some bullshit about me staying behind with all the other ladies."

"Shame on me. You'd better get cracking, then. We leave in thirty minutes."

Houston, Texas

ANTHONY SET THE phone down, with satisfied smile. That would take care of Vincent for a while. He knew the Mexican lord didn't trust him, but he wouldn't be able to ignore the possibility that the intel was right, either. He'd have to check it out, maybe try to contact someone in Patrizia. But no one would answer. Anthony's allies had seen to that. And they'd also arranged a very nice welcoming party for Vincent when he raced to the rescue. Which he would. He'd have no choice.

Vincent would be out of the picture, and Duvall would be on his own. Now, if Scoville could just find his balls long enough to do his fucking job, the tide would turn, and Christian Duvall would be the one drowning.

CHRISTIAN LEANED back on the pillows piled against the headboard of his oversized bed. One arm was wrapped around Alon, holding the new vampire back-to-chest in front of him, while his other arm was against Alon's mouth, held there by the fangs dug deep into his vein. He closed his eyes, feeling every tug as Alon sucked down the rich bounty of his blood. The new vampire probably wouldn't remember much of this night, might even be embarrassed if he did. Taking blood was inherently sexual, even between vampires. The euphoric didn't hit them the way it did humans, but it was still a deeply sensual act.

It was also exhausting. Both for the new vampire, whose body was still undergoing massive changes, courtesy of the vampire symbiote, and for Christian who had to give far more blood than would normally be the case. In the coming days, after he'd become Lord of the South, he'd undergo a similar ritual many times as vampires in his new territory swore allegiance. But while the mechanics were the same, the amount of blood required was far less than that required to create a new vampire. His new vampire subjects would take only a little of his blood, in order to bind their lives to his. And not every vampire would have to do so, only the stronger ones whose loyalty Christian would need to be sure of.

But while it was fatiguing to create a new vampire, Christian didn't regret it. He couldn't. The link between Sire and child was too powerful. It didn't allow for regrets. Alon was already *his*, and Christian would throw down his life to save him.

The door opened quietly, and Marc stood there, cell phone in hand and a very troubled look on his face.

"What is it?" Christian asked softly, a sinking sense of inevitability nearly swamping him. Whatever it was wouldn't be good.

Marc lifted the phone. "Scoville just called. I told him you couldn't be interrupted."

Christian was too tired to deal with any more of Anthony's half-assed challengers. "What the fuck did *he* want?"

"He'll only talk to you, but . . . no bullshit, Christian, he sounded panicked. I think you should call him back."

Christian glanced down at Alon, whose sucking was falling off rapidly. He'd sleep for several more hours now, through the rest of this night and right into tomorrow's daylight sleep. Tomorrow night would be his first true awakening, and then they'd discover exactly what sort of vampire he would be. But for tonight, he was dead to the world.

He maneuvered Alon's sleep-heavy body to the bed, then stood and walked over to join Marc. Taking the phone from him, he hit the Call Back button and waited.

"Christian, thank God."

Marc was right, Scoville *was* panicked. Hell, he sounded scared shitless. And from the noises behind him, he might have a good reason.

"We're under fucking attack, man. We need help, or this place will be overrun."

"Where are you? What the fuck is going on?"

"We can't fight these things. We're all going to die if—"

"Snap out of it," Christian yelled. "I need information. Facts. How many of you are there?"

"We started with twenty-five." Scoville's voice was quieter, but there was a hitch in his voice, like he was fighting the urge to cry. "Twenty-five," he repeated in a whisper. "Now? They're killing us. Swarming like bugs. They don't feel pain, nothing stops them."

Christian was moving, the phone pressed between his ear and shoulder, while he started pulling things out of his closet. He turned and his eyes met Marc's questioning look. He nodded in response to the unvoiced question, *"Are we going?"*

Marc immediately spun away, racing down the hall. He'd be making arrangements, lining up transport, but to where?

"Damn it, Scoville, calm the fuck down." *Merde! This guy had wanted to be Lord of the South?* "Tell me where you are."

"Laredo," he said dully. "Anthony put me in command down here. It was my punishment for not killing you." He laughed bitterly. "Or for not dying while trying to kill you."

"Laredo," Christian repeated for Marc's benefit. "Did you call Anthony?" he asked, switching back to Scoville.

"He's not answering. I don't even know where he is, or whether he'd even come if I found him."

"What about his fighters? You must be able to get some of them moving."

"A lot of them went with Anthony, which means I can't reach them either. And the rest won't move without his say so. He's totally fucked us!"

"Anything from Vincent?" Christian asked calmly, hoping it would rub off on Scoville.

"He's coming, but he'll take hours to get here. We'll never last that long. I think this is it, man. Hubert's on his way."

"Why call me? We're not exactly friends."

"Because we need help, damn it. And there's no one else to call. My people are *dying,* do you get that? And when we're all dead, they'll go right up the 35 to San Antonio. They're like locusts. There'll be no stopping them."

Christian's thoughts were racing. He knew Hubert's creatures, and Scoville was right. They were an infestation that needed to be wiped out. And Hubert needed to be stopped before he could create more.

Scoville was right about Vincent, too. It would be hours before he rallied his people and got them on the scene. He and Marc were a lot closer, but there were only two of them. Granted, he could bring the kind of power that won battles, but could he trust this? He sure as hell didn't trust Anthony, but Scoville had no reason to love his Sire. And there was no faking the screams or the sounds of battle he could hear over the vamp's terrified breathing.

It was the screams that settled it for him. He wasn't going to stand by while vampires died fighting for a territory that he would soon call his own. Vampires who would be his people, if they survived.

Fuck it.

All right," he said, as though just deciding, although in his heart, he'd decided the moment he heard that first scream. "We'll be there."

Marc ducked into the room, yanking a heavy black turtleneck over his head to join the black combat pants he was already wearing. He sat on the bed to pull on his socks and boots. Christian stripped off the jeans and T-shirt he'd donned to greet Natalie earlier, then washed the blood from his already healing arm and started pulling on clothes more suitable for fighting fucking zombies.

"I've got a chopper on the way," Marc said. "The flight time is longer, but they'll pick us up at the local high school, five minutes from here, and drop us right at the location. Saves time overall."

"I can't leave Natalie alone here with Alon," Christian said, sitting to put on socks and boots.

Marc stood. "Don't even think about leaving me here to—" he started to say, but Christian interrupted him.

"Hell, no. I need you to keep anyone from stabbing me in the back while I'm fighting fucking zombies for them." He stood and stomped his feet, settling into the boots.

"Alon's out for the night, right?" Marc asked.

Christian nodded. "Until tomorrow night."

"So we shut the vault, and lock the house down. Natalie's smart. And after last night, she'll stay put."

Christian didn't like it, but he didn't see any alternative. There was no one he trusted enough to give them access to his lair, not even this temporary one. Besides Marc was right. Once he activated the house's full security suite, no one was getting inside unless he wanted them to. "I don't think we have a choice."

"Right. You need help with the big guy there?"

"No, I've got this. I'll be out soon, and I'll talk to Natalie."

NATALIE KNEW something had happened the minute she looked up from her computer to find Christian and Marc both storming into the kitchen dressed in black from head to toe like a couple of special ops guys from a summertime action flick. Her heart was doing its best to crack a few ribs as she slipped off the kitchen stool and met Christian's somber gaze.

"What is it?" she asked him breathlessly.

"Hubert hit the border outpost south of Laredo," he said briskly, striding past her to the alarm panel where he started punching buttons. Shutters she hadn't noticed before began sliding down over all the windows, including the big sliding glass door. And these weren't the fancy, decorative kind of shutters, either. They looked more like the heavy metal barriers that some people installed against hurricanes back home in Louisiana.

"What are you doing?" she asked in alarm.

"Activating a total lockout. Stay in the house and you'll be fine."

"Stay . . ." she repeated slowly. "Are you *leaving*? Where are you going?"

"Alon's downstairs—"

"Stop!" she shouted. "I know where Alon is. Now, tell me what's happening."

Christian walked over and put his hands on her shoulders, squeezing lightly before moving his grip down to her arms. "Scoville called from Laredo. Hubert is on the move, and Anthony is MIA. Marc and I are flying down to help Scoville and his team hold the line until Vincent can get there with some serious fire power. You'll remain here with Alon."

"I thought you said—"

"He's already fed, and will sleep until tomorrow night."

"Then why can't I go with you?"

"It's a war, Natalie, a *vampire* war. There will be no humans on the field."

"I know you think I'm useless—"

"I do not."

"—but I can sh—"

"I need you safe," he almost shouted, cutting off her protests. "Marc and I will be on our own out there," he continued in his regular voice. "With allies who will probably be as happy to stab us in the back as fight by our side. I can't keep you safe and watch Marc's back at the same time. Do you understand that?"

Natalie *hated* it, but she understood. Except... "You're trusting *Scoville's* word on this?"

"Never. I trust no one but Marc. He has my back, and I have his. For the rest . . ." He shrugged. "As long as they're willing to kill our enemies, I'll stand by them. But trust? No."

"I understand. I do, but—" Her attention was dragged away from an argument she already knew she wasn't going to win, at the sight of Marc upending a bag of blood over his mouth and sucking it dry. She stared, more fascinated than she would have thought possible. "You can drink that stuff?" she asked, turning back to Christian.

"That *stuff* is human blood, though we prefer the warm, fresh kind," he said, a small smile playing around his lips. He caught a full bag that Marc tossed his way, broke the seal, and gave her a warning look, as if to say, *"This is your last chance to look away."*

Natalie shook her head. This was an important part of Christian's life. If she turned away from it, she might as well walk out the front door and never come back.

He shrugged, then tilted his head back and drank, just as Marc had before him.

She glanced over at Marc, and asked, "Where'd you get that? I didn't see any in there." She gestured at the big stainless steel refrigerator where her perfectly ordinary food was stored.

"Vegetable crisper," he said, grinning. "A special compartment in the back."

"Oh," Natalie said faintly, and turned back just in time to see Christian finish off the bag and toss the empty to Marc. "So what's with the DEFCON 1 security?" she asked him. "You never did that before."

Christian licked his lips before answering. "Normally, I drop the shutters every night. But I didn't want to freak you out before I managed to seduce you." He grinned at her scowl, and continued. "It's for your protection. Anthony still wants you, *chére*. Never doubt it. We don't know where he is, and we can't be sure what's really happening down in Laredo."

"Then why are you going? Shouldn't you wait—?"

"Because whether it's a trap, or a real threat, vampires are dying down there. I can't stand by and let that happen."

Natalie was scared out of her mind, and trying not to show it. Not for herself, though. She had the gun Leighton had sent her. If Anthony tried anything, she'd shoot him and be done with it. But she was terrified that something would happen to Christian. And then what would she do? She'd just found him. She couldn't lose him now.

"Chopper's five minutes out," Marc said, standing in the short hallway that led to the garage. He was plainly ready to leave, staring at the two of them, as if urging them to get on with it.

"Natalie," Christian said softly, squeezing both of her hands and drawing her attention back to him. "The security system is fully armed, every door and window locked down. No one can get in or out without the code."

"What if there's a fire?" she asked, trying to be rational, to be calm. She'd be fine. He needed to worry about himself.

He let go of her hands to write a number down on a sticky note and press it against the counter next to her laptop. "If you need to get out, enter that code on the alarm panel next to the front door, or the sliding door here. It won't work anywhere else. You'll only be able to open that door, but all of the window shutters will be accessible from inside the house. Everything will lock down again after sixty seconds, or when the door is closed, whichever comes first."

"But what about Alon? He's too heavy for me—"

"If you're in danger, don't worry about Alon. You get out and call Jaclyn. She'll help you."

"I'm not leaving Alon in a burning house!" she said, staring at him in shock.

He gave an impatient growl, gripping her shoulders again and shaking her slightly. "There's not going to *be* a fire. But if there *is*, Alon will be safer than you. He's locked in a fireproof vault in the basement."

"Oh. All right, then." Privately, she was thinking that meant she could leave anytime she needed to. Not that she would readily abandon Alon, or defy Christian either. But as long as Alon was protected, she could think of several scenarios where she'd have to break out of this prison, er, safe house. None of which she shared with Christian, who was regarding her with evident concern.

"We'll be fine," she told him. "You worry about yourself and Marc. I don't trust any of Anthony's people."

"Neither do I. But if this is Hubert's grand move, he needs to be stopped. And I need to be there when it happens."

She nodded again, then wrapped her arms around his neck, pressing herself into the already familiar comfort of his muscled body. Fighting tears she was determined not to show, she kissed his cheek, then the corner of his mouth. His arms were bands of iron around her.

"Come back to me," she whispered.

"Always."

He was trying to be patient, trying to give her what she needed. But she could feel the same tension in his body that she'd noticed in Marc's. She stepped back with a forced smile.

"You, too, Marc," she called over to him. "I want you both back here in one piece."

"Yes, ma'am," Marc said, but he tossed a set of keys up into the air, catching them impatiently.

Natalie surprised herself by laughing. "Okay, the girlfriend drama is over. You're free to go."

Christian speared his fingers through her hair, tugging her head back, before settling his mouth over hers in a luxurious, lazy kiss that held everything sensuous and loving, and nothing of his need to leave.

"You be good while I'm gone," he murmured against her mouth, then kissed her one last time, and turned away to stride down the hallway. Marc was already in the garage, the door swinging shut as Christian caught it with one hand. He turned and gave her a final wink good-bye, and then he was gone.

Chapter Eleven

Patrizia, Mexico

VINCENT LEANED out the open door of the helicopter, studying the small coastal town. It was suspiciously quiet. The streets were dark and empty, despite the warm weather and relatively early hour. He considered the fact that this was a fishing village, and that fishermen tended to go out early in the morning, and, hence, would go to bed early, as well. But his vampire senses were telling him something different. There were humans down there, but not as many as there should have been. And they were all huddled behind closed doors and windows.

His chopper was a big Sikorsky, outfitted for military transport, not comfort, so he was able to fit eighteen of his best warriors on-board, in addition to the two pilots and Lana. If it was up to him, Lana's fine ass wouldn't leave her seat, but he knew that wasn't likely. The best he could hope for was to keep her far back from the front line, which was where she could do the most good anyway. She couldn't go hand-to-hand with a vampire, not even one of Hubert's zombies, but she was very handy with a gun, and had excellent tactical sense.

He sat down and flicked the switch on his headset to open the command channel, which would connect him with only Lana and his lieutenant, Michael. "Something's wrong down there," he said.

"I think that's a given," Lana said dryly. "Why else would we be here?"

Vincent gave her a dirty look. "There are humans in the town, but not many, and no vamps," he clarified. "Mikey, have the pilot circle wider. Hubert's army has to be here somewhere." He watched Michael switch over to the pilots' channel, then turned to Lana. "Whatever goes down tonight, you hang back, and use your gun. Try to find a spot where you can assess the battle for me."

"Uh huh," she said, nudging him with her elbow. "You're not fooling me, babe. But I'll go along with it, because this time, you're right."

"This time?" He couldn't hear her snort in response, but he could see it.

"Here we go." Michael's voice came back on the channel as the helicopter banked, taking them wide over the foothills, which formed a

187

narrow crescent-moon around the small village. There was a strip of flat-land, a little over a hundred yards deep between the last houses and the first hills.

As they flew, Vincent closed his eyes. He didn't need to *see* where they were going. Not with his eyes anyway. He opened himself to the extraordinary senses of his vampire nature, and the world narrowed and opened up at the same time. He was exquisitely aware of every one of his vampires around him, of the powerful link he had with Michael as his first child. But stronger and brighter than any other was his mate bond with Lana. She was in every beat of his heart, the very fire in his blood. How could anyone have ever doubted his feelings for her?

But he put that aside for now, stretching his awareness beyond the helicopter, searching for his enemy. He'd never met any of the European vampires, but Hubert had a reputation, and both Raphael and Christian had confirmed that rep. That he was powerful went without saying—he was centuries old and a vampire lord. But his notoriety went beyond that. He was ruthless and cruel, caring for nothing but his own lust for power. The very fact that he used up humans in order to create vampires who were barely deserving of the title, and who had no purpose but to be torn apart in the grinder of his ambition . . . that said it all.

They'd nearly finished the first pass of the foothills, when Vincent's senses twinged in awareness. Without opening his eyes, he spun his raised finger in a circle, and heard Michael giving the pilots directions. The chopper banked again, sharply, and Vincent stood, drawn closer to the open door. The sign he was looking for suddenly blazed across his vampire senses. It wasn't a gradual thing. It was more like a door that had been shut was suddenly opened.

Flicking the command channel open, he said, "That's it, almost directly below us. Get us close enough to deploy."

He opened his eyes then, physically searching the crumpled land of the foothills. There were a hundred places for even a large group to hide down there, but only from human eyes.

"My lord?" Michael stood next to him in the doorway, matching Vincent's searching posture.

"More than thirty so far," Vincent said absently, still counting. "They're clustered together, and their presence is weak. It's difficult to get a good count. Hubert's zombies, I'm thinking."

"But no Hubert?"

"There's a stronger presence, but just one. And it's muted, as if he's trying to hide." Vincent swore softly. "I wish I'd met him before, or at least touched his power."

"Who else could it be?"

"Good question."

The pilot's voice came over the channel. "Going down, my lord. Topo display says there's a valley down there. I should be able to hover at twenty feet."

"That'll do," Vincent responded, taking his seat next to Lana.

"Can we light it up?" the pilot asked, requesting permission to clear the chosen landing zone by using the chopper's two six-barreled machine guns, one on each side. They could fire 4000 rounds per minute, and were more than enough to clear a landing space for Vincent and his troops.

"Do it," Vincent said, then nodded at two of his vampire fighters who took up their stations at the Miniguns, waiting for the pilot's signal. Vincent clicked off his headphone and signaled for Lana to do the same. It was about to get very noisy up here.

Vincent caught the slight tensing of the gunner's muscles, and touched Lana's thigh in warning an instant before the guns opened up. Vampires cursed as hot cartridges spit from the feeder, a few of them bouncing around the compartment before making it out the door. He caught one in his bare hand as it flew at Lana's head, and tossed it into the open air, pretending like his hand wasn't burning like fuck. Lana took his hand and kissed the raw palm, which almost made it all better. He turned with a grin, and she rolled her eyes at him, mouthing the word, *"Men."*

He gave her a quick, hard hug. He was a vampire, not a man, but it was too noisy in the chopper to tell her that right now. He'd have to remember it for later.

The pilot's voice came over his headset, on the broadcast channel, giving everyone the head's up. "Ten seconds."

Over at the door, Michael had his hands up where all of the fighters could see them, counting down.

When he hit two seconds, Vincent stood. He would be the first one out. Michael's expression told him what his lieutenant thought about that, but they both knew it had to be this way. Vincent led from the front. He never asked his people to risk more than he did.

The ground was suddenly there. Vincent stepped into the open air, dropped the twenty or so feet, and landed easily. Vampires didn't need ropes, not at this height. Lana did, but she hated to be the only one. He eyed the chopper closely, waiting for her slender figure to fill the doorway.

And there she was, one arm above her head, gripping the header over the door. Behind her, Vincent could see Michael, making sure Vincent was waiting for her, ready to grab her if necessary. Vincent waved a hand, knowing Lana wouldn't be able to see it in the dark. She'd have a hissy fit if she knew he was watching out for her. The rope slithered out the chopper door. She grabbed it and jumped. And Vincent's heart jumped with her.

He didn't catch her as much as he braced her, hands on her waist, easing her impact with the hard, rocky ground, as she released the rope. Her knees bent to absorb the shock, and she immediately straightened, giving him a narrow look. Vincent merely shrugged. He wasn't about to let her break a leg to make a point, no matter what she wanted. As the chopper lifted away, he put his mouth to her ear, and said, "Remember your position."

She stiffened to attention and raised her hand to snap off a sarcastic salute, when suddenly her eyes went wide and attitude went out the window.

Vincent spun, and stared at what was coming at them. They'd all been calling Hubert's creations zombies, for lack of a better word, but that's exactly what they looked like. Red-eyed and blank-faced, but moving well enough, as they scrambled down the surrounding hillsides, heading toward Vincent and his people. Some were sporting very un-vampire-like wounds that should have healed by now. From the reports he'd read, it had been hours since this group had fought anyone, and longer still since their attack on the town. Even a low-level vampire would have been able to heal anything short of a lost limb by now. But whatever these creatures were, their vampire symbiote was so weak that they weren't healing properly. Vincent didn't think he could have created vampires like this. Didn't know how it was done. Was this Hubert's special talent? The equivalent of Vincent's ability to read memories? Could such a thing be called a talent? It was an atrocity.

But whatever else these primitive vampires were, right now they were the enemy, and there was no doubt of their intent. They were here to kill anyone who got in their way.

Vincent did a quick survey of the battlefield. They were in a relatively clear space, surrounded by sloping hills of sandy rock. The ground beneath them was flat, but littered with small stones and gritty dirt, made worse by the "clearing" they'd done before landing. But the moon was bright behind scattered clouds, casting more than enough light for his vampires to fight by.

Michael stepped up to his side, his gaze never leaving the approaching army. "More than fifty, *jefe*."

Vincent nodded. His people were probably outnumbered three to one, but numbers were often the least important factor when it came to vampire battles. Vincent's fighters were bigger, stronger, and sure as hell more capable than these poor creatures, many of whom had probably been fishermen only yesterday morning.

"I'm going after Hubert. You know what to do," he told Michael. The two of them had fought side-by-side for decades. There was no one he trusted more at his back, except perhaps Lana. But not when it came to this battlefield.

Michael pulled his attention away from the approaching army long enough to exchange a manly embrace with Vincent. "Kill the fucker," he said with a vicious grin.

Vincent matched his grin, then looked over Michael's shoulder. Lana was perched on a rock outcropping, fifteen feet above the battleground, guns laid out beside her. He sent a surge of energy across the clearing, surrounding her in warmth. She looked up, searching for him, smiling when the moon emerged strongly enough that she could see him. He wanted to climb up there and kiss the hell out of her, wanted to taste her skin, feel the heat of her body against his one more time. Just in case. This was war, and he was going up against another vampire lord. Anything could happen.

But because this was war, he settled for blowing her a kiss before closing his mind to everything except the coming battle. Spinning away, he put on a burst of vampire speed and smashed through the approaching zombie vamps, as he went to confront their master. Those few who got in his way, he simply tossed aside, ripping off limbs as necessary, picking up one, and using him as a club to batter another at one point. None of them tried to stop him. They seemed incapable of recognizing that he was a greater threat than any other vampire on the field. He was merely one fighter, while their focus was on the larger group behind him. Their directions from Hubert were clear, and just as clearly one-dimensional. Once Vincent was through their lines, he was forgotten.

The sounds of battle rose behind him, as he started his climb. The zombies had come from somewhere within these hills, so it made sense that Hubert was concealed up there, directing the fight from the safety of his hiding place. Finding a spot beneath a heavy overhang, he sent his awareness outward, searching for the single, strong presence that would be Hubert. As before, when he'd searched from the chopper, the lone signal was bright, but muted, as if Hubert was attempting to camouflage his presence. It would have worked if Vincent hadn't been a vampire lord himself, or if he'd sent someone else to head up this offensive. If the present battle was any indication, that's what Hubert would have done. There he was tonight, hiding in the hills, letting his vampires die to protect him. Maybe he had assumed Vincent would do the same, and so had counted on his camouflage to shelter him from the actual fighting.

But Vincent *was* a vampire lord, and he was fucking powerful. He cut through the fog Hubert had walled himself behind, and started climbing. Turning Hubert's own game on him, he kept his power signature locked down tight, so that the other lord wouldn't know who was coming at him. Let him think Vincent was a soldier, a master vampire, but nothing more.

He scrambled up and over a final outcropping of rock so loose that, had he not had the enhanced physical abilities of his vampire nature, he almost certainly would have slid right back down the hill, probably breaking a few bones in the process. Hubert was a coward, but he had the smarts to choose a good hiding spot.

Vincent came over the edge cautiously, and crouched low, with senses wide open. A bolt of power blasted across the open space, pulverizing the rock behind him and sizzling by so close to his head, that it seared his cheek in passing.

"Fuck that," he snarled. He snapped his shields into place, and straightened to force the challenge. Releasing the full measure of his power, he shuddered under the exquisite pleasure of it, feeling it flow out and around him in a rush of ecstasy that rivaled sex. In his mind's eye, the power embraced him, caressing his skin like a lover, before soaring into the night to surround him. But this was no time for poetic musings. He had a vampire lord to kill.

"Fucking coward," he called, aiming the taunt at a tight cluster of ancient prickly pear cactus that rose higher than his head, their big blooms shining yellow in the moonlight.

He waited for Hubert to answer his challenge, to come out of hiding and confront Vincent with a display of his own. But the only response was another bolt of sizzling energy that shot across the clearing and splashed harmlessly against his shields.

"If that's the way you want it, old man," he muttered, and sent a ball of vampire-fueled fire roaring into the cactus cluster, igniting it like a giant torch, with flames blasting twenty feet into the sky.

Hubert gave a high-pitched yell, and darted away from the conflagration, giving Vincent his first direct sight of the enemy. He'd never seen Hubert before, and hadn't thought to ask what the vampire looked like. Physical appearance wasn't important; only power mattered. And that's what Vincent focused on when he studied the European invader. He could see the rainbow shimmer of the lord's shields in the glimmer of the flames, could feel the unrelenting pressure as Hubert probed for a weakness in Vincent's shields, as well. But other than that probe, his attack was curiously passive, his energies concentrated on maintaining his shields.

It wasn't what Vincent would have expected from a lord as old and experienced as Hubert, and he wondered if the invader was a victim of his own strategy. The power necessary to maintain control over his zombie fighters might be taking such a toll on his strength that it was leaving him vulnerable to the far more dangerous enemy right in front of him.

But at the same time, Vincent knew that Hubert had a whole village full of blood donors sitting down below like a human buffet. The European should have been at peak strength.

All of these thoughts raced through his mind in an instant as he calculated the fastest way to dispose of Hubert and get back to his fighters, and to Lana. If Hubert was weakened by his own actions, then all the better. It was time to get this fight started.

Shifting his gaze to the tumble of rocks behind Hubert, who remained curiously unmoving, Vincent seized them with his power and sent them flying down the hill. They slammed into Hubert, who flinched visibly on impact. His shields held, but they wavered as he stumbled forward, nearly going to his knees. He grimaced in pain, his fangs flashing, as he struggled to regain his feet.

But this wasn't an old-fashioned human sort of duel, with rules of honor and chivalry. Vincent struck while his enemy was down. Striding over the empty space between them, he curled hands together in front of his chest and shaped his power into a massive cudgel of energy. Swinging it around his head, building momentum as he drew closer, he stomped to a halt just before he would have hit Hubert's shield, and powered the cudgel downward at the vampire lord's head.

There was a fraction of resistance, a bare slowing of his downward stroke as the weapon penetrated Hubert's shield. And then there were blood and brains splattering everywhere, trapped within the shield for a gruesome few seconds as Hubert struggled to stay alive, before his shield collapsed, and he crumpled to the ground.

Vincent stared, shocked at the ease of his victory, but not so stunned that he paused in delivering the final blow. Reaching into the gory mess, he punched a hole in Hubert's chest, ripped out his heart, and tossed it onto the burning cactus. Seconds later, Lord Hubert of Lyon was gone, an unlamented footnote to the history of Vampire.

And yet . . . something wasn't right about this. Vincent had never doubted he would prevail in this fight. This was his territory, and he knew his strength. But he'd expected more of a challenge. He thought again of the zombie vampires, and the toll they might have taken on Hubert's strength. And perhaps that explained it, but it did nothing to ease the pebble of unease that was building in his gut. Turning, he raced for the plateau's edge and started downward.

He could see the battle still raging down below, could catch glimpses of movement as the moon flirted with the clouds overhead. He heard the crack of Lana's rifle as she fired repeatedly, systematically. The closer he got, the more individual sounds carried up to him, the roars and grunts from his own fighters punctuating the almost steady keening growl that rose above Hubert's zombie vampires.

The pebble in his gut became a boulder. He needed to get back to his people. The feeling of wrongness was driving him forward with a frenzy that had him leaping from foothold to foothold, rocks skidding beneath his feet in a shower of dirt and stone before him. Lana was down there. Michael and all of his fighters were, too. But Lana was so much more vulnerable, her connection to him too new to save her if the unimaginable happened. What if she'd been the ultimate target? What if Hubert hoped to destroy Vincent by killing his mate?

It would work. Vincent couldn't imagine surviving the agony of losing Lana, couldn't imagine wanting to go on without her.

Reaching the flat, he tore across the battleground, tearing through Hubert's zombies, tossing them aside, ripping out hearts and tearing off heads in his urgency to destroy them all before disaster struck. He couldn't have said what the disaster would be, couldn't envision whatever Hubert's plan had been. What kind of vampire lord weakened himself so severely that he couldn't survive a challenge? What horrible revenge had he hoped to inflict?

Vincent reached the giant boulder where Lana was secured, her gun still firing at an almost inhuman pace. As he climbed, he could hear the battle winding down behind him. Even Lana's steady gunfire was slowing. She rolled over in alarm when he made the final leap to her side, her gun coming up, finger on the trigger. She froze, eyes wide, when she recognized him, then lowered the weapon with a curse.

"God damn it, Vincent! I almost shot you. What the fuck?"

Vincent didn't waste time on words, just gathered her up, and stretched his shields to cover them both, staring out into the moonlit night and listening as the battle was reduced to the muted growls of his fighters and the dying cries of their enemies. There was no mercy in vampire society. Vanquished enemies were destroyed. There was no other outcome.

"Vincent," Lana said, drawing his attention with the soft intensity of her voice. "What's going on, babe?"

He dragged his gaze from the battlefield where he'd been counting his fighters, noting each face, scanning for injuries.

"*Querida*," he said fervently, stroking a hand over the long braid of her black hair.

"Vincent? You're scaring me."

He shook his head. "I don't know. Something's wrong with this. I was convinced Hubert had a surprise planned, something we hadn't thought of, but . . ." He scowled, still unable to put words to his fear. "Come on," he said suddenly. "I need to talk to Michael."

He waited while she secured her weapons and slung the two rifles over her shoulder. Then he gripped her around the waist and stepped to the edge of the boulder.

"Hold on," he warned her, and stepped off the rock, dropping them to the ground fifteen feet below. His knees bent, thighs flexing as he absorbed the impact. Lana uttered a tiny squeak, and gripped his arms briefly, but she couldn't have been that surprised. She knew what he was capable of.

"Asshole," she whispered. "A little warning next time."

Vincent kissed the top of her head in apology, but his mind wasn't on it. His arm tightened around her when she would have turned for the landing zone where they'd be meeting the helicopter. He was still consumed with the need to protect her, still waiting for the unknown to happen. Lana glanced up at him, but didn't say anything, and didn't try to break away.

"*Jefe*," Michael said, coming toward him with a victorious grin. Behind him, Vincent's warriors were dispatching the few remaining fallen enemies, and slapping each other's backs in celebration. If they'd been in the city, the blood bars would be going wild tonight, his fighters pumping adrenaline and blood lust so thick, it would color the air.

"Michael," Vincent said tightly, his attention never leaving the hills around them as he continued to scan with all his vampire senses.

"What is it?" Michael asked, suddenly tuning in to Vincent's tension. "Hubert?" he asked, turning to mimic Vincent's search of the surrounding area.

"Hubert's dead," Vincent said sharply, and that quickly, he realized what was bothering him. "They should have died," he muttered, halfway to himself. "Why didn't they die?" he asked louder, looking at Michael.

"Who?"

"These," he said, waving a hand at the dead and dying zombie vamps. "Look at them. They're so newly turned that they're not even dusting. Their bodies will lie there until the sun destroys them in the morning."

Michael nodded. "Okay," he said, still not getting the point.

"So why didn't they die when I killed Hubert?" Vincent asked quietly. "They shouldn't have been able to survive the shock of his death. But when I came back here, you were still fully engaged, as if nothing had happened, as if . . . Fuck me," he swore fervently.

Michael understood then. Without a word, he flicked on his headset and called the helicopter back. "Where to, my lord?"

"I don't know yet. Let's just get the fuck out of here for now."

"What?" Lana was demanding, pounding a fist on his chest where he was still holding her tightly. "What happened?"

"That wasn't Hubert I killed," Vincent said bitterly. "I knew something was off. I just thought . . . Fuck." The helicopter came into view, hovered briefly, then settled just above the ground. With no enemies alive to contest their arrival, the pilots could risk coming in closer.

Vincent steered Lana back to the chopper, boosting her up and in, before following her inside. As they donned their headsets against the noise, his thoughts were churning, playing back the sequence of events that had brought him here, to this remote fishing village, considering all the players and their reasons for wanting him distracted and out of the way.

"Anthony," he growled.

"What about him?" Michael asked over the command channel, as he settled onto the seat on the other side of Vincent.

"He had a reason for sending us here. Get us to the airport. I need to call someone, and find out what the fuck is going on."

Chapter Twelve

Houston, TX

NATALIE WATCHED the door close behind Christian, heard the heavy shutter roll down with the subdued rumble of well-oiled gears. Tiptoeing over, she peered through the peephole, and realized she could still see the outside. No one was there. She rolled her eyes. Of course, no one was there. And why was she tiptoeing?

"Get it together, Nat," she whispered. But she couldn't stop staring at that door, couldn't stop thinking about how trapped she felt in this big empty house. Just to reassure herself, she crossed to the keypad and entered the code that Christian had given her.

The shutter responded instantly, raising itself with the same rumble of noise that had closed it. She opened the door and glanced outside. The neighborhood was quiet, the elegant homes each perched above a gently sloping lawn, most with soft light shining through windows, testifying to their occupation.

She breathed in a dose of the fresh air, then stepped back and closed the door. Christian was right. She needed to be smart and safe, even if Anthony was in hiding. He was sneaky and accustomed to getting his way. She punched in the code, and took comfort in the solid sound of the shutter dropping securely down again.

"Well, you can't stand in front of the door all night like a dog, waiting for him to come home," she muttered, then turned to survey the house. The entrance opened into a split-level living room that was filled with furniture. It was elegantly appointed, and probably very expensive. But she preferred the kitchen, where Christian's giant espresso machine ruled the room. Her bedroom, or rather, the one she was using, was comfortable and nicely furnished, and now that she'd been there a few days, it was also cluttered with the stuff of daily living. She imagined the basement was like that, too.

That reminded her of what Christian had said about Alon being secure in a locked vault downstairs. She stared down the hallway on her right, contemplating the closed basement door, and what lay beyond it. She could go down there and see for herself. No one else was in the house, no one would ever know. She started in that direction, then stopped. No. It wouldn't be right to snoop around while Christian was gone. She wouldn't like it if he did that to her. She'd just have to wait, and ask him when he came back if he would show her what was down there.

She wrinkled her nose in irritation. Being a good person was a pain in the ass sometimes. She sighed and tried to decide what to do. The living room had a full entertainment suite, and she'd bet Christian had cable, or some equivalent. Probably hundreds of channels. She could find a movie to watch. But that didn't hold any appeal. She was too nervous about what Christian and Marc would find when they reached the border, too worried about what might happen to them. She needed to distract her brain, or she'd drive herself crazy.

"Work," she decided. Her work required full concentration. Once she started on a trail, she lost track of time and everything else. She stopped in her bedroom long enough to grab a sweatshirt and her laptop, then headed back to the kitchen.

She set her laptop on the kitchen island, and grabbed a Diet Coke from the fridge. She was going to need a lot of caffeine, and for all the beauty of Christian's machine, cup by cup wasn't going to do it. It was times like this that her Mr. Coffee was made for. Brew a pot and mainline the whole damn thing. Fortunately, she'd bought a twelve pack of Diet Coke when she was at the store. It's not like the vamps needed all that room in the fridge anyway.

Scooting onto one of the kitchen stools, she opened her laptop and logged in. She was about to open her work files when the new folder she'd created for the files purloined from Anthony caught her eye. She'd intended to discuss them with the guys, was going to argue for them letting her handle the research and general ferreting out of info, while they focused on the stuff she couldn't do, like fighting and all-around intimidation. Other issues—like a full-blown street battle and an enemy invasion—had intervened before she could talk to them about it. But there was no reason she couldn't get started.

She clicked the folder open and scanned the document list. There hadn't been enough time to be picky. She'd simply grabbed everything she could, and still didn't know exactly what she had. She hadn't discussed any of this with Christian, but it didn't take a rocket scientist to figure out what they were looking for. Anything that incriminated Anthony. A nice confession would be good. Maybe a heartfelt diary entry . . . *I can't live with the lies anymore. I have to tell someone.* She snorted her opinion of *that* happening. Anthony was one of those people who could justify just about anything, as long as it served his purposes.

Her eye trailed down the list of documents. She'd used her access to the network, and her more or less authorized knowledge of everyone's password, including Anthony's, to log onto his computer and copy everything generated in the last two weeks. The files were from several different folders on his computer, but for the sake of expedience, she'd dumped them all into a single folder on her flash drive. That left her with a jumble of file names and dates. She clicked the heading to sort the docs by date, which at least gave her a place to start. The most recent documents were likely to be the most relevant.

She went through the files systematically, one at a time. Most were routine stuff, but she did learn one thing. Anthony kept a record of everything, including personal notes and observations. Forget that diary, this was way better. He didn't like e-mail, and he never texted, preferring a face-to-face conversation or a phone call, but apparently, he'd fully embraced the use of his computer as a personal journal. Getting inside a person's head and discovering how they thought was half the battle in figuring out what they were hiding, and where. Anthony's notes were like a roadmap for someone like her.

As she skimmed down the list, looking for more journal entries, she came across a sub-folder that she must have grabbed without realizing. It was titled "Faxes," and she opened it expecting to find . . . faxes. Lots and lots of faxes, going all the way back to when Anthony first came to the estate. Who used fax machines these days? E-mail was much more efficient and easier to keep a record of. But it was also easier to track and hack. This was probably more of Anthony's paranoia peeking through, but it worked for her, so she started opening files. They were all the same format—a document that someone had created for Anthony to use as a fax cover sheet, with an auto-fill function on the appropriate lines. And several had been written in the last two days. In fact, it was a flurry of faxes. Heh, heh.

Most had to do with arrangements for Anthony's personal belongings to be packed and shipped to New Orleans, and for various details of a house he'd apparently purchased in that city in anticipation of his move. Her family would be sorry to see him return. Was it wrong for her to hope he never made it back?

She opened the next one in order and was surprised to see Christian's name on the subject line. Reading down, she realized it had never been sent. There was no one on the "to" line, but the bulk of the text was all about the battle down in Laredo. In fact, based on what little she knew, it seemed almost prescient in its details. She frowned. Scoville was the one who'd called Christian, and he'd said Anthony was MIA. So why would Anthony know so much about what was happening?

Making a series of notes to herself, she stayed with the fax files, and eventually found one that had been sent to Vincent just a few hours ago. It was in Spanish, which frustrated her a little bit. She could get by in the language, but she was far from fluent. Still, she read through the text, using a translation app when she hit words or phrases she didn't understand. And the more she read, the more worried she became. This e-mail had the same urgent tone as the one Anthony had written to Christian, but it urged Vincent to go far south into his territory, all the way down to the Gulf of Mexico. It warned that Hubert had established a foothold in a small fishing village there, that he was turning locals, and creating an army in preparation for a move against Vincent.

But how could Hubert be in a village on the Gulf of Mexico if he was attacking the border outpost in Laredo? And hadn't Christian mentioned that Vincent was on his way to Laredo?

More importantly, why did Anthony know so much about Laredo?

She picked up her cell to call Christian. Foremost, he needed to know that Vincent wasn't coming. But he also needed to know that Anthony might be involved, and that the situation might not be what Scoville said it was.

She called his cell phone, but there was no answer and no voicemail. "Damn it," she swore softly. He should be off the helicopter by now. She'd been working for several hours already. But that meant he was probably in the middle of a fight, and not exactly paying attention to his cell phone.

She stood there for a moment, staring at the floor, not seeing anything, deciding what to do next. But the answer was obvious. She had to go down there and warn him herself. She knew all the arguments against her going. She wasn't a fighter, and blah, blah, blah. But she wasn't as helpless as everyone seemed to think, either. Christian would still be furious, but better that than dead.

And bottom line, she couldn't trust anyone else to do it. Everyone had an agenda around here, including her. The difference was that the only line on *her* agenda was keeping Christian and Marc alive.

Her mind switched to planning mode. No emotion now, just logistics. She knew the air charter company Anthony used. She could call and arrange transport using her authority from the estate. She could also use the estate's money, which was both handy and karmically satisfying. But first, she needed an update on the situation. It wouldn't do any good if she zipped down there, only to stumble into a bloody mess of a battle.

Information, information, she thought as she scrolled through her contacts, and stopped on Jaclyn's name. With Jaclyn's connection to Raphael, she'd certainly know what was going on. Natalie pressed the button, and listened to the phone rang.

"Hi Natalie," Jaclyn answered with her usual lack of formality. "Are you coming in tonight?"

Natalie frowned, surprised that Jaclyn would expect her. Between Anthony's unknown whereabouts, and a full-on battle on the border, the estate house was the last place she'd be expected to be.

"Probably not," she said slowly, "what with Christian rushing off to Laredo."

"Laredo? What's happening down there?"

Fear seized her, and her heart stopped beating for a long moment. "There was an attack on the outpost tonight," she said, her throat so tight she had to fight for the words. "Scoville called Christian in a panic, begging for help. It sounds like Hubert's about to launch a full-scale invasion."

"I haven't heard anything about this," Jaclyn said, her words laced with impatience. Her voice abruptly faded as she turned away from the phone. "Cibor," she said, "what's going on in Laredo?"

Natalie couldn't make out what Cibor replied, but it wasn't what Jaclyn wanted to hear. "Well, get hold of someone down there, and find out what the situation is. I want it five minutes ago." Jaclyn's irritated voice came back to her. "What else do you know?" she demanded.

"I only know what Christian told me about their phone conversation. But there's something weird going on, because—"

"Hold up," Jaclyn snapped, and then didn't say anything for a long time, while the deep rumble of Cibor's voice could be heard in the background. And then Jaclyn was back.

"Something odd is going on," she told Natalie, her tone both worried and distracted. "No one here knows anything about an attack. And *no one* is rushing to defend the border."

"Jaclyn," Natalie said urgently, "it's way more than odd. Look, I hacked into Anthony's private files, and there are faxes and stuff. I think—" She drew a deep breath through her nose, fighting for calm. "I think Hubert really will attack tonight, but Scoville's working with Anthony, and they lured Christian down there to face Hubert and his whole damn army all alone. They want Christian dead."

Cibor could obviously hear every word, because he said something to Jaclyn, and then Jaclyn said to Natalie, "I think you're right. But the only way to be sure is to fly down there ourselves, and I can't go. I'm too closely linked to Raphael, and we can't get in the middle of what some might consider a territorial challenge. But I'm sending Cibor down to eyeball the situation. If there really is an invasion, he'll be a good addition to Christian's side. And if not, he'll at least be able tell us what's really going on."

"I'm going with him," Natalie said, sliding off the kitchen stool and heading for her bedroom. "But you'll have to stay here with Alon, just in case."

"Stay there? Wha—Wait! Who's Alon?"

"My dojo master. Christian turned him after he nearly died when Marcel Weiss tried to kill Christian last night," she said, speaking rapidly.

"Marcel tried to kill Christian? What the fuck?"

But Natalie wasn't listening anymore. "Alon won't be any trouble, because he's asleep and locked in a vault. But I can't leave him here all alone."

"Well, good, because you're not going anywhere."

"Can you get a helicopter?" she asked Jaclyn, ignoring her pronouncement. "Marc told Christian that a helicopter worked best, because of airport hassles and stuff, so—"

"We've got this, Natalie. Cibor will take care of it."

She ignored that, too. "—how long before you and Cibor can get here?"

"Look, I'm not sure—"

"About what?" Natalie demanded. "Christian and Marc are out there all alone against who knows how many enemies. They need help, and I can do that."

"How, Natalie?" Jaclyn asked softly, her voice full of compassion. "I understand you want to help him, but you can't fight vampires, sugar. I don't care how much karate or whatever it is that you do. You'll only get hurt or worse, and that won't help him."

"I appreciate what you're saying, but you don't know—"

"And Christian?" Jaclyn persisted. "Do you think he wants you in the middle of a vampire battlefield? Do you have any idea what that's like? He locked you in his house, didn't he? I bet you're sitting there with all the shutters deployed, and not even a window to look out of. Tell me I'm wrong."

Natalie tightened her jaw, hating to admit Jaclyn was right. But she still didn't know everything that Natalie knew. "You're not wrong about the house, but it doesn't *matter*. Christian doesn't know that he's on his own. Scoville told him that help was coming, that *Vincent* was coming. But he's not. Anthony sent him to the other side of Mexico! I have to warn Christian."

"Did you try calling him?' Jaclyn asked patiently.

"Of course, I did," she snapped. "It was the first thing I thought of, but he's not answering."

"He probably turned everything off. No distractions on the battle-field," Jaclyn mused. "It's what I would do."

"Well, whatever his reasons, I can't reach him, which means I have to go there—"

"And become the biggest distraction of all."

That gave Natalie pause. Jaclyn was right. Christian would worry more about protecting her than himself. And that could get him killed. But she couldn't sit here and do *nothing.* "Christian needs what I know," she insisted.

Jaclyn sighed. "He's probably figured it out by now, but I'll send Cibor to be sure. And you're not going, even if I have to lock you up. Cibor can get there faster without you, and he's one hell of a fighter."

Natalie's heart was urging her to go, to find her own way there and rush to Christian's side. But her very excellent brain shut that idea down almost before it started. Jaclyn was right. Christian needed Cibor right now a lot more than he did Natalie.

She sighed deeply, and mumbled, "Okay."

"It's for the best, sugar. But I'll come over and keep you company, anyway. We're on our way."

Laredo, TX, on the Mexican border

CHRISTIAN STARED out the window as the helicopter swooped low over the border outpost. Its belly lights illuminated an adobe-style building that appeared abandoned. There were no guards in sight, despite the chopper hovering noisily overhead, and no lights were on anywhere in the building. What the hell had happened here? Had Hubert already attacked and moved on?

As the helicopter circled, he swept the area with his power, searching for life forms of any kind. He caught a drift of something strong enough to bring all of his senses to full alert, but then it was gone, like a scent blown in from far away, and stirred up by the chopper blades. He frowned, considering the possibilities. It could be nothing, a trace left over from the many vampires who'd occupied this outpost. Or it could be Hubert. The ancient vampire might have clamped down on his power a second too late to conceal it from Christian, which meant he was close. The possibility made him uneasy, but not as uneasy as the abandoned outpost did. Where were the vampires who should have been stationed here? Where was Scoville?

Christian studied the lone outpost building, looking for answers as the helicopter made its landing approach. The structure was big enough to hide a lot of vampires, and there was certain to be a basement. Maybe Anthony's people had hidden themselves down there, wanting Hubert to think the place abandoned, so they could spring an ambush.

He continued his sweep of the area, probing as deeply as his considerable power would let him. He found nothing and no one, until the helicopter dropped low enough to land, and then he faltered under the assault. The outpost was a graveyard. It stank of very recent violence and death. Everyone who'd been here in the last twenty-four hours was dead. Friend or enemy, it didn't matter.

The chopper settled on the ground, skids sinking into the soft dirt. Christian slapped Marc on the shoulder, then stepped out, adopting a crouching run until he cleared the rotor blades, then straightening to look around.

"I'm not sensing anyone," Marc said quietly, his voice troubled as he came up next to Christian.

"There's nothing to feel but death," Christian told him, then stiffened to attention and spun around.

"You're too late," a rough voice said from within the darkness of the open door.

Christian stepped in front of Marc as a figure appeared. His face was in shadow, but Christian could read the exhaustion in his body language, could see the blood draining from multiple wounds in his chest that obviously wouldn't heal.

"Who—" he started to say, but then the person emerged fully, and he recognized him. "Scoville?" he said in surprise. "What the hell happened here?"

Scoville smiled bitterly, and took a stumbling step forward. Marc rushed over to help, slinging the other vampire's arm over his shoulder and easing him over to a nearby wall to sit. Christian watched without saying anything, while Scoville tried to catch his breath. He must have been shielding like crazy to conceal himself from Christian's initial sweep. Why?

"I didn't know who you were," Scoville said, anticipating Christian's question. "I thought it was Anthony, coming to make sure of his work."

"You're saying *Anthony* did all of this?"

Scoville spit a gob of blood onto the muddy ground. "Not in person. He leads from the rear, especially if the front involves dying. But it wasn't supposed to be like this. *You* were supposed to die, not everyone else."

Marc stood with a hiss of anger, distancing himself from Scoville, putting himself between the injured vampire and Christian.

Christian touched Marc's shoulder, and moved around him. He needed to talk to Scoville, needed to see the vampire, to judge what he was saying. "So this was all a trap. You wanted me down here." He shrugged. "Here I am. So what happens next? And why shouldn't I kill you right now?"

He laughed bitterly. "Go ahead. I'm a dead man either way. Anthony told me to call you, said he'd send a chopper to get me before you ever got here. Everyone else was supposed to die. He *wanted* you to see this, to see what Hubert could do and be afraid. He wanted you to *die* afraid. But he lied . . . again." Another laugh, this was weak and breathy, as if the recitation was taking his last strength.

"I don't know why I'm surprised. All he does is lie. There was never a chopper to whisk me away to safety. You were right all along. I was never more than a stalking horse, a sacrifice to make things look good. But Anthony's had another candidate in mind all along."

"Who?" Christian demanded. None of this was making sense.

"Hubert," Scoville said, his face bleak as he raised his head to stare at Christian. "Anthony made a deal with Hubert in exchange for New Orleans. Raphael wanted out of the South, and Anthony knew he couldn't hold the territory on his own. So he called Hubert. Anthony gets the greater New Orleans region as a new territory of his very own, not beholden to Hubert or anyone else. And Hubert gets all the rest of the South."

"Fuck," Christian said softly. That made a terrible sense, especially coming from Hubert. That's the way it was in Europe, a hundred little territories in the same amount of space where in North America, there would be only one. It was why the European continent was so damn crowded, and why they wanted North America so badly. But Anthony? Jesus, he'd sacrificed his own people, *murdered* his own people, to further his greed and ambition. Had he really believed the North American Council would accept him after this? That they'd add a seat for the Lord of New Orleans, as if nothing had happened? He was fool. Raphael was already gunning for him over what he'd done to Cibor. Add this to his crimes, and the entire Council would hunt him down and execute him. Vampire law stated that might was right, but not when you butchered your own people to gain territory.

"What about Vincent?" he asked Scoville. "Is he a part of it?"

Scoville shook his head slowly. He was slumped over, barely able to sit, as if the effort of talking to Christian had drained what little strength he had left. "Sorry," he gasped. "I used everything I had left to hide from your scan." He swallowed dryly, then said, "Anthony didn't confide in me . . . obviously. But I knew Vincent pretty well when he was still Enrique's lieutenant, and I don't think he'd go along with this."

Christian glanced up and met Marc's worried gaze. "I wonder if he even spoke to Vincent?"

"So, let's get the fuck out of here," Marc suggested.

But Christian shook his head. We're not done yet," he said, remembering that brief whiff of power he'd detected. "Anthony didn't trick us down here for nothing. Hubert's on his way, and it's up to us to stop him somehow. Our friend here lied about everything else, but not that. If we don't manage to stop Hubert, he'll march up the 35, killing as he goes. It's what he does."

Scoville gave another weak cough, and Christian eyed the injured vampire. He required blood, but the only humans available were the chopper pilots—assuming they'd even volunteer, which he doubted. Besides, they'd be needed at full strength later to do their job. He grimaced. He hated giving his own blood to save the bastard, but he needed vampires, and Scoville was the only one available. Assuming he'd step up and fight.

"What's your plan, Scoville?" he asked. "What's next?"

"There is no next. I'm dying. It's a question of minutes, not hours."

"What if I agreed to help you?"

"Why would you do that?"

Christian shrugged. "I need firepower, and you're it. I assume you can fight, and I've felt your power. You have enough to make a difference if we all stand together. If not . . . your dust will be a fine addition to the landscape."

Scoville didn't say anything, just hung his head and breathed for long enough that Christian thought he might be dying right now. But then he lifted his head, and said, "I'll stand with you. I'll fight. Not because I give a fuck about you or your ambitions. Because of the vampires who fought and died here tonight believing help was coming, believing their rightful lord was on his way. I give a fuck about *them*. And I want to see Anthony pay." He was gasping for breath after that speech.

Christian eyed him for a moment, then sighed, knowing what he had to do. He pulled off his leather jacket, and shoved up the long sleeve of his T-shirt.

Marc put a hand on his arm, and said, "Let me."

But Christian shook his head. "This is my duty, not yours, *mon ami*." He lifted his forearm to his mouth and dug in his fangs, opening a vertical slash down the center to his wrist. Scoville's head came up at the rich smell of blood, his eyes taking on a yellowed gleam. This was the blood of a powerful vampire, a vampire strong enough to rule a territory. It was ambrosia, catnip to a vampire's senses. And it was life itself to a vampire as wounded as Scoville.

"You have a name besides Scoville?" Christian asked tightly.

Scoville shook his head. "Not anymore, my lord."

Christian nodded. "All right. Scoville, do you come to me of your own free will and desire?"

He nodded, his yellowed gaze never leaving the rich bounty of blood now dripping down to pool in Christian's cupped palm. "I do, my lord," he whispered.

"And is this what you truly desire?"

"It is my truest desire."

"Then drink, Scoville, and be mine."

Scoville cupped Christian's hand in both of his, holding it reverently as he leaned forward to lap up the blood. He licked Christian's palm nearly clean, then followed the flow of red up to his wrist, where he latched on and began sucking.

Christian imagined that he could feel every tug of Scoville's mouth from his vein all the way to his heart. This was going to cost him before the battle was over. He needed all of his strength for what was coming, but he couldn't simply let Scoville die. He wasn't Anthony. He lifted his other hand, ready to tap the vamp out, to tell him that it was time to stop . . . When suddenly there was a surge of power nearby.

"Scoville," he said urgently. "Enough." He disengaged without waiting, holding his wrist, and squeezing the two sides of the wound together. It would heal fast, but not fast enough. Not for what was coming. "Marc," he said, turning to his lieutenant. "I need to wrap this right now."

Marc nodded and ran for the chopper, which was still on the ground, rotor still turning. There was a first aid kit in there. Christian had noticed it on the flight over. Marc disappeared into the helicopter briefly, then jumped down with the white metal box in his hand. He opened it and set it on the wall. Scoville had slipped all the way to the ground and now sat there, breathing slow and heavy, almost as if he was drugged. Which he was, in a way. Christian only hoped he'd come around before Hubert attacked.

Ripping open a roll of gauze, Marc wrapped Christian's torn wrist, layer after layer, using almost the entire roll, before he ripped the material off and dropped the roll back into the box. Tearing the end in two, he tied off the bandage, then looked up to study Christian carefully. "Are you good to go?" he asked.

Christian nodded, flexing his hand and wrist as he yanked his T-shirt sleeve back down. "It takes more than this to knock me out of a fight."

"That's good, because if what I'm feeling is right—"

"It is," Christian confirmed.

"Then hell itself is about to descend on us."

Christian agreed completely with Marc's assessment. Hell was indeed about to descend on them, and all he had to fight it with was Marc and a blood-drunk Scoville. "I'll take Hubert," he told Marc. "You and Scoville—" He looked down at the sated vampire. "You ready to fight?" he asked.

The vampire sucked in a deep breath, shook all over like a wet dog, then climbed to his feet slowly, but with surprising grace. "Ready and willing, my lord," he said, his voice gravelly but strong. "Let's kill those fuckers."

"Fuckin' A," Marc agreed.

Christian smiled, despite the grim circumstances. "I don't know what Hubert's bringing to the fight, but I guarantee we'll be badly outnumbered. So we fight as a team, covering each other's backs. Once Hubert shows his face, I'll go after him. We have a history, and he'll want to settle it. I was supposed to be fighting *with* him, not against him. But no one checked with me first. I had no interest in gaining the South for *him* when I wanted it for myself. That didn't make him happy. So I think he'll want a one-on-one. That means I shouldn't have to worry about his other vampires coming at me while we're fighting, but stay alert in case I'm wrong."

Marc didn't look happy about the plan, but he nodded his agreement. Scoville's nod was more matter-of-fact, a warrior obeying orders. Christian was his sworn lord now. That two-minute ceremony was all they needed. Everything else was irrelevant.

"Do we have any guns?" Marc asked Scoville. "Those would help even the odds."

He grunted an affirmative, but said, "Guns aren't the problem. It's ammo. We used everything we had in fighting off Hubert's creatures. Have you seen those fuckers? They're vampires, but not like anything I've ever seen. They're like—"

"Zombies," Christian supplied, and Scoville nodded.

"That's exactly it. It's like they're alive, but not. Like they don't have a mind of their own."

"I don't think they do. I've seen Hubert do this before, though on a smaller scale. The poor souls he turned had no purpose other than to serve him."

"Fucking creepy is what it is. But they're effective. They swarm like insects, simply overrun you until you can't even move. We must have killed thirty or forty of them, injured more, but it didn't stop them. As long as they could crawl, they kept coming."

"But you killed some of them, and they're too new to dust when they die. Which means they carried away their dead," Christian observed thoughtfully. "Hubert didn't know you had survived, and he didn't want me to see the bodies. Maybe he feared I'd retreat right away to wait for reinforcements, and he doesn't want that. He wants me here, with no one but Marc to back me up."

"And me," Scoville reminded him.

"But you're supposed to be dead."

"I nearly was, and I'd prefer he didn't get another go at it. So let's talk ammo. We can probably salvage four mags, thirty rounds each. The weapons are MP5s. You know how to operate one?" he asked Marc.

"Of course," Marc said, his tone conveying his insult at the question. Marc had been in the military when Christian found him, and he remained a military man, through and through. Even though he was a vampire now, with power and strength he'd never had as a human, he still kept up on human weaponry of all kinds, big and small.

"Had to ask," Scoville said, by way of apology. "Let's see what we can round up." He turned for the deserted building and Marc followed.

Christian remained outside while the two of them disappeared into the outpost. He kept a mental eye on Marc. Scoville had sworn to him, but Christian didn't fully trust him yet. Not with Marc's life. Standing in the yard, he studied the battlefield, hands braced on his hips. The outpost was in a desolate area, with no other structures for miles on all sides. He could see the dim lights of a single structure in the distance, probably industrial from the number and location of the lights. Far beyond that were the much brighter lights of Laredo. It was unlikely anyone would come from there to investigate. He hoped not, because humans could only die in the coming battle, and this wasn't their fight.

Turning his head to look in the other direction, Christian saw nothing but endless black desert, dotted with clumps of cactus in the moonlight. There were plenty of low hills out there in the darkness, more than enough to hide an army. Christian opened his senses to a cautious probe, but he was immediately swamped with the life force of so many vampires that he couldn't count them all. And hiding behind them, or driving them forward, was Hubert. Christian knew Hubert well. He and Mathilde had been friends of a sort, and Christian had spent decades in Mathilde's court. He knew the taste of Hubert's power, the feel of his mind. And he had no doubt that it was Hubert he'd be facing tonight.

"Marc," he called, then waited until his lieutenant poked his head through the open doorway.

"Time's up. They're coming."

"Right," Marc acknowledged, and Christian could hear him calling to Scoville deep inside the building.

The helicopter had been idling beyond the yard, far enough away that their rotor wash didn't blow everything to pieces. Christian did a crouching run over there, climbed into the passenger compartment, and donned a headset to talk to the pilots. "You need to get out of here," he told them. "Do you have a place in Laredo where you can wait for us?"

The co-pilot nodded. "Yes, sir. How long?"

"An hour or two at most."

"We'll fuel up while we wait. You have our number?"

"I do." Christian climbed out of the chopper, and moved away, watching as it flew off toward Laredo and was soon out of sight. He heard footsteps behind him.

"That was our ride back," Marc observed.

Christian had trouble concentrating on what Marc was saying, his senses nearly overwhelmed by awareness of the vampire army now bearing down on them. He stared out into the darkness, unable to see them yet. But they were coming.

"They'll come back when we call," he told Marc absently, as they started walking back to the outpost. He glanced over, his gaze sharpening as he noted the HK MP5 that Marc now wore on a combat harness in front of him. Christian nodded his approval of the gun. "Get ready," he said. "They're coming."

He'd just reached the yard of the building when a flicker of movement caught his eye, and the first enemy vampire appeared in the near distance. "Hold your fire," he told Marc quietly. He didn't want anyone killing this vamp before he had a chance to scan it, to ferret out what Hubert had done, so he could figure out how to kill them.

The vampire was quickly followed by another, and then several more. But Christian kept his attention on that first outlier, digging deep into the creature's brain to determine what made him tick. He was Mexican, more indigenous than European in appearance, probably some poor farmer Hubert had captured and changed. The vampire's eyes glowed a dull red, but seemed focused on nothing. And while he moved well, it was slowly, as if he had difficulty getting his body to obey his brain.

But then, there wasn't much brain left, at least not if one only counted the functioning parts. Christian smashed easily through the vampire's natural shield, the bare minimum that every vampire was born with, and immediately saw what Hubert had done. It was the same here as in Europe. He'd turned all of these vampires, then starved them of blood, giving them only enough for their basic instincts to kick in. Since the most basic instinct of all was a vampire's link to his Sire, these creatures would do anything Hubert asked, without question or any sense of self-preservation. They would be merciless in their defense of him, and from what Scoville had said, they were vicious fighters.

Christian fired off a sharp jolt of power, and took down the vampire he'd been scanning. The vamp dropped to the ground in a boneless heap, but he didn't turn to dust. As Christian had surmised, they were far too new to dust upon death. The bodies would lie there until the sun rose. More incentive to make this short and brutal.

The vampire's abrupt death had no effect on the army behind him. They plowed on, stepping over, on, and around their former companion's body, as if he were no more than a rock in their way. A steady noise emanated from their throats, a high-pitched keening that seemed never to stop, as if they didn't need to breathe. Or maybe it was just that there were so many of them, he couldn't detect the break when the creatures drew breath.

"Now, my lord?" Marc asked, coming up to stand next to him.

"Now," Christian agreed, as Scoville took his place on the other side of Marc.

The night came alive with the sound of the two submachine guns. With ammunition so short, they didn't go to full auto, but their vampire-enhanced vision and reflexes made their single-shot rhythm sound every bit as fast as automatic fire. The two vampires swept their weapons from side to side, taking out one zombie vamp after another. But despite the carnage they were wreaking, none of the approaching vamps made any attempt to evade their fire. They didn't even slow down. They just kept coming.

Christian didn't try to count, but instinct told him there were at least a hundred of the zombie vampires still out there. He resisted the impulse to grab a gun, or even to drop a few of the oncoming zombies with his vampire abilities. He could sense Hubert out there behind his fighters, and didn't want to give the European lord any more data than necessary about his power. He figured Anthony had probably shared whatever he knew, but fortunately, not even Anthony knew everything that Christian was capable of.

When the main force finally reached them, however, Christian knew the time for caution was over. He stood side-by-side with Marc and Scoville, sending bolts of his power to take down the zombie fighters as they charged forward. A small contingent made a dash for it, trying to outflank Christian and his small team. But Christian caught their charge, and dropped them mid-stride. Despite his success, however, it seemed inevitable that they would be surrounded in relatively short order. There were so many more of the creatures than the hundred he'd estimated at the beginning of the assault. Their power levels were so low that they barely pinged against his vampire senses even now, when he could see them in the flesh. As a group, they were noticeable, but as individuals, they were barely there.

"We need to pull back," Marc yelled, dropping the mag from his MP5, checking to verify it was empty, then slapping it back in. "I'm out."

"Same here," Scoville called. He slung his weapon over his back, freeing his hands to fight.

"Back to the outpost." Christian had to shout to be heard over the unceasing and high-pitched growl of the enemy. "On my mark." He killed another two zombie vamps who tried to slip behind them and cut off their retreat, before shouting, "Now!"

The three of them ran back to the outpost and the horde followed. By the time they put their backs to the building, they were trapped. The only way out was through the bodies of their enemies. So be it.

The fight was brutal and bloody. The attacking vampires had no weapons but their bodies, and they used them without regard for survival, launching themselves into the air, fingers curled into claws, nascent fangs protruding through bloodied lips. With no ammo, Marc and Scoville fell back on their own vampiric powers. They weren't as strong as Christian, but they weren't lacking, either. Together, the three of them fought systematically, taking out vampire after vampire with controlled bursts of power. Christian knew that eventually the other two would run out of juice. Their strength would drain well before his did. He had the power to end it before that happened, to mow these pitiful creatures down with a single massive blow. It would kill most of them, and knock the rest senseless. Marc and Scoville could then deliver the *coups de grâce*. But while it was tempting to get it over with, he was wary of using up too much of his power in a fight against these weaklings. Not with Hubert still lurking out there somewhere.

Christian had every confidence he could defeat the French lord, but victory could not be taken for granted. Hubert was powerful and ruthless, and Christian would have to be at his best. Which was why he had to resist the temptation to end this part of the battle quickly.

One of Hubert's vamps suddenly came roaring through the swarm. Bigger than the others, his red eyes bore a gleam of intellect that the others lacked, and it seemed to drive him forward. He made straight for Marc, rolling beneath the bursts of destruction being generated by all three of them. He managed to tackle Marc around the legs and send him tumbling to the ground, where he wrapped gnarled fingers around his throat, and bore down. His face was contorted with hatred, fangs gleaming, and ropey muscles straining, as he tried to choke the life out of him.

Christian spun around, grabbed the vamp by his long, greasy hair, yanked him off Marc, and tossed him through the air. He landed on top of the horde who immediately began attacking him, biting and clawing, seeming not to understand that he was one of their own, knowing only that he'd come from the enemy. And all the while they kept up that weird keening growl.

"Marc?" Christian asked, his attention fixed on their enemy, killing any of them who ventured too close.

"I'm good," his lieutenant said, jumping gracefully back to his feet. His neck was bleeding where the vamp's fingernails had dug into the skin, and, at any other time, Christian would have pulled him out of the fight to treat those wounds, which were surely filthy. But not tonight. It was only the three of them, and everyone had to keep fighting. But even with all of them giving their best, Christian knew they couldn't stand against these creatures for the rest of the night. Exhaustion would take its toll, and he was wasting his power on these pathetic vampires when no matter how many he took down, more would come to fill the gap.

He had to end this grueling stand-off. He had to find Hubert and kill him.

It was a struggle to search for Hubert, while fending off the horde, but he managed. He'd no sooner begun, however, than he heard the low buzz of a helicopter rotor, growing louder by the second. He had the brief thought that their pilot must have come back to evacuate them, but dismissed that quickly. The pilot was human. He'd have no idea what was happening here. And if he did, he'd take one look at Hubert's zombie army, and get the hell out of there.

He had the even more unlikely thought that the approaching copter was Anthony sending help. But that was such a ridiculous idea that it was there and gone before he could draw the breath to laugh about it.

The zombie vamps didn't seem to care either way. If they noticed the helicopter, they didn't react to it. Christian had nothing but his peripheral vision to spare for the new arrival, and it showed him a single, large male jumping from the helicopter when it was still well above the ground, which meant the jumper was a vampire. But friend or foe?

"What the fuck?" Christian muttered. Like he needed anything to make this night worse.

But the vampire who burst through the horde, sword in hand, slicing left and right as he strove to join them, was definitely a friend. Cibor hacked a path to Christian's side, put the building at his back, and wordlessly joined their defense, wielding his sword and his power with deadly accuracy. He fought with a confidence and grace that were the product of his history. He'd been born in a time when men fought with swords, and he'd wielded a blade from the day his hands were big enough to hold one.

"Jaclyn sends her regards," Cibor said finally, not even glancing aside as he cleared a cluster of vampires, slicing them open, then stabbing them in the heart to be sure they were truly dead. It was much easier to know such things when your enemy simply dusted upon death. With these zombies, you had to make sure.

Christian raised his eyebrows in surprise. He hadn't expected Jaclyn's aid, not with her close association to Raphael. But he was happy to have it. "I'll thank her personally when this is over," he said.

"You think you'll survive this?" Cibor asked, as he lifted his chin to indicate the seemingly endless army of zombie vamps.

"I know I will," Christian assured him.

Cibor tossed his head back and laughed. "I gotta say, Duvall. You've got balls. Speaking of which—" He paused to take out three vampires who were attempting to take advantage of what they thought was his distraction, clearing enough space that he could get more than a few words out. "Listen,

Natalie found something in Anthony's files. Vincent isn't coming to this party. Anthony sent him on a wild goose chase in the opposite direction." He grunted as a vampire came flying out of the pack, vaulting over his fellow zombies in his eagerness to die. Christian raised his power to destroy the vamp, but Cibor lifted his sword first. He impaled the vamp through the chest, then tossed the body off his blade and back into the fray with a flick of his wrist.

As if that was a signal of some sort, the zombie vampires abruptly pulled back a few yards. They crouched low and hunched together, their red eyes staring straight ahead, never blinking, never veering. Hands were curled into claws, and their fangs dripped saliva along with their own blood, from where they'd sliced up their lips. These were very new vampires, and it made Christian furious that Hubert was using them this way.

"Creepy bastards," Cibor muttered, whipping his sword through the air to strip the blood off. "What the hell are they doing?"

Christian had a pretty good idea, but first.... "Is Natalie okay?" he asked.

Cibor nodded. "Completely safe. Jaclyn's with her."

Relief washed over Christian, giving him a boost of energy. His worry for her had been a distraction he couldn't afford. Knowing she was okay was like getting a shot of power that he badly needed. He scanned the crouching vampires.

"Time to end this," he said grimly. Tightening his shield around him, drawing on all of his power, he blasted a message into the ether. *"Hubert!"*

His answer came almost instantly. The zombie vamps parted like the biblical Red Sea, murmuring something rhythmic, their eyes lifted to the upper end of the opening pathway. Christian listened carefully, and realized the vamps were chanting Hubert's name over and over again. Creepy didn't come close to describing this scene.

The last of the vamps cleared the pathway, and Hubert was suddenly visible at the top of a small hill, standing there soaking up the worship of his admirers. A brilliant smile crossed his face when he swung his gaze over and found Christian watching him.

"Christian Duvall," Hubert said. "What a delightful surprise. I'd expected Anthony. This is his territory, after all."

"Bullshit. You know exactly where Anthony is," Christian replied. "He's back home safe and sound while you kill his enemies for him."

Hubert shrugged. "Anthony is a weakling. But then . . . we can't all be me," he said, and laughed at his own jest. He sobered abruptly. "You should have sided with me when you had the chance, Duvall. I would have given you whatever territory you wanted."

Christian chuckled. "Once you're gone, the entire South will be mine, old man. I don't like to share."

"You think you can take me? You're an infant, compared to me."

"I'm old enough."

"As you wish," Hubert said casually, then flung his arm out, sending a huge blast of power bowling down the pathway.

Christian yelled a warning and shoved Marc and Cibor aside, as his own shields hardened in defense. The strike hit him like a thousand pound medicine ball, crashing against his shields, but not breaking them.

Christian matched Hubert's smug smile as he revealed the full force of his vampire nature for the first time that night. Power swelled inside him, hardening his shields, screaming down his nerves, strengthening his muscles, until he felt ten feet tall and bursting with energy and confidence. He roared his defiance and slapped aside Hubert's attack, sending a return volley sizzling up the open pathway in a stream of blue fire. Zombie vamps screamed as they were caught in the blast, charred in an instant. The fireball crashed into Hubert who was standing there like a king, the dying screams of his minions washing over him while he ignored them. He staggered under the assault, then straightened with a howl of rage. Furious eyes shot copper flames, huge fangs glared white in a snarling grimace. He strode closer, every foot pounding into the soft ground, arms reaching out, firing shot after shot of pure power, each one stronger than the last, each one hitting Christian in a different place in a bid to break his shields.

Christian turned to Marc and the others. "Get away," he said. "This is between the two of us."

"I won't leave you," Marc growled furiously.

"He'll use you," Christian insisted. "He'll kill you just to weaken me."

"Fuck," Marc swore, then leaned in to say grimly, "Draw on me for power, Christian. Use whatever you need."

"It won't come to that," Christian assured him. "But I'll use you if I need to," he continued before Marc could protest. "Now leave this battle to me."

Marc's jaw tightened, but he nodded, and joined Cibor in grabbing Scoville, who was sagging badly. They moved off into the dark next to the outpost, far enough away to avoid getting caught in the back splatter, but close enough to see what was going on. Christian could feel them there, still too close. But he knew Marc would never leave altogether.

"It's sweet how you care for your child and the others," Hubert sneered. "You protect them now, but do you think I won't kill them once you're dead?"

Christian didn't bother to answer the taunt. "Enough talk, Hubert. This has been building since the day we met. Let's finish it."

Hubert's vampires shifted en masse, shuffling in a wave to cluster behind him, growling their weird noise, straining forward with fangs dripping as if hungry for their enemy's blood.

Tired of the posturing, Christian paced forward deliberately to close the distance between them. He knew Hubert, knew that he liked to fight from a distance, with power lobbed like baseballs, slamming into his enemy and breaking his shields, until he launched the fatal blow. But Christian wasn't going to let him get away with that. He was going to force the older vampire out of his comfort zone and into his.

Calling on the discipline of his Krav Maga training, Christian drew his power into a solid core deep inside his chest. Nothing was wasted, nothing was random. Even his shields were pulled in close to his body, until they were a hard shell of defiance. Raising his arms before him, hands as stiff as blades, he pushed deliberately into Hubert's space until their shields touched, buzzing like a flight of angry bees as they strained against one another. It hurt like hell. But Christian ignored the pain, and shoved even harder until he was close enough to see fear beneath the rage in Hubert's eyes.

Hubert fought back, slamming a fist into Christian's ribs. But this was not the fighting style he was accustomed to, and the blow lacked power. He shrieked in rage, and several of his minions collapsed as the vampire lord sucked away their life force to power his own.

But while Hubert was focused on killing others to recharge his strength, Christian was focused on killing Hubert. Stiffening his fingers into a weapon, and putting all of his considerable strength behind it, he slammed it through Hubert's shields and into his neck, ripping through skin and tendon and shredding his veins.

All around them the zombie vamps keened as Hubert staggered, eyes wide with shock as blood poured from his neck. Teeth bared, he came after Christian, taking advantage of their closeness, fingers spitting power as he plowed a fist into Christian's gut, trying to dig through and reach for his heart.

Christian went to his knees, groaning under the assault. Every tear to his flesh, every rip in his organs was agonizing. But this was it; this was his moment. If he failed now, he would die, and Marc would die with him. He thought of Natalie, of what Anthony might do to her when he was gone, of how he would use her family to get what he wanted from her.

Never.

Forcing himself to his feet, dragging his arms upward, and drawing from Marc who had left himself wide open as a well of strength, Christian clapped both hands over Hubert's ears, putting enough power behind it to rattle his brain. Hubert's shields buckled under the concussive force, and he screamed in pain. He fell back, blood streaming from his ears and neck, hatred spilling from his eyes. He gathered his power once more, and the minions closest to him collapsed, sucked dry to feed their master. Hubert aimed a smug smile at Christian.

"You have your one," he taunted, his face a gruesome visage above the bloody ruin of his neck. "But I have many."

Christian staggered backward as Stefano Barranza sprang up from his concealment amidst the zombie vamps. His sword was a blur of movement, and Christian was forced to defend himself, forming a sword of his own, energy against steel. He girded himself for a fight, knowing the danger of turning his attention away from Hubert. But before Barranza could attack, Marc was there. Lobbing fireballs at Barranza from the side, he forced the other vampire to defend himself or die. Marc's pain speared through Christian when Barranza succeeded in closing the distance, aiming that deadly blade at Marc's belly, but he danced away easily, and Cibor stepped in, matching Barranza blade for blade.

A tingling awareness spun Christian around a moment too late. Taking advantage of Christian's preoccupation, Hubert renewed his attack. Fed by his remaining zombie vamps, who were dying around him in waves, he gathered all of his remaining strength, and threw it at Christian in a single, boulder-sized ball of power.

Christian groaned when it crashed into his shields. That fucking *hurt!* He stumbled to one side, and nearly went down, cursing himself the whole time for getting sidetracked, grateful that his shields had managed to protect him. No more distractions. Marc and Cibor could more than hold their own against Barranza. His job was to get rid of Hubert. The European was the key to everything.

Hubert had to die.

Christian stared at his enemy through shuttered eyelids, his lips stretched into a grim smile as he gathered his power and considered his options. His thoughts churned over everything he'd learned in the last few minutes, everything he'd known about Hubert before this clusterfuck got started. Foremost was the realization that Hubert's shields were weaker than they should be, much weaker than he'd expected. He shouldn't have been able to get through them with that neck strike early on in the fight. He knew he could use that, if he could only think how. And he had to think quickly. As powerful as he was, his strength wasn't endless. He was still hurting from Hubert's successful attacks, and his gut felt like it had been chewed up and shoved back into his skin.

An idea blinked to life. He needed to turn the tables on Hubert, to distract him just long enough for his plan to work. Because if he failed, they would all die.

He started forward grimly, closing the space between them once again, intent on taking away the security of distance. Hubert shouted his defiance and charged ahead, his teeth bared in confidence as he brandished a sword of pure, sparkling energy before him. Howling in victory, he stabbed Christian repeatedly, easily penetrating his shields and piercing his already damaged gut.

Christian staggered, grunting in pain. He'd counted on Hubert's response and anticipated the strike, but not the agony. Had he thought the earlier attack had hurt? That was nothing compared to this. Forcing himself to concentrate, he gathered his remaining strength for one final blow, putting everything he had left into it. Curling his right hand into a fist, he crashed through Hubert's shields and struck his chest right over his heart with the full force of his power. The blow was hard enough to shatter ribs, hard enough to stop Hubert's heart for a few precious seconds.

Hubert's eyes flashed wide and he fell to his knees, gasping for air. No heart pumping meant no blood flowing, and no vampire symbiote racing through his body. It sent his entire system into chaos for a brief moment, giving Christian just enough time to utilize the unique power that was his alone, the power granted him on the night he became vampire. He wrapped his fingers around Hubert's throat and squeezed, draining his power along with his life, drinking it up to bolster his own flagging strength. The infusion of power bumped Christian's strength to unheard-of levels. It wouldn't last forever, but it was his for now. And more importantly, it was no longer Hubert's.

Hubert stared, life fading from his eyes as he gazed up at Christian. "What did you do?" he whispered. And then he smiled, almost in admiration. "Mathilde never told me."

"Mathilde never knew," Christian said flatly. He opened his fingers and released the vampire lord's neck as his body became nothing more than dust mixing with the corpses of his army.

Christian spun back just in time to see Marc slice Barranza's neck with his own blade, then shift his grip, and stab him in the heart. Marc sagged to one knee, and Christian started for him, but stopped when the fine hairs on the back of his neck all came to sudden attention.

"What the hell was that?" demanded an unfamiliar voice.

Houston, TX

NATALIE HADN'T known what else to do, so she'd sat on the bed in her room and worked, digging into Anthony's files, reading them one by one. Despite her efforts, however, she hadn't found anything as condemning as the fax Anthony had sent to Vincent. But what she *did* find didn't paint a lovely picture of Anthony. He'd been working with an outside accountant, looking for ways to steal money from the territorial accounts without her noticing. Unsuccessfully, of course. She *did* know her job. But it made her wonder if that was the real reason for his obsession with her. Maybe he'd thought to seduce her into helping him abscond with funds.

The idea made her shudder in disgust.

Needing something to cleanse her mind, she got up and walked over to the open bedroom door, intent on going to the kitchen for a snack. She was about to step into the hallway, when the front doorbell rang.

Natalie stilled, somewhat alarmed at the unexpected sound. She stepped quietly back into the bedroom, then spun around and hurried over to her bed where she'd been working. Slapping her laptop shut, she stared around the bedroom looking for a hiding place. Maybe she was being paranoid, but too many crazy things had been happening lately, and a little paranoia might be a good thing. Under the mattress was too obvious, as were the drawers. Peering behind the elaborate headboard, she saw there was a slight ledge where the headboard met the bed frame, and there was just enough space between the headboard and the wall that it might work. She was on her knees on the bed, shoving the laptop down into the narrow space, when she heard Jaclyn's heels on the wooden floor heading for the front door.

With the laptop reasonably secure, she tiptoed over and pulled the bedroom door nearly closed, leaving it open just enough for her to peek down the hall. She watched as Jaclyn checked out their visitor through the peephole, then entered the code—which Natalie had given her for safety reasons—and opened the door.

Everything happened so fast after that that Natalie had trouble ordering the events in her head. Jaclyn opened the door, greeted someone with a friendly, "What are you doing here?" And then three shots sounded, and Jaclyn stumbled backward, blood blooming on the back of her designer sweater.

Natalie managed to stifle her gasp. She ducked back into the room and pushed the door nearly closed, just as three vampires rushed into the house. She had to get out of there. Christian had told her the shutters could be opened from inside once the code was entered. She could go out the window, and run until she found a safe place to hide and call Christian. She slid her shoes on, and grabbed her jacket and purse. Acting on impulse, she ripped open the box with the gun that Cynthia Leighton had given her and shoved the gun and a box of ammo into her purse, then slid the box under the bed. She wished she had her cell phone, but it was sitting on the charger in the kitchen. She got the window open and had just cranked the shutter release when the door to her bedroom was pushed open so hard it hit the wall with a loud crack. Natalie spun around, her back pressed to the unopened shutter.

"Going somewhere, little human?" the vampire asked. He was huge, bulked out with muscle, his eyes cold and mocking. She recognized him vaguely as one of Anthony's security people. But there were so many vampires around Anthony, she'd never paid attention to them, unless they came into the office.

"What do you want?" she demanded, trying to be tough. After all, he had no right to be here, but she did.

He grinned, his fangs on full display. "You," he said simply.

She opened her mouth to tell him to go to hell, but he was across the room with his big fingers gripping her arm before she could get the first word out.

"What are you doing?" She struggled, knowing it was pointless. She had to try.

"I'm taking you back where you belong," he growled. "Your little whoring vacation is over. You belong to Lord Anthony."

Natalie blushed hotly at his description, even though he was wrong. She didn't belong to anyone, and she sure as hell wasn't a whore. But at least she understood what was happening now. Anthony had arranged for Christian to face Hubert alone down in Laredo, hoping and planning for him to die there. And as long as he was gone, Anthony figured he might as well swoop in and claim Natalie, so she could play her part in his ridiculous idea of their future together. He might be a powerful vampire, but he was losing his mind if he thought she would ever agree to live with him. No matter how much he tried to mess with her brain.

As for the gorilla currently squeezing her arm tightly enough to leave bruises, she knew the Borg from Star Trek had been right. Resistance was futile. So she didn't try. Her time would come, and she would be ready for it, but that time wasn't now. Slinging her purse over her shoulder, she gripped the strap tightly, and let him drag her out the door.

"I've got her," he said, loudly enough that the other two vamps came rushing back from wherever they'd been searching in the big house.

Natalie almost panicked when she thought about the basement, and about Alon sleeping down there, totally helpless. But then a female vamp came running down the hall and said, "Good thing she wasn't in the basement. He's got a fucking vault down there."

"Didn't do him any good now, did it?" her captor sneered. He pulled her to the front door, and she got her first good look at Jaclyn.

"Jaclyn," she whispered and tugged at the grip on her arm, wanting to check the female vamp. She'd been shot, but vampires were tough, and Jaclyn was a very strong vampire.

"She'll live," her captor growled. "Don't want Raphael involved in this."

Natalie was pretty sure that just *shooting* Jaclyn would be enough for Raphael to *get involved*. But it wasn't only Raphael that they needed to be concerned about. Jaclyn had bodyguards, including her lover, Cibor. And they wouldn't take kindly to her being hurt.

"Let's go." He dragged her out the door, not bothering to close it behind him. Natalie thought about Jaclyn lying there vulnerable, and sent a private prayer to whichever god protected vampires that she would be safe.

Laredo, TX

CHRISTIAN HEARD the power behind the unfamiliar voice, and braced for one more battle. God, he was tired. He turned to face his enemy . . . and stared. Three SUVs idled in the shadows beyond the yard. All of the doors stood open, and vampire fighters waited in readiness before them. He'd been so engrossed in his fight with Hubert, and then his worry over Marc, that he hadn't heard their arrival, hadn't even sensed their presence. He was aware of Marc and Cibor rising to stand at his back, ready to face the newcomers, whoever they were. The tension was thick enough to ripple the air between the two groups, but no one moved.

Christian studied each vampire in turn, noting their readiness, their discipline as they waited for orders. Their obvious leader was the one who'd spoken. He noted the vamp's confident posture and watchful eyes, and the depth of his power despite efforts to conceal it. And that quickly, he knew. This was Vincent, Lord of Mexico.

He bit back a sigh. What the fuck? Wasn't it enough that he'd had to fight an army of creepy zombie vamps, deal with Barranza's sneak attack on Marc, and finally kill that asshole Hubert to end it all? Now he had to face down Vincent? The boost gained from Hubert's power was the only thing keeping him on his feet right now. And *that* was actually the biggest problem. The talent that had let him drain Hubert was the "what the hell" that Vincent was asking about. No one knew about Christian's talent, except Marc. He sure as hell hadn't confided in Mathilde, because she'd have killed him in his sleep if she knew. It was vampirism taken to a deep, dark level, the ability to drink the power of other vampires, the way every vampire drank human blood.

Christian eyed Vincent carefully, not sure yet if he was friend or foe. "That was me defending my future territory," he said bluntly, addressing Vincent's question at face value. And then a thought occurred to him. "It also made me Lord of Lyon in France, if I wanted the territory, which I don't."

Vincent stared back at him, blinking a few times, then he grinned. "Vincent Kuxim," he said, taking a step closer, and holding out a hand. "I'm sorry we couldn't get here sooner."

Christian regarded the vampire lord, considering. He didn't know Vincent other than their brief phone conversation, but he knew from Natalie's discovery that Anthony had sent him on a false trail to make sure Christian faced Hubert alone. They'd both been used by Anthony and Hubert, and that made them allies of a sort. And Christian could use allies. Especially the kind who shared a border with what would soon be his new territory.

He met Vincent halfway and gripped his hand. "Christian Duvall," he said. "That was Hubert, by the way," he said, gesturing in the direction of Hubert's pile of dust.

"I guessed as much. Anthony had us chasing him all the way down near Cancun. I don't know who the sacrificial lamb was that they sent in his place, but he never had a chance."

"That seems to be a theme with Anthony and his friends," Christian said calmly. He was still waiting for Vincent to demand answers about what he'd seen him do to Hubert, but, surprisingly, he didn't seem to care anymore. That might change once he reported to Raphael, as Christian had no doubt that he would. But that worry was for the future. Right now, he had more important things to think about, like getting Marc away from here, and killing that fucker Anthony.

"My apologies, Lord Vincent," he said politely. "But time is short, and Anthony is still at large." A helicopter sounded in the distance, and Christian glanced back at Cibor, who nodded. He'd called in their transport. "That will be my pilot. We should talk another time. Once the dust settles."

Vincent laughed. "Is that any way to talk about Anthony?" he asked cheerfully, but then, his mood changed in an instant. "Don't worry. If you don't kill the asshole, I will. No one fucks with me like that."

Christian nodded. "Very kind, but I doubt your services will be necessary."

As quickly as Vincent's mood had changed before, it shifted again as an attractive, dark-haired woman walked up to him, and he slung an arm around her shoulders. "My fiancée, Lana," he said. "*Querida*, this is Christian Duvall, our new neighbor." He shifted his attention to Christian again. "You should come to our wedding. Bring your woman, if you have one. I'll send you an invite."

Christian blinked, not knowing what to say. First, vampire lords did not get married, they mated. And secondly, he barely knew the couple. But what the hell?

"I look forward to it," he said, then shook hands with Vincent once again, before the Mexican vampire lord signaled his people, and they all climbed back into the waiting SUVs.

Christian waited until the three big vehicles had disappeared back into Mexico, then glanced over at Marc who was standing next to him, one arm banded protectively over his gut. Christian pulled him into an embrace, using the contact to share some of Hubert's power and speed his healing.

Marc strengthened almost at once. Christian drew back, but kept a hand on his shoulder. "He invited us to his wedding," he said, still puzzled by the encounter.

"I heard. You going to go?"

Christian thought about it. "I think I will. I'll take Natalie, and you, too."

"Should be interesting." Marc turned as the helicopter settled to the ground. "Are we going after Anthony tonight?"

"Hell, yes. I need to find whatever hole that bastard crawled into, and then I need to kill him. By the time the next sun rises, I'll be Lord of the South."

Cibor helped load the badly injured Scoville into the helicopter, then climbed in after him. Another shot of Christian's blood would have helped him heal, but he was going to have to do it the old-fashioned way this time. Christian had no blood to spare. A gnawing certainty was telling him that this battle wasn't over yet. Something else had happened. Something they hadn't anticipated.

He glanced over and saw Cibor on the phone. It was nearly impossible to have a conversation with the helicopter noise, but maybe he was texting, or checking messages. Which reminded him . . . he pulled out his own phone, and saw there were multiple calls from Natalie. He listened to the most recent one, and heard her warning him about Anthony, and that Vincent wouldn't be coming. He experienced an unexpected warmth, pride for what she'd accomplished with her stolen files. Without her discovery, Cibor wouldn't have shown up at the critical moment, and his presence had made a huge difference. Plus, Christian's encounter with Vincent might have turned out very differently, if he hadn't already known that Anthony had misdirected him.

Speaking of Cibor, however, he noticed the vamp scowling at his cell phone as if he was thinking about chucking it out the door. Clicking on the comm channel, he gestured to get Cibor's attention, and pointed at his headset. Cibor reached up and clicked his on.

"Something wrong?"

"I don't know," Cibor said, obviously troubled. "I have a really bad feeling, and I can't reach Jaclyn."

"Bad cell connection?" Christian asked, hating the coincidence, and sensing his own *bad feeling* growing ominously.

"No. It goes right to her voicemail. And she never does that with me."

"Could she be in a meeting?"

Cibor shook his head. "She was going to stay at the house with Natalie."

At the mention of Natalie's name, Christian's fear solidified into knowledge. Something was wrong. He switched over to the pilot's channel and asked him to speed it up. Whatever the cost, he'd pay it. He needed to get back to Houston.

Houston, TX

NATALIE DIDN'T protest all the way back to Anthony's estate. She was a little surprised that was where they took her, but apparently Anthony was so confident in his scheme to kill Christian that he thought the house was safe for him again.

The vamps dragged her out of the Suburban, although *dragged* was probably too harsh a word. They were being very careful, for all that she was a prisoner. Probably more of Anthony's orders. He had this image of her as a delicate flower who would bruise if you touched her too hard, and she wasn't about to enlighten him.

The only real surprise was when they herded her to the stairs down to the basement, instead of up to the office. She'd never been down here. At least, not to the part that was occupied. Like everyone else, she'd seen the half of the basement that was empty—big spaces and white walls. Not much to see.

But that wasn't where her captors were taking her. They turned right at the bottom of the stairs, passing through a set of doors that looked like normal heavy wood. But if you looked closely—as Natalie did because she was thinking of her escape—you could see the panels had a thick metal core. They were open now, but would probably close before sunrise just like Christian's shutters. Natalie didn't plan on being here that long.

A short walk, and they hit a branching. To the left was a long hallway with multiple rooms on both sides. But they went right, down a short passage with a single room at the end. Natalie guessed this led to Anthony's private quarters. At least she hoped so, because it would be much easier to break out of that than a prison cell. She could deal with a wooden door, but not a set of iron bars. Lock picking was not something they'd covered in her finance classes.

One of her guards went ahead of her, and it was obvious from the moment she stepped inside that she'd been right—these were definitely

Anthony's quarters. The room was decorated much the way his office had been, except for the self-congratulatory photos hanging on the walls. The style was old New Orleans, with rich fabrics and dark woods, and the furniture looked like it might be antique.

Her guards didn't linger, but kept her moving through the outer room, pulling her into a small office that had only a desk and two chairs. An oil painting of the New Orleans harbor circa mid-1800s hung on the wall above the desk, and bookshelves lined the rest. Her guards shoved her down into one of the chairs and left her there, closing and locking the door with an obnoxiously loud click when they left.

Natalie stuck her tongue out at the door, then waited a few minutes and tiptoed over to listen. Vampires were stealthy, so she didn't expect to hear their footsteps, but even vampires had conversations, and their clothes made noise like everyone else's when they shifted around. She listened intently, with her ear to the nonexistent crack between the doors, but she didn't hear anything. What troubled her, though, was that she hadn't heard the outer door close. That could mean all kinds of things, from her guards leaving it open, to them sitting right outside, or simply a really quiet latch.

She wished she knew which one it was, but it didn't really matter. Because she had a gun, and she knew how to use it.

Going over to the desk, she set her purse down carefully, not wanting the heavy gun to make a sound, just in case. With a furtive glance at the door, she pulled the Glock pistol out, released the magazine as quietly as she could, then checked the weapon over. She would have felt better if she'd had a chance to take it to the gun range before putting her life on the line, but it seemed in good order. And from everything she'd heard about Cynthia Leighton, she doubted the woman would send her anything but a fully functional weapon. She loaded the mag with the Hydra-Shok ammo and slapped it back in, masking the slight noise with a loud cough.

With the gun in hand, she went over to the door and examined the lock. Her granddaddy had complained a long time ago about all those movies that showed people shooting out locks. He said any decent lock would be a lot tougher to destroy, while at the same time grumbling that most locks were shit. But Natalie could still hear the loud click of this particular lock engaging, and so she bent over to see exactly what she was dealing with.

It was a deadbolt, and looked almost too heavy for the door. She'd checked as best she could when they'd hustled her in here, and the door had appeared to be an ordinary inside door, even lighter than the one in the outer room. The lock, on the other hand, was pretty damn serious. But that was okay, because Leighton's Hydra-Shok ammo was serious, too. She might not be able to shoot out that lock, but then, she didn't have to. She could just blow the door to pieces and climb through. It would make a lot of noise, but that's what the rest of her mag was for. She'd never shot a person before, but that didn't mean she wouldn't. Especially if that person had kidnapped her and was now holding her against her will.

She stiffened to attention when she heard voices outside. They drew closer, and she recognized one of them as Anthony's. Her fingers tightened on the gun. She could shoot him when he walked through the door. But what about his guards? She wasn't exactly Rambo, and these were vampires. She doubted she could shoot fast enough to hit more than one of them, even if that one was Anthony. On the other hand, she was really worried about Anthony's immediate plans for her. If he tried to bite her as some sort of claiming ritual . . . Just the thought made her sick to her stomach.

She shoved the gun into her purse just in time, as the door opened and Anthony walked into the room.

"Natalie, darling," he said, taking her hands in his, raking her over from head to toe. He frowned as he took in the artfully faded and torn jeans, her Nikes, and slouchy sweater. "Not your usual mode of dress, my dear. But we can buy you something more appropriate once we're home."

Natalie bit her tongue to keep from telling him what he could do with his "usual mode" comment. But then the full meaning of what he'd said penetrated.

"Home?" she asked. What did he mean by home? Where was he taking her?

"New Orleans, of course. We'll be leaving within the hour." He chuckled at Natalie's puzzled expression, and said, "I'm sure this is all very confusing for you. It's certainly not what I planned, but events have overtaken us, and we must move quickly."

"Events?" she repeated. "What sort of events?"

"I'm sorry to tell you this, darling," he said solemnly. "But Christian Duvall is dead. He fought bravely, but his opponent was much older and more powerful, and he never had a chance."

"Dead?" Grief swelled, crushing her heart and lungs, until she could barely breathe. But even as she swayed under the pain of it, part of her doubted Anthony's words. She and Christian had a connection, didn't they? They weren't mated or anything, but he was a powerful vampire, and he'd taken her blood more than once. She'd even taken a little of his, too, just a few hours ago, when she'd bit his shoulder. But even more than that, she *loved* him. Her thoughts screeched to a halt as she realized it was true. She loved him. Which made her even more certain that Anthony was lying. But she couldn't stop the tears that welled up, and didn't even try. They rolled down her cheeks, and she couldn't find the will to wipe them away.

"I know you cared for him. You're young and innocent, and he had that French charm, but trust me, darling Natalie, you'll forget him once we start our life together."

Natalie froze. She could feel Anthony's mind pushing at her again, trying to persuade her to his way of thinking. Or, more likely, to take away her will and force her do what he wanted. The bastard. Well, too bad for him. She knew what it felt like now, and Anthony held no dominion over her. Christian was the only vampire in her heart *and* her mind.

A thought suddenly occurred to her. If Christian was still in her mind, if their connection was still protecting her from Anthony's sleazy manipulation, then he had to be alive. Either Anthony was lying, or he didn't know the truth of what had happened down in Laredo. Either way, her best bet was to pretend to go along for now. Let Anthony think she was his . . . whatever the hell he thought of her as. Slave? Minion? Lover? She shuddered inwardly at the very idea, but she had to convince him she'd been whammied. She dug up an engaging smile and plastered it on her face as she listened to his crazy ass plans.

"The house is ready, with all the necessary upgrades for our safety. I've even spoken to your parents, and they've given their blessing. You'll be immortal, my darling, just as I am. We'll have several lifetimes together."

Good Lord. She barely managed to keep her reaction from showing. He'd talked to her parents? What the hell? Was he stuck in the fourteenth century? But it didn't matter, because she knew he was lying now. Her father would *never* have given his blessing to a relationship with Anthony. He'd have been on the phone five seconds after Anthony left, yelling at her to get her ass home so he could set her straight.

"I know this has been an emotional night for you, and I wish I could give you more time. But you can rest on the way, and you'll feel better once we reach New Orleans. Now, relax as much as you can, and I'll be back to escort you to the plane very soon." He pulled her into a tight embrace, and she had to force herself not to shove him away. "We're going to be so happy." He said it with so much emotion, that she was convinced he believed it. Yikes.

It was almost painful to maintain her fake smile, as she watched him hurry out of the room, his guards in tow. The door closed, and she heard the click of the lock. She blew out a relieved breath, massaging her jaw, which was stiff from that stupid smile. She walked over and tested the knob. Definitely locked. Apparently, their impending connubial bliss didn't stop him from holding her prisoner. And what was the big hurry in leaving for New Orleans tonight? Could it be that someone was on his way back here? Someone like Christian?

She heard the outer door close this time, and the noise snapped her out of her thoughts. Who cared about why Anthony was going to New

Orleans? The only thing that mattered was that he believed he was taking her with him, and that wasn't going to happen. She was going to be long gone before he came back.

The possibility that Christian might actually be dead briefly threatened to derail her new determination, but she fought it back. If Anthony was lying about one thing, he was probably lying about it all. But she needed to get out of there to uncover the truth.

THE FLIGHT BACK to Houston seemed to take days rather than hours. Christian checked his cell phone obsessively, calling Natalie far too many times, and never getting her. By the time the chopper reached his neighborhood, he was standing in the open hatch staring down as if he could see what was happening by force of will alone.

The pilot headed for the high school athletic field, but Christian tapped his shoulder. "Drop us at the house, we'll jump."

The man swiveled to give him a disbelieving look, then shrugged. He'd probably figured out by now that his passengers weren't exactly your run-of-the-mill humans. If they wanted to jump from a helicopter, that was their business.

"I can't hover any lower than twenty-five, thirty feet in that neighborhood," he warned Christian. "There's a rope back there if you want to rappel down."

Christian nodded. One rope for the four of them would take too long, but maybe Scoville would need to use it. He was still far from full strength.

Having heard the conversation, Marc stood and dug around behind the seats. Finding the rope, he looped it through a D-ring tie-down on the floor of the chopper, then knotted it securely. Scoville stared at the rope unhappily, but gave a reluctant nod. He probably hated being the weak link, but he wasn't stubborn enough to break a few more bones trying to prove something that didn't need proving.

Christian's house came into view, and it didn't look good. Every light was on and the front door was wide open. As the pilot maneuvered into place, Christian noticed that one of the bedroom shutters was also cracked open, which meant someone had gotten out that way. Or at least tried to.

Fear settled in his gut. What the hell had happened? He looked over at Cibor, whose face reflected the same emotion. His lover was down there, a woman he'd been with for decades, if not centuries.

"This is the best I can do," the pilot said over their headsets.

Christian leaned out the open door and nodded. "This will do." He ripped off the headset, and leapt. Cibor was right behind him, then Marc, and finally Scoville slithered down the rope.

The minute his feet hit the ground, Christian was running, his senses wide open, scanning the house for signs of life. He found only one, faint but there. A vampire.

Where the fuck was Natalie?

"One vampire," he snapped as Cibor raced up beside him. "Badly injured."

Cibor growled and shoved into the house ahead of Christian, falling to his knees at what he found. Jaclyn lay facedown on the floor, blood staining her sweater and pooling around her from a wound they couldn't see. Her head was turned to one side, her pale face bruised, her eyes closed.

"Jaclyn, *moje serce*," he cried, lifting her delicate frame into his arms.

Christian didn't know much Polish, but he knew that one. "My heart," he'd called her, and the agony infused into those two words told Christian more than anything he'd learned from Natalie about the love shared between these two vampires.

"Let me help her," he said gently, going to his knees in front of the couple. There was no point in searching the house for Natalie. She wasn't here. And he wasn't prepared to find her body, so he didn't look.

Cibor crushed Jaclyn closer to his chest, with a hostile look. Christian understood the vampire's dilemma. His instincts were telling him to defend her, but reason was telling him Christian could be trusted, and that he could help her. Cibor just had to get past the fierce possessiveness that was riding him hard right now.

Christian waited patiently, meeting Cibor's gaze, gently urging the other vampire to *think*.

"Let him do it," a weak voice said, and both vampires dipped their heads to stare at Jaclyn. Her lips parted in a bloody grimace. "My body's trying to fix itself, but I've lost too much blood."

Christian snapped his gaze back to Cibor. Jaclyn might want his help, but he still had to get past her lover.

The big Polish vampire finally nodded, but he didn't release his grip on Jaclyn.

"She needs to drink, Cibor," Christian said matter-of-factly. He wasn't a lord yet, but he had far more power than Cibor did, which meant his blood was more powerful, too. He shoved the long sleeve of his shirt up to his elbow, then bent his head to rip open a vein. Blood welled instantly. Cibor's nostrils flared, as Jaclyn turned her head, instinctively seeking the flowing bounty. She growled, and Cibor finally loosened his hold just enough for her to roll in Christian's direction.

Christian didn't wait. Not wanting to push Cibor's protective instincts past the limit, he scooted only close enough to extend his arm, and place his wrist over Jaclyn's mouth. She latched on at once, mostly lapping the blood at first, then sucking more vigorously as her strength returned. Which didn't take long. Jaclyn was a powerful vampire, and Christian's blood was potent. After only a few minutes, she gave a final long lick and released Christian's arm. He could already see the strength returning to her, her face once again animated by her own power.

She sat up, still leaning on Cibor, but clearly far better than she had been.

"What happened?" Christian asked as patiently as he could.

Cibor gave him an unfriendly look, but Jaclyn patted her lover's hand and turned to Christian. "It was my fault," she said. "A friend came to the door, one of the few women on Anthony's security squad, and someone I thought could be trusted. I opened the door to her, and the bitch did this." She dipped her chin at her abdomen and the bloody ruin of her shirt. "But I was just in the way," she said, meeting Christian's gaze intently. "It's Anthony, Christian. He still thinks Natalie is his."

The rage in his chest was so consuming that Christian thought it would destroy him. He rose to his feet. "How long ago?"

Jaclyn shifted her gaze to the clock on the mantel, a clock he'd barely known was there.

"An hour, I think. He won't hurt her," she said, wincing as she tried to sit up. "But I think he's leaving Houston for good this time. I don't know who's supposed to take over—"

"He was giving the territory to Hubert," Christian said tightly. "But Hubert's dead."

Jaclyn's eyes widened. "You?"

Christian nodded. "I have to get to the estate."

"The chopper," Cibor suggested.

"It's long gone. We'll have to drive."

Cibor looked up, indecision tightening his expression, torn between his need to stay with Jaclyn and keep her safe, and his hatred for Anthony which was urging him to continue this fight.

Christian shook his head. "Stay with Jaclyn. Keep Alon safe. I'll handle Anthony.

Marc," he said turning to his lieutenant.

"Sire?"

"We're taking the BMW, and fuck the speed laws."

Marc laughed grimly. "Music to my ears."

NATALIE LISTENED at the door for a long time, before she was convinced that they were really gone this time. Walking over to the desk, she retrieved her gun, and slung her purse over her shoulder again. It seemed weirdly light without her laptop in it, and she wondered if they'd found the computer. Or if they'd even looked. But she set that aside with everything else. She had only one purpose—to get the hell out of there.

She tapped on the door experimentally, concentrating on the area around the lock to determine how far the metal plating extended. Hydra-Shok ammo was designed to destroy flesh by creating a shock wave as it passed through the body, expanding tissue and leaving permanent muscle, vascular, and nerve damage. It left a small hole going in, and a big one going out. She wasn't sure how it would work on a wooden door, but she was sure it had enough punch to do some major damage. Her plan was to shoot out the wood all around the lock, then employ her best judo move and kick the lock right out of the door. Five shots should do it, but they'd also draw the attention of anyone nearby—why hadn't Leighton included a damn suppressor with the gun?

Natalie stepped back. She'd have to be fast and accurate. She hadn't fired a gun in a while, but she could still sure as hell hit a target from a foot away.

She took a minute to listen again at the door, then raised her gun, and her courage, and fired five shots in succession without stopping, her aim moving right around the lock. Her ears were ringing when she finally stepped back, and took a quick look at her work. The doors were sagging, the lock connected by the thinnest of raw wooden shards. Not wasting any time, she gave the lock a solid side kick and the doors popped open, the lock falling heavily to the carpeted floor.

Once in the outer room, she hurried directly to the hallway door, considering for the first time that it, too, might be locked. But luck was with her, and the knob turned easily in her hand. She opened it cautiously and peered out. So far, the corridor outside was empty, but she was pretty sure that wouldn't last.

She ran for it. She had no strategy, no secret ninja powers of concealment. Her idea was to run as fast as she could, find a stairway, and make it to Jaclyn's office on the second floor. Theoretically, that was Raphael's territory, and she should be safe there, even if Jaclyn wasn't in. The too-vivid memory of Jaclyn lying in a pool of her own blood flashed across the back of her eyes, and she nearly stumbled on the first step. Damn, she hoped they'd been telling her the truth about that, and that Jaclyn would recover.

She made it to the first floor. It was quiet, weirdly so. She peeked around the corner of the stairwell and found no one. This was odd. Apart from her own rather noisy escape, simple routine business usually kept this corridor busy. Something was definitely up. Maybe it was because Anthony was leaving. Maybe all of his people were off packing or doing whatever the hell they did for him when he traveled.

But then, she really didn't give a fuck why. It was good for her and that was all that mattered. She burst into the hallway and ran for the main staircase to the upper floors. She was halfway up the first flight, when there was a shout and the sound of heavy footsteps pounding up behind her.

Natalie stuck her hand in her purse, reaching for her gun, but a hard arm circled her, pulling her back against a thick chest and trapping her arms at her sides.

"Got you, you little bitch," an unrecognizable voice growled in her ear.

Natalie gave an angry shout, and jabbed her elbow into his gut. His grunt was satisfying, but it did nothing to loosen his hold on her.

"That wasn't nice. I'd teach you better, but Anthony wouldn't like that." He squeezed her hard enough to hurt, and she gasped. "But then, people get hurt all the time by accident."

"Is that was this is?" she managed to ask, her voice high and tight from the pressure he was putting on her. "An accident?"

"Close enough, bitch. Close enou—" His words became a grunt of surprise, and the next thing she knew she was covered in dust.

THE GATE AT Anthony's estate had been wide open. No guards in sight.

Tires skidded on the perfect green grass as Marc pulled right up to the front porch and slammed the car into park.

Christian was out of the car before it stopped moving, If Natalie was in there, minutes could make a difference. By the time he reached the porch, Marc was right on his heels. But even as he ran, he registered the weird silence of the estate. No guards, no one walking around. Momentous events were at play, and no one was here to observe them. Did Anthony even know what had happened in Laredo? Or did he think his plan had worked, that Christian was dead and Hubert on his way to claim the South?

He slammed open the front door and heard a woman's angry yell. Natalie? He turned in the direction of the cry, striding down the main hallway toward the center stairs, and there she was, being manhandled by some asshole.

Christian took the stairs in a single leap, still running on the high of Hubert's death. He rammed his hand into the asshole's back, smashed through his ribs, and crushed his heart. Natalie froze as the vampire's dust covered her. She turned to face him, and he waited for her to react. It was pretty disgusting.

But she didn't seem to notice the dust. Her face split into a huge smile and she threw herself into his arms. "You're alive."

Christian hugged her close. "Why wouldn't I be?"

"Anthony said you were dead."

"Anthony's a traitor and a liar. Where is he?"

She shook her head. "I don't know. He locked me up in the basement, but I broke out—"

"He wouldn't expect that," he said.

"He thought he vamped me, but you were already there in my heart, and he couldn't—"

"You're mine, *chère*. No one else's."

"But he didn't know—"

Their reunion was cut off by the thundering arrival of Anthony's security force. They swarmed down from the second floor, filling the landing between two flights. Christian shoved Natalie behind him, pushing her against the wall. "Stay there," he ordered, then turned to face the arriving vamps. There were ten or more, the best of Anthony's guards, his inner wall of security. They belonged to Anthony, body and soul, and would fight to the death to protect him.

Christian was still burning with the power boost he'd gotten from Hubert's death. He waded into the crowd, using his fists as much as his power, disabling one after the other, knocking them unconscious and reinforcing it with his power to keep them down. He was aware of Natalie, holding her position against the wall behind him, aware of Marc, fighting by his side. He heard the distant slam of the front doors, and then a new contingent of vampires arrived, launching an attack from below. With a mental warning to Marc, Christian spun to confront this new threat. He raced past Natalie, and leapt down to the floor before the new arrivals could set foot on the stairs. He fought without thinking, moving on instinct, his vampire senses warning him of each new danger as he whirled from side to side, crushing skulls and stopping hearts, sparing lives where he could.

He'd just dropped the last opponent when he heard Natalie's furious scream. He turned as if in slow motion to see his worst nightmare coming true. Marc was down one knee, muscles straining as he struggled to rise. Above him stood Anthony, his face a determined grimace as he poured all of his power as a vampire lord—the power of all the Southern vampires he still ruled—into destroying Marc. He lifted his gaze to Christian, and his expression turned gleeful as he pulled a stake from behind him, and raised it over Marc's bowed back.

Terror seized Christian as he raced up the stairs, knowing he couldn't get there in time, knowing Marc was about to die. He threw everything he had into a blast of power, but Anthony's shields were flush with power, and Christian had no time to craft a better weapon. He saw the stake coming down, caught the strain on Marc's face as he fought to break free.

Christian howled as the stake flashed downward . . . and then a gun boomed, and the stake fell from nerveless fingers. Anthony clutched at the bloody hole in his stomach, then looked up to stare at Natalie in disbelief, betrayal written clearly across his face. The wound wasn't enough to kill him, but it disabled him for just long enough.

Christian was on him a second later, gripping his neck, taking away his breath and draining the once Lord of the South of every ounce of power remaining to him. He held on until the asshole was little more than a shriveled husk. And then he ripped his head off, and tossed it down the stairs where it dusted in mid-bounce.

Christian dropped immediately to his knees next to Marc, placing a hand on the back of his neck and gripping tightly. He held his position until finally Marc looked up and met his eyes.

"He was too strong. I couldn't—"

"Stop," Christian said. "You fought three battles while that fucker was packing his bags for New Orleans. And then he had the balls to suck power away from the very people he was getting ready to abandon. You're strong, *mon ami*, but not even you can hold out against the power of an entire territory."

Marc nodded, his exhaustion visible, even after the power infusion he'd gotten from Christian. He needed blood and sleep. Christian squeezed the back of his neck in reassurance, then leaned forward to kiss the top of his head. It wasn't until then that he looked up to see Natalie watching.

He rose to his feet, worried about what her reaction would be to the way he'd killed Anthony, despite the soft look in her eyes for Marc. "I'm sorry you had to see—"

"What?" she interrupted. "That pervert Anthony turned into a shriveled mummy? Or the other jerk who called me a bitch turned to dust? Fuck that. They deserved it. Although, I wouldn't mind a shower. The dust thing was a little icky."

Christian started to laugh, but then the weight of the territory crashed into his brain, and he fell to his knees. Natalie cried his name, but it sounded distant, as if she was miles away. And the deep rumble of Marc's voice was sound without words. All he could hear were the thousands of vampires who comprised the Southern territory, a jumble of voices arguing, begging, shouting, and none of them understanding what was happening. Anthony had been loosening his hold on the territory for weeks in anticipation of Hubert's takeover, and it showed in the confusion of his people. Christian forced himself to concentrate through the pain, to stretch out his awareness into the cacophony of voices and emotions. He embraced the whole and the individual, wrapping them in compassion, confidence, and above all, control. He was their lord and they would, by God, *stop fucking whining!*

Silence. Followed by a low murmur of agreement and relief that slowly faded away into more of a feeling than a noise. Christian sucked in a deep breath. He sat back on his heels, hands limp on his thighs, head hanging.

This had been one hell of a night. All he could think about was blood, sex, and sleep. Hopefully in that order, and all with the same person.

A soft touch to his cheek had him raising his head to find Natalie kneeling next to him, with a worried look on her face.

"Time to go home, *chére*," he said wearily.

"What do we do about all of this?" she asked, gesturing to the piles of dust and the occasional disintegrating body part.

Christian looked around. "It'll all be gone by morning. Let's go."

Natalie helped him to his feet, which wasn't necessary, but it felt good, so he let her do it. He reached down, and gave Marc a hand up, and together the three of them walked slowly down the hall. Just before they reached the front door, Natalie asked a question she seemed afraid to have answered. "What about Jaclyn?"

Christian's arm was around her shoulders. He squeezed briefly and said, "She's fine. Cibor's with her."

Natalie blew out a relieved breath, as tears filled her eyes. "I thought maybe—"

"I know," he said, kissing away the tears. "But Jaclyn's tougher than she looks. By tomorrow night, she'll be pissed as hell, and good as new."

They walked out into the last hours of the night, and over to the BMW, which was parked right where they'd left it. Natalie looked at the car, and the two dark furrows of dirt left by Marc's emergency route over the grass, then held out her hand for the keys. "I'm driving," she announced.

Marc didn't argue, and neither did Christian. All he wanted was to get home, and get Natalie in bed before sunrise. If she thought driving them home herself would get them there faster, he was all for it.

"Keys are in the car." He walked around to the passenger door, while Marc climbed into the back and stretched out.

The estate seemed almost deserted as they sped down the long, curved driveway and out through the wide-open gate. Christian would have to come back tomorrow night to count the casualties, and comfort the survivors. But for now, he simply relaxed into the BMW's fine leather seat and reveled in the knowledge that he was, by his own hand, Lord of the South.

NATALIE DROVE QUICKLY, but without the flash she associated with Marc's driving. He had vampire reflexes on his side; she was just human. But she didn't regret that for one minute. Because it was her humanity that Christian wanted, her human blood that he needed. She'd seen the lust burning beneath the exhaustion in his eyes, and it made her hunger for him in a way that would have had her own eyes burning if that had been possible. Who would have believed that her father's good little girl would be sitting here right now, squeezing her thighs together in anticipation of getting home and into bed with a vampire?

There was so little traffic that the trip was short, despite her sensible driving, and it wasn't long before she was turning down Christian's street. The house was completely shuttered up. She pulled into the driveway, and Christian pushed a button on the overhead console to open the garage door. She found herself worrying about the security risk posed by the ordinary garage door, until she saw that the door to the house was shuttered as tightly as all of the other doors and windows.

Christian held her hand while he flipped up the cover on an alarm panel, and entered a release code that was a lot more than six digits. This was clearly a custom system, and, moreover, obviously designed for vampires. Apart from the shutters, which weren't exactly standard in the upscale Houston neighborhood, the multiple codes for different functions were something she'd never seen before. Anthony had been proud of his vault down in the basement, but he didn't have anything like this. She shuddered suddenly, remembering her recent imprisonment, and Anthony's plans for her.

"Don't think about it," Christian murmured, pulling her closer to his side.

Natalie glanced at him. How the hell did he know what she was thinking? She'd have to ask him sometime when they weren't all dragging their feet with exhaustion. The heavy shutter rolled up with a muted hum, and Marc pushed through and into the house. Christian and Natalie were right behind him.

The house was quiet, mostly dark, except for a light on in the kitchen. Why was it always the kitchen light that people left on? Even vampires left it on, and the kitchen was hardly a gathering place for them.

The basement door opened, and Cibor emerged, looking more worn than she'd ever seen him. She looked up, meeting his tired gaze. "Jaclyn?" she asked.

"She's sleeping it off. Between her own recuperative ability and Christian's blood, the damage is almost healed. What she needs now is sleep."

"She needs *you*," Natalie corrected him softly.

He gave her a crooked smile. "She's *got* me." He shifted his attention to Christian and asked, "Anthony?"

"Dust in the wind," Christian informed him.

Cibor smiled, and gave a little bow. "Lord Christian."

"Call me that tomorrow night. I might have the energy to believe it."

The big vampire laughed, then turned and started back down the stairs. Marc moved to follow, and Natalie tensed. Would Christian walk her to the guest bedroom and leave her there again? Had she earned enough of his trust that he would let her sleep next to him, wake next to him in his own bed?

He waited until Cibor and Marc had both disappeared down the stairs, before turning to pull her close, his arms around her waist, his fingers resting at her lower back, just above her butt. She put her hands on his chest and looked up at him in question, her stomach doing backflips, as she waited for the inevitable rejection.

"Do you love me, Natalie?" he asked, surprising the hell out of her.

Natalie stared up at him, her heart pounding so hard, she thought his vampire ears must be able to hear it. Did she love him? Of course she did. The pain she'd felt when she thought he was dead had forced her to acknowledge that. But could she admit it to him? Could she lay herself open and risk being torn apart? If she didn't, if she told Christian she wasn't sure or some other bullshit, she'd never see him again. And she would regret that forever.

"I love you," she said, and the mixture of terror and relief those three words conjured up had her body so confused, that it didn't know whether to run or stay.

Christian gave her his beautiful smile, and tightened his arms around her. "*Mon cœur est tien, Natalie.*"

My heart is yours. She knew enough Cajun French to understand that, and her heart squeezed so much that it hurt.

"Christian," she breathed. And he kissed her, his lips touching hers gently at first, then harder as the kiss was filled with all the passion and terror of the previous hours. She clung to his broad chest, her fingers clenched in the thick cotton of his shirt, kissing him back until her lungs were begging for air. She rocked on her feet when he finally lifted his mouth, and she rested her forehead against him as she sucked in air.

He hugged her, chuckling softly. "Can you breathe?"

Natalie looked up at him with a smile. "I can now, but it was worth it."

"That's good to know. Shall we go to bed? The sun is very nearly up, and I have plans."

She grabbed his hand and turned toward her bedroom. "Let's go," she said, but he pulled her back.

"Not there, *ma chère.*"

Her eyes widened hopefully. "Are you sure?"

"Are you? Once that door closes, it doesn't open until sunset, and I'm not exactly a lot of fun in the meantime."

"Oh," she said suddenly remembering. "Let me get my laptop!" She hurried down the hall to the bedroom that had been hers, grabbed her laptop, her toothbrush, and a nightgown, then ran back to where a bemused Christian was waiting for her. "I'm ready."

He took the laptop from her, grabbed her hand, and led her down the stairs.

A zing of excitement shimmered along Natalie's nerves, and she had to admit it wasn't just the thought of getting Christian naked. She was going to see the secret room! It was like taking a tour of the bat cave, and she was endlessly curious.

Christian led her past a huge vault-like door at the foot of the stairs. He set her laptop on a nearby counter, then turned to shove the heavy door shut. While he punched in yet another code to lock the door, Natalie examined the room they'd just entered. Computers were lined up on a table against the far wall, and screens filled the space above them, with the largest one being a huge, wide-screen TV monitor. She noticed a couple of different game consoles, and tried to imagine Christian and Marc down here playing Tomb Raider or Witcher. Actually, after seeing them in action, she could totally picture those two getting into Call of Duty. The thought made her want to laugh, but she swallowed it. She didn't think laughter was the reaction Christian expected from her first sight of the bat cave.

He picked up the laptop, and took her hand to pull her through the computer room and down a hallway. There were two doors on each side of the corridor, and a door at the far end. The first two doors to either side, and the door at the end, were closed, but Marc stepped out of the open door on the far left. He smiled at her, then said to Christian, "Cibor and Jaclyn are there." He indicated the closed door next to the one he'd stepped out of, then pointed at the door opposite. "Scoville's in that one, and Alon's still in yours."

"Alon?" she said eagerly. "Can I see him?"

"Tomorrow," Christian told her. "He's sound asleep right now."

"But he's okay?"

He nodded. "He's fine. But, Natalie," he said, giving her a serious look. "He'll be different. He's a vampire now."

"I know," she said, although she was beginning to suspect that she really didn't. "But he'll still be Alon. I'm just happy he's alive."

Christian gave her a skeptical look, but didn't push her on it. Either because he figured she had to see it to believe it, or maybe because he didn't want to spend the little bit of time they had before sunrise talking about Alon's new life as a vampire.

"Did Marc say Scoville was here? I thought he was with Anthony?"

"Anthony hung him out to dry, so he's had a change of heart. He's with me now."

She had questions about that, but decided she was too tired to pursue them tonight, as Christian wrapped his hand around her hip and urged her into the room opposite Marc's. "See you at sunset," he called to Marc. He pushed her all the way inside and closed the door behind them.

Natalie found herself in a room that wasn't all that different from the guest room upstairs, except that the bed was bigger, and the décor much more masculine. Lamps on either side of the bed gave off a slight golden glow through pleated tan shades, and the lamp bases were porcelain with an elaborate gold and maroon design. The bed itself was a simple black leather headboard, with bed linens in two shades of gray, and lots of pillows. An en suite bathroom opened off to one side, and there was a good-sized closet behind a sliding, mirrored door.

Christian set her laptop on a low, six-drawer dresser, then walked toward the bathroom, pulling off his T-shirt as he went. "I need a shower," he said from inside the shirt as he yanked it over his head. When he emerged, his hair was tousled and he gave her his sexy grin. "Join me."

Natalie smiled slowly. It wasn't a question, but she didn't mind. She was too riveted by the thick muscles padding his shoulders and arms, the flat planes of his chest tapering down to a perfect set of abs and a flat belly. She sighed with pleasure at the sight of him, and he laughed. It was the sound of unabashed male pride, but she couldn't blame him. Not with the way she'd been ogling his body. Her smile widened. "I'm ready for that shower."

Two minutes later, they were both naked under the pounding rush of some really hot water. Natalie stood under the spray, washing away the slimy feel of Anthony's touch. Not to mention the traces of the vampire who'd dusted all over her when Christian killed him. Yuck. She'd just slathered shampoo over her hair, when Christian's strong fingers took over the job, massaging her scalp as he rubbed it into her hair. Natalie leaned back against him, stretching her arms behind her to wrap around his hips, and caress the strong curves of his firm butt. The position also had the side benefit of pressing his equally fine erection against *her* butt, which she didn't mind at all.

"I could get used to this," she murmured, mostly to herself.

"Rinse," he said, reaching over her head to unhook the removable shower attachment. Natalie turned around and tipped her head backward, enjoying the combined pleasure of the hot water and his strong fingers as they threaded through her hair.

Once he was finished rinsing, she patted his chest. "What's next?"

He got a wicked grin on his face, and said, "I thought I'd fuck you up against that wall until you screamed."

Natalie felt a rush of heat low in her belly that quickly sank even lower.

Her cheeks flushed, and she admitted to herself that she wouldn't mind that scenario at all. But that's not what she'd meant when she'd asked him. She stomped a foot impatiently, laughing when he instinctively twisted to protect his balls from her knee. She reached between them, and cupped his balls in her hand, giving them a fond caress that ended with a firm stroke of his cock. "You don't have to worry about protecting these guys," she told him. "I like them way too much."

Christian snorted. "That's good to know, but I've seen you in action, *chére*. A man can never be too careful."

Natalie patted his chest again. "What I meant to ask was, what happens next with your vampire stuff? Will you move to the estate now?"

"Hell, no. We'll stay here in the short term, but I have to start building a security force, and that will mean a much bigger house. The estate is the right size, but I hate that place. I'm thinking of moving to Santa Fe. I like it there."

Natalie made a noncommittal noise. She wanted to know what came next with them, too, but she wasn't going to ask about *that*.

"Hey," he said, lifting her chin with one finger. "You want to help me pick out a new house?"

"You mean like, as a financial expert? That's not really—"

"No, Natalie. Like . . . as my mate. I love you. I want you to stay with me."

Natalie's heart leapt so hard, it felt like it was lodged in her throat. Tears filled her eyes, and Christian's eyebrows rose at the sight. She forced herself to swallow, in order to croak, "Happy tears."

"Ah. Does that mean you're saying yes?"

She nodded, glad that she'd already showered her mascara off, because the tears were now streaming down her face. She gathered herself enough to say, "My father will want a real wedding."

Christian threw his head back and laughed. "A wedding he'll have then."

"You mean it?"

"Of course. All I care about is having you by my side and in my bed every night."

Natalie rolled her forehead against his wet chest. She was so happy she could hardly contain it. "I love you," she whispered, then looked up at him and said it again. "I love you."

"Je t'aimerai á jamais, ma Natalie." I will love you always.

Christian bent his head to kiss her, then said against her lips, "Now, about fucking you up against that wall . . ." He reached down and grabbed her butt, lifting her as he backed her against the tiled wall of the shower.

Natalie sucked in a surprised breath, but responded quickly, wrapping her legs around his hips and squeezing, pulling him against her. Christian growled his approval, hitched her a little higher, then gripped his cock and slipped it into her slick and ready pussy, going deep with a single, gliding thrust.

"So nice and wet for me," he murmured, his deep voice a hum of sound over her wet skin.

She shivered and tightened her hold on him, wrapping her arms around his neck, and locking her ankles over his butt, pulling him even further into her body. Her nipples scraped the soft hair on his chest, and she lowered her mouth to his shoulder, kissing the thick skin over solid muscle, licking her way up to his neck.

He did the same to her, his tongue a hot rasp over her flesh, until his mouth closed over her vein, and she felt the hard brush of his fangs.

She moaned in anticipation, sucking the strong tendon between his neck and shoulder, giving in to the temptation to bite, her teeth sinking in until she tasted blood. She froze in shock at what she'd done until she heard Christian's groan.

"That's it," he ground out. "Taste me."

Natalie's whole body shook with desire. She bit down harder until her mouth was filled with his blood. She swallowed automatically. The orgasm came from nowhere, storming through her body, and shaking her bones, until she thought she'd break apart. Her nerves were on fire, her body clamping down on Christian's cock, as she cried out again and again, ecstasy rippling over her in growing swells until she could only cling to Christian and ride it out. His arms were banded around her like steel as he slammed his cock into the tight glove of her pussy, until, with a shout, he plunged deep and stayed there, the hot wash of his release filling her, as his fangs sliced into her vein and sent her screaming into climax all over again.

Natalie bucked helplessly, her emotions spilling out in sobs while she clung to his massive shoulders, her face buried against his neck. Christian hummed his pleasure as he drank her blood, and in the midst of her orgasm, she found a sensual satisfaction in knowing that she was keeping him strong and alive.

Eventually, the tremors slowed, and stopped. She felt the warm scrape of Christian's tongue on her neck, and then he lifted her away from the wall, and reached out with one hand to turn off the water. Stepping out of the shower, he grabbed a huge, fluffy towel and wrapped it around her, then carried her into the bedroom. He pulled the covers back and laid her down on the bed, then joined her.

Natalie stirred enough to say, "We're all wet."

"And soon we'll be dry," he replied, unconcerned. "Come on, you'll catch a chill." He wrapped her in the towel, tugged the covers over them both, and pulled her into his arms.

Natalie snuggled against him, too exhausted to do anything else. She'd worry about wet sheets later. Right now, she just wanted to curl up against Christian and sleep.

"Natalie," Christian said softly, forcing her tired eyes to open again. "Where'd you get the gun?"

"Cynthia Leighton sent it to me," she mumbled. "I think she wanted me to kill you, though," she added without thinking, then froze, realizing what she'd said.

But Christian only snorted, and said, "That woman really knows how to hold a grudge."

"A grudge?" Natalie asked, feeling her consciousness slipping away.

"Later," he murmured, rubbing a soothing hand up and down her back. "Go to sleep."

CHRISTIAN KNEW the moment Natalie drifted off. What little tension had been left in her body disappeared, and she slept curled up against his chest as if she couldn't get close enough. Which was fine with him. His need to protect her was stronger than anything he'd ever felt before, stronger even than his feelings for Marc. He had to fight against the urge to hold her closer, for fear he'd break something.

Rolling over to his back, he pulled her against his side, and laid his head on the pillow. The sun was already tipping over the horizon. It was a testament to his power that he'd been able to remain awake this long. But he'd wanted to see Natalie asleep before he fell himself.

Once the full power of sunrise hit him, he'd be literally dead to the world. He only hoped she would sleep until he woke. If she didn't, if she woke before he did, she'd learn the hard truth of sleeping with a vampire lover.

NATALIE OPENED HER eyes in the unfamiliar room, her memory slowly coming back to fill in the blanks. This was Christian's bedroom, and they'd gone to sleep together. She rolled over, expecting to find him sound asleep, and admittedly curious to see what he looked like when he did his vampire sleep thing.

Except . . . he wasn't there. She blinked in surprise. If he was already awake, that meant it was after sunset, and she'd slept through the entire day—something she'd never done before. Of course, she'd also never been kidnapped, shot her way out of a locked room, and then helped kill a powerful vampire before either. Add sex in the shower with Christian, and suddenly, she wasn't all that surprised she'd slept so long.

She heard voices outside the room and rolled out of bed. She made a quick trip to the bathroom to take care of necessities, then moved over to the sink to wash her hands and face. Once there, however, she got a good look at her hair and had to stifle her shriek of horror. Her hair had been wet when they'd gone to bed, which meant it now looked like someone had shocked her with a few hundred volts sometime while she slept. And all she had with her was her toothbrush and her purse.

Her purse, at least, had a brush in it, so she managed to tame her hair into a tight braid against the back of her head, tying it off with a scrunchie, also from her purse. She brushed her teeth, washed her face, and put her clothes back on from last night, minus the underwear. She didn't mind pulling on the same clothes, but she drew the line at day-old underwear. Besides, it was only until she could get upstairs to change.

Checking her reflection one last time, she opened the bedroom door, and walked out into the hallway, which was now completely empty. The voices were still there, but they'd already moved upstairs. In the kitchen, probably, where Christian's beloved espresso machine lived.

She considered stopping at her room to change first, but then she caught Alon's voice among the others, and rushed into the kitchen instead.

"Alon!" She ran right into his outstretched arms, hugging him tightly as he rocked her from side to side. When she finally pulled back, she had tears in her eyes. "Are you okay? Really okay?"

"Never better, Nat. I feel great."

Natalie was hugging him again, overcome with happiness at seeing him alive, when she heard a dry cough from behind her. She glanced back and found Christian staring at the two of them with eyes that were deadly serious.

Oh, right. Vampire possessiveness. She turned, and gave Alon a smacking kiss on the lips, then spun around with a grin and walked over to Christian.

"Good evening, my lord," she said teasingly.

His arm snaked out to snag her around the waist and yank her against his body. One hand dropped to her butt with sharp smack, before stroking it possessively. He gave her a knowing look, obviously feeling the absence of underwear, and a hot blush crept up her face.

To cover her embarrassment, she went up on her toes and kissed his unresponsive mouth. "I missed you when I woke up," she murmured against his lips. His expression softened, and he kissed her back, this time with feeling, uncaring about who was watching. When he finally released her mouth, Natalie was a little wobbly, and had to cling to his shirt. His smile said he knew the effect he had on her, but she didn't care as long as he held her the way he was now. She turned in his arms, and took in the other two people in the room.

"Hi, Marc," she said.

"What? No kiss for me?"

Christian growled a warning, but she just laughed. The other vampire standing with him was vaguely familiar, but she didn't know his name.

"Natalie, meet Scoville," Christian said. "Formerly in Anthony's service, now sworn to mine."

Natalie nodded her head politely at Scoville, not really understanding what the vamp was doing here, when he'd been the one whose lie got Christian down to Laredo. But if Christian was okay with the guy standing in his kitchen, she had no complaints.

"What happened to Jaclyn and Cibor? Are they still sleeping?"

"No," Christian said. "They left already. Jaclyn needed to be with her own people."

"But she's okay?"

"Fully healed, but it may take a few days before she's feeling that way. She was hit pretty hard."

"I should call her later, and ask if—"

They all stopped at the sound of the doorbell, turning almost as one to stare in that direction.

"Are we expecting company?" Marc asked, glancing at Christian.

"Not that I know of."

Christian's hold on her tightened when Marc went to answer the door, almost as if he was preparing for the need to defend her. Natalie glanced around the kitchen, and saw that the house was still at DEFCON 1, with shutters over all the windows and doors. She also noticed that Alon and Scoville had both gone hyper alert, their attention riveted on the doorway that Marc had taken. It made her long for her gun.

Marc opened the front door, which Natalie took to mean that the person ringing the bell posed no threat. The vampires all seemed to read it entirely differently, though, if the shift in their body language was anything to go by. Christian pretty much shoved her behind him, not relaxing until the door closed again, and Marc came into view down the hallway.

"Express delivery," he said, indicating the FedEx-type envelope in his hand. Except the colors were wrong, and it couldn't be FedEx because they didn't deliver this late in the day. Not usually anyway. Maybe vampires had their own version of a guaranteed delivery company. VampEx. Natalie stifled a laugh. Somehow, she didn't think Christian would see the humor right now.

Marc stared down at the envelope, as if wishing he had x-ray vision, then looked up at Christian with a shrug. "Seems innocuous enough."

Christian lifted his chin at Alon, and passed Natalie into his care, despite her protests. Sure, she was the most vulnerable person in the room if that envelope decided to blow up or something, but Christian could at least talk to her before passing her off like a football.

"Relax, Nat," Alon murmured in her ear. "He's just protecting you."

She elbowed him in the side, hard enough that he grunted. "I know that."

Christian's concern was infectious, and her fingers pinched Alon's arm as she watched him pull the zip strip on the envelope, and tip it upside down until the contents fell into his other hand.

It was a white envelope, about the size of a nice greeting card, and made of quality paper. It looked like an announcement of some sort to Natalie, and she wondered briefly if this was how vampire lords were welcomed to the fold. But Christian's puzzled expression told her that wasn't it.

He ran a finger under the sealed flap, pulled out the heavy stock card inside, and started laughing.

Natalie frowned, then shoved away from Alon, walked over to Christian, and pulled the card out of his hand. She'd read only the first few words, "Ms. Lana Arnold and Lord Vincent Kuxim request . . ." before Christian hugged her close and told everyone, "We're going to a wedding."

Chapter Thirteen

Mexico City, Mexico

CHRISTIAN WAS THE last to arrive, and he suspected his fellow Vampire Council members had planned it that way. He scanned the gathered vampire lords. Sophia was missing again. And there was no Rajmund, but Lucas was here this time, his long frame slumped over one of the big conference room chairs, looking like a bored teenager. Aden stood against the far wall. Christian wasn't a small man, but Aden was huge, and he was eyeing Christian with thinly veiled hostility. Christian had never met the Midwestern lord, so this had to be more carryover from someone else's crimes.

"Christian," Vincent said, speaking first as the host of this gathering. He came over and offered his hand. "You're looking better than the last time I saw you," he added with a grin.

"A hot shower does wonders," Christian joked, shaking hands.

"You know everyone, of course."

Christian nodded, then walked over to greet Raphael. The North American Vampire Council was, strictly speaking, a council of equals. But everyone in this room knew who was really in charge.

"Raphael," Christian said, with a bare tip of his head. He would have loved to know how much Vincent had told Raphael about Hubert's death, and Christian's talent. But he wasn't about to ask.

"Christian," Raphael responded, smiling. "Congratulations on your victory. A double victory from what I've heard. Hubert and Anthony both in one night."

"I had a good team."

"And hidden talents," Raphael said, telling Christian all he needed to know.

Christian eyed him carefully. "It's always best to hide one's skills from one's enemies."

"But not from one's allies."

Christian nodded, conceding the point for the present. But then, they hadn't been true allies before tonight, had they?

"No Sophia?" Christian asked, changing the subject. He waited to see if Raphael would follow his lead, or push for more.

"We're all worried about her," Lucas called from across the room, sounding completely alert despite his less than attentive posture.

Christian turned, concealing his surprise. It was still difficult for him to reconcile this gathering of powerful lords with the fact that they really were allies. And yet, there was no doubting the sincerity of Lucas's concern.

"No one's heard from her yet?" he asked, remembering Duncan talking about her absence during the challenge gala.

"Not a word," Aden chimed in, sitting at the table and no longer radiating hostility. As if now that Raphael had given his blessing, they were all old friends.

Christian took a seat at the table, more than willing to go along with the lowered level of tension in the room. "Is that unusual?" he asked.

"Unusual enough," Duncan said. He was different than the other lords, his persona one of quiet, calm confidence, rather than bristling power. Not that he lacked power—he just didn't broadcast it the way the others did, including Christian himself. "Raj has tried to reach her several times, with no success, and his spies have reported a lot of movement among her people in Toronto."

"My Cyn is quite concerned, as well," Raphael commented. "She is . . . friends with Sophia's mate," he added, and Christian noted a distinct flavor of distaste in Raphael's tone. "Could it be another European plot?" Raphael asked Christian directly.

Christian thought about his answer. He wasn't aware of any plans to challenge Sophia, but that didn't rule out the possibility. He was familiar with the schemes of Mathilde and her friends, but they weren't the only Europeans eyeing North America, and he said as much to his new allies. "Mathilde made no secret of her plans for this continent, and there were those who, while not allies of hers, would certainly try to take advantage of the disruption she caused to further their own goals."

"Berkhard is also in the wind," Raphael commented. "He was there with Mathilde and Hubert at the beginning in Hawaii, but, like Hubert, he left soon after I was . . . temporarily subdued."

"I don't know any of his specific plans, but I do know Berkhard. He would view Sophia as an easy target because she's a woman."

"That would be a mistake," Aden rumbled, and Christian noted the amused glances that some of the others gave him. There was a history there. Christian would have to find out what it was.

"Will she call if she needs help?" Duncan asked quietly.

"Eventually," Raphael replied darkly. "I just hope it's not too late."

"Well, gentlemen," Vincent said, standing from his place near the doors. "This has been fun, but I've got a wedding to attend, and a bride who's waiting for me. So, welcome to the club, Christian. Now, let's go party."

"SHE LOOKS SO beautiful," Natalie said, sniffing quietly. She dabbed her eyes with a tissue, and rested her head against Christian's shoulder.

Christian lowered his chin to look down at her. "You don't even know her," he murmured.

As if that mattered. Lana Arnold was a *bride*. But even in a world where all brides were beautiful, she stood out. Her dress was in the romantic style, gorgeous ivory lace with wide, off-the-shoulder lace straps. It was fitted through the bodice and down to her knees, where it ended in a mermaid swirl that trailed into a short train. Her veil was mantilla style, sheer silk that flowed down to her knees, with a matching lace trim. The ivory color was beautiful against her mocha skin, and her hair beneath the veil was a flow of black silk that rivaled the veil for beauty.

But it wasn't her beauty that brought tears to Natalie's eyes. It was the glow of happiness she radiated as she started down the aisle on her father's arm. She had eyes for no one but Vincent, and he had the same for her. If Natalie hadn't known better, if she hadn't known that Vincent was a tough-as-nails vampire lord, she might have thought she was seeing a sheen of tears in Vincent's eyes, too.

A low chuckle rumbled from Christian's chest as he shifted to put his arm around her. He kissed the top of her head, and whispered, "You're far more beautiful, *mon amour.*"

That did nothing for the state of her emotions. A new rush of tears welled, and Natalie opened a fresh pack of tissues. At this rate, she'd have no mascara left by the end of the evening. On her other side, Marc gave a suspicious cough that sounded a lot like laughter. She gave him a narrow glance, and his return look was one of wide-eyed innocence. She rolled her eyes. As if.

Up at the front of the room, the couple were exchanging their vows. It was short and sweet, just the way she liked it, and soon, the officiant was pronouncing them husband and wife. They exchanged a passionate kiss that brought everyone to their feet with cheers, then bells were ringing, and Natalie was crying all over again.

Christian hugged her against his chest. She could feel his body shaking with laughter, but she didn't care. She was where she wanted to be, in his arms. And very soon, she'd be the one walking down the aisle on her father's arm, with her Uncle Clovis presiding. Christian would have to meet her family before then, of course. But everything would be fine. As long as they were together, they'd always be fine.

"*Je t'aime, Natalie,*" Christian whispered. And that was all that mattered.

Epilogue

Vancouver, British Columbia, Canada

SOPHIA STARED at the picture, her hands shaking so much that the image blurred. She was furious, but she was also scared to death. They had Colin. She didn't know how this had happened. Colin was deadly, a warrior from head to toe. He was invincible. She scolded herself, knowing that last one wasn't true. No one was invincible, not even her. But Colin was never alone, never without vampire guards. So, how had they'd gotten to him?

The answer was as enraging as it was bitter. Someone had betrayed him, betrayed them both. Someone who was close enough to Colin that he'd trusted him. Trusted him enough to have dismissed his other guards and met alone with the traitor.

She studied the picture again, and her heart broke. They'd beaten him, at least. And probably done far worse things that she couldn't see. There were horrible things a vampire could do to a human, terrible ways of torturing not just his body, but his mind. Her Colin was tough. He was a Navy SEAL, trained by the best to withstand torture, to resist attempts to get information out of him. But no one was invincible, she repeated to herself.

She put the awful picture down, and her hand hovered over the phone. She needed help, and didn't know whom among her own people she could trust. If one was a traitor, couldn't there be others? She needed to call Raphael. She could no longer pretend that the other vampire lords didn't know something was wrong. They'd have missed her at the challenge launch in the South, and at the Council meeting in Mexico to welcome Christian Duvall as the new Southern lord. Hell, if nothing else, Cynthia Leighton had been calling Colin nonstop, and getting no response. She'd have brought her concerns to Raphael by now.

And wasn't this exactly what their new and historic alliance had been crafted for? For when everything was on the line, and one of them needed help? There might be a price. But there was no price she wouldn't pay to save Colin's life and sanity.

It was Colin himself who worried her the most, however. He would never betray her. He'd die first.

And that was what terrified her. That he'd die before she got there. She picked up the phone and called Raphael.

To be continued . . .

Acknowledgments

As always, I want to thank my editor, Brenda Chin, for her patience and expert input, both of which made this a better book. A big thank you also to Deb Dixon for another amazing cover. I love my Christian!

Thank you to Sophie Wogc (Rebel Love!) who improved Christian's French, which is a good thing, because my high school French just wasn't going to cut it. You know that Saturday Night Live skit with Alec Baldwin? Yeah, well, that was me. Rest assured that any mistakes in Christian's language are mine! Thanks again to John Gorski, who always bails me out when it comes to guns and bullets. Natalie needed his help this time around. Without him, she'd still be trying to get out of that locked room.

And once more I must thank my fellow writers Steve McHugh and Michelle Muto (more Rebel Love!) for their invaluable input to everything I write. We started together so many years ago, we've written and read so much together, and they're my first line of support when the writerly front gets dark . . . and yet we've never met in person. Someday, someday.

Love and thanks to Karen Roma for all of her efforts on my behalf, from beta reading, to Tim Tams, to her tireless promotion of my books. Another good friend I'll meet someday for sure.

Hugs also to Annette Romain Stone for all her help. Being a writer these days means staying active on so many fronts, and Annette keeps me sane while I juggle all of that, and try to keep writing at the same time. Thanks also to the wonderful members of my Street Team, who do such a great job of getting the word out about my books. I couldn't do it without you.

Special thanks to all of my readers who make it possible for me to do what I love. I'm a lucky, lucky woman.

And finally, love always to my family who cheer me on and keep me going. And love to my darling husband, who made my life complete on the day he said, "I love you."

About the Author

D. B. Reynolds arrived in sunny Southern California at an early age, having made the trek across the country from the Midwest in a station wagon with her parents, her many siblings, and the family dog. And while she has many (okay, some) fond memories of Midwestern farm life, she quickly discovered that L.A. was her kind of town, and grew up happily sunning on the beaches of the South Bay.

D. B. holds graduate degrees in international relations and history from UCLA (go Bruins!) and was headed for a career in academia, but, in a moment of clarity, she left behind the politics of the hallowed halls for the better-paying politics of Hollywood, where she worked as a sound editor for several years, receiving two Emmy nominations, an MPSE Golden Reel, and multiple MPSE nominations for her work in television sound.

Book One of her Vampires in America series, *RAPHAEL*, launched her career as a writer in 2009, while *JABRIL*, Vampires in America Book Two, was awarded the RT Reviewers' Choice Award for Best Paranormal Romance (Small Press) in 2010. *ADEN*, Vampires in America Book Seven, was her first release under the new ImaJinn imprint at BelleBooks.

D. B. currently lives in a flammable canyon near the Malibu coast with her husband of many years, and when she's not writing her own books, she can usually be found reading someone else's. You can visit D. B. at her website, dbreynolds.com, for information on her latest books, contests, and giveaways.

Made in the USA
San Bernardino, CA
04 September 2019